SMALL FAVORS

ALSO BY ERIN A. CRAIG

House of Salt and Sorrows

SMALL FAVORS

ERIN A. CRAIG

DELACORTE PRESS

Text copyright © 2021 by Erin A. Craig
Jacket art copyright © 2021 by THERE IS STUDIO

All rights reserved. Published in the United States by Delacorte Press, an imprint of Random House Children's Books, a division of Penguin Random House LLC, New York.

Delacorte Press is a registered trademark and the colophon is a trademark of Penguin Random House LLC.

GetUnderlined.com

Educators and librarians, for a variety of teaching tools, visit us at RHTeachersLibrarians.com

Library of Congress Cataloging-in-Publication Data
Names: Craig, Erin A., author.
Title: Small favors / Erin A. Craig.
Description: First edition. | New York : Delacorte Press, 2021. | Audience: Ages 12 and up. | Summary: In the secluded town of Amity Falls, Ellerie has the chance to have her secret wishes come true, but there is a price to pay in this retelling of Rumpelstiltskin.
Identifiers: LCCN 2020033380 (print) | LCCN 2020033381 (ebook) |
ISBN 978-0-593-30674-1 (hardcover) | ISBN 978-0-593-30675-8 (library binding) |
ISBN 978-0-593-30676-5 (ebook)
Subjects: CYAC: Magic—Fiction. | Wishes—Fiction. | Fairy tales.
Classification: LCC PZ7.1.C715 Sm 2021 (print) | LCC PZ7.1.C715 (ebook) |
DDC [Fic]—dc23

ISBN 978-0-593-48509-5 (B&N edition)

The text of this book is set in 11-point Adobe Caslon.
Interior design by Ken Crossland

Printed in the United States of America
10 9 8 7 6 5 4 3 2 1
2021 Barnes and Noble Edition

Random House Children's Books supports the First Amendment and celebrates the right to read.

For my mama—
Thank you for never backing down when
I challenged you to tell a scary story.
But also . . . thank you for always
making the endings happy.

IMPORTANT FAMILIES
OF THE GATHERING

The Downings
Gideon (apiarist) and Sarah,
Samuel, Ellerie, Merry, Sadie

The Danforths
Cyrus (farmer), Rebecca, Mark

The McClearys
Amos (Elder and owner of the general store) and Martha

The Dodsons
Matthias (Elder and blacksmith) and Charlotte

The Schäfers
Leland (Elder and shepherd) and Cora

The Briards
Clemency (parson) and Letitia, Simon

The Buhrmans
Calvin (tavern owner) and Violet

The Lathetons
Edmund (carpenter) and Prudence

The Fowlers
Gran (poultry farmer) and Alice (schoolteacher)

THE RULES

*as drafted by the Elders and Decided
by at the first Gathering of Amity Falls*

1. A rope of great cords will not fray, snap, or weather.
   The Falls stands strong if we all bind together.

2. Tend your land, your beasts, your field,
   and prosperous bounties the Falls will yield.

3. Fifteen harvests children sow,
   then to the Gathering let them grow.

4. Seek not to harm your fellow men,
   for Amity's wrath circles round again.

5. Let from your lips no false words pour,
   damning characters evermore.

6. When neighbors reach for helping hand,
   extend your own, as God commands.

7. Enter not the forest deep.
   Beyond the Bells, the dark fiends keep.

INDIAN SUMMER

1

THE SMOKE SMELLED OF BURNING PINE NEEDLES, DARK and sweet. It seeped from the hive box in front of me and danced across the fields, caught on a balmy breeze. Papa pressed down on the bellows to release another cloud, training it carefully toward the tall wooden structure's entrance. His head bobbed as he silently counted the passing seconds. Finally he nodded.

Even though my hands were completely covered, they shook as I approached the hive. I'd never been allowed to help remove frames before, and I wanted to make sure I did everything exactly as Papa said. With a muffled groan, I strained to hoist the heavy lid before setting it aside in the grass, careful to avoid three drowsy bees crawling across its top.

After puffing more of the smoke deep into the box, Papa stepped back, allowing me full access to the hive. "Take out one of the super frames and we'll inspect it." His voice was muffled under the thick netting swagged about his face.

Though I could only see the limned highlight of his profile, he looked pleased. Proud, even. I prayed I wouldn't let him down.

Usually I was in the kitchen with Mama, Merry, and Sadie during harvests. Samuel helped Papa, bringing in the heavy, honey-laden frames for us to process. I'd hold them upright while Mama

ran a wide knife down the combs, slicing off waxy caps with practiced ease. The dripping frames would go into a large metal drum,
and Merry and Sadie would take turns cranking the handle until
all the honey had spun free and was ready to be filtered.

I glanced toward our farmhouse now, imagining my sisters jostling for space around the hearth as bottles were boiled clean and
set out to dry. They'd be squabbling and begging for Mama to let
them go out. It was too pretty a day to be spent over a hot fire and
iron pots. A hawk screeched overhead in tacit agreement, spinning
lazy circles in the late-August sunshine.

"Ellerie," Papa prompted, drawing me back. "The first frame
can be the trickiest. Sometimes the bees seal the edges over with
resin. You might need to chisel it free."

"Won't that upset the bees?" I peered down through the slats of
the frames. The ever-present hum had died down, but I could still
see some movement in the lower boxes.

"Not if you do it right," he teased unhelpfully. I sensed his
smile behind the netting. "The first time my father let me take the
frames out, I was stung six times. It's a rite of passage."

Growing up with beekeepers for parents, I'd certainly been
stung before, but it wasn't an experience I cared to repeat. I'd kept
the entire household up with my first sting, sobbing through the
night—not for my swollen hand but for the poor bee who had
died in the process.

Reaching under my own heavy netting, I wiped at the sweat
trickling down my face, debating where to start. There were eight
frames in this section, each spread out with uniform precision. I
chose one near the middle and gently wiggled it back and forth,
testing the sides. It moved easily enough. I held my breath as I
pulled it free, careful to not brush it against any of the others on
the way out.

"Let's see, then." Papa leaned forward, studying the bees' work.

Lacy patterns of honeycomb sheeted over the frame, some filled and capped but most empty.

He clucked his tongue, considering. "Not yet. Could be a late harvest this year. Too much snow last winter. Put it back."

With the utmost care, I eased the wooden frame back into its slot, then breathed a sigh of relief.

"Now the next."

"We check every one?"

His head bobbed. "If you go through the trouble of smoking the bees, you need to make sure to thoroughly inspect the hive. Honey isn't the only thing we're concerned with. We're stewards for the hives, protectors of these bees. We need to make sure they're healthy and their needs are being met."

He set the smoker down and lifted the top box, peering into the lower chambers. After setting aside the first box and counting the second's frames, he took one out, and gently brushed aside two bees clinging drunkenly to the combs.

"Tell me what you see."

I squinted through the veil. There were more honeycombs, as golden as a stained-glass window. At the center of almost every cup was a tiny white speck, no bigger than a barley seed. "Those are the eggs, aren't they?"

"Very good. What do they tell us?"

I felt uncomfortably on the spot, like a knobby-kneed schoolgirl no older than Sadie. "That the queen is laying?" He made a noise of affirmation, encouraging me to go on. "So if she's laying, that's good, right? A healthy hive?"

He nodded. "It means the hive is queenright." He pointed to the eggs, his usually sure and swift movements hampered by the thick gloves. "Eggs this size mean there was a queen here at least three days ago. When you check the boxes, you always want to look for fresh eggs. A box without them is a dying swarm."

He deposited the frame back and removed another, showing me the grubs, fat white blobs that looked nothing like the buzzing honeybees soaring about our yard. Another frame contained the pupas, cocooned away in caps of honey, growing and dreaming.

"Those will break free in only a few days' time," Papa said approvingly. "New workers or drones. Our hive is thriving, Ellerie. Let's put everything back together and let them wake up. We'll check on the honey next month."

"And they'll all be okay?"

I hated the note of worry in my voice. I knew they would be. Papa had never lost a colony before. But seeing how everything fit together, up close and right in my hands, reinforced what a fragile existence these bees had. Leave a frame out by accident, and the bees could crosscomb, filling up the extra space with so much honeycomb, you'd destroy the box trying to free it. Set the lid off-kilter, even slightly ajar, and the bees wouldn't be able to regulate the internal temperature. They'd work themselves to death, fanning and buzzing to heat the hive.

"They'll be just fine. You've done well today."

My face flushed with pleasure. I'd wanted to impress him, to show him I was every bit as capable as Samuel was. Samuel should have been here, should have been wearing this veiled hat, not me. But he'd slipped off after breakfast this morning, and Papa's face had grown as dark as a summer rainstorm sweeping across the mountain peaks.

Samuel had changed over the summer, racing off the farm with his best friend, Winthrop Mullins, as soon as chores were finished, sometimes even leaving the last of them to be divided up among us girls. He often quarreled with Papa, bickering over little annoyances until the two stood hot-faced, their noses curled into sneers. Mama said he must be sneaking off to see a girl, but I was at a loss to guess who it could be. We never kept anything from each other, my twin and I, and it seemed absurd to imagine him storing secrets now.

Once the box lid was securely tightened, I swooped down to pick up the metal smoker before Papa could, offering to carry it back to the supply shed for him. When we were a good distance away from the hives, he pulled off his hat, then balled up the netting and his pair of gloves into its center.

"I think this will be a good winter," he predicted, swinging his arms back and forth as we walked. I smiled as he whistled a song through his teeth, hopelessly off tune.

"What's that flower there?" he asked, pointing to a patch of pink blooms sprouting along the path.

I removed my hat for closer inspection. "Fireweed," I exclaimed proudly.

He clicked in disapproval. "Its real name?"

I tried remembering the species, written in tiny scrawl in Papa's botany book.

"Epilobium angustifolium?" I guessed, stumbling over the Latin.

Papa smiled. "Very good."

"Maybe . . . maybe I could help with the next inspection too?" I asked, keen on taking advantage of his happy state.

He nodded, and my heart leapt. Papa was a man of few words unless you got him talking about his bees, and then he'd prattle on for hours.

I envied Sam, born just minutes ahead of me—and a boy. He'd stroll after Papa to the shed without a backward glance, confident and certain of his place in the world.

Not like me, stuck in the house, forever poised and waiting for the next step in my life. Waiting for a boy to come along and ease me into my next purpose. A wife. A mother.

Waiting.

Waiting.

Waiting.

Until today.

Inside the shed, I held on to the veiled hat for just a moment longer, fingers sunk deep in the netting. I was scared to let go and release the magic of the afternoon. But an angry vibration buzzed against my thumb. A stray bee was entangled in the mesh. I struggled to gently sort through the layers, trying to free the honeybee as her legs squirmed in rage.

"Don't sting, don't sting," I whispered to her. "I'm only trying to help. You're nearly free. . . ."

The stinger sank into the side of my finger as the air split in two with a howl of anguish.

It hadn't come from me.

Papa rushed outside as more cries and shouts rose. This wasn't the sound of a children's game turned too rowdy. This pain wouldn't be patched with a splint or a kiss on the knee. It echoed across the valley, becoming a confusing cacophony of desperate heartache.

"Ellerie, get your mother. We're going into town." Papa was already halfway to the path leading into Amity Falls.

Another scream rang out, sharp and shrill, and a cold sweat trickled down my neck despite the warm afternoon. My feet remained still and unmoving. I did not want to know what was behind such torment.

"Ellerie!" Papa urged, sensing I wasn't behind him.

I tossed aside the hat, my finger swelling uncomfortably. The body of the honeybee spilled free from the netting and fell into the dirt, already dead.

2

SAMUEL WAS THERE, ALREADY A PART OF THE CROWD gathered around the porch of Elder Amos McCleary's store. Across from the clapboard schoolhouse, the general store was centered at the heart of Amity Falls. It was the place where good news came to be spread and bad news was met with instant comfort.

Mama and Papa pushed their way through the wave of bystanders, and I grabbed at Sadie to keep her from trailing after them. Merry stood next to me, tall and slim, coming nearly to my shoulders. I felt her stiffen as she caught sight of what everyone had circled around.

Molly McCleary—Amos's daughter-in-law—stretched across the body of her husband's prized stallion, Samson. He was an absolutely enormous beast, standing nearly nineteen hands tall, but he seemed less now, lying in the middle of the dusty road, chuffing in pain. Molly clung to the beast, her sobs buried in the wadded saddle blanket. The ends of the fabric were ripped ragged and stained with dark brown splotches.

Blood.

The air was tainted with the biting taste of copper pennies.

"Merry, why don't you take Sadie and some of the other children over to the schoolyard?" I asked, my hands fluttering uselessly about my little sister's face as I tried to keep the scene from her. The supply train had left just a day before, with Jebediah McCleary and Samson at the lead. Whatever had happened since then didn't need to be heard by a seven-year-old, no matter how very grown-up she fancied herself.

Sadie squirmed to avoid my grasp, blond braids flying. "I want to stay," she protested. "I'm not a baby anymore."

"No one said you were—" I started, but Merry skillfully cut me off.

"Look, there's Pardon and Trinity." She pointed to Sadie's friends. They also lingered on the outer edge of the group, standing on tiptoes to catch what they could. "Did you hear, Trinity picked up five jacks last week? On just one swipe."

"That's impossible!" Sadie scoffed, eyeing her friend with outright suspicion.

Merry shrugged. "It's what she said."

Sadie reached into her pocket and removed a handful of metal trinkets. "I've got mine. Let's see if she can prove it." She always kept a set of jacks on her, and we all knew it.

I offered Merry a grateful smile as our little sister loudly challenged the girls to a game of jacks. They were soon out of earshot, spreading their lightweight voile skirts across the schoolhouse steps. Though Merry immediately joined their game, engaging and distracting them, I felt her worried stare like a tangible weight.

"You won't! You won't!" Molly screamed, railing at Elder Matthias Dodson and snapping my attention back. The blacksmith stood over her and the horse, pistol in hand. "Jeb would never allow it."

"Molly, look at his leg. The bone is shattered. There's no way to fix that. He'll never walk again."

"He came back here, didn't he? It can't be as bad as you think."

My breath caught as I spotted the broken hind leg. It twisted to the side at an impossibly wrong angle. Matthias was right. The bones would never properly heal. Samson would have to be put down. It was criminal, allowing him to linger in such blatant misery.

Approaching thirty, Matthias was the youngest of the three town Elders, and he rubbed at the back of his neck like a little boy, clearly wishing someone else would intercede. "I don't . . . I don't know how he made it this far, but we can't—"

"Jeb will never forgive me. No. No, you can't." Her hand ran across the stallion's sleek black hide. It came away wet and red.

"Molly, it's not just the ankle. . . ."

"I said no!" She was on her feet in an instant, pushing at him, pushing at the gun.

The crowd took an uneasy step back. Molly had covered the worst of the stallion's injuries, and the front of her dress was slick with the animal's blood. His side was clawed open by four deep marks, revealing sinew and bone. Samson shifted uncomfortably, his breathing labored. Flecks of white foam gathered in the corners of his velvety lips.

Mama stepped in, her hands out to show she meant no harm. Her voice was low and soothing as she rubbed comforting circles across the woman's back, just like when we were too sick to leave bed. "Samson is hurting, Molly."

She nodded miserably.

"I know it's hard, but he's trusting you to be brave, to do the right thing."

"I know." Molly's voice croaked out. "But Jeb . . ."

"Jeb will understand."

Shivering, Molly threw herself into my mother's arms, staining her dress. "He'll want to do it himself. He has to do it. He'd never forgive me if . . ."

Mama turned, her clear blue eyes searching the crowd. They

met mine for only a moment before shifting on, looking for a man who was not there. "Then, where is he? Was he taken to Dr. Ambrose already? Where's the rest of the party?"

Matthias's jaw clicked. "No one else came back. That poor horse came tearing down the road, eyes rolled nearly to the back of his head. Never seen anything like it . . . but Jeb wasn't with him."

I glanced toward the tree line as if the rest of the supply train might come bursting forth at any moment, racing away from whatever had mauled the fallen stallion. But the pines loomed over the Falls like watchful sentinels, tall and unmoving.

Molly fell to the ground with a violent shudder, grabbing at the saddle blanket and burying her screams within it. They welled up deep within her, as pointed and sharp as barbed thorns, tearing at everything they could on the way out. "He'd never leave that horse. Not if he were . . ." The sobs broke her words apart.

Mama knelt beside her, whispering things too soft for us to hear. Eventually she helped the suffering woman to her feet, and they slowly made their way up the steps to the general store. Before Mama disappeared over the threshold, she turned back with a firm nod to Matthias. "Do it."

The bloody business was over before we had a chance to look away.

A tarp was thrown over the body so we didn't have to look at the poor beast.

But I couldn't draw my eyes away, watching four red lines bloom across the canvas, even as Samuel slipped in beside me, like a matching bookend. Though obviously not identical twins, with our fine golden hair and soft gray eyes, there was no doubt we were kin.

"What happened on that supply run?" I whispered, my insides turning and twisting. If there was something out in the woods that could have taken down a horse of Samson's size, I shuddered to guess what it could do to a person.

He adjusted the brim of his straw hat, scanning the forest. "I don't know."

"The other men . . . do you think they're—"

"I don't know, Ellerie," he repeated firmly.

"Where were you this morning?"

"I was . . . I was over near the shoreline, and we heard shouting. By the time I got here, Samson was already . . ." He pointed to the tarp. "With that gash, and the ankle . . . But it's like Matthias said, there weren't any others. . . . Just him."

"Who's 'we'?"

He dragged his eyes from the trees. "Hmm?"

"You said 'we heard shouting.' Who's 'we'?"

A short, middle-aged woman pushed her way to the front of the crowd before Samuel could answer me. "It obviously was an attack of some sort," Prudence Latheton, the carpenter's wife, guessed. "Wolves, probably."

"Never seen a wolf with claws that big," Clemency Briard said, running his fingers over the tarp where the marks had bled through. Even with the parson's fingers spread as wide as they could, the wound was bigger still. "Must have been a bear."

"But the howling . . ." Prudence trailed off. Her faded blue eyes looked about the group, seeking confirmation. "You've all heard it too, haven't you? In the night? It's been . . . just awful. And so close to town."

I knew what she spoke of. For the past three nights I'd awoken to the sound of the wolves. Their cries haunted the dark, horribly pitched and chilling. Even though I knew I was safe in our loft, I'd press myself against Merry's back, snuggling close, unable to warm myself.

"There was a grizzly near the tree line just last week," Cyrus Danforth confirmed. "Biggest damn thing I ever saw." He gestured to his shoulders, estimating its height. "And that was just on all fours. It was nosing around the Abels' smokehouse. Didn't think it'd . . . Not this."

"Where are the other Elders?" Papa asked, looking to Matthias. "We should be forming a search party."

The blacksmith scratched at his beard, as dark and shiny as a beaver pelt. "I haven't seen Leland Schäfer. Cora said he went out along the western ridge with the flock this morning. He wouldn't have heard any of the commotion from out there."

"And Amos?"

We all glanced back uneasily to the general store. We could hear the old man's sobs even from here.

"He and Martha ought to be with Molly now," Matthias concluded. "And, Parson Briard? Perhaps they'd appreciate some comforting words from you?"

Clemency's thick lips twisted with dismay. He clearly wanted to stay and watch the drama unfold. With a sigh, he gathered himself up, stretching as tall as his squat frame would allow, before giving out a benevolent nod. "I suppose you're right, Matthias. Keep the McClearys in your prayers. Good Blessings to you all."

"Good Blessings," we repeated as he headed toward the store, his steps now charged with purpose.

"We'll organize this on our own," Papa said, returning to the problem at hand. "If there was an attack, bear or otherwise, the supply train could have scattered. People may be injured and lost."

"The hell we will." Cyrus spit out a sluice of tobacco, narrowly missing Prudence's hemline. She jumped back, disgust wrinkling her nose. "That fool stallion probably threw Jeb and crossed paths with the bear before he could make it home."

Papa shook his head. The Danforth farm bordered along our fields. Our families had years of disagreements stacked between them, never truly forgotten. Papa and Cyrus could put on civil faces when needed, but the animosity was always simmering beneath the surface, threatening to boil over. "We owe it to the supply train to at least search the nearby woods."

"Look at that stallion. Torn to ribbons. You want that to happen to you, Downing? You want your wife and daughters seeing your riderless horse?"

Papa narrowed his eyes. "Of course not. But if there's a chance others could be alive—"

Prudence's husband, Edmund Latheton, reached out to Papa. He was even shorter than his wife, and his auburn beard was kept square and neat. "Gideon, maybe we should wait—the run should be back in another week or so . . ."

"If you were out there, would you want us waiting a week?"

Edmund swallowed, his jutting Adam's apple bobbing up and down like a ship at sea. "I . . . no, but . . . we've seen things too. Not a grizzly," he quickly clarified as his wife began to protest. "Or maybe it was. . . . I don't know. It was big, with silver eyes—"

"Glowing silver eyes," Prudence added.

"Glowing silver eyes," he agreed. "And it was fast. Faster than any bear I've seen." He opened his mouth once, twice, clearly unsure how to finish the story. "Yes, if I was out in those woods, I'd want someone to come find me . . . but having seen that . . . thing . . . I don't want to be the one going after them."

"Glowing silver eyes," Cyrus repeated, waggling his fingers theatrically. "You sound as nutty as your pa did, Latheton."

Papa's eyebrows shot up. "Is that you volunteering, then, Danforth?"

Cyrus wiped a sodden handkerchief across his forehead.

"Hardly. I'm not about to get myself killed for Jebediah McCleary. I don't care if he is an Elder's son. He knows the risks he takes every time he goes over the pass. And so does every other fool who went with him."

"You don't benefit from those runs?" Papa asked, his voice heavy with skepticism.

"I'm a self-made man," Cyrus said, his chest puffed out as wide and important-looking as it would go, undoubtedly to try to make up for the several inches of height Papa had over him.

"A self-made man who took sugar with his coffee this morning," Samuel muttered, his nostrils flaring with derision.

I was listening so intently to the argument that my brother's comment first slid over me, unnoticed. But like a burr, it caught in my mind, prodding for recognition.

I leaned in toward Samuel, lowering my voice. "How do you know how Cyrus Danforth takes his coffee?"

"What?" he asked, unmoving. His eyes were fixed on Papa with a sudden intensity as if he couldn't bear to look away.

"You just said he had sugar this morning," I pressed. "Why were you at the Danforths'?"

"I—wasn't."

Samuel was an awful liar. The tips of his ears always grew pink, and his sentences were reduced to stammering messes.

A bit of movement at the edge of the group drew my attention, and I looked over to see Rebecca Danforth joining the crowd. My best friend raised her fingers with a small wave, and my own hand echoed in automatic response before I noticed that Samuel's did the same.

He'd focused wholly on Rebecca. When he dragged his eyes back to me, his smile died away and his cheeks turned a faint red.

"Did you go see Rebecca this morning?" I hissed, my voice softer than a whisper. A bolt of realization struck me, leaving me aghast. "Is *she* why you've been sneaking off all summer? Rebecca Danforth?"

"No!" he insisted. "Let it alone, Ellerie."

"Are you courting her?"

"I said let it alone."

"But—"

"Enough!" he growled. The thick lines of his eyebrows leveled into an angry ledge, and his face was splotchy.

I snuck one last peek at Rebecca, my mind racing. When Mama had supposed that Samuel was off visiting a girl, it had never occurred to me it might be her. It just wasn't possible.

By all rights, we never should have become friends. The bad blood between our families went back generations, to even before her great-grandfather had killed mine. But as Danforths and Downings, we were always paired as desk-mates at school, and proximity can often create the best of relationships. We'd grown up sharing our pail lunches, weaving each other chains of clover, and swapping stories in the wildflower fields that separated her house from mine. Though we were no longer little girls, we still shared everything—books, recipes, even the few bits of jewelry we owned. She couldn't have kept a secret like this from me.

And Samuel . . .

He was my twin. I should have sensed this; I should have known.

But looking between them now, I knew I'd missed it. Whatever bond I'd shared with them wasn't as strong as I'd imagined it to be. I'd been completely in the dark, without even an inkling of suspicion. My own cheeks heated and my stomach churned as I imagined how my cluelessness must have amused them.

When had it begun? Rebecca had stayed overnight just last week. We'd slept in the barn's hayloft, giggling about the boys in town till the moon had sunk behind the mountains. She must have thought it was such a good joke, never letting on about the truth. She must have thought I was the biggest fool, never guessing her secret.

"I'm going into the woods," Papa stated, firm enough to bring me back to the present. "Jeb would never have let that horse out of his sight—we have to assume something on that run went terribly, terribly wrong. . . . I can't make any of you come with me, but I can ask. It's the right thing to do, no matter what might be out there."

"A fool's errand," Cyrus sniped. "And I'm no fool. I won't be a part of any of this." With a snarl, he released a final slug of tobacco. "Somebody bury that horse before it starts to smell."

He stalked off, muttering to himself. Rebecca's lips pressed together into a thin line.

Papa scanned the crowd, his dark gray eyes lingering on every man present. He paused, clearly hoping for others to volunteer. "Judd Abrams?"

The tall rancher ran his hands through silvering hair, tousling it uncomfortably. "You know I would, but I've got a field of pregnant heifers, due any day. I can't leave them."

Papa ran his tongue over his teeth. "Calvin Buhrman?"

Violet grabbed her husband's elbow, silently pleading with him to stay. After a moment of indecision, the tavern owner shook his tight, dark curls.

"Matthias Dodson? Will you ride with me?"

I hated the look of crushed hope in my father's eyes as the Elder waved aside his plea. "You know I can't leave town, especially with Amos in such a sorry state."

The three Elders were tied to the Falls in a way that none of its other citizens were. They were the keepers of law and tradition, justice and order. While Parson Briard might have been in charge of nurturing and nourishing the soul of Amity Falls, the Elders protected its head and heart.

"I'll go with you, Papa."

I heard the words before realizing it was my own voice that spoke.

There was a nervous titter from the group, but I didn't care. I'd been there this morning to help him, and I wanted to help again now.

I'd show him I was every bit as capable as Sam was.

More so even.

Because I was there. Here.

I could be the reliable one he needed.

My face burned crimson as Papa shook his head.

"I could be of help. Even if it's just . . ." I racked my mind, searching for something to lift the weight of defeat from his shoulders. "The brush Samson ran through! It's bound to be bloodied. It'll need to be burned away, or it'll draw all sorts of things. Let me at least do that."

"I need you at home, Ellerie, looking after your sisters."

"Mama would have your hide if she knew you were going into the forest by yourself. And what about the Rules?" I persisted after Papa as he turned to go. "You can't go alone."

Matthias opened his mouth, undoubtedly ready to offer some sort of dispensation he truly couldn't make without the other two Elders, but Sam spoke up first.

"She's right, Papa."

Rebecca had stepped to his side, her hand curved just inches from his.

"You can't go by yourself."

"I didn't hear you offering to go before. In fact, I've not heard you offering to do much of anything all summer," Papa shot back.

"I . . ." Any words that were to follow dried in Sam's mouth as Papa's eyes fell to Sam's and Rebecca's almost-held hands, missing nothing.

"I see there is much to discuss when I return."

Samuel pushed aside Rebecca's hand and ran after our father. "I'm coming with you."

"Sam!" Rebecca's voice was soft and pleading, but my brother didn't stop. He whizzed past me, and I had to step out of the way to avoid being hit.

Papa chewed the inside of his cheek. "Fine. Fill a pack, but be quick about it."

3

MY FIST STRUCK THE DOUGH, SMASHING INTO ITS THICK, warm pliancy with a satisfying thud. I struck it again, leaving a giant dent before gathering it up into a loaf. It still looked misshapen. I hit it once more.

"Whose face are you imagining right now?" my mother asked, coming around the tall kitchen table with a tray of hot bread. She deposited the loaves onto the cooling racks before bustling back to the oven.

"I don't know what you mean," I said, slamming the dough back onto the table. A burst of flour rose into the air, mixing with sparkling dust motes as they danced in and out of the late-afternoon rays of sun that painted the kitchen orange.

"Something's been bothering you since we came back from town yesterday," she observed. "You've nearly pounded that loaf into oblivion."

Using the back of my hand, I pushed aside a stray ringlet of hair that had pulled free from my bun. I only ever wore my hair up on baking days. Our kitchen simmered with yeast and heat, far too hot for my usual thick braid.

"There's nothing wrong with having a bad day," Mama continued, crossing back to the table. She grabbed the dough from me and worked it into a more manageable shape. "And there's certainly nothing wrong with taking out frustrations while baking. I do whenever your father does something to vex me. Why pick a fight when you can bake a loaf of bread?"

She slammed the dough into another loaf pan, adding an exclamation to her point.

"Mama, we make bread almost every day."

Her eyes twinkled as she tapped my nose, dusting it with flour. "Exactly."

Mama sold her baked goods in town—to the Buhrmans' tavern and at the general store. Her sourdough was good enough that even the most tightfisted misers would fork over the shiny dime Amos McCleary charged per loaf.

But it was her honey cakes that had all of Amity Falls lining up.

She only made them once a year—just after Papa harvested the combs, and all the honey had been extracted and bottled. He'd make sure our larder was fully stocked for the winter and would then sell the surplus in town—charging a whole dollar a bottle. Though people claimed to be scandalized by the price, he never had a shortage of customers, and the honey was always sold out before day's end.

All but three bottles.

He saved those for Mama.

Mama's cakes were deceptively simple. Flour, spices, fresh cream, and three eggs each. No nuts or chocolate or sugared icing. She never added anything to take away from the true star of the dessert—Papa's honey.

As the story went, shortly after they were married, Mama brought her first honey cake to a church social, and all the women in town nearly stampeded her to get the recipe. But no one could ever correctly replicate it—even using the precious honey they'd bought from Papa. When people demanded to know how to achieve the impossibly thin and moist layers or the perfectly caramelized tang, Mama would smile mysteriously and say it was just a pinch of love.

Some claimed it was more like a touch of magic. Even Parson Briard—after his wife had made a particularly disastrous cake—said Mama must have been blessed by the angels of Heaven. There was no other way to account for it.

I'd watched her make them for years, studying every step—down to the way her fingertips danced across the rolling pin—but I'd never been able to make an exact match. Maybe Mama did have a bit of magic in her.

"Tell me all about it," she said, scattering another scoopful of flour across the table before starting on the next round of dough.

I toyed with a hangnail, worrying it back and forth till it broke free. I didn't know what to say. Samuel and Papa had left while Mama had been tending to Molly. She hadn't heard who my brother had been sneaking off to see all summer, and as mad as I was at him, it wasn't my story to tell.

"You're worried about Sam," she guessed, and it felt impossible to disagree. "And your father."

We'd watched the brushfires burn late into the night, shimmering through the trees. She hadn't said so, but I knew that Mama had thought they'd return yesterday.

"Do you . . . do you ever wonder what life is like outside of the Falls?" The question bubbled up from deep within, surprising me.

"Out of the valley?" Mama asked. I nodded. "I can't say it's never crossed my mind. Especially when I was around your age. I wanted to go off and see so much more of the world. See a big city skyline. Buy a fancy dress and have tea in a proper restaurant."

"Why didn't you?"

She raised her shoulders. "Other dreams became more important."

"Papa?"

"And you. Your brother. Our home here." She paused, rolling the dough between her hands thoughtfully. "Your father left the Falls once."

"When Uncle Ezra went missing." I knew the story well.

My father's younger brother, Ezra, had gone hunting by himself one summer, venturing out past the Bells. He'd never returned. Townsfolk had searched for him for over a week before giving up.

"Gideon wouldn't let it rest. He said he knew Ezra was still alive, out there someplace. He went over the pass, looking for him in nearby towns, even going into the city."

"But he didn't find him," I concluded. We grew up with tales of Ezra and his adventurous spirit, spoken in hushed tones.

"Your father still thinks Ezra's out there, that he'll come back one day. As big and wide and wondrous as the world can be, everyone eventually wants to come home."

Before I could answer, telling her how much I wanted to leave, how much I wanted to find my place in that wide and wondrous world, Sadie's tabby cat flew out from nowhere and landed on the table with a hiss.

"Sadie, how many times have I told you to keep Buttons out of the house while I'm baking?" Mama cried, hollering loud enough for my sister to hear her in the barn.

We saw her small silhouette race by the windows. Her footsteps clattered across the porch's splintered planks, further aggravating the cat. "Sorry, sorry!" she exclaimed, bursting into the kitchen. "We took him to the barn, but he got scared."

"Can't imagine anything horrible enough to scare that monster," I said, jumping back as he swiped at me, claws bared like tiny knives.

Sadie had found him when he was a kitten, no more than a few days old. He'd been trapped in a bag near the creek that ran behind Papa's hives. She wasn't supposed to play near the boxes, but she claimed to have heard crying. We all assumed he'd die before the day was over, but Sadie fed him drops of milk every hour and cuddled him close at night. He was well and truly her cat, despising the rest of us. Papa said he had no use for an animal so full of hate, but Buttons had proved to be an excellent mouser so was allowed to stay.

"I think he saw that thing with the silver eyes," Sadie started as Merry came in, arms weighed down with two pails of milk. She let the screen door crash shut. It spooked Buttons, who leapt off the table with a miserable yowl. "Trinity says she sees them outside her window at night. I think that's what Buttons saw too."

"Bessie kicked at him," Merry corrected Sadie, her eyes wandering over the cooling racks, looking for an easy snack to grab. "That beast tried swiping at her ankles, poor cow."

"My sweet, practical girl," Mama said, cupping Merry's chin and giving her cheek a fond pinch. Mama turned to Sadie. "Don't pay any attention to Trinity Brewster's stories. That girl has a penchant for the dramatic."

Sadie made a noise of agreement. "It's true. She couldn't even pick up three jacks today."

"It is strange, though, don't you think?" I asked, scattering fresh flour onto the table as Mama grabbed the basket of brown eggs, preparing to make another batch. "The Lathetons mentioned something with silver eyes too. Why would so many people imagine seeing the same thing?"

Mama's voice was full of sage authority. "It's a small-town problem. In the big cities, with so much going on, people have more to talk about. But here, everyone knows what everyone says— sometimes only minutes after it's been said. We can't talk about the things we really want to, so people invent other things to discuss. It's easier to have a problem with something out in the pines than with the person who lives next door."

"Like Mr. Danforth?" Sadie asked, plopping onto one of the stools. Buttons lay in her arms, purring contentedly and looking for all the world like a sweet cat. I swear he smirked at me when our eyes met.

"Like Mr. Danforth," Mama agreed, sifting flour and yeast into the bowl.

"Wilhelmina Jenkins says that Sam is going to marry Rebecca Danforth. She said she saw them kissing down by the lake last week." Sadie's legs swung back and forth. "Do you think Mr. Danforth would interrupt the ceremony?"

Mama burst into laughter. "I can't imagine a less likely bride for Samuel than Rebecca Danforth. Wilhelmina Jenkins ought to have her eyes examined."

I drew a series of spirals in the flour. Mama was as in the dark as I had been, then. It should have made me feel better, but instead my stomach ached, squirming uncomfortably as I withheld the truth.

Mama reached into the basket and neatly cracked open an egg with just two fingers. I'd always admired her ability to do that.

"Look," she said, gesturing to the bowl. "Double yolks. That's a sign of good luck."

Sadie leaned over the table, straining to see. Two yellow circles peered up at us like eyes.

Mama grabbed a second egg. Her breath hitched as she dropped the insides into the bowl.

Another set of double yolks.

Curiously, I fished out an egg for myself and studied it. It didn't look any different from the others in the basket. I broke it open, using the side of the bowl to crack the shell, then cast it from me as if it was something horrid and squirmy.

We emptied out the entire basket, ruining Mama's dough and wasting over a dozen eggs in all. Each contained two yolks.

"I've never seen anything like this," Mama murmured darkly, studying the sea of yellow before us.

"Maybe we're just extra lucky?" Sadie asked. "That's good, right? With Papa and Sam in the woods? I'd be so scared to go in there, especially with all those monsters running around."

"There are no monsters," Mama said, pushing the bowl away with one final look. The insides steamed. "It was just a bear that wandered too close to the Falls. Maybe a rogue wolf or two."

"But there *used* to be monsters," Sadie pressed. "Abigail told me all about them."

Sometime at the start of summer, Sadie had created an imaginary friend for herself. She was called Abigail and—by Sadie's account—was as beautiful as a princess, dressing in fine gowns and silk slippers. She often whispered town gossip to Sadie, who tended to relay it to the rest of us at the most embarrassing moments. I'd overheard Mama fretting about Abigail's existence to Papa early on. She'd worried Sadie was far past the age when it was acceptable to have a made-up friend, but Papa didn't mind. We didn't live directly in town, the way the rest of Sadie's friends did, and if she wanted to have a companion to chat with while milking the cows or racing about the farm, it was all right with him.

"Some think that, yes," Mama said, tactfully avoiding all mention of Abigail.

"Don't you?"

"I think . . ." She pushed wayward strands of hair off her forehead with a sigh. "I think when the founders first came to the Falls, they were exhausted and under an immense amount of strain. They'd lost so many people to animal attacks on the journey and wanted to blame something that was as big and wild as the land was. So they saw monsters and they hung the Bells. But time went by, and there's not been even a glimpse of those creatures for decades. You know that."

"Because of the Bells," Sadie said, a firm believer in Amity Falls's legends.

"Because there were never any monsters to begin with," Mama said, dusting off her hands. Buttons saw this as a direct threat to himself and flew out of Sadie's lap, then disappeared into a dark corner. "If that cat lands in the dough, he's staying outside tonight."

"Not with the monsters!" Sadie howled, leaping after him. "Abigail said they'd love to eat him right up!"

"There are no monsters," I said, echoing Mama.

An eerie cry spread across the valley as if to prove me wrong.

Another joined in.

And another.

This wasn't a lone wolf wandering too close to town. This was an entire pack, and they sounded on the hunt. I thought of Papa and Sam out in that forest, so near the wolves, and shuddered.

Even Mama paused. "Not Gideon, not my Gideon," she repeated in a whispered prayer.

When the howling came to an end, she looked at each of us, weighing our fears. "We should light the Our Ladies."

A chill raced over me, setting my arms to gooseflesh even in the stifling kitchen. We hadn't had cause to use them in months. Not since the great blizzard in March, which had blanketed the entire town in flakes so thick, it had been nearly impossible to see anything but the biting, burning white.

Merry froze. "The Our Ladies?"

Mama threw a damp towel over the last of the dough. "It'll keep till I return. Ellerie, you're in charge."

"You can't leave us!" Sadie said, dropping Buttons to fling herself into Mama's skirts. "Not with the monsters out there! You heard them!"

Mama struggled to extricate herself from my little sister's grasp. "I won't be gone even an hour. I'll start on the eastern edge, and by the time a few are burning, people in town will see and light the rest."

"I'll go." The words left my mouth before I'd even made up my mind. "I bet I can have five lit before dark."

My mother's eyes softened and she grasped my hand. "That's very brave of you, Ellerie."

Merry's eyes were wide. I could see she was trying to muster the courage to volunteer as well.

I squeezed her hand. "I'll grab a lantern and be back before you know it."

The Our Ladies were a series of giant bonfires built along the edge of Amity Falls, just yards away from where the tall pines sprouted and the boundary ceded from town into the unbroken wilderness.

Three generations ago, when the town was being settled, the Latheton family had created the first wave of them, perfecting the materials and shape so that the fires could burn all through the night without needing to be fed. Morbidly, they resembled tall, elegant women, their wide bases resembling skirts, so the structures had been christened "the Our Ladies." Just like the Holy Mother protects her flock, the Our Ladies held the darkness back from the Falls with the purity of their flames' light.

At first, the Falls had burned through dozens of bonfires every night to keep the creatures of the woods cowering in the pines. But as the town had grown and the land had been tamed, the Our Ladies were only used during storms or if someone was foolish enough to venture into the forest and lose their way. Unburnt pyres dotted the perimeter of our town, the virgin wood jutting from the stacks like curved rib cages, waiting to be called into service.

When lit, the fires brightened the whole area with their amber glow. Long, flickering shadows raced across the valley, like hungry hands stretched out, ready to snatch away anyone unlucky enough to be lost in the woods.

As I made my way through fields of our wildflowers, the sun was already dipping its blinding edge behind the western range of Blackspire. Made up of four mountains, with a solitary fifth to the south, the cluster was often referred to as God's Grasp. Amity Falls lay across the valley's heart line and did inspire a certain peacefulness, as though we truly did reside in our Heavenly Father's palm.

The Falls's founding families had been traveling by wagon train, toward the promise of abundant land under the western sun. Their party had been plagued by misfortune, losing cattle and even a couple of teamsters to the tricky trail and deadly mountain predators. When Matthias Dodson's great-grandfather had discovered the beautiful shores of Greenswold Lake and the miles and miles of land, lush and ready for farming, the wagon train had set up camp and never left. They'd hung the Bells—any bits of brass or silver the settlers could spare—along the edge of the forest, claiming the purity of the chimes would hold back the shadowy terrors. More families arrived to clear the surrounding woods. More trinkets were hung, bells with bowls and clappers, and the so-called monsters were driven from the settlement. Amity Falls grew from outpost to village to town.

Dusk stole across the land, and the constant droning of the cicadas faded away. It wasn't until the riot stopped that I realized how loud they'd been. The sudden silence set my teeth on edge.

Even the Bells were still.

Twilight didn't linger long in the mountains, and I didn't want to be tripping over tree roots and briar bushes in the dark. Our fields came to an end, and I paused for a moment, on tiptoes and with bated breath, staring out at the sea of wheat in front of me.

This wide swath, grown yellow in the summer sun, was all that separated me from the pines. The stalks were even taller than I was, and once I was among them, the only thing I would have to guide me would be the scattering of stars pinpricking the sky. If anyone was out there, if anything was after me, I'd never know it was coming. I tried pushing aside thoughts of silver-eyed monsters but nearly jumped out of my skin as a prickly tuft brushed my cheek.

A slight breeze rustled through the field, breaking the oppressive heat and setting the wheat to whisper. It waved at me, as if beckoning, beseeching me to join it. The center of my throat was dry and sticking.

I stepped in.

The stalks pushed aside with an easy pliancy as I slipped between them. I was only a few feet in but already felt swallowed by their magnitude.

A crack sounded from deep in the midst of the swaying stalks. I paused, straining my ears to hear it again. John Brewster, Trinity's father and one of the Falls's farmers, said you could stand in a field of corn and actually hear the plants growing, crackling, and popping as they shot skyward.

Was wheat like that too? Or was there someone else in the field with me?

"No," I reprimanded myself. "Stop this foolishness and light the Our Ladies."

I pushed on, keenly aware of a rustling to my left. It kept pace with me, speeding up when I broke into a sprint, pausing when I stopped. The stalks were too dense for my lantern's light to penetrate, but I thought I heard a soft in and out, like someone catching their breath, just beyond where I was.

Or was it only the wind?

The wheat could drive a person mad.

Nearing the end of the field, I could finally make out the pines looming, as formidable as a fortress. They blocked out the scope of sky and starlight.

A tinkling of Bells rose as I broke free of the wheat. A few stalks clung to my skirts, desperate to pull me back into their ranks. The first Our Lady was just ahead of me. Twelve feet tall and ten feet wide, she towered over the landscape, her arms outstretched to beckon wayward travelers home. If Papa and Sam were still in the area, they would have to see her.

The ground around the Our Ladies was razed, scorched from previous fires. Fallen limbs, lashed together with old rope, made up the structure. The base was stuffed with logs, broken bits of furniture too far gone to save, and an outer layer of twigs and dried leaves. The whole thing reeked of tar and varnish—a special concoction the Lathetons had perfected.

I set my lantern upon the blackened soil and fumbled to free a bit of kindling from her skirt. It caught quickly and I fed it into the base, gently blowing on the sparks to strengthen the flames. There was a quick flare as the tar lit and the fire danced up the structure, bringing light into the world once more.

I watched her burn for a minute, maybe two, until I was satisfied she was well and truly ablaze, then turned toward the next one. The Our Ladies dotted the boundary lines, spread out every half mile or so. It was going to be a long night. Hopefully others in town would see that the eastern Our Ladies had been lit and would rush to help, setting fire to the ones in the far west.

When I reached the second structure, I caught a bit of movement at the periphery of my eye. A girl emerged from the wheat, pushing aside and parting the stalks as if they were the Red Sea. She was too far away to properly identify and traveled without a lantern, but her dress glowed pale blue under the light of the rising moon.

My eyes flickered to the Danforths' farm, only a mile or so away. The cabin was at the top of a rolling hill, and I could just make out the glow of candles from within.

Rebecca.

I raised my hand in greeting but couldn't tell if she noticed. She wandered over to the Our Lady closest to her—two structures down from where I stood—and paused before kneeling. Moments later there was a spark of metal against flint and the Our Lady caught fire. Rebecca circled around to the far side, disappearing behind the burning edifice.

I turned back to my own Our Lady and grabbed a fistful of kindling from it. Others along the perimeter lit as I worked, and I whispered a prayer of gratitude for the swift feet of our neighbors.

As more and more Our Ladies caught fire, the valley warmed, growing bright and golden. I imagined the pack of wolves racing through the forest, pausing at such an unusual sight before slinking back into the safety of the night, far from Papa, far from Sam.

I started the trek to the next pyre, but a burst of clattering chimes from the pines drew my attention.

Something was moving within the shadows, caught in a tangle of Bells.

Something big.

I raised my lantern, squinting against its glare. A figure, then another, stumbled from the tree line. They were a disjointed mess of dark smudges against the black earth, and for a moment, I couldn't tell if they were human or wolf.

"Ellerie?" a familiar voice called out. "Is that you?"

"Papa!" I shouted, and broke into a sprint, racing toward him. He and Samuel huddled against one another, holding each other up. There was a makeshift splint on Sam's ankle, and though it was tightly lashed with strips of torn shirt, the skin was swollen enough to have split open.

They both stank, covered in a mixture of blood, old sweat, and above all, the stench of fear.

I'd never seen my father look like this. He seemed to have lost ten pounds overnight. His cheeks had a hollowed gauntness, and his eyes were shaky and haunted.

"It's okay. You're home now. You're safe," I said, embracing him. I tried to not wrinkle my nose, feeling the cold, wet grime cling to his shirt, cling to me. We'd have to use an entire bar of soap to get the stink from their clothes.

I took the moment to peek over his shoulder, searching for the others from the supply run. No one else followed them out of the pines.

"Is there—did you find . . . ?" I trailed off, knowing there was no decent way to phrase a question I already knew the answer to.

"Not . . . not now, Ellerie."

The gritty coarseness of his voice chilled me. He must have spent all day and night shouting for the missing men. Even his breathing had a harsh rasp to it.

Samuel groaned. His eyes were glazed over, and a light seemed missing from within him. He stared ahead with dull incomprehension. I don't think he even registered where he was.

"Let's get you both home. Mama and I have been making bread all day—and there's stew. And I'll heat water for a bath—you won't have to do a thing. And then—"

"Samuel? Sam!"

Rebecca Danforth came racing across the field, her hair swinging wildly behind her. She sounded near hysterics.

"You're hurt," she exclaimed, kneeling to examine his ankle. "What happened? We've been so worried. We—"

"We need to get them back to the house," I said, cutting her off. "Can you help us?"

"Of course, of course." She slipped beneath his arm, pressing herself against his side, and together they stumbled off.

I snaked my arm around Papa's waist and started after them.

"Hang back, Ellerie," he mumbled. "Give them a moment together. I think Sam needs it."

We watched as they staggered off. At first, Rebecca did all the work, propping my brother and all but dragging him alongside her. Just as they stepped into the wheat, he seemed to come back to his senses, and his hand fell across her back, tracing fond circles.

I paused, squinting at his fingers. They stood out in stark contrast to the floral print of her dress.

Her dark floral print.

With confusion, I glanced back to the row of burning Our Ladies, but the girl in the pale dress was gone.

4

I DREAMT OF A FOREST GLADE, SHROUDED IN SHADOWS and dotted with eyes.

Silver glowing eyes.

Waking up, I lashed out, caught in a confusion of tangled bed-sheets, fighting against one twisted around my ankle.

"Stop it, Ellerie," Merry muttered, still asleep as she snatched the quilt from me, leaving the cold to sober my racing mind.

I sat up, grumbly and miserable. We hadn't gone to bed until long after midnight, and judging by the gray sky, dawn was still an hour away.

Rumors of Papa's return had spread quickly through the Falls, and the three Elders had raced to the farmhouse to pepper him with questions.

Had he found Amos's son?

Had he seen evidence of the attack?

What exactly was in those woods?

Papa had gently pushed off their barrage, saying he'd found the remains of a campfire, remains of the tents, and finally, nearby, the remains of the men themselves.

Amos's dark skin had turned ashen before he'd suggested that a town meeting be set for the next morning. The Elders had left with deeply furrowed brows, whispering uneasily among themselves.

I rolled out of bed and tiptoed to the window, careful to skirt the two squeaky floorboards in the middle of the loft. The room was tight quarters, and my siblings were all notoriously light sleepers. Sadie huddled on the other side of Merry, snoring gently. Samuel's bed was wedged into a dark corner, as far from us girls as he could get. An old sheet had been hung a few years ago, as our bodies—once so familiar to one another—had taken on lives of their own. Though it afforded us a modicum of privacy, the faded check print was thin enough that we heard every toss, turn, and mumble he made.

I peered out the small diamond-paned window and across the still fields. The Our Ladies were nothing more than smoking piles of embers and ash now. They'd have to be cleared away at dawn's light. A team of volunteers would be needed to scour the outer edges of the forest, looking for fallen branches, before Edmund Latheton could start on their replacements.

After Papa spoke at the town meeting, I wondered if anyone would be brave enough to offer their assistance.

Papa and Mama had talked into the early hours of the morning. I'd heard their hushed whispers carried up the stairs, though I hadn't been able to make out actual words. That worried me more than anything else, I think. Papa was always early to bed. He'd wake before the sun rose, to start his work around the farm. I couldn't begin to imagine how Mama would budge him from bed this morning.

From behind the curtain, Samuel coughed once and rolled over.

My eyes fell on the Danforth farm. Their crops bordered along our garden, and it never ceased to amuse me that even Cyrus's rows of corn ran perpendicular to Papa's tomatoes and beets. The cabin was dark and still, and the windows met my gaze with a vacant, hollow stare. It reminded me of the expression on Samuel's face as he'd staggered from the pines last night, and I looked away.

The color of Rebecca's dress still gnawed at me. Someone in a pale gown had lit that Our Lady, I was certain of it. But who could it have been? Rebecca wouldn't have had time or cause to race home to change, and there were no other women who lived in the vicinity. Rebecca's mother had died giving birth to her little brother, Mark, and—as the Danforths supplied most of Amity Falls's produce—their property was enormous. Their next neighbor was miles away.

"Ellerie, is that you?" Samuel whispered.

I filled a cup of water from the pitcher at the bureau and slipped behind the sheet. Sam was sitting up, struggling to adjust the pillow beneath his swollen ankle.

"Let me do that," I offered, giving him the water before plumping the battered pillow.

A tattered book jostled free and fell to the floor.

"Heroes of Greek Myths," I read, before tucking it near him. "I haven't seen that book since we were children at school. Remember how we used to pore through it?"

"Sadie brought it home—I thought I'd borrow it for a bit." He downed the water in one long swallow before beckoning for me to join him. My knees creaked as I knelt beside the bedframe, and I suddenly felt so much older than eighteen years of age. I was grateful when Samuel handed over one of his blankets, and I wrapped it around my shoulders to ward off the morning's chill.

"How are you feeling?"

His eyebrows, golden and thick even in the dimly lit loft, furrowed together as he winced, sinking back under the quilts. "The ankle hurts, I'm not going to lie. But it'll be all right. I don't think anything is broken."

After Samuel had eaten last night, Mama had pried him away

from Rebecca and helped him up the stairs. She'd snuck him a shot of Papa's whiskey to help him sleep, and he'd been gone to the world before the Elders had arrived. Rebecca had stood peering up at the loft, chewing on the inside of her cheek, until Papa had gently suggested she return home. Her eyes had met mine, wet and miserable, until I'd offered a small smile. She'd returned it with a tentative one of her own, and for a moment, all had felt right between us.

"What happened?" I asked, pushing aside the memory of my friend's worry.

"We found Samson's trail easy enough. There was so much blood. Swathed all along the brambles and the trunks . . . It was even up real high." He paused to gesture with his fingers. "Dripping down from the pine needles. . . . How'd it get way up there? Then we . . . we got separated. It gets dark early in the forest, you know?" Samuel continued. "One minute Papa was right behind me, trying to pull down some of those . . . branches to burn . . . and the next, I couldn't see him anywhere. It was just me and the fires and all that blood. I shouted for him but never heard a reply. I tried . . . I tried following the flames—he'd have to be at the end of them, right? But he wasn't. It was just . . . those things."

"The wolves?" My nightmare lingered uneasily.

He shook his head slowly. "Those weren't like any kind of wolf I've seen before. They were big, Ellerie, so big. Bigger than a bear, bigger than the hive boxes, big enough to swallow the world whole."

A patch of icy unease formed at the back of my neck, and grew large enough to plummet down my spine like raindrops on a windowpane. Growing up, I'd assumed that the legends of monsters in the woods were nothing more than elaborate fairy tales, stories told to keep foolish children from getting lost in the pines.

Were the stories true?

Were the monsters real?

"Whatever they were, they went after me, but it wasn't like a chase. They were too fast for that. I could have never outrun them. I twisted my ankle, trying to get away. But it was . . . it was almost like a game to them. They were playing with me, laughing at my fear."

"You heard them laugh?" The words fluttered from my mouth, as insubstantial as autumn leaves caught in a brusque wind.

Samuel scrunched his eyes shut. "I hear them laughing even now."

Sweat beaded across his brow, and I dabbed it away with a corner of my blanket. His skin was flushed hot. A fever and nothing more.

"Don't think about that now, Sam. You're at home and you're safe and those things can't get you here."

I glanced out the window, pleased to see soft gray light filtering through. Mama would be up soon. She'd know what to do, what medicines Samuel ought to have.

Medicines.

Jeb and all those men had been on their way out of the mountains to secure supplies for the Falls. Runs usually took place twice a year—as soon as the ice melted away, ensuring the pass out of God's Grasp was clear, and again at the end of summer, before early snows could set in, making travel impossible. We hadn't had a group head out since April. How low were Dr. Ambrose's supplies?

Another group would have to be sent out, and soon. It was as simple as that. Medicine wasn't the only thing brought back. We relied on those runs to get supplies that couldn't be procured in town.

Guns and bullets. Cloth and thread. Books. Sugar. Tea. Coffee. They simply couldn't be produced in a town so small.

Selfishly I'd hoped for fabric for a new dress. I'd shot up two inches since spring. Mama thought it must be my final growth spurt, and I prayed she was right. No clothing hung properly on my frame. Bodices stretched uncomfortably as I went about my chores, and my wool stockings could be seen, peeking above the leather of my black boots. I was already taller than Mama, and the only cloth at McCleary's were two bolts of floral batiste. They were beautiful, to be sure, but would do nothing to keep me warm once leaves began to fall.

"Ellerie?" Samuel whispered.

His lips were chapped, and I fished a tin of salve from the rickety table near his bed. Mama made balms and lotions with the abandoned beeswax after harvest.

"You believe me, about the monsters, don't you?" His gray eyes were glassy, but I couldn't tell if it was from the fever or if he was about to cry.

"It must have been terrifying," I answered carefully.

He grabbed my hand. "I thought I'd never see you again."

I squeezed his fingers. It was only his fevered imagination, but my heart thunked out of rhythm as I envisioned a world without my twin.

"You'll keep me safe, won't you? You've always kept me safe. Ever since we were little."

He sounded little now, younger than even Sadie. A sad, small, lost boy, desperately in need of protection.

"Of course."

"I couldn't . . . I couldn't stand the thought of being without you. We've never not been together. It just . . ." He broke off into a sob.

"Don't think like that, Sam. We're a team, right? You and I. You know I'd never let anything happen to you."

His eyelids fluttered shut as he slipped back into the uneasy embrace of exhaustion.

I could count on one hand the number of times I'd seen Samuel cry. Though I was sorry he'd hurt himself, and had such a frightening experience in the woods, I wondered if this moment would be a turning point for us. All summer we'd been growing further apart, me remaining at home while he snuck off on adventures unknown. But now . . . perhaps everything could go back to what it had been like before.

I watched his chest rise and fall, a satisfied peace settling over me as I counted to one hundred before deciding it was finally late enough to wake Mama.

But when I tried slipping my hand from Samuel's grip, he tightened his hold.

I flexed and twisted my fingers but couldn't squirm free. Though his face was slack, his grasp was as tight as a bear trap. I tried prying loose, to no avail.

Samuel's lips were moving. Just barely.

I leaned in close, pressing my ear to hear the refrain he whispered over and over, like a prayer, an entreaty.

"They're coming for you. *She's* coming for you."

My breath hitched, caught in the hollow of my throat. "Sam, what are you saying? Who's coming? Who's 'she'?"

I glanced out the window, half expecting to see a figure perched on the sill, pressed up and leering through the panes. A figure long and lithe. A figure wearing a pale dress. But there was only a cool lavender sky.

He made a small whine, already deep in another dream. I was about to wake him, demand answers, but heard a rustle behind me.

"Ellerie, what on earth are you doing up so early?"

Mama poked her head around the curtain, squinting. Her hair was still in its nightly braid, hanging long over her shoulder.

"I couldn't sleep. I kept having nightmares."

"I shouldn't wonder, after last night. You didn't wake up Sam, did you?"

I shook my head. "He stirred earlier but then . . ." I nodded back to him. His mouth hung slack, bits of drool wetting the corners. His hand fell from mine, as if he'd not been clenching it just moments before.

"Why don't you come downstairs and help with breakfast?" she asked, pulling me to my feet. "We'll make a pot of coffee for just you and me first. It's going to be a long day for everyone. We might as well make sure we're fortified."

"That hit the spot," Papa said, pushing aside his empty plate with a contented sigh. "Thank you, Sarah. Ellerie."

Mama and I had made a veritable feast: eggs as yellow as sunshine and freckled with cracked black pepper; thick slices of ham; tomatoes fresh from the garden and fried so perfectly that the tangy insides burst in our mouths; and towers of pancakes, drizzled with the final dregs of the maple syrup jar bought from the Vissers' orchard last winter. Sadie ran her pancake over her plate, wiping up every last bit of the sticky sweetness. She smacked her lips, clearly longing for more.

Mama accepted a quick peck from Papa as she reached in, collecting his plate and cutlery.

"The girls can clear the table," he said, drawing her back to sit on his lap while my sisters and I locked eyes, trying not to giggle.

She tweaked his nose before rising. "I'll wash up as you all go to the town meeting."

"You're not coming with us?" he asked, surprised.

"Someone needs to stay home with Samuel and Sadie." Mama picked up a plate heavy with ham drippings.

"What? No fair! I want to go too!" Sadie's fork dropped with a painful clatter.

"You can keep me company and help watch after Sam. We might even make a batch of ginger cookies," Mama promised, crossing into the kitchen. "Besides, you know you're not old enough yet."

"Then Merry should stay home too!"

"I'm sixteen now," Merry reminded her, gathering the rest of the table's cutlery.

"Barely," Sadie shot back. "Please, Papa, let me come. I want to hear you speak."

He stood up, ruffling her hair till the fine strands stood on end, creating a golden corona around her like drawings of saints in Parson Briard's books. "You know they wouldn't let you through the doors, little love."

The founding families had drawn up a list of seven rules designed to help nurture Amity Falls from a field of backwater campsites into the bustling town it was today. In a place so removed from the rest of the world, we had to be able to rely on our neighbors, to know that their intentions and hearts were pure. Every house had the list of Rules tacked near the main entrance—all carefully copied in Old Widow Mullins's elaborate copperplate—to remind us of our duties as we went into the world each day.

In truth, I barely noticed ours anymore. They garnered no greater acknowledgment than my mother's prized but faded wallpaper or the cross-stitched pillows on the threadbare settee.

The Rules ranged from mundane (no one under the age of sixteen was admitted into the Gathering House) to ones so practical that it seemed silly to list them in the first place (no one was to ever enter the pines on their own) to outright warnings (sabotaging a neighbor, be it family, property, or livelihood, would be punished with swift justice). We were too small a community to warrant an appointed judge and too isolated to care about big-city strangers ruling over our lives.

When crime did occur in the Falls—however rarely—the town dealt with it on its own.

I watched Papa follow Mama into the kitchen. What was he going to tell the Gathering? There would be a Deciding, that much was obvious, but what would we be voting on?

He kissed Mama's forehead before picking up two buckets from beneath the old metal washtub and swinging them out to the pump. Last night he'd seemed so haunted and beaten down that I'd worried he would never recover. Today he was practically giddy. His whistle could be heard all the way across the yard.

"Papa seems in an awfully good mood," I observed, returning the crock of butter to the icebox.

A soft smile lit Mama's face as she gazed out the window. Papa was busy at the pump, drawing water from our well with the long iron handle. He worked with an easy efficiency, the muscles in his back and arms shifting smoothly, always ready for whatever was required.

"He's happy to be home. They wandered in the pines for so long. If you hadn't lit the Our Ladies when you did, Ellerie . . ." Mama trailed off, unwilling to finish that dark thought. She reached out and squeezed my hand. "We're all very glad you did."

"If you want to go to the Gathering House, I can stay behind with Sam and Sadie," I offered, wistfully hoping she'd decline, even as the words left my lips. I didn't want to miss whatever was said.

Mama shook her head. "Sam's splint will need to be rewrapped, and between you and me, I could use a quiet morning."

I studied her with fresh interest. There *was* a certain weariness I hadn't noticed before. Though her eyes sparkled, the skin around them was dark. I hadn't seen her look like that since . . .

"You're pregnant," I guessed with a hushed gasp. I'd been too little to remember what it had been like with Merry, but when she'd carried Sadie, we'd often had to help with extra chores and keep the house quiet. She always said the first three months were the most draining part of the process. "And that's why Papa's so happy too. You must have told him!"

Her smile deepened into a grin. "I never can get much past those eagle eyes of yours."

I threw my arms around her. "Mama, that's wonderful! How far along are you?"

"It's still in the early stages. I only noticed a few days ago myself. Don't tell your sisters yet. Or Sam. We want to wait a bit longer."

I nodded gravely, promising to keep the secret. Mama had had two miscarriages before, and they'd devastated the household.

I counted the months. "So, April, then? Maybe May?"

"Maybe," Mama agreed, and raised a swift finger to her lips as Sadie came in carrying the empty milk pitcher.

5

"*Rule Number Three: Fifteen harvests children sow,*
then to the Gathering let them grow."

THE HALL WAS NEARLY AT FULL CAPACITY BY THE TIME
Papa, Merry, and I made the trek into town. Matthias Dodson and
Leland Schäfer pulled Papa over as soon as we entered, leaving
Merry and me to scout out seats on our own.

The Gathering House was a long building on the northern
outskirts of town. The windows, lining three of the walls and normally shuttered tight against the cold, were open today, offering an
unbroken view of the pines looming all around us.

At the front of the room was the Founder Tree. It had been
an impossibly large black walnut, boasting three trunks at its base.
Stories claimed it was the reason why the wagon train had veered
off-trail to rest in the palm of God's Grasp in the first place.

Decades ago, a terrible storm had come across the mountains
without warning. Through the gales of wind and rain, the settlers had seen bolt after bolt of lightning strike the behemoth tree,
seemingly without harming it. They'd watched the shadowy creatures that had terrorized their travel run in fear from the flashes of
white heat. The wagon train leader had viewed the tree as a great
protector and had decided they would set camp there once the
storm had passed.

Most of the smoking walnut had been hewn down, leaving

behind the wide trunk as a centerpiece for Amity Falls's Gathering House to be built around. But its unmarred image—full branches and full roots spread wide, reminding us of our connectedness—was everywhere. Carved into the buttons of the Elders' cloaks, carved across our thresholds, carved into the very staff Amos used to walk the Falls every day.

The rest of the room was crowded with rows of plain wooden benches, divided into sections by an aisle. Spotting an empty length of bench, I slid in, pulling Merry after me before anyone else could claim it. So relieved that we wouldn't have to stand for the whole meeting, I hadn't bothered to glance at who I'd sat next to.

"Oh. Rebecca."

Her face, normally a soft peaches-and-cream complexion, turned bright crimson as she saw me.

"Good morning, Ellerie, Merry."

Her eyes betrayed her, darting away to see who else had come in with us.

"Sam is at home." My voice fell, flat and clipped, the words painfully angled as they spilled free. "He couldn't have walked here with so bad a sprain."

"Is he hurting very much?"

I paused, weighing out how exactly to answer.

Rebecca squeezed my knee, her eyebrows drawn together in a worried line. "I . . . I wanted to tell you, Ellerie, truly I did. It felt wrong keeping something so big from you. You're my best friend—we've always told each other everything. Always shared everything."

Beside me, Merry sniffed. "Apparently."

Rebecca let out a small noise that was both gasp and sob. "Sam said we would. Eventually. He just wanted to wait."

"Wait? What on earth is there to wait for?"

She shook her head. "I don't know. He always just said it would be better, later on. For—for a while, I worried he wasn't serious about the courtship. Why else wouldn't he announce it? I thought he was playing a joke on me—"

"Sam would never do something like that." My tone was sharp enough to slice her sentence in two. No matter what secrets Sam had kept, I ought to stick up for my twin.

Rebecca combed her auburn hair behind her ears as she nodded in agreement. She still wore it long and loose, like a little girl. The locks fell into perfectly formed curls, brushing over the black floral pattern of her dress.

"I know that now. But at the time it just—"

"You had on that dress last night, didn't you?" I asked.

Her expression darkened with confusion. "I—yes."

"Did you have any visitors over?"

"What? When?" She looked positively bewildered.

"Last night. Before the Our Ladies were lit. Was there anyone at your house?"

"Papa and Mark, of course. Who else would there be?"

"That's what I'm trying to figure out. You're sure that—"

I was cut off as the three Elders marched to the front of the room. They took their place in the row of padded leather chairs facing us. Papa trailed after, filling the space between us and them. Every trace of the joy he'd shared with Mama was gone, replaced with a heavy and grave responsibility.

He ran his fingers over his beard, gathering thoughts before proceeding. Papa was well respected in town, admired even. I ached for him, about to deliver such dreadful news, standing all alone. But he didn't look scared or uncertain. He knew exactly what needed to be done. He always had.

"Good Blessings to you," he began, his words carrying clearly throughout the hall. "As most of you know, earlier this week,

Jeb McCleary left with five others on the summer supply run. And just a day later, his stallion returned, fatally injured and riderless."

I looked around the room to find Molly or her children. They weren't here, and my heart warmed with gratitude at whoever had thought to keep them away. If Papa's story was anything like Sam's, Jebediah's family didn't need to hear it.

"My son and I ventured into the woods following the trail they would have taken. We found what I believe to be their last campfire, only a few miles from the Falls. They didn't get very far before . . . it happened."

"What 'it'?" The question came from the back. I couldn't tell who had spoken.

Papa's jaw tightened and his front teeth clicked together. "It was hard to make out what truly took place. . . . It appears the men were attacked while sleeping. Their tents were torn to shreds and the men were missing."

"Could it have been bandits?"

Papa shook his head. "I believe it was animals, of some kind."

"That bear," Cyrus Danforth said, standing.

"No bear could have done what we saw. And . . . whatever it is . . . there's more than one. Perhaps a pack."

"Wolves." Edmund Latheton spoke up.

"That feels more plausible. Leaving the camp, we found . . . parts of the men dragged away. It seems no one got far. The creatures must have been extremely fast."

"Wolves," Cyrus conceded. "So why the theatrics? Send a team of men to root them out and be done with it."

"Now, wait just a minute," Gran Fowler said, standing now too. "We all saw that stallion. Those slashes on his side were enormous." He spread his fingers as wide as they could go. "They were certainly bigger than anything I could cause."

Cyrus let out a chirp of laughter. "Good news, everyone. Fowler isn't the murderer."

The chicken farmer's eyes narrowed. "I'm just asking, what wolf has paws bigger than a grown man's hands?"

Papa nodded. "None we've seen before. And . . ." He rubbed the pads of his thumbs over the rest of his fingernails. "Sam and I started burning away the surrounding brush. We didn't want anything else drawn to the blood, especially with the camp so close to town. As we started lighting the fires, we saw the creatures, just out of range. The fires' light caught their eyes, making them glow bright and silver. They'd been there the whole time. Watching us."

He reached up to scratch the back of his neck. It was the first time since taking the floor that he looked nervous.

"I couldn't make out their exact shape—they blended in with the pines' shadows—but whatever they were, they were monstrous in size. Well above my height."

I bit down on the corner of my tongue. Papa was one of the tallest men in the Falls. I tried to picture a wolf bigger than him. I could imagine the scruff of its back, raised with a sinister growl, or the massive paws, with moonlight reflecting off clawed tips, but the pieces wouldn't go together to create a whole beast. My mind refused to assemble such an abomination.

"That's impossible," Cyrus snorted.

Gran looked uneasy. "It does sound rather far-fetched, Gideon. Is there any proof?"

Papa's eyes flashed, indignant. "Proof? What proof more do you need than my given word? Everyone here knows me to be a man of integrity and honor. I'm not prone to flights of fancy or exaggeration. If I say that's what I saw, you can be certain it's exactly what's out there."

Looking around the room, I saw several people exchange guilty glances. They weren't convinced.

Papa evidently caught them as well and sighed. "Samuel saw them too. He'll tell you the same thing."

Sam's story from this morning flitted across my memory. He had admitted that he'd seen giant beasts in the woods.

He'd also said they'd laughed at him.

"Latheton," Papa said, finding the carpenter in the middle of the room. "You say you've seen them too. How big would you guess they are?"

After a moment of urging from his wife, Edmund rose unsteadily to his feet. "I . . . I couldn't say for sure . . . but they are much larger than regular wolves. Faster too. The one we saw . . ." He glanced back to his wife. She reached up and squeezed his hand. "The one we saw, it was out near my woodshed, on the far side of the property. You know that little spot where the creek cuts in?"

Several people nodded, drawn into his story.

He gulped a big mouthful of air, and I noticed a slight tremble in his hands. "We saw the eyes—just like Gideon said—shining silver. Something must have spooked it. It raced across the field to hide behind the barn. That's nearly five hundred feet, and it made it in only seconds. I . . . I've never seen anything move like that."

Prudence stood up. "He's telling the truth. They both are," she added, glancing back to affirm Papa.

"So what do you propose we do about these monstrous wolves, Gideon?" Cyrus asked, joining Papa at the front of the room. His stomach jutted over his pin-striped pants like the prow of a ship. "You make it sound as though half the town will be needed to take one down."

Edmund paled. "I don't think even that would be enough."

Papa murmured an agreement, his eyes wary. "I . . . I believe the monsters our forefathers spoke of have returned."

Murmurs of disbelief spread through the crowd.

"That's impossible," Parson Briard said, jumping to his feet, his brow furrowed into deep lines. "While my family was not here when the town was settled, those stories have always sat wrong with me. Fanciful fairy tales to scare children at bedtime. God would not allow such creatures to exist."

Matthias frowned. "Sit down, Clemency. You're making a fool of yourself. There were many documented sightings. They were real. But, Gideon . . . you know as well as I, there's not been a sighting since—"

"Since now," Papa cut off unhappily.

The Elder's nostrils flared. "Then these devils need to be eradicated."

Papa shook his head. "I'm not proposing we hunt them. There're too many and we don't have nearly enough ammunition . . . which brings me to our biggest issue today. We must send out another group for supplies."

There was a snorted scoff in the back of the room. "You can't be serious. If you really believe those things are real, that they're back, you can't expect anyone to volunteer. It's certain suicide."

"No more than attempting to make it through winter without a run," Papa said grimly. "Dr. Ambrose says his stocks are low. That bout of croup in May had children guzzling ipecac by the bottle. Are you confident you've got enough meat smoked to last till next spring? We need more bullets. More everything." His face softened. "We'll take better precautions. We'll send more people."

"More people to die," the dissenter shot back.

I turned in my seat and spotted Calvin Buhrman. The tavern owner's dark eyes burned brightly. Jebediah McCleary had been his brother-in-law. I was mildly surprised that Calvin hadn't remained at home with his grieving sister.

"I see no children here today," Cyrus said, peering about the crowd. "I take it we're meant to vote on this foolhardy expedition?"

Papa turned to address the Elders. "Surely we don't need a Deciding for a supply run? I called the adults here because we need to assemble a group of volunteers." He looked over his shoulder, offering a small smile to us. "I'll be the first to do so."

"Papa, no!" I shouted, leaping to my feet. "What about Mama?"

"His own daughter doesn't think it's a good idea," Calvin said, pouncing. "I vote no. Surely we can rough out one winter. Our forefathers did it all the time. Let the creatures starve. They'll be gone by spring, off for better hunting grounds. We'll send a supply train then. Hell, I'll lead it myself."

The room erupted into too many discussions, some shouted across the aisle, others hissed in fervent tones between spouses. Merry pawed at me, asking about Mama. I waved her off, knowing Mama would be disappointed if I didn't keep her secret.

From the circle of Elders, Amos McCleary raised one dark and shaky liver-spotted hand. He was the oldest man in all of Amity Falls and the head of the Elders. Cataracts clouded his once brown eyes a milky blue, and he used a long walking stick to help him navigate the Falls. On its top was a miniature replica of the Founder Tree, before it had been struck down by lightning. The carved leaves had lost much of their detail, and were polished as smooth as a lake's surface.

"It seems to me," he said, speaking with a papery-thin creak, "several questions must be asked before the Deciding can begin." Amos glanced toward the other Elders. "Are we in agreement?"

The men nodded.

"The first . . . do we believe that Gideon and others in town have seen these . . . creatures? Let those who do raise their hands now."

My hand and Merry's shot into the air, along with a little over half the room. Beside me, Rebecca hesitated, worrying her fingers around a twist of hair.

"Sam saw them too," I hissed at her. "You'll have to start dividing your loyalties eventually."

After a long beat, she raised her hand, though her fingers curled with timidity and she immediately looked down, avoiding her father's glare.

"All counted," Matthias said, marking the number down in his ledger.

"Very good," Amos said. "And those who do not believe them, will you now raise your hands?"

A smaller amount did. Parson Briard not only hoisted his hand into the air but stood up, making sure everyone could see his vote.

"Then it's decided," Amos continued. "We believe the creatures exist. Now, . . . do we believe they seek us harm? Do we believe they are responsible for the deaths of Jeb—" His voice faltered, breaking. "Of my son, and the rest of the supply train? Let those who believe this to be true indicate it."

Our trio of hands rose once more.

"And those who don't?"

Cyrus Danforth and the parson were the only ones to move.

Amos gripped the handle of his cane, hoisting himself with obvious effort. "Very well. Now we are ready to begin the Deciding. As you all know, we cast our Decision publicly, so all the Falls may know our mind. We are one community, relying on ourselves and our neighbors, so it's only fitting that we know each other's true minds."

Leland Schäfer stood up. "The Decision before you, then, is this: We believe the woods surrounding Amity Falls contain a pack of creatures, fast and large. We believe them to be deadly, having already killed some of our own. We have not restocked our supplies since April last, and the winter snows will soon be here. Should we send out a supply run now or wait until spring, when the creatures may have moved on?" He glanced at each of us before continuing. "Are we prepared to cast our votes?"

After a long pause, several heads nodded.

"Then come forward and ready yourselves accordingly. Yellow for a run now, red for waiting till spring."

Row by row, the town of Amity Falls shuffled to the stumps of the Founder Tree. Beaten copper bowls rested across two of its ringed surfaces, and on the tallest trunk lay a book. Nearly four feet wide when opened, the book contained the votes of every Decision the town had ever made.

Papa cast his vote first, pressing the palm of his hand into one of the bowls. It came out a bright saffron, stained yellow by a mixture of turmeric powder and water. He stepped toward the book, then pressed his hand onto the right side. As he stepped back, allowing others to vote, he caught my eye and smiled encouragingly.

Merry watched the proceedings with rapt attention. It was her first Deciding, and when she got to the front, she hesitated before dipping her hand into the yellow dye. The handprint she left in the book was smudged, from nerves.

I stepped up after her, studying the two bowls before me. I absolutely believed that Papa and Sam had seen some sort of animals in the woods and that those creatures were responsible for the deaths of our fellow townsmen. But did I think there should be a run? Logically, one was needed. Supplies were low; supplies were necessary.

But at what cost?

What Calvin had said was true—our forefathers had made it through winters in the mountains with much less than what we had now. It would be a rough few months, but if we banded together, sharing with our friends and neighbors, sacrificing a little now for a greater good, we could manage it.

On the other hand, how did we know the creatures would leave before the spring run? How could we be sure that, as snow fell and game became scarce, they wouldn't venture into town?

We couldn't. We would need more ammunition, more guns, more bullets.

But if we sent a caravan now, Papa would be at the head of it. What if something should happen to him? Mama would never recover. Grief would kill the baby and then her.

The two bowls stared up at me. The yellow turmeric was to the right; the red liquid, made from the dyes of beets and crab-apple bark, to the left. The dyes wouldn't easily wash away. The founders had wanted to make sure everyone understood that their actions affected the community as a whole. Whatever I decided now would be worn on my hand for days to come, like a brand.

I glanced toward the book, easily picking out Papa's and Merry's prints on the right. The left was evenly full of red marks, full of people who would rather wait and hope for a better spring.

Which was the right choice?

The weight of my decision crushed into my chest, like boulders falling down the mountain slopes, until I snapped into action.

My fingers pressed into the dye and onto the page, and it was done.

I stepped aside, allowing Rebecca to cast her vote. As I took my seat, I felt Papa's eyes on the back of my neck, as persistent as a sunburn.

Once everyone in the hall had voted, making their marks in the great book, Matthias counted up the handprints and whispered the outcome to Amos.

"The Decision has been reached," Amos said, standing before the crowd, clutching his cane as a tremble shook through him. "This was not an easy Deciding, I know, but a majority was

reached and the majority will be carried out. The red marks out-
number the yellow by just one. We will stay in the Falls and wait
until spring for another run. Amity Falls has spoken."

We trekked home in silence, Papa between Merry and me but not
actually walking with us. He was always a step or two ahead, eyes
cast to the ground, lost in thought. Merry shot curious glances
between us but remained silent, rubbing at her yellow palm.

Once, I tried reaching out to Papa. With a flick of annoyance,
he jerked away, as if the mere sight of my red-stained fingers ab-
horred him.

6

I RAKED PAPA'S SHIRT UP AND DOWN THE WASHBOARD, once, twice, three times, before stopping to examine it. I'd gotten nearly all the blood out of the cotton, but one stubborn spot remained. After running the bar of soap over the corrugated metal board once more, I started again.

Three days had passed since the Deciding, and Papa still wouldn't look at me. I'd tried to make my penance, quickly volunteering for any household chores to most help Mama. I took the heavy knotted rugs to the laundry lines and beat them with switches, shaking free every bit of dust until my shoulders quaked. I'd flipped the mattresses, filling them with new straw, fresh feathers, and even handfuls of dried lavender to bring pleasant dreams. I wanted to volunteer to help with the bees again, but didn't dare ask.

Today was wash day. I'd carried two metal tubs down to where the creek cut through our farm. There was a fire pit there, and I'd soon had one tub full of hot soapy water. The second was for rinsing. Once the clothes were free of soap, I hung them on the half dozen lines stretching alongside the stream. Lunch was still an hour off, but I already had four lines full. Our clothes shifted in the breeze like a troupe of ghosts come to dance. My fingers ached and my skin was scoured raw, but no amount of scrubbing would get rid of that damned telltale Deciding stain.

My knuckles scraped across the metal ridges, and I hissed, jerking backward. Papa's shirt fell into the water, disappearing under the bubbles as I grabbed my hand, massaging the stiff muscles.

"Are you all right?"

I jumped, certain I'd been alone. Peering through the wavering lines of shirts and petticoats, I expected to see Sam, propped against a pair of roughly hewn crutches, but no one was there.

"Over here."

My head snapped toward the creek.

Standing on the far bank and near the tree line was a stranger.

He was tall. Quite tall. Even from all the way across the water, I could tell I'd barely skim his shoulders if we stood side by side.

"I didn't mean to startle you," he continued. "It looked like you might have hurt yourself?"

"It's fine. I'm fine." I held up my hand in proof, though the knuckles were sore and red.

"That looks painful. Anything I can do to help?"

He stepped out from the shadows of the pines and dropped a large rucksack to the dirt. It landed with a heavy thud. Sunlight flecked across his dark hair, bringing out burnished highlights. His face was striking, long and chiseled with a proud, vulpine nose dominating his other features. It had been broken before, maybe more than once. The crooked lines of it gave him a piercing intensity at odds with his youthful frame.

I leapt to my feet as he took another step nearer. Warning bells rang in my mind, racing through my blood, and I fought the urge to flee. Visitors to Amity Falls were nearly nonexistent, and every possible worst-case scenario skittered through my imagination. I glanced over my shoulder, trying to catch a glimpse of our farmhouse, but the laundry lines obscured it, which meant no one at home could see me either.

"Stay right where you are," I shouted back, far louder than necessary. I hoped my words would carry across the field and over the hum of the bees. No matter how angry Papa was with me, he'd come running if he knew I was in danger. "You're trespassing."

The boy raised one eyebrow and looked back at the trees. "Am I? I wasn't aware the forest belonged to anyone." Amusement colored his deeply tanned face, and the corner of his lips twitched as if fighting an impulse to smile.

"It doesn't, but our property starts right at the water's edge," I said, wishing I'd thought to bring along the family rifle. During the hottest months of summer, Papa had us carry the gun to the creek when we did the wash. Bull snakes and rattlers were drawn to the hot flat stones lining the riverbed. Mama usually brought it with her, but she'd been resting when I'd hauled the tubs and baskets down, and I'd forgotten all about it until now. Though I'd never actually killed a snake, he didn't know that, and I longed for the reassuring heft of the barrel in my hand.

He looked down as though the boundary could be visibly seen, and checked his feet with exaggerated movements. "So . . . I'm *not* trespassing, then?"

My jaw tightened. "Who are you? What are you doing here?"

He pointed over to a large rock overhanging the stream. "Just to be clear, that rock is on the forest's side of the creek. I won't be crossing any line if I sit there, will I?"

His voice was light, on the verge of laughter. I wasn't sure if he was mocking me or trying to work his obvious charms in his favor.

Without waiting, the stranger plopped onto the lip of the rock and began removing his boots. Leather cords held the tops of them to his knees, and he whistled as he loosened the knots.

"What on earth are you doing?"

He took one boot off, then the other. "I've been hiking for hours."

"Hiking from where? You're not from Amity Falls."

"I'm not," he agreed, tossing aside a pair of mud-stained socks and flexing his toes. He rolled up the legs of his buckskin trousers, revealing a pair of muscular calves, and groaned in pleasure as his feet dipped into the rushing waters. "Oh, I needed that. I could stay here all day, just like this." Leaning back on his forearms, he dangled his legs into the stream with a languid grace. Basking in the sunlight, without a care in the world, he looked like some god of old we'd read about in school. Pan, or the one who liked wine and dancing.

Dionysus, I remembered after a moment.

"Then where are you from?"

He peered at me through slitted eyes. "You're awfully persistent."

"And you've evaded every question I've asked."

His right eyebrow raised into a perfect arch. "Have I? How rude of me! I'll answer whatever you ask next, I swear it." He swiped his fingers over his heart, making a solemn oath. "Go on; this is your chance. Ask whatever you like."

I folded my arms over my chest. "What's your name?"

The boy wrinkled his nose. "Oh, not that! You can ask me anything you want, and you choose something so wholly pragmatic? No, no, no. I'll let you try again."

I couldn't help my snort. "Are you serious?"

"Always." He clapped his hands. "There, I answered something for you. Now you owe me one."

"I owe you nothing. That wasn't even a real question!"

"I beg to disagree. You posed a challenge, daring me to give an answer. Is that not the very definition of a question? Besides"—he smirked—"your voice went up at the end. Everyone knows that's the true mark of a question. Now, I gave you an answer. So give me one in return."

"Fine. What do you want to know?"

The corners of his eyes crinkled as a smile burst across his mouth, full and wide and utterly incorrigible. "What's *your* name?"

"Truly?" I raised an exasperated eyebrow at him before relenting. "Ellerie."

"Ellerie . . . ?" he drew out, clearly seeking more.

"Downing."

"Downing," he repeated. "Your father is the apiarist in these parts, isn't he? I was told I absolutely must purchase a bottle of honey from him if I found myself here come harvest time."

"From who?"

He cocked his head as if he didn't understand the question.

"Who told you about Papa? And the honey?"

"You get a chance to redeem yourself, and those are the questions you choose?" He sank back again. "You're really, truly awful at this game, Ellerie Downing."

"I didn't realize we were playing a game."

"Of course we are. Isn't everyone?"

Though his voice was as light and breezy as ever, a trace of overfamiliarity set my nerves on edge, and I glanced through the lines of laundry once more, wishing a great wind would come along so Papa could see this strange boy.

"Then, what's your name?" I asked, suddenly ready for the conversation to be over. "You know mine now; it's only fair."

"Games are rarely ever fair, honey-haired girl." His teeth winked as he smiled.

His audacity was maddening. I turned away from him, busying

myself by rinsing the shirt and hanging it on the line. I'd finish the rest after lunch, bringing Papa with me in case the stranger was still there. He'd be able to get answers out of this infuriating man.

"Ellerie?" he prompted, once it became clear I was ignoring him.

I stacked the empty baskets together and hoisted them onto my hip before daring to look his way. "I don't need another question. I already know everything I need to about you." With a satisfied puff of pride, I turned on my heel and pushed past the first line of clothes, going home.

"I very much doubt that," he called after me, but I steeled my resolve and didn't turn back once.

"There was a stranger down by the creek," I announced after we'd sat down and prayed over the food before us.

Everyone turned toward me, even Papa.

"He came out of the woods while I was washing clothes."

Mama's gaze shifted over to Papa, her eyes round with worry. He tapped the table, debating what to do with the information. With a trace of a smile, I imagined Papa grabbing the gun from over the mantel and storming down to the stream. We'd see how long the stranger could avoid answering simple questions with the length of a rifle trained on him.

"I told him where the property line was. He never crossed it," I added, to be fair.

Papa reached for the bowl of hard-boiled eggs and spooned two onto his plate. "What'd he look like?"

I started to say "handsome," but caught myself before the treacherous word fell. "Tall. About my age, I think. He had on boots."

Papa nodded. "Probably a trapper. Jean Garreau passed last

winter. I expect we'll be seeing a few new faces around the Falls this autumn, wanting to stake a claim on his territory."

"Should we tell him about the monsters?" Sadie asked, straining her neck to see over the windowsill to catch a glimpse of the trapper.

"We might ought to," Papa said, still considering. "Trappers usually keep to themselves till they've got pelts to sell. But if he's out in those woods, he needs to take care." He glanced at me. "You see any weapons on him?"

I frowned, trying to remember details. I hadn't seen a gun, but if he was a trapper, he'd surely have a set of knives. And there was that large rucksack, chockful of something.

"I don't think so. But he had a big pack."

Papa's eyebrows furrowed together. "After lunch, show me where he was? He's probably gone by now, but just in case."

"Want me to go with you, Papa?" Samuel asked. It was the first day he'd ventured downstairs, carefully aided by Merry and Sadie.

"We'll be fine," Papa said, stabbing at a potato. "But I need you out at the hives this afternoon. Think you can hold the smoker?"

My heart sank. I'd hoped, with Sam laid up, I'd get another chance with the bees. I hid my red palm beneath the table as if that could take back the last three days or my foolish vote.

Samuel frowned, his eyes darting to the crutches propped against the wall. "I . . . I can try, but . . ."

"Just take Ellerie," Mama said. "This contention between you two has gone on long enough. She cast her vote, as she's allowed. Let it lie, Gideon."

The words behind Papa's lips piled up like water in a dam. Just as I was sure they were about to break through, drowning us all, he swallowed them back and released a long sigh instead. "You done with all your chores today, Ellerie?"

"There's one last basket of clothes."

He let out a noncommittal grunt, then asked for the biscuits. Mama picked up the plate but wouldn't release it until he met her stare.

"After the wash is done . . . why don't you help me with the hives?" His teeth gritted together so hard, I feared they'd crumble to powder.

I looked down meekly, but inside I was a mess of nerves. I so badly wanted the chance to show him I was just as capable as Samuel, but not like this. Not when he would rather anyone else but me beside him. Things could go so horribly wrong. He'd be tense, and the bees would sense it. They'd attack, and we'd lose half a hive before the afternoon was over. And it would all be my fault.

A warm hand landed on my knee and squeezed it. Mama offered me a small smile. She looked so full of encouragement that I dared to wonder if I might be able to fix the mess I'd made. Perhaps I could use our forced togetherness to explain why I'd done it, why I'd voted against him.

And at least within the beekeeper's suit, my hands would look exactly the same as his.

7

"AREN'T YOU TAKING THE RIFLE?" I CALLED AFTER PAPA as he slipped through the doorway. I'd just dunked the last plate into the rinse water and was handing it off to Sadie to dry and put away.

Through the kitchen window, I saw him pause on the steps leading to the side yard, back to the house. I couldn't read his expression, but his shoulders seemed to soften as he considered the question.

"You think we really ought to?"

I wrung out the washcloth before joining him on the porch. "Maybe. Just to be safe?"

Papa turned. "He say anything that makes you think we need it?"

I remembered the stranger's tone of voice, the way he'd always seemed just on the verge of mocking me, and how badly I'd wanted the rifle in my hands. Looking back, I could clearly recall the feeling, but not what inspired its urgency. After a moment's reflection, I shook my head. "I guess not."

Papa glanced up at the sun. "It *is* an awfully warm day. Why don't you go get it for me anyway? There could be snakes."

The prickly ball of worry that was lodged in my stomach eased, like a porcupine lowering its guard. Papa would be able to get all the information he needed from that boy.

If he was even still around.

⋘⊰⊱⋙

We spotted him as we wove through the lines of clothes. Still laid out on the rock, feet still in the water. He'd covered his face with a dark wool hat and was so utterly motionless that I assumed he'd fallen asleep.

"You might want to be careful dipping your toes in that creek there," Papa called out, warning our approach. "Water snakes liable to think your toes are salamanders. They're not poisonous, but that won't make a bite hurt any less."

The boy removed the hat and used it as a sun block to peer at us. With a languid stretch of his back, he sat up, keeping his legs resolutely in the creek. "Water snakes, you say?"

Papa nodded.

After a moment of wary silence, he eased his feet out of the creek. "All pins and needles anyway."

"I'm Gideon Downing," Papa said. He'd stopped a few yards from the waterline, making no attempt to hide the rifle from the stranger's view.

"The beekeeper," the stranger said.

Papa leaned against the butt of the rifle. Though his stance seemed casual, there was a wiry energy racing through him that set my teeth on edge and made every word of their banter feel weighted with tension. "Passing through, or are you aiming to stick around?"

"Making the rounds," the boy answered noncommittally.

"With your folks?"

"Just me . . . and my partners," he allowed.

"That so?"

The ambling speed of their conversation was maddening. My fingers itched to grab the rifle, shoot a warning shot into the sky, and demand that actual answers be given.

"We've got a little campsite up a ways." He pointed toward the mountain farthest west. "I was following the creek when I stumbled across . . ." He drew his sentence out as if he'd already forgotten my name. I was surprised at how much that stung my pride.

"Ellerie," Papa supplied.

"Ellerie," he agreed. "Didn't mean to scare anyone. She set me straight on your property line. I'll make sure to stay far from it. Don't want to be stepping toes onto anyone's claim by mistake. Man could get himself shot over less in these parts."

"You shouldn't run into trouble with anyone in the Falls," Papa said, his stance relaxing, degree by nearly imperceptible degree. "We keep clear of the forest unless we're heading out of the pass."

The stranger rubbed his chin thoughtfully, looking pleased.

"It's actually why I wanted to speak with you. There've been some sightings of . . . wolves recently. They overtook our supply train last week. Six men died."

The boy whistled through his teeth. "That a fact?"

Papa hummed an affirmation, the set of his lips grim.

"Awful sorry to hear that. Haven't seen any traces of wolves, but I'll certainly keep my eyes out. Appreciate you warning me."

Papa scratched at the back of his neck, his gaze falling on the stranger, as sharp as a razor. "I don't believe I caught your name, son." The last word rang out, flat and atonal, an unspoken threat, and I wanted to cheer, knowing he hadn't fallen for the boy's tactics.

"You wouldn't have; I never said it." There was an uneasy beat before he let out a laugh, breaking the tension. After brushing off his pants, the boy waded across the creek, reaching out a friendly hand. "The name is Price."

It wasn't.

In Amity Falls, every name seemed to have a pragmatic purpose. Names were weighty, seared to the identity of the person or place as if with a branding iron. Tall dark mountains? Blackspire. A lake choked verdigris with blooms of algae? Greenswold. The rightness of a name was woven into the very essence of the thing itself.

Whoever this person was, he wasn't Price. The name "Price" rested atop his elongated frame like an ill-fitting coat, puckered and gaping.

If Papa noticed the lie, he didn't comment. He shook the boy's hand, and they fell into an easy discussion about God's Grasp. Price, as he called himself, hadn't been raised in these parts and said he'd be grateful for any tips Papa could impart. When Papa asked about his home, Price glanced my way with a chuckle.

"Out west," he said, skirting around another answer.

"Where?" I interrupted. "Out west where?"

"Ellerie," Papa scolded. "He'll tell us if he wants."

Price laughed once more, but it sounded strained. "Along the coast."

"But where?" I pressed. "It's a big country. There's an awful lot of coast out west."

"Curiosity has always been one of Ellerie's strong suits," Papa apologized.

The stranger looked me over with fresh eyes. He was finally close enough for me to make out their color. They sparkled, clear and light, like the creek behind us. Soft gray one moment and amber the next. Hints of green crept in as they squinted into a smile, pleased at whatever they saw in me. "Tenacity too, I reckon."

Papa gave him a knowing look in agreement. "Will you be near the Falls long?"

"Thinking of it. My first tour has been promising." His eyes drifted back toward the pines. "Quite promising. Could be my best season yet."

"If you do, you ought to join us for supper sometime. Cooking over a campfire for too long can be rough on a young man. There's also a tavern in town—run by Calvin Buhrman—good food, good company. Stop in one night. I guarantee you'll have customers if your pelts are good quality and your prices are right."

"I do love cutting a deal," he said with a laugh. "I'll make sure to stop by the tavern. And I appreciate your kind offer. I certainly hope honey cake will be on the menu? I truly have heard talk of them up and down the mountainsides."

"I'm sure my wife could be persuaded," Papa said, and offered his hand once more, putting an end to their conversation. "Welcome to the Falls, Price."

"Thank you, sir," he said, shaking Papa's hand with a firm grasp.

"Ellerie? You've got laundry to finish?"

He knew I did.

"Why don't I help pull the sheets off the lines? Get you home earlier."

It was a strange offer for him to make. He never helped with the wash, always leaving it to us girls. Price took his cue from it, though, and waded across the river to put his boots back on.

"See you around, Downings," he said, raising a hand in farewell before throwing on his pack and slipping back into the pines.

We paused in silence, watching until it was impossible to discern him from the trees. Only then did I turn to the scrubbing tub, its bubbles long gone. It felt strange to have Papa here, watching me work, and I think he felt it too. His hands hung awkwardly at his side, clearly wanting a task to fill them.

"I'll rebuild the fire," he offered, kneeling next to the circle. The flames had died to ash in my absence. Papa picked up a piece of flint but made no motion to strike it. He tapped his thumb against it instead, the yellow stain on his skin as bright as the day he'd pressed it into the Deciding book. His face was cloudy and unreadable. I couldn't begin to guess at the words he was measuring out in his mind.

"Back out east, when my grandfather was not much older than you are now, his father decided to harvest a few extra bottles. It had been a tough year. The spring rains had swollen the river near their cabin, and it rose up, overwhelming everything. They lost so much in that flood. Great-Grandpa saw the harvest as a chance to recoup their losses. He took an extra frame, then another. There'd been an early spring that year; it was expected the next would be too. But it wasn't. Snow plagued the plains well into May. The hive didn't have enough honey to survive on their own and the bees starved. They lost every single bee that winter. All so Great-Grandpa could sell those bottles."

"What happened next?" I'd never heard this story before and was horrified to be so enthralled by it.

He shrugged. "Great-Grandpa knew that the only way they could ever hope to dig themselves out of the mess was to start over. They'd heard tales of free land up in the north and joined a wagon train heading west. Grandpa met Granny in that caravan, and when she wanted to stay put in Amity Falls, he did too." He rubbed at his mouth. "They settled the land, started the town, and built up our hives. Grandpa repeated that story to my pa every year at harvest. When I wanted to pull out an extra frame one year, Pa told it to me. . . . Sometimes we have to overlook our own desires for the betterment of the hive as a whole." His eyes fell to my hidden hand.

I could see what Papa meant. We were all striving to build our town from the wilderness. If one area failed, it could jeopardize everything else. Every individual action had a direct effect on the community at large. My hand felt hot with shame.

"We'll be okay for just this winter, won't we, Papa?" My voice quavered, and I felt as though I were all of five years old again, creeping into my parents' room during a storm, scared of the dark and seeking comfort. Protection. A story to hold back the terrors of the night.

"We might be," he said, sounding unconvinced. I supposed if I was old enough to cast my voice at Decidings, I was old enough to not be coddled with wishful thinking. "With the late summer there'll be a rush to get the harvest in—for everyone. If we can set aside enough food and ration out every bit of it, we'll be just fine."

I leaned in, resting against his shoulder.

Papa pointed to the basket of dirty clothes. "Is any of that absolutely necessary to clean today?"

"I . . . I don't guess so." I ran my eyes down the lines. "Just some of Sam's wool socks, but he's not been wearing them with the splint."

Papa waved off my worry and pushed himself up. "What say we get Merry and Sadie to come down and fold up all these lines while you and I check the hives?"

"Truly?"

He offered out his right hand, the one stained yellow, and I placed mine in it. The sunlight painted the world in such rich bronze highlights that when I glanced at my empty hand, I couldn't even see the red.

8

"HAVE YOU HEARD ABOUT THE STRANGERS?" PRUDENCE Latheton asked, snipping off a length of thread. Without skipping a beat, she had it through the eye of her needle.

Mama had marched us to the parsonage bright and early that morning, where Letitia Briard was hosting a sewing bee in honor of Alice Hazelman's impending nuptials to Gran Fowler.

Alice had taught at Amity Falls's schoolhouse for twenty-eight years. Well past forty, everyone had assumed she'd never marry, but one Sunday morning—just as Parson Briard had asked for joys or concerns to pray over—the chicken farmer had stood up and declared his undying devotion to Alice. Their wedding was set for the end of the month, and all the women in the Falls were scrambling to help fill the schoolmarm's hope chest.

For the first time in my life, my stitches had been deemed worthy enough for me to work with the older women, taking up a small section of the brightly colored log cabin quilt. But after listening to a litany of Old Widow Mullins's ailments and a slew of marital advice for Alice that made my cheeks burn, I found myself watching my sisters' group of girls with envy. They were pressed together on a long bench, hunched over sets of pillowcases, and stifling fits of giggles as Wilhelmina Jenkins told a story in hushed whispers.

"Strangers?" Letitia Briard repeated from her position of honor at the head of the quilt. Despite the warmth of the parlor, her calico dress was still crisp and neat, its pleats pressed with a precise care I couldn't ever seem to muster with mine. I'd never seen the parson's wife with so much as a hair out of place.

"A pair of men stopped in at the store yesterday, wanting to see if my Edmund could take a look at a busted wagon wheel. I've never seen a cart worn so hard. It near split at the seams, rolling up to the shop."

"Strangers in Amity Falls?" Charlotte Dodson asked. "Matthias never mentioned anything about it. Pass the scissors, won't you?"

Prudence handed her a pair. "New trappers, apparently. Wanting to try their hand at Jean Garreau's territory."

Letitia sniffed with disapproval. The Briards' contempt of the Frenchman was well known throughout Amity Falls. He'd never been seen sober, and had strung together phrases so colorful that even hardened ranch hands had blushed.

"Did they say anything else?" I dared to ask.

My cheeks felt as warm as baked apples as thoughts of the stranger who called himself Price danced into my mind. The memories were filtered through a sun-dappled haze as though it had been months, not days, since I'd met him. Logically I knew I probably misremembered the golden hue of his skin, the sootiness of his thick eyelashes, and the sharpness of his wit. I painted him with far more charm than he deserved.

Still, part of me hoped he somehow might have mentioned me.

"They were curious about what game to expect in the forests."

"There are more things out in those woods than any of us could ever dare imagine," Charlotte said, tying off her line of stitches.

"Amen," Letitia said, and we all settled into a moment of reflection.

"Did you hear about Judd Abrams?" Cora Schäfer asked, her voice dropping to a theatrical whisper.

I leaned in closer. "No."

"Maybe I ought not say anything. It's terribly gruesome."

"Just tell the story, Cora. It's clear you want to," Prudence said.

The Elder's wife shrugged. "Three of his horses dropped foals last week."

Prudence raised a delicate eyebrow, unimpressed. "That story is hardly worth telling once, let alone repeating."

Cora continued on, unperturbed. "Judd said none of the mares had shown signs of being pregnant before the births, and they'd not been around any of the stallions this season. He'd penned them up in the north field, all the mares and fillies together, see? But stranger yet . . ." Her voice dipped even lower. "The foals were . . . *wrong*."

A light of interest sparked across Alice's face. "Wrong how?"

"One of them had eyelids fused shut—"

Charlotte frowned. "That's a common birth defect. Matthias's mare had a stillborn like that just last year."

"It wasn't stillborn," Cora said, clearly vexed by the interruptions. "And the eyelids were strange—translucent, Judd said. He could see the foal's eyes moving around, staring right at him. He said they followed his every movement, absolutely aware he was there."

I paused, my needle stabbed halfway through the quilt's batting, as a shudder ran through me.

"What about the other foals?" Prudence asked.

Cora *tsked*, tying off a knot. "Just terrible." She took her time searching the sewing basket for another spool of thread, allowing the suspense to build. "The spine on the second one was outside the body, all the vertebrae poking through like quills on a porcupine. When it tried to stand, the bones fractured, shattering into splinters, and it keeled over dead, thank God. And the third was even worse! Judd said—"

Beside me, Bonnie Maddin dropped her section of the quilt and scurried away from the group, pressing fingers over her mouth.

"Perhaps we ought to change the topic, ladies," Mama suggested with practiced tact. Even she looked slightly green, and I wondered if the topic upset her. I said a swift prayer for the baby within her, that it would grow healthy and strong. "Surely there must be something more pleasant that will pass the time. Letitia, we spotted your zinnias coming in. I don't believe I've ever seen bigger blooms before."

The conversation shifted, and Mama caught my eye. She nodded toward the door, indicating I should check on Bonnie. Excusing myself, I left the circle and slipped into the kitchen, where the queasy girl had raced.

Rebecca was there, washing teacups at the large basin sink. Her eyes were fixed out the window, watching with amusement as Bonnie threw up all over Letitia Briard's prized flower beds.

"The parson will have a fit when he sees that," Rebecca guessed, as Bonnie's friends raced over to pull her toward the outhouse. When Rebecca turned to see who it was, her face fell. "Ellerie."

"Rebecca," I said, echoing her flat tone. An uneasy beat passed between us. "Do . . . do you need help?"

Her mouth twisted. "I suppose you could dry if you like."

Minutes passed as we worked alongside one another, the clinks of cups and saucers saying more than we did. Words piled in my throat, half-thought-out sentences and discarded statements cramming in on top of each other until I couldn't hold them back any longer.

"I'm sorry," I started, just as Rebecca broke her silence too.

"Forgive me, Ellerie, please."

There was a pause, hope knitting a tentative bridge between us as we both laughed.

"I never wanted to keep this secret from you," she said, placing her hand on my forearm.

"It doesn't matter, Rebecca. I shouldn't have been upset. It just took me by such surprise. I never—"

"I never—" she agreed, and our words ran out. She returned her attention to the sink, fingers dancing over the soapy bubbles.

"He makes you happy?" I asked, taking a dripping saucer from her and toweling it off.

"He . . ." Her face brightened with pleasure. "He truly does, Ellerie. I never knew it was possible to feel like this."

A flicker of envy flared in me, pulsing just behind my sternum, and I did my best to push it back. I didn't want to begrudge my friend her happiness, but I also didn't want to imagine her locked in a tender embrace with my brother either. It made me feel . . .

Alone.

Just weeks before, Rebecca had stayed overnight and we'd whispered secrets and stories up in the hayloft until the wee hours of the morning. I'd been worrying over the autumn to come—it was the first we wouldn't go off to school with the other children of the Falls. We both had turned eighteen earlier that year and were now considered adults, but the reality of it had yet to sink in. With no suitors of my own and the summer lingering sweetly on, it had seemed as if nothing had truly changed. Rebecca had predicted that once the harvest came in, and the young men in the Falls knew exactly how much they'd have to offer, we'd have beaus lined up for miles.

Her words had been such a comfort then. But how easy it had been for her to say them. She already had a suitor.

There were plenty of boys in town, young men my age whom

I'd known all my life, but I'd never once wondered what it would feel like to have their eyes meet mine, heated with happiness, crackling with desire. I'd never pictured walking together down a moonlit lane, stealing kisses behind the schoolhouse. I couldn't imagine being offered a flower, a ring, a heart.

I'd always thought Rebecca and I would experience this together. Finding suitors, giggling over first kisses, celebrating betrothals. Knowing she'd gone ahead with this new stage of life without me hurt in unexpected ways, a knife dug in deep beneath my ribs, twisting with every breath.

"That's . . . wonderful," I heard myself say, back in the moment at hand, here in the kitchen with my best friend, who I was in no way jealous of.

"It is," Rebecca said, all but beaming. "And . . . there's something else. Something . . . I don't even know quite how to say. I haven't told Samuel yet. . . . I wanted you to know first. You're more than my friend, Ellerie. I've always thought of us as sisters, you know?"

"Of course." I squeezed her hand. She was shaking.

"I . . ." She bit her lips even as she grinned. "I'm pregnant."

"Pregnant," I echoed, mindful even through my shock to lower my voice. "With a baby?"

She giggled. "I certainly hope so. It's . . . it's not that I ever planned for such things to happen this way. I always knew I was going to wait, but Sam . . . he just . . . he's so—"

Her cheeks stained bright pink, and I held up my hand, derailing her train of words before they could smash into me. "I don't need to know all of those details," I assured her.

Rebecca laughed again. "Of course."

"But . . . you're going to tell him, though? Soon?"

She nodded. "I actually was hoping you might be able to help with that. . . . I'm just so nervous."

"Nervous? He loves you."

Rebecca met my eyes and smiled. "I know. It's just . . . this is such a big moment. We haven't really talked about . . . big moments. I always assumed he'd propose once the harvest was over, but now . . ." Her fingers twisted together anxiously. "I just want him to be happy about it, is all. It's a lot to spring on a person."

"But if—you've already . . ." My sentence stammered to an embarrassed end. "Surely he must be thinking about that next step."

I felt nauseous, speaking so lightly of it. It wasn't just a step, a small pacing of footprints. Sam and Rebecca were so far ahead of me in their life's course, it felt like miles separated us. They were off together in some mysterious great unknown, while I was stuck where we'd always been, all on my own now.

I glanced toward her stomach. Her apron bib covered her front, and I wasn't sure if she wore it loose to keep her clothes neat or if she was already trying to conceal a bump. "How far along are you?"

She shrugged. "Not at all. I only noticed a day or two ago. I thought my monthlies were just late, but I feel different, you know?"

I didn't. And a small part of me worried I never would.

"You won't say anything, will you, Ellerie? Of course you won't. I know you wouldn't," she continued on, her sentences tripping over each other in their haste to spring free.

"I'd never," I promised. "But *you* need to say something to Sam, and soon. Aprons won't cover that secret forever."

She nodded fervently, and a titter of laughter burst from the other room as the older women continued with their sewing and gossip, unaware of the very real scandal that had just unfolded in the parson's kitchen.

"Just think," Rebecca breathed happily. "The next quilting circle will be for me." She kissed my cheek and headed back to the parlor, leaving me with a row of cups to put away.

∞❊∞

A sign was posted on the door of the general store, hammered in place with two tacks. The unseasonable heat had made the edges curl in on themselves, obscuring the message. We trudged across the dusty road, Merry carrying our sewing box under one arm and Mama scanning her shopping list.

We didn't need much, she'd promised as we'd left the quilting bee. Mama always thought it better to kill two birds with one stone if you were able.

Sadie was the first up the steps, standing on tiptoe to smooth the crinkled paper.

"No credit accepted. Cash only," she read aloud wonderingly. "What's that mean, Mama?"

Mama reached into her pocket and pulled out some coins. She never left the house without a bit of money—just in case—but her forehead furrowed as she counted it. "It means we're not getting everything I wanted." She tapped her finger on the list, weighing out the importance of each item. "Ellerie, why don't you get the sugar? Merry, the tea."

"What about me?" Sadie asked, twisting back and forth. Her skirt twirled about in the manufactured breeze.

"You can come with me to check on Molly McCleary," Mama said. She took Sadie's hand and led her toward the side of the building and up the stairs to the apartment Molly and Jebediah kept above the store.

Had kept.

It was only Molly now. I hadn't stepped foot in the store since the supply run had left, and I wondered if the tragedy would somehow be marked there, imprinted on the shelves, a shadow of sadness and despair.

But the little brass bell on the door chimed out our entrance as brightly as ever.

The store clerk, a young man named Joseph, called a brief hello, clipped as the bell rang again. Rebecca ducked in, side-stepping into the nearest aisle. Papa and Samuel were meant to pick us up in the wagon, and I knew she hoped to see my brother.

The door opened once more and several girls from Merry's class at school entered. They stood in a tight circle, whispering with glee as they spotted Joseph at the counter.

"Afternoon, ladies," he said. They fell into giggles and his face flushed nearly as red as his hair.

The door opened once more, and Prudence Latheton barged in with Cora Schäfer at her heels. "What's this about McCleary not accepting credit?" she snipped, ignoring Joseph's attempt at a greeting.

His face fell a smidge. "Amos has taken over all the accounts since Jeb . . . well, you know. With no supplies coming in till spring . . . I think he just wants to feel a bit more secure. I'm sure it'll go back to normal once the accounts are settled."

Prudence sighed. "That Elder. Well, I only need a spool of thread today. Linen, if you've got it."

I made a beeline for the dry goods, noting the diminished selection and sparsely filled shelves. There were only three bags of flour along the floor. Usually the aisle was so crowded, they fell into the walkway, catching people's ankles and coating everything with a white dust.

One lone sack of sugar remained on an upper shelf. It was only five pounds, smaller than what Mama had written out, but I grabbed it. I'd ask Joseph to bring another five pounds from the storeroom before we left, and let him know the shelves needed restocking.

Prudence was still fussing through the crate of bobbins,

holding the colors to the sunlight with a critical eye. Joseph flipped through the great ledger opened up before him.

"This will do, I suppose," she finally conceded, and fished out a dime from deep in her apron's pocket. She slid it across the counter and nodded good day.

"Actually, Mrs. Latheton," the boy squeaked. "It's a bit more than that."

Throughout the store, every woman stopped her browsing and shifted attention toward the counter.

"More?" Prudence questioned, eyebrows arching.

The clerk was visibly uncomfortable. "Well, because of . . ." He tapped at the ledger, finding the Latheton name.

"I paid in cash just now; you all saw me."

"But there is debt on the account. . . . I'm afraid that will need to be paid before you can purchase anything else."

There was a gasp from the far corner of the room, and I turned to see Merry's friend Jane set down the canister of coffee she'd been intending to buy.

"That's absurd!" Prudence snapped. "You can't spring changes on people without giving them ample warning. I don't carry that sort of money on me. No one does."

Joseph took the bobbin of thread from her. "I can set this aside for you until you do."

I think it was kindly meant, but Prudence's face flared with embarrassment and rage. She opened her mouth to hurl out something undoubtedly pinched and icy, but nothing sputtered from her. After a tense moment, she turned on swift heel and left, letting the swing door slam shut behind her.

The handful of coins Mama had pressed into my palm felt insubstantial as I stepped up to the counter. I sensed the eyes of everyone in the store watching us, waiting to see how this would play out.

"I think you need to restock some of your shelves," I said, trying to squelch down my nerves. I had no idea what the state of our account might be and didn't want all of the busybodies behind us judging Mama or Papa. "We'll need another five pounds of sugar, and my sister is getting tea. . . ." Merry scurried up to the counter and set the metal tin down with a sharp click.

Joseph scanned the ledger for our name. "You're all paid up." He jotted down our purchases and tallied the total. "That'll be two dollars and twelve cents."

"And the other sack of sugar," I prompted, my fist still tight around the money.

"There isn't any."

"What?" I glanced past his shoulder through the open storeroom door. Boxes and sacks were stacked on large shelves with orderly efficiency. Barrels of gunpowder sat alongside a crate clearly marked SUGAR. "There must be. There's a crate right there."

The clerk leaned over the counter, keeping his voice lowered and his gaze fixed on a whorl in the wood grain. "It's empty. Nearly all of them are. We were meant to get more in with the supply run, but . . ."

"Oh." I looked over the storeroom with fresh eyes. It had seemed stocked to overflowing just moments before. Now it looked sad and abandoned, empty crates waiting for a merchant who would never return.

"Do you still want that sugar?" he prompted.

"Of course," I said, my fingers digging into the sack's burlap sides. I counted out Mama's coins, and Merry and I took up our purchases.

Little whispers filled the store as we left. Despite Joseph's quiet divulgence, the women of Amity Falls had heard everything.

"What does this mean?" Merry hissed as we hopped down the front steps. "Surely there must be more stock somewhere. The shelves were so empty!"

I spotted our wagon several buildings down. Zenith and Luna were tied to a hitching post, but the cart was empty. I tucked the sack of sugar beneath the buckboard seat but paused before hoisting myself up. "Where do you think Papa and Sam got off to?"

Merry scanned the road, still clinging on to the tea. Before she could guess, a commotion rose from Matthias Dodson's livery. Horses whinnied and shouts rang out, calling for others to come and see.

"Might as well," Merry said, shrugging.

A crowd of people gathered in the yard at the blacksmith's stables. Most of the men were pressed together, circling about something I could not see. There were too many bodies jostling for space. Merry and I edged around the group, nearing Matthias's forge. There were fewer people to contend with in the scorching heat, and I was able to make out a form lying in the dirt.

I tilted my head, unable to make sense of the snippets I saw.

It's an elk, I thought. *A stag.*

The McNally boys had gone on a hunting party this morning. Their sister Florence had mentioned it at the quilting circle.

But it was the wrong size for an elk.

It was the wrong *everything*.

A fifth leg jutted from the carcass, painfully truncated and twisted. Rather than ending in a cloven hoof, five claws curved from the stump, like a set of talons on a bird of prey.

The hide was too thick, the hair bristly and coarse, the body too small.

And the head . . .

I gasped as I glimpsed the antlers. They started at the stag's forehead like clusters of toadstools, likely obscuring his vision as more and more sprouted down his muzzle. It was a wonder the poor creature had ever been able to lift his head under the weight of so many horns. I counted at least five dozen points, tangled round each other like tree limbs starved for sunlight.

"You shot this up on the eastern ridge?" Calvin Buhrman asked, kneeling down to examine the legs. He ran a finger over the hook of one claw, whistling through his teeth.

Orin McNally nodded. "Never seen anything like it."

"I have," Martha McCleary said, stepping through the crowd with care. Her twists of hair were snow white, and she leaned heavily on her cane. It was nearly an identical match to the one her husband, Amos, used. "My pa shot something like that back when this town was nothing more than a couple of families living in tents, trying to fight back the wilderness." Her lips, papery thin and creased with deep lines, pressed together as she dredged the story up through decades of memories. "Pa said there were whole herds of them, dotting the meadow where the Pursimons' farm now is. All too small. All too strange. Can't eat the meat, and the hide is too thick to wear. Best to burn it. Burn the body and scatter the bones."

"What's wrong with the meat?" Orin asked. The crowd had fallen into a still hush as Martha had spoken, and his question sounded as loud as a gunshot.

Her face wrinkled into a grimace. "It's wrong. It's all wrong."

"Were there more of them?" someone in the group called out.

"Just this one," Pryor McNally said, circling the body. "We ought to keep the head at least. Won't that be something, hung above the mantel?"

"Something indeed," Martha agreed, though her words did not match the look on her face. "Do as you wish; you young people always do."

With a shake of her head, she toddled out toward the main road, then disappeared around the corner, no doubt taking the news back to the general store. The Elders would be here soon.

Before I turned my attention back to the creature, I spotted Samuel near the entrance to the yard.

He'd strayed away from the group and was speaking with Rebecca, half-hidden in the shadows of the portico. Her fingers twisted through his, and smiles played on both their lips as they whispered to one another. Though their secrecy had initially stung, seeing them so happy together warmed my heart, healing its wounds.

It would be a busy autumn, planning a wedding, helping them settle into their new life together. Would they build a farmhouse of their own, or remain with us? I pictured Rebecca and me sitting beside the hearth as snow fell, knitting tiny hats and socks, quilting small, cozy blankets. I imagined them pink. Sam would undoubtedly want a son first, but I hoped it was a girl. A little girl with blond hair and stormy gray eyes.

But something was wrong. Sam's face slowly fell, turning ashen as his smile faded. He shook his head once, a sharp dismissal before stepping away from her.

"No," he said, his voice traveling on the breeze. "You're wrong."

Rebecca tried to take his hands, but he jerked them to his chest, darting to the side to avoid her. His head shook again, once, twice, three times, as he was backing up, backing away, backing as far from Rebecca as he could get.

Rebecca trailed after him, unable to see that she was only making it worse.

Accusations, hissed too softly to draw the crowd's attention from the stag, were hurled back and forth until Rebecca reached out and grabbed Samuel to her. Her fingers softened, running down his shoulders, holding him in place. For a moment, I thought she was going to kiss him, ending the fight, ending the misunderstanding, and all would be forgiven.

Instead she served him a hard slap across the face and stalked off without a backward glance.

9

"Rule Number Five: Let from your lips no false words pour,
damning characters evermore."

"WE NEED TO TALK," I SAID, LINGERING IN THE OPEN doorway of the barn as Samuel unharnessed the horses.

"About what?" he grunted, hoisting Luna's bridle over her ears.

He hadn't said a word the whole ride home, sitting in the back of the wagon and rubbing at his cheek as though Rebecca's handprint still stung. Sadie had chattered about all the gossip she'd overheard at the sewing circle, drowning out any chance of a conversation. No one else seemed to realize anything was wrong with Sam.

I glanced toward the house. Mama and Merry were in the kitchen, and Sadie was out on the side porch, sweeping circles of dust about her skirts and laughing. Papa had been quiet as he'd ferried us home, and then had said he needed an afternoon walk to clear his mind. For the moment, it seemed Sam and I were alone.

"I saw you and Rebecca fighting," I started, twisting the corner of my apron around my finger.

He froze, his back tense as he waited for more.

"I . . . I know what it was about," I ventured.

He snorted. "I really doubt that, little sister."

I crossed in, splitting the distance between us. "Rebecca told me everything . . . about the baby . . . about everything."

He shifted into motion once more, placing the harnesses on a stack of hay bales. The tack would need to be cleaned and oiled later. "She tell you who the real father is? Because it's certainly not me."

I gasped. "Of course it is! She loves you—"

Samuel led the horses to their stalls for a rubdown. "She loves a lot of boys in town. I was the only one stupid enough to love her back."

My mouth fell open in surprise. "That's not true!"

"Not what I heard. Not what a lot of people have heard."

"People? What people?"

He pushed back a lock of hair. "I was at Buhrman's earlier. Winthrop Mullins said he saw her down by the creek with that Pursimon boy." He snorted in disgust. "He's not even in Merry's grade."

"Then it couldn't have been whatever Winthrop thought it was. He was probably just teasing you or—"

"It wasn't just Winthrop. Even that new trapper was going on about it," he snarled.

Had Price been at the tavern today? He'd been running into everyone in the Falls. My heart twanged, uncomfortably concerned I'd missed seeing him, but I pushed back those thoughts. "The boy I saw down by the creek?"

He shrugged. "I don't know. Him or one of his friends. He was dressed funny—he had this fancy black hat like he was on his way to the opera, but buckskin breeches and hair down his back."

Not Price, then. Someone else from his camp.

"He said he was setting traps along the north ridge and came across a couple in the woods. It was Rebecca and Simon Briard. The parson's son! And judging by the state of their clothes, they hadn't been praying."

I remembered Rebecca's face from earlier that morning, flushed with love for my brother. "I know that's not true!"

"Oh yes, you know so very much, Ellerie. I've been sneaking around with her all summer, and you just bothered to figure it out. Forgive me if I don't have much faith in your skills of deduction." He slapped Zenith's rump, trying to get the stalled horse moving again.

I stepped back to let him work, giving him space and a moment to cool his temper.

"What will you do, then?" I asked when the silence had drawn long.

"Do? Do about what? It's not mine. I'm going to forget I ever had anything to do with her and move on." He slammed the half door shut, punctuating his thought.

"They need to be rubbed down," I reminded him.

His face was splotchy with anger. "Why don't you do it, then? Since you're so full of ideas about what others ought to be doing."

With a sigh, I picked up a large flat paddle brush and started in with Luna first. "How . . . how do you know it's not yours?" I tried keeping my voice smooth even as I wanted to cringe.

After a pause, Sam took up a comb and began brushing off Zenith. "You really want all the sordid details of my love life, Ellerie?"

"Of course not, but Rebecca is certain you're the father, and I can't imagine her straying from you." I picked at a particularly nasty tangle in Luna's mane, focusing my attention on a problem I could solve.

"Well, she did. Just like the trapper said. And Winthrop. I don't doubt there are others too. She's probably familiar with half the boys in the Falls."

I peered into the neighboring stall with a withering stare. "Sam, you can't believe that. This is Rebecca. I've seen how she looks at—"

He pointed the comb at me. "Don't tell me what I ought to believe. Stop sticking your nose into things that don't concern you."

We glared at each other for a long moment before I turned back to Luna. She swayed back and forth as though listening in and unable to pick a side.

"Everything all right in here?" Papa asked, suddenly appearing in the doorway. "I heard your yelling all the way from the creek."

"It's nothing," Samuel said, working the brush over Zenith with sudden diligence.

"Actually—"

Sam was up and over the half wall before I could continue, his hand raised as if to slap my words away. I cried out in surprise and ducked around the mare to avoid him.

"I swear to God, if you breathe a word of this to anybody—" he began, but was yanked back as Papa rushed into the stall, stopping him before his hand could fall. "Let go of me!" Samuel shouted, enraged. He cast aside Papa's arm. The momentum threw Samuel off balance, and he crashed hard against a post.

"Sam!" I cried out in concern, even as I hid away.

Papa stepped forward with an outstretched hand, ready to help.

"Get away from me," my brother growled, scrambling to his feet. "I'm so sick of everyone in this family always reaching for me. Everyone always in my face, wanting more and more. Just leave me alone!"

Before Papa could stop him, Samuel raced from the barn.

"What in the world happened?" Papa asked, whirling back to me.

His face softened as he spotted my building tears. Growing up, Sam and I had squabbled often—as twins, we were often seen as one person even when our thoughts were wildly divergent— but we'd never come to physical blows before. He was changing, growing angry and hard. I didn't understand why. Was this simply part of growing up—growing separate and apart?

"Sam—" I stopped short. This was a problem, a big problem, but it was Sam's, and Sam's alone to fix. I wouldn't run tattling to Papa like a little girl, out of breath and braids flying. "It's nothing."

Papa looked me over. "Are you all right?"

I stepped from the stall.

A long sigh fell from his mouth. "I don't know what to do about that boy. It's like pulling teeth to get him to do an ounce of work this summer. He needs bigger opportunities, bigger responsibilities. When I was his age, I was already wed with the two of you on the way. He needs to grow up, become a man."

I swallowed uncomfortably.

Sam and I were twins. We were supposed to be at the same stage of life. What bigger opportunities did Papa think I was meant to take on? Why wasn't he concerned that I wasn't married, wasn't grown-up?

I wasn't a man.

My place in the world was nebulous, a malleable concept only given definition by the space I occupied. When I was in the classroom, I was a schoolgirl. At home, I was a daughter. When someone eventually courted me, I'd be a wife, a mother.

But until then, what was I?

Who was I?

I had no answers and once again felt the sharp loneliness of being left behind.

By my own twin, the one person I was meant to go through the world with.

I opened my mouth, but Papa chuckled to himself, unaware of the torment he'd summoned within me. "If he's not proposed to that Danforth girl by the end of the summer, I might just do it for him."

◦❀◦

Sam didn't come home for dinner that night, and in the morning, his bed remained crisp and completely untouched. We didn't see him that day, or the next.

We didn't see him for a whole week.

Though they didn't comment on his absence, I caught Mama fretting in moments of solitude, chewing on the side of her cheek as she peered out the window. Papa couldn't seem to muster the energy to worry.

Crops needed tending.

Animals needed care.

And finally, the honey was ready to be harvested.

The morning of the harvest, he tapped me on the shoulder, letting me know I was needed. My excitement loomed so large, I could barely eat my breakfast.

Papa and I donned hats, veils, and gloves and worked from sunup to sundown, putting hive boxes to sleep and extracting out the honey-laden frames. We carried them back and forth across the field with trembling arms. Each section of a hive box could weigh up to eighty pounds when full of capped honey, and I think it surprised but pleased Papa to see I could keep up with him and never once slowed down the process.

It felt good to put in a hard day's work. My muscles ached each night, but I went to bed so content, I almost never noticed Samuel's empty corner of the loft.

◦❀◦

"Mama, please!" Sadie exclaimed. "I'll do anything, I promise!"

Days before Sadie's eighth birthday, Trinity Brewster had loaned her a tattered book of fairy tales. Every night, I'd read the stories out loud while Sadie hopped about the loft reenacting them for us and making Merry join in whenever a handsome prince or evil queen was required. "Hansel and Gretel" was her favorite, and she studied the illustrations with rapt attention while pondering what the three-tiered cake at the center of the witch's table must taste like.

At first, she thought it must be a strawberry cake, so thick and moist that it would take a circus strong man to slice through it. Then she decided it was a pecan cake, with toasted nuts and caramel drizzle. Finally she declared that Abigail had told her it was chocolate, with a generous scoop of cocoa powder dusted across the frosted tiers.

Once Abigail had conjured such a cake, Sadie could think of nothing else.

"I'll only turn eight once—shouldn't we celebrate with chocolate cake?" she wheedled the morning before her birthday, more persistent than a starving dog after a bone.

"You can say that about any birthday," Merry said, fanning herself with her straw hat. We were out in the garden picking sugar snap peas for dinner. "I'll only turn sixteen once, and I didn't even have a cake! It was that blackberry cobbler—which was delicious and I loved it," she added quickly, throwing a look of apology toward Mama.

"Even if we could find chocolate in Amity Falls—which is this side of impossible—I'm sure we'd never be able to afford it, little love," Mama explained, tossing another handful of pods into the basket.

"I wish Trinity had never shown me that story," Sadie moaned, and she plopped herself to the ground with a petulant thump.

"You've loved reading the stories," I reminded her gently. "We all have."

"Stop being such a baby, Sadie." Merry swiped a fistful of peas from the plant nearest her. "You can't get everything that pops into your head. Don't you think we all want things as badly as you want that cake? Ellerie needs new dresses, and I'm dying for new books, and Mama . . ." She paused, her delicate eyebrows knitting together as she pondered what Mama could possibly want. "Mama could use a whole lot of new things."

"I'm happy with everything I've got," Mama said. "And I truly wish there was a way to get you your chocolate cake, Sadie-Bird, but I don't see how it will happen this year." Mama reached out to cup Sadie's cheek and rubbed her thumb back and forth across the downy peach fuzz. "I'll tell you what. . . . We'll spare an extra bit of sugar, and I'll make a honey cake in three layers—just like the one in the picture—and come spring, when they send out the next supply run, I'll make sure Jeb—"

Though done by pure habit, she still blanched at her mistake.

"I'll make sure whoever is running the store has chocolate squares on their list, and we'll make a cake then too. With chocolate frosting so frothy, you'll have to eat it with a spoon."

Sadie folded her arms over her chest, clearly interested but unwilling to accept at first glance.

"And I'll make you a crown to wear tomorrow," I threw in. "Just like the one the princess wears in the book!"

"Which princess?" Sadie asked, as though it truly made a difference.

"Any of them, you goose," I said, laughing, then helped her out of the garden row.

She brushed her skirts off with as much dignity as a pouting almost-eight-year-old could muster and looked at Merry. "What will *you* give me?"

Merry opened her mouth, undoubtedly to reply with something clever and biting, but Mama shook her head. My sister twisted her lips, thinking. "I'll set the table for you for the rest of the week," she offered. "So you can rule over your kingdom like a princess ought to."

Sadie cocked her head to the side, as if listening to a voice the rest of us could not hear, before clapping her hands with glee. "Abigail and I accept! And we want the crown to be as golden as sunlight!" she added, turning to me.

I pushed myself up, peas all picked. "Then golden you shall have!"

Even after the honey was harvested, we were never allowed to pick the flowers growing in our fields. Once the combs had been cut away and we left the bees to prepare for winter, Papa would wade out into the fields, picking the annuals to extract their seeds. He liked to experiment with different combinations of flowers come spring. Every type of flower pollen produced a different taste in the honey—some giving flowery notes so sweet, it made your teeth ache. Others tinged the honey with a rich smoky flavor perfect for pouring over hardtack biscuits and dry bread.

The preparation of the flower fields was one of Papa's favorite duties. He often admitted it would be much easier to allow the bees to forage for pollen in the wild, but he knew that the honey would be unpredictable and unremarkable. I think he liked imagining himself as a French winemaker, toying with varieties of grapes to create the perfect blend to ferment. He kept journals of his experiments, drawing pictures and writing detailed notes on which flowers produced the best flavors. It was a homemade field guide any botanist would envy.

So when I went to pick flowers for Sadie's crown in the early afternoon of her birthday, I left the farm behind, wandering west toward the trio of waterfalls feeding the Greenswold. There was a large patch of wood sorrel there that would be the perfect shade of gold for a flower crown.

It was another hot day, and once I'd situated myself among the flowers, I unbuttoned the top two clasps of my dress and fanned myself. The mornings were always cold, on the verge of a hard frost, but as the sun blazed over the valley, it grew sweltering and miserable, feeling more like July than September.

I wove together a small circlet of reeds and ivy for the wreath's base and was just about to start adding flowers when a voice called out, startling me.

"Beautiful afternoon, isn't it?"

A figure moved through the trunks of the pine trees, almost as sleek and dark as the shadows themselves. As he stepped into the sunlight, I could see it was the mysterious trapper who called himself "Price."

His pack jingled with an assortment of tools and a large machete, undoubtedly used to hack back the forest's undergrowth. It also boasted an impressive collection of rabbit feet dangling on a string, a rather morbid bunch of fur and claws. I wondered why a man would ever feel compelled to carry so much supposed luck wherever he traveled.

"Hot, though," he added, and plunked himself on the ground just feet from where I sat. A sheen of sweat dotted his brow, and his sleeves were rolled up to his elbows, revealing tattooed bands of dark green ink circling his wrists like bracelets. There was a pattern within the bands, but I couldn't quite make it out.

After rummaging through his bag, Price pulled out a round canteen and shook it once before offering it to me. When I passed, he downed it himself. I tried not to notice the way his Adam's apple bobbed as he slugged back long swigs of the water.

This boy was too attractive by half.

He recapped the canteen and wiped his lips on the back of his hand. "Hungry?" he asked, pulling out a small pouch from the bag. It was full of jerky and smelled spicy and delicious.

I shook my head. Back home, Mama was preparing an absolute feast for supper, and I didn't want to spoil it.

With a shrug, he dug in. "More for me, then. So tell me, Ellerie Downing, do you fancy yourself a fairy queen?"

"I—what?"

He pointed to the half-assembled wreath in my lap. "If you don't mind me saying so, you really ought to use different flowers. Those yellow ones are all wrong for you. You need something that better matches the pink of your cheeks." He snatched up a creamy, white clover blossom and held it close to my face to compare. "This suits you better."

"It's not for me," I said, ducking away, lest he guess how much I hoped his fingers might accidentally brush against my skin. "It's for my sister, for her birthday."

"Today?"

I nodded.

"Be sure to wish her many happy returns for me."

"And who shall I say is wishing?" I asked, feeling recklessly bold.

He hesitated for a moment, his eyes warm and amber today as they studied me. "Why, Price, of course."

"That can't truly be your name."

He smiled, and I noticed two deep dimples situated perfectly in the centers of his cheeks. "Can't it?"

"It doesn't suit you," I said, using his words against him.

The dimples flashed again, and I grabbed a fistful of yellow flowers so that I'd have something else to occupy my thoughts.

"All right, fine. I lied to your father. You're terribly perceptive, you know." He picked a second clover blossom and tied its stem to the other. "I rather like that."

"Why would you lie?"

He added another flower to his chain and another after that. "I'm new here. I don't know anyone. No one knows me. Why should I freely offer my name?"

"So people can get to know you."

He shrugged. "You're welcome to learn all you like about me. My name hardly changes who I am."

"What about your family name?"

He scoffed, his voice turning dark. "My family name has absolutely nothing to do with who I am."

He'd told Papa he was traveling without parents, and I wondered why. Had he left voluntarily, or had they been taken away, captured, or killed? Amity Falls didn't receive much news of the outside world, but I did know that bandits roamed the West, robbing wagon trains, stealing supplies and life savings before riding off in clouds of dust. Some of their names were even more famous than the men who stopped them. Was this boy's father one of those bandits? Was his surname tainted by crimes he'd not committed?

"Tell me all about the birthday girl," he said, skillfully leading the conversation away. "Younger or older?"

"Younger. She turns eight today." There were several Old-Man-of-the-Mountain sunflowers poking up from the rocks near him, and I stretched out to pluck one free. It would be the perfect center jewel for Sadie's crown.

"And her name?"

My eyebrow arched skeptically at him. "Really?"

"Hand me that one, will you?" he asked, pointing to a perfectly white clover blossom near my thigh.

"I wouldn't have guessed you knew how to make flower crowns."

"I've many, many hidden talents, Ellerie Downing." He tied off another loop. "My sister taught me how."

"Younger or older?" I asked, mimicking him.

"Much younger. I was already thirteen when Ma had her. Amelia loved picking flowers. Could spend a whole afternoon out in a field, making crowns and necklaces and bracelets for everyone she knew."

"And you wore every one of them, didn't you?" I noticed he'd slipped into the past tense, speaking of her, but I didn't comment. This was the most information he'd ever volunteered about himself.

He laughed. "I did. . . . She got sick," he added, sensing my curiosity.

"I'm sorry to hear that."

With a shrug, he finished off his chain, tying it into a circle. "Perfect for a fair-haired fairy queen," he said, settling the wreath atop my head. He nodded approvingly. "I was right, those are the perfect flowers for you."

My cheeks flushed red beneath the weight of his twinkling stare, and I grabbed at the first flower I spotted, just to have the chance to look away.

"I'm sure your beau will appreciate them tonight."

"Tonight?" I echoed, not bothering to correct him.

"Pretty girl like you, I'm sure you've got at least one suitor serious enough to join your family celebration. What do you think he'll bring little . . ." He trailed off, obviously hoping I'd slip up and fill his silence with my sister's name.

"There won't be any gift, I'm sure," I said, and he wrinkled his nose, amused I hadn't fallen for his trick.

"What a cad! If I was lucky enough to court someone as bright and lovely as you, you can be certain I'd bring your sister a grand present."

"Would you?" I tried picturing him sitting on the porch as we shared our gifts, sipping a cup of punch and listening to one of

Sadie's jokes. The image filled me with an acute sense of longing, hitting me hard along my sternum.

He nodded seriously before swooping down like a bird of prey and plucking up a bit of green. He spun it between his fingers with an admiring twirl as I leaned toward him, straining to make it out.

"For luck in the coming year."

His thumb brushed over the length of my forefinger as I took the tiny treasure from him.

"A four-leaf clover!" I exclaimed. Though I'd spent many afternoons in my childhood searching for them, they'd always eluded me. It was a beautiful specimen—each leaf a deep shade of emerald and perfectly identical to the others. "However did you see it?"

He shrugged, mustering more modesty than I would have given him credit for. "I've always been good at finding them."

"This is the first time I've seen one. . . . Sadie will love it," I admitted, before realizing what I'd done. I clapped my hand to my mouth.

"Tell Sadie Downing I wish her every happiness today," he said around a wide grin.

I carefully tucked the precious sprig deep into my dress's pocket, then ran my fingers over the clovers in front of me, searching for one of my own. A sea of three-leafed plants stared back.

"Can I give you a tip?" he asked, taking the opportunity to kneel next to me, so close our thighs bumped against one another. He bent over the clover, resting on his forearms as he searched. "You can usually find them on the outskirts of the patch."

"The outskirts," I repeated, and leaned down, looking again with fresh eyes.

"Luck can't be covered away or contained within a crowd," he murmured, raking his fingers through the edge of the clover. "It won't blend in. It wants to be found. You just need to know where to look."

As quick as a wink, he snatched up another clover and displayed it in the center of his palm. He raised one eyebrow, daring me to take it.

When I reached out, he snapped his hand shut, closing it around mine, rough and warm. His touch, so strangely intimate, brought a mess of flutters shimmering beneath my skin, like light dancing across the waves of Greenswold.

"Does your beau hold your hand like this?"

Our eyes met, and a hot flush crept up my neck. I found myself unable to move, unable to breathe, unable to do anything but stare back into his amber depths. My heartbeat couldn't decide where it belonged, first soaring high in my throat, only to plunge to the depths of my belly. I knew my cheeks must have been glowing, but the rest of me felt delicious, nauseating shivers of delight and worry. I was wholly divided, savoring his presence and wishing he'd leave before I could do something to embarrass us both.

"I . . . I don't have one," I finally admitted, slipping my fingers free and leaving the clover behind.

A lazy smile grew across his face, crinkling his eyes with merriment. "Is that a fact?" He contemplated the little clover for a moment. "Go on and take it. Luck already seems to be working in my favor today."

I jabbed one final flower into Sadie's crown and stood, brushing off my skirts. "I ought to be heading home."

He leaned back on his elbows, peering up at me. "So soon?"

Deep within my boots, I curled my toes in and out as I thought through my next move. "Would you like to come with me? Papa did say you're welcome to have dinner with us . . . and Mama will have made plenty to share. You could even give this to Sadie yourself."

He tilted his head, pondering my offer. "Dinner at the Downings'. . . . Dinner with Ellerie. . . ." He was up on his feet in one sharp moment. He moved like a cat, all languid sprawl one moment and graceful action the next. "I'll need to make myself a bit more presentable. What time should I join you?"

This was the first time I'd stood next to him and realized just how much he towered over me. Though I'd been the tallest girl in my class, the top of my head barely skimmed his shoulders. For a moment, I imagined him pulling me into an embrace. I'd fit perfectly beneath his chin, tucked in the secure circle of his arms and . . .

I shoved the wild thoughts aside. "I'm sorry. . . . We usually eat around six."

He nodded. "That sounds just fine. My camp is up that way," he mentioned, pointing to a break in the pines about a half mile away.

"Is it safe up there?" I asked, setting off. I noticed how he slowed his pace, shortening the length of his stride to better suit mine.

He scratched at his ear with a rakish grin. "Are you offering to join me?"

The heat in my chest, which had fallen to a low simmer, flared again, staining embarrassment all over my face. "Of course not! You know, you ought to be careful talking that way around here. There are many fathers who'd shoot a man for speaking to their daughters like that."

He looked delighted. "Would Gideon?"

"Probably."

He bobbed his head approvingly. "And I respect him all the more for it."

"How have your traps been?" I asked, eager to change the subject. Imagining the stranger—*my* stranger, as I was coming to think of him—filling other girls' ears with outrageous flirtations made my stomach pulse with a jealousy I wasn't familiar with.

"I've caught a few little victories," he said, jumping over a fallen branch. "I'm still waiting on something grand, though."

"A buck?" I guessed, unsure of what trappers would consider the biggest prize.

His teeth winked in the sunlight. "Much grander than that, Ellerie Downing."

I paused, weighing out my next words. "I still don't know your name."

"Of course not," he replied, the corner of his mouth twisting with wit. "I've not said it."

I waited, assuming he would offer it now, but he ambled through the tall grass, seemingly content to walk along in silence. When he glanced up, he caught me staring at him, and his eyebrows rose in a dare.

The joke was wearing thin, becoming more awkward the longer he carried it out. "It doesn't matter to me what your family name is. . . . I think a person ought to be free to make their own way in the world . . . no matter who their parents are . . . or what they might have done."

"How magnanimous of you."

I swiped my braid back over my shoulder. "I only meant—"

"I know what you meant, Ellerie. And . . . as someone whose family has done an awful lot of awful things . . . I do appreciate it."

I'd been right! I instantly conjured up a sweeping and romantic backstory for him—a little boy raised in the dangerous world of stagecoach robberies and highwaymen. I wondered if Papa might have heard of the stranger's bandit father.

"But it would be nice to be able to call you something—anything, really," I persisted. The seconds ticked by unfilled. "You're truly not going to tell me?"

"No," he laughed. "I'm really not. There's a power in names, don't you think? Once your name is given away, you can't help but be pulled along by those who have it."

My footfall landed on an uneven rock, and I stumbled forward. He grabbed my arm to keep me upright. "I don't—I don't think I underst—"

"Ellerie Downing!" he exclaimed, his voice raised, bursting from his chest like cannon fire. My eyes snapped up from his hands encircling my wrist, and his nose wrinkled. "You see. Power."

He had a point, but I wasn't ready to admit it. "You're impossible."

"I suppose I am. And, for now, this is where I must leave you."

We paused at the opening of the pines, and I suddenly couldn't seem to remember what I ought to be doing with my hands. They felt too large and ungainly and, no matter how I held them, unnatural. "I'll see you later on this evening, then . . ." I trailed off, allowing him ample time to fill in the gap. "This is absurd. I have to be able to call you something."

"Why?"

"Because things . . . important things . . . have names. They just do. I can tell you the name of every flower in the Falls, all of those trees," I said, gesturing behind him. "And it's infuriating that I don't know what to call you."

He held up his hands, utterly guileless. "I tried giving you a name, and you didn't like it. Call me whatever you want, then. It doesn't matter what you choose."

"But it does! It should! There's a reason why I knew that 'Price' wasn't your name. It didn't fit you. Names are meant to have meaning."

"You can bestow on them all the meaning you want, but in the end, does it ever really matter?" He pointed down to a bright orange marigold near his boot. "I don't know the name of that flower, but I know it smells sweet, and if I burn myself, I know it will take the sting away."

"It's *Calendula arvensis*. A field marigold," I added softly.

"Now you're naming things in Latin?" He rolled his eyes away to the woods, and I feared I'd pressed too hard. "What's 'Ellerie' mean?"

I paused. "Cheerful."

He rubbed at his chin. "And I can see I've made you anything but." When his eyes met mine, they were darker, tinged nearly as green as the—

"Whitaker," I decided suddenly. "I'm going to call you 'Whitaker.'"

His eyes crinkled with amusement. "You look at me and see a Whitaker?"

"I looked at them." I pointed to the hundreds of trees behind him. "You probably don't care, but those are white firs. They can grow over a hundred feet tall, and their branches are thickest at the base, covering the forest floor. Without a path, it would be almost impossible to walk through even an acre of them all clustered together. Completely impenetrable. Just like you."

He stared down at me, his gaze fixed with an intensity so strong, I wanted to look away, but felt too pinned in place to move. "'Whitaker' it is." He reached his hand out as if we were meeting for the first time. "Hello there. I'm new to Amity Falls. Name's Whitaker Price."

"Ellerie Downing," I said, placing mine around his to shake.

"Pleasure meeting you, Ellerie Downing."

As he pulled away, I caught a glimpse of the four-leaf clover he'd pressed to the center of my palm. He strode down the trail without a goodbye, but just before he disappeared into the trees, he turned back to wink at me.

10

"WE'RE HAVING A GUEST AT DINNER TONIGHT," I AN-nounced, bursting into the kitchen through the back door.

Mama looked up from Sadie's birthday cake. As promised, she'd modified her recipe to create a truly spectacular tiered masterpiece. I'd never seen such thin cakes, perfectly balanced by the same amount of custard cream. There was a large base and a smaller middle. At the top of the tiniest tier were eight pink candles no bigger than matchsticks. I knew Papa must have dipped them especially for Sadie. We usually never bothered to dye our candles. The natural amber tone from the beeswax created a warm and happy glow all on its own. It didn't need altering.

But Sadie loved pink. And Papa loved Sadie.

"A visitor?" Mama asked. She set down the sifter of cake crumbs to give me her full attention.

"That new trapper. Papa wanted to invite him over for supper sometime, and—"

"On Sadie's birthday?" she interrupted, a frown marring her expression.

"Well, no. I ran into him while I was out getting flowers for her crown. I invited him, not Papa. I knew you were making a lot of food, and it seemed like the kind thing to do. He's been at a campsite all this time."

She picked up the sifter with a knowing look and continued dusting the cake. "And is this lonely, friendless trapper also masquerading as a handsome young man?"

I pressed my lips together, trying to hide my smile. "Maybe. Though I'm sure he's also an excellent trapper."

Mama's gaze flickered over the chain of clover blossoms still tangled in my hair. "Looks like it."

"Where's Merry?" I asked, glancing about the empty kitchen.

"Oh, out there . . . again," Mama said, gesturing to the flower fields.

I peered out the window.

Merry stood in the middle of the fields, her arms outstretched wide to the sky. Her face was pointed toward the sun, like a morning glory seeking warmth. Her eyes were closed, and her lips moved with fervent repetition.

"Is she . . . singing?"

"Praying."

"Praying? For the flowers?"

"Maybe. Or a boy," she reasoned, amusement coloring her voice.

Mama wiped her hands on her apron and joined me at the window. For a moment, we leaned against one another in companionable silence, watching Merry. "That girl feels things with every ounce of her soul. All my children do," she added, tweaking my nose.

There was a rustle behind us as Sadie twirled into the kitchen.

Mama turned, smiling. "Well, what do you think of the cake? I looked over that picture in the book for inspiration—I think it turned out rather well, don't you?"

"Oh, Mama, it's so pretty!" she said, swooping in to plant a kiss on Mama's cheek. "Even better than my first cake!"

"First?" I glanced at the counters, but only pans and bowls lay scattered across them.

"You've got something on your face, Sadie-Bird," Mama said, returning the kiss. "A smudge of dirt or something. . . ." She licked her thumb and wiped at the offending blemish. "That's . . . not dirt." Mama pulled her closer, sniffing. She rubbed Sadie's skin once more before tentatively bringing her finger to her lips. "Sadie Elizabeth Downing," she chastised. "What have you been eating?"

"A birthday present," she said, visibly bewildered by Mama's outburst.

"What present?" I asked, kneeling next to her. The corners of her lips were brown and her cheeks smudged. "You weren't making mud pies, were you? You know better than to eat those."

"I'm not a baby anymore!" Sadie exclaimed, and a sweet aroma wafted from her as she glowered at me.

"What is it?"

"It's chocolate," Mama said, rubbing the residue between her fingers. "Where on earth did you find it?"

Sadie's small face scrunched into an ugly mask as tears began to fall. "Why is everyone being mean to me? It's my birthday. All I did was eat my cake!"

Mama frowned. "Chocolate cake? You found chocolate cake?"

Sadie let out a shrill sob.

"Where is the cake now, Sadie?" I asked, trying to stop her panic. She stared pointedly at me. "You ate it? All of it?"

"It was small! Only this big." She pantomimed something the size of a muffin.

"Where was it at?"

"On my milk stool—in the barn!"

"Was anything else on the stool?" Mama asked. "A note or card, maybe?"

"Just this," she said, pulling a small bundle from her apron pocket.

It was a little rag doll, dressed in checked blue with a matching bonnet. Its yarn hair was every bit as fair as Sadie's, nearly a perfect match. But its face gave me pause. Most of Sadie's dolls were blank—tiny figures made from corn husks or scraps from Mama's quilting basket.

But this rag doll was different.

Its creamy muslin surface was marred by two red Xs stitched across where eyes should have been. The unseeing face was ghastly in its simplicity, horrifying me the longer I looked at it.

"Where on earth did you get this?" I asked, grabbing it from her.

"Abigail made it for me. For my birthday."

"Mama, did you make this doll?" I asked. Relief flooded through me as she took the awful visage away.

"Of course not. What ghoulish eyes." She ran her thumb over the scarlet thread with a shudder.

"I like them," Sadie said, unconcerned.

"Where did it come from?" Mama asked.

"I told you—Abigail."

Mama pressed her lips together, her patience waning. "Did you borrow it from one of your friends? Trinity? Or Betty Neally, maybe?"

"Abigail made it," she insisted.

"There is no Abigail," Mama snapped. "Tell me where you got this!"

"I didn't do anything wrong!" Sadie cried, bursting into a fresh set of tears.

Mama softened instantly, pulling her into a hug. "I'm sure you didn't. . . . I just wonder where the cake came from." She pushed back the hair plastered against Sadie's forehead. "Was it very good?"

Her eyes lit. "It was!"

"Better than my honey cakes?"

"Just . . . different," Sadie said, as diplomatic as she was ever likely to be.

"And there truly is nothing left of it?"

She shook her head, then brightened. "There was a little pink candle with it! One of Papa's. It's still in the barn."

How had one of Papa's pink candles ended up on a chocolate cake? Mama looked as confused as I felt. "Can you get it, Ellerie? I need to start on the green beans if we're ever going to have supper tonight."

Once outside, I ran headfirst into a dark shape hurtling up the path to our house.

"I'll kill him, I swear I will!" Cyrus Danforth growled and grabbed at my shoulders. "Where is he?"

The air in my lungs froze. He must have discovered Rebecca's secret.

"I don't know—let go of me!" His nails were long and unevenly cut, digging into my sleeves like jagged razors. I tried to squirm from his clutch, but his fingers, riddled with arthritis, hooked into my arms like talons. I could feel the bruises already beginning to form.

"I'm certain he's off hiding somewhere like the vile snake he is," Cyrus snarled, spittle flying from his lips. There was a burst of red dotting his left eye—a blood vessel had ruptured—making him look half-crazed.

"What is the meaning of this?" Papa roared, running up behind me. He had a canvas bag slung across his chest and was wearing his widest brimmed hat. He'd been out in the fields, harvesting the flower seeds.

"Let go of my daughter!" he snarled, casting aside the bag. His hat knocked off and rolled under the porch.

Cyrus's grip tightened, digging into the already tender underside of my arm. I struggled to slip free, biting my lip to stifle tears. With a cry of utter rage, Papa ripped Cyrus from me and hurled him into the side yard.

Cyrus stumbled backward, swinging his arms in wild circles before landing hard on the sunbaked earth. His head slammed into the ground, and for a moment he appeared cross-eyed, pupils swaying off-kilter. With a grunt, he pulled himself up. Charging at Papa, he let loose a string of words I'd never heard issued from a gentleman before.

Papa pushed me toward the house before ducking out of the way.

"Get inside, Ellerie," he ordered, his hands up and fingers splayed, ready to defend himself. "Now!"

I was edging toward the back porch—it was the closet entrance by far—when Cyrus regained his balance and ran at Papa again, fist drawn for the blow. Papa darted to the side, missing the first punch, but he wasn't fast enough to counter, and Cyrus fell on him, his left hook catching Papa hard in the stomach.

"Papa!"

"Enough!" a voice bellowed, and then a gunshot cracked the air in two. We froze and turned to see Mama standing on the porch, holding the rifle out, pointing it skyward. "Step away from my family, Cyrus Danforth."

"I will not."

Mama adjusted the aim of the rifle and peered down the length of the barrel. "Get off my husband," she said, warning enunciated in every weighted word.

After an uneasy moment, Cyrus shifted away, brushing his pants as if he'd been sitting in the grass at a church picnic. "Have it your way, Sarah. I'll let the Elders deal with him—and that worthless scrap of flesh you call a son."

Papa sat up, wavering from side to side.

"Elders?" he repeated, and began to laugh—giant and wild laughs that heaved from the depths of his belly. Blood filled his mouth, reddening his teeth. "You show up on my land, attack my daughter, and *you're* going to the Elders? On what grounds? Sam has done nothing to you."

A sharp bark of laughter burst from Cyrus. "Nothing? My daughter's heart is broken, and my winter stores have been wiped out. And you call it nothing." Cyrus wrinkled his nose into a sneer and spat, aiming the phlegm at Papa's feet.

My father's face grew grave as he listened. "What the devil are you talking about, Danforth?"

"My storeroom—as if you didn't already know. Completely ransacked. Canisters of flour and sugar, scattered to the wind. Broken jars of molasses and beans, a giant stinking mess."

"I'm sorry to hear that, Cyrus. But you know us. You know me. We'd never—"

"I *thought* I knew you, Downing." He shook his head as if disgusted by the sight of us. His eyes couldn't seem to find a spot to focus on, drifting back and forth like puffs of dandelions dancing in the wind. "I assumed it was your boy at first, working alone, but now I wonder. . . . If you think destroying my stock will get me to vote for that damned supply run, you're sadly mistaken. I've got money—lots of money—and I'd sooner buy out the whole of McCleary's and watch the town starve than ever agree with the likes of you."

Mama let out a slow hiss, shaking her head. "You're the one mistaken. No one in my family would ever do such a thing. You're wrong."

Cyrus's lips pulled into a grimace. "I'm not wrong about your boy. It's a damn shame she was, though."

Papa frowned, clearly puzzled. "She? Who's she?"

"My Rebecca."

"Why would Samuel do anything to harm Rebecca? He's been courting her half the summer."

"You call that courting? Sneaking out of the house, shirking her chores so she can fool around in the hayloft with your boy? And now he says he never wants to see her again. Says he never wanted her for a wife. So that's the end of that. She'll never find herself a man with the stink of your boy all around her." He looked to Papa, eyes glassy and vague. "I bet that gave you a great laugh, didn't it? First your son destroys my daughter, her good name, her future, and then you go and try to wreck mine. You've been plotting this for years."

"Gideon has been in the fields all day," Mama said, her finger twitching on the trigger. "I think you ought to reevaluate your story."

Cyrus held up his hands, palms open and questioning. "But I don't see your boy here. Where is he? You can't deny the part he's played in this. Soon everyone will see evidence of his sins—my daughter won't be able to keep them hidden forever."

Mama gasped. "She's not . . . Surely you don't mean . . ."

"She's in the family way, there is no question of it."

"But we don't know that Sam—" Papa stopped as Mama glared daggers at him.

"Cyrus, I don't know what we can say to ease any of this, but Rebecca will not go through this alone. Of course they will be married—Samuel will do his part and—"

"He's already done his share. That boy will bring us all down."

"Now, look you here," Papa said, standing over Cyrus and pushing his pointer finger into his chest. His face was red, and I saw his hands trembling with rage. "It's a terrible thing that has happened, but your daughter played just as big a part in it."

Cyrus scoffed. "I should never have let that good-for-nothing into my home. I knew he was trouble from the moment I saw him toddling about the yard, hanging on to his mother's apron straps. He was always weak. Weak, spineless, without an ounce of character in him. But I don't suppose it's all his fault. You can't blame the apple for the tree's worms."

Papa narrowed his eyes and clenched his jaw. "Samuel has committed some very grave mistakes—but as God is my witness, he was not in your storeroom."

"Don't waste your breath. There's only one way to be certain. He will go before the Elders, look them in the eyes, and speak his truth. Then they'll see. Then they'll judge. You can try to secret away all sorts of sins in the dead of night, but you can't hide a guilty conscience. Not from the Elders, not from the Falls. Now . . . for the last time, where is he?"

Papa stared at him, hardening his face. But after a long moment, he glanced to Mama, giving away his uncertainty.

"Ha!" Cyrus pounced. "You don't know either! The Elders can decide for themselves. It's been a long time since we've had a hanging. . . . Isn't it funny how the wheels of history turn?"

Glaring at us with contentious triumph, Cyrus veered toward town, and ran straight into Samuel's fist. He'd appeared suddenly, running up from the side yard when no one was watching. A spray of blood and teeth burst through the air, and the late afternoon sun turned the droplets to shimmering rubies.

Recovering with remarkable efficiency, Cyrus whirled around and swung at my brother, bringing him to the ground as they traded blows.

"Sam!" Papa rushed over to pull him off Cyrus but was struck across the face by an errant fist. Papa persisted, grabbing Samuel by the waist and hoisting him free of the brawl. "We never settle anger with violence."

"I didn't do a thing to that storeroom, and that baby is not mine," Sam protested, squirming free. "It's lies! All lies! You want to let him lie to the Elders?"

On exhausted, wobbling legs, Papa swayed between the two men, keeping them apart as Samuel circled about, trying to find his next opening. Cyrus clutched his jaw, stooping in the grass for his teeth.

Samuel wiped away a bit of blood from his cheek. A diagonal cut, undoubtedly from Cyrus's unkempt nails, slashed his face, weeping and red.

Cyrus pushed himself up, waving off Papa's offer of assistance. "If I see any of your family on my property again—ever again!— I'll fire without question. You understand me, Downing? Keep away from my family and off my land!" With another curse, Cyrus Danforth stormed off, his faltering footsteps taking him directly into town.

"Are you sure you don't want to have the doctor look at that?" Whitaker asked once again, wincing as he studied Papa's battered face. "I could ride into town and be back in no time at all. I think you might have broken your nose."

"And I'm certain of it," Papa said, touching his nose gingerly even as he waved Whitaker's offers aside.

"Papa, let me go," Sam said, trailing after him into the sitting room. "I'll find Dr. Ambrose and—"

"I said it's fine." He gestured toward one of the chairs, indicating that Whitaker should join him. "Sam, don't you think you ought to help your mother in the kitchen?"

His eyes darted to me. "Ellerie can."

I'd been leaning against the doorframe, trying to not get caught staring at our guest, and doing a poor job of it. He'd already winked at me twice.

But at the mention of my name, I startled into motion. Mama did need help.

"Ellerie may stay. She's been here all week, hauling frames and bringing in the harvest. It's your turn to lend a helping hand, don't you think?"

Sam watched on for a moment, a low anger kindling in his eyes.

As he slunk back into the kitchen, I heard Mama light into him, her ire spitting out in whispered hisses.

"Samuel Elazar Downing, what on earth were you thinking? Bedding Rebecca Danforth? And abandoning her? Mark my words, we're setting this right."

"Mama, I—"

Merry entered the sitting room, carrying a tray of glasses and a pitcher of sun tea. She almost tripped over the threshold, peering back to watch the turmoil. She winced, seeing whatever Mama had done to stop Sam's protest.

Sadie skipped into the room, twirling about in her best pinafore before stopping short. "Oh, Papa, your face! Does it hurt? Did Mr. Danforth do all that?" She stole a quick glance toward the kitchen. "Did Sam?" She froze, suddenly noticing the stranger in the room. "Who are you?"

"Merry, Sadie," I said. "This is Whitaker Price."

11

THE FLOWERS WOKE ME FIRST, QUIETLY TIPTOEING into my sleep and casting a sweet floral filter over everything. I felt myself smile, breathing in the soft bouquet.

Then came the smoke.

Black, burning, and unforgivably present, it wafted in with an acrid bite, curdling my dreams into nightmares. My eyes flashed open and instantly watered as I stared into the rafters.

Was that shouting?

I kicked my legs over the side of the bed, slowly coming back to consciousness. It was surprisingly bright outside, and I briefly worried I'd overslept. But my sisters still dozed next to me, and I could hear soft snorts from Samuel's corner.

Why was it so bright?

I stumbled out of bed to peer outside, and gasped. An apocalyptic landscape greeted me, burning so many shades of orange and red and hot white. Flames licked the sky, reaching higher and higher as if to devour the world whole.

The flower fields were on fire.

"Sam! Sam!" I cried out, desperate to wake my brother.

"What is it?" he grumbled, wincing as I threw back the curtain.

A shaft of that awful orange light fell across him, and he held up his hands, shielding his eyes. "Why is it so bright?"

"Fire! The fields are on fire!"

"What's going on?" Merry asked with a groan.

"We have to get water. The flowers are burning! Sadie, wake up!" Sam sprung out of bed, grabbing at his pants and socks.

"There's no time for all that! We've got to tell Mama and Papa!" I was already halfway down the stairs.

Their room was empty, the sheets shoved to the foot of the bed in a hurried tangled mess. Through their window, I spotted Papa's form, silhouetted black against the firelight, kicking dirt at the edge of the flames.

My boots were at the back door, and I shoved my feet in, not bothering with the laces, before flying into the night. My nightdress glowed bright gold, bathed in the light of the climbing flames. I should have been riddled in gooseflesh, but the fires threw off so much heat that it felt like a warm afternoon.

"We need to keep the fire from leaving the fields," Papa said as I joined him. His voice rasped, harsh and metallic. He'd breathed in too much smoke. "We haven't had rain in weeks. If even one spark gets into the grass . . ."

He stomped out a patch of fire, but I knew what he would have said. If the fire broke free, it was a quick path to the house, to the supply shed, and to our hives. The buildings could be rebuilt, but we needed to protect the bees at all costs.

"Your mother is at the pump. She's been filling buckets but I can't leave to get them." He flung a blanket at a new bank of flames. For every one he smothered, it seemed two more popped up in its place.

"I'll take over there," I assured him. "Sam and Merry and Sadie are on their way."

I raced across the side yard, the tops of my boots flapping wildly and catching at the hem of my nightgown. It had seemed like a waste of precious seconds to tie them, but now I worried I'd trip and snap an ankle, and then what help would I be?

"Ellerie, thank God," Mama cried out. Three buckets already full of water circled the pump. "They're too heavy for me to lift, and I just—" She bent over, gasping for air.

"I'm here to help. Stop and rest. Sam!" I hollered, seeing him on the porch, struggling with his boots. "Water is here! We need you!" I turned back to Mama and grabbed at the next empty bucket to fill. "What happened?"

She leaned over, her hands on her knees. "I can keep going. . . . You should help Gideon. . . . I just need a moment."

"Mama, I've got it."

"At first I thought lightning must have struck, but there's no rain." She panted, drawing air sharply between each word. "Please, God, send us rain!" She clutched at her side with a grimace.

"Rest, Mama. Sam will get these to Papa."

I cranked the handle up and down, drawing water from deep in the well.

"What's going on?" Sam asked as he joined us.

"Heat lightning, maybe," I said around each pump. "We need to soak the yard, contain the flames. Bring these to Papa."

With a nod, he hoisted two buckets up, then carried them to the burning fields. His ankle still bothered him, and as he limped across the wide yard, I fought the urge to leave. Mama would only take up the pump again, and I feared she'd already placed too much stress on the baby.

Merry and Sadie slipped out into the yard and immediately went looking to see where they were needed most.

Wind whipped across the valley, warm and worrisome as it fed the flames, twisting them into little spinning cyclones of ash and embers.

"Mama, they need more buckets. I'll take this set over," I decided, already worrying over my decision. "I'll send Merry to help fill more. Please, please rest."

"I need to do something," she insisted.

"There are warming blankets in the supply shed," I said, grabbing on to the idea. "We can use them to beat back the flames. Do you think you can make it there and back?"

Mama swallowed back exhaustion and rushed off, holding her belly with a firm hand.

I picked up two buckets and made my way across the yard, trying to not slosh all the water out. Papa met me halfway and took the load, then handed me Sam's buckets, already empty. "More! We need more!"

I tumbled over on my way back to the pump, tripping on one of my loose laces. With a curse, I tied them into quick knots and went to work, filling the buckets once more. Sam flew out of the darkness, snatched them away, and left more to fill.

Again and again the buckets were taken and filled, taken and filled. It seemed like hours had passed, though I knew they'd not. The sky above was as dark as ever, and Mama hadn't even returned from the supply shed.

My shoulders ached, and a dull pain spread across my back, throbbing with every gasp for air. I glanced toward town. Surely someone had seen the flames by now. We couldn't keep fighting this on our own.

When a sharp gust of wind raced across the field, it ripped through the fire, shattering it into sparks and carrying the embers away. Some of the falling cinders took root on the far side of the house, and Papa raced after them. Mustering the last bit of strength left in my trembling limbs, I bolted off to help.

"Why isn't anyone coming?" I shouted over the crackling roar. After I emptied the bucket, I used it to scoop dirt onto the blaze that remained. "Cyrus and Rebecca must smell it, even if they're asleep."

The firelight's shadows cast the swelling and crags of Papa's face into sharp relief as he frowned, like a gargoyle come to life. "That bridge has burned, Ellerie." He snorted over his poor choice of words but kept beating at the flames. "We need more water! Take these and go," he said, tossing me his pails.

Merry was at the pump, filling up the wheelbarrow, and I took the moment to push sweaty, sooty hair from my forehead. I was light-headed, dizzy, and breathing in more smoke than air.

This wasn't working.

The world seemed to tip on its axis as a series of ragged coughs ripped my chest open. With watery eyes, I watched Sam's and Sadie's silhouettes in front of the flames. They almost seemed to be dancing. Stars swirled across my vision, angry dots of white and lightning blue. Merry was suddenly around me, her arms clinging to me as the coughs racked my frame.

Through my nauseous stupor, I spotted two shapes, far across the fields, set away from the burning chaos.

Whitaker.

Whitaker and a man even taller than he was, wearing a strange, black top hat.

The other trapper Sam had met.

"We saw the flames all the way from our campsite," Whitaker said as they raced toward us. "Go help the little one along the edge of the field."

The man in the top hat nodded once and disappeared into the sizzling dark.

Whitaker's attention fell to me. "What can I do?"

Another series of coughs sputtered up, and I curled around my knees, unable to answer.

"She's breathed in too much smoke," Merry said, her hand

rubbing circles at my back. "Can you stay with her? Sam needs the wheelbarrow."

Whitaker was already hoisting the handles. "I've got it; you look after Ellerie. I'll be back for those buckets."

Merry nodded gratefully. I struggled to sit up, watching him go.

"Water," I said, raspy and raw. "Please."

She brought a half-filled pail to my lips. The cold water soothed my throat, calming back the coughs. After a few deep breaths, I struggled to my feet, ignoring the small voice inside pleading to rest. "I need to get back to Papa. Keep pumping the water, Merry. Keep . . ." I trailed off, another cough bubbling up. With a groan, I took up the buckets once more.

"The trappers spotted the fire," I told Papa as I returned to the side yard. "Others in the town must have too. More could be on their way."

As if in response, shouts rose, caught on the wind. It was our neighbors and friends, hurrying to the farm and ready to help. They carried old tarps and buckets, spades and metal cans. Dr. Ambrose, still wearing his nightcap, held his medicine bag in one hand and a pail in the other.

"Stay with this fire?" Papa ordered before rushing to meet them.

He broke the volunteers into groups as they reached our property, sending most to fight the flames at the edge of the fields. Others formed a bucket brigade to help pass water more quickly. Over the crackles and pops of the inferno, Papa shouted that he was going to check on the hives.

Out of water and without a blanket, I stomped at the patch of fire nearest me, kicking sprays of dirt over it. Every part of me ached. I had a strange sense of dissociation, my hands and feet repeating the same motions over and over while my mind slipped into some sort of hazy, waking sleep. The yard was a sodden mess of scorched grass and mud. The flower fields were a lost cause, too far gone to salvage, but at least the bees were safe. And our house. And the shed.

The shed.

Mama.

I scanned the yard, trying to spot her nightgowned form.

Suddenly, above the swirling chaos, I heard Papa scream.

12

"THE BANDAGES, ELLERIE, PLEASE," DR. AMBROSE RE-
quested, already holding out his hand.

Eagerness to comply flustered me, and in my haste, I knocked
one of the metal instruments off the tray. It clattered onto the bed,
nearly striking the figure on top of it.

No.

Not the figure.

My mother.

Mama.

What was left of her.

Sparks from the fire had landed on the supply shed while
Mama was inside searching for the hives' warming blankets. By the
time Papa had spotted the flames, it had been too late to stop the
inferno.

Dr. Ambrose said she must have fainted, her lungs filled with
the heat and smoke. The ceiling had fallen in and a beam had
crashed down, pinning her legs in place as the fire had begun to
devour her. We'd had to cut the remains of her nightdress away,
carefully peeling back sections where the cotton had fused with
her skin.

The cotton wasn't always the only thing that ripped free.

I tried not to acknowledge the blackened skin, the way it split and flayed back, revealing bloody muscle and white tendons. My eyes avoided the clusters of blisters swelling on her like heads of mottled cauliflower. And I completely refused to focus on the burn wrapping around her neck, like a fiery hand had taken hold of her and squeezed. Dr. Ambrose said it was only an illusion, simply the way the fire had traveled across her skin, but once I'd spotted the five fingers seared into her flesh, I couldn't envision anything else.

I looked at her face instead.

Her eyes were closed and her forehead tightened in pain, but it was still my mother's face, whole and untouched. Whatever else the fire had taken from her, her face was still hers, and hers alone.

Papa had been certain she was dead. He, together with Matthias and Leland, had lifted the heavy rafter, burning their hands in the process. Papa hadn't even noticed. He'd scooped Mama's limp body from the burning cinders and carried her out into the night, releasing his grief in howls so loud that they'd echoed across the valley.

It wasn't until he'd gently laid her on the porch that we'd realized she was still breathing.

Just barely.

"The bandages, please," Dr. Ambrose repeated, shaking his hand at me.

"Of course. I'm sorry," I said, my voice as raspy as an old iron gate. Between the smoke and tears, my throat felt impossibly swollen.

"Here's the honey!" Papa burst into the bedroom with a jar held aloft.

Dr. Ambrose said that keeping the burns loosely covered and clean was the best way to prevent infection. Honey would keep the wounds moist and also help to lessen the sting of the minor burns.

Looking over the ruined landscape of my mother's body, I didn't think there was a thing on earth that could help *that*.

"Sarah?" Papa leaned over her, scanning her face for any sign she'd heard him.

"Let her rest, let her rest." Dr. Ambrose nudged him out of the way so he could begin applying the honey.

Papa, usually so strong, blanched white as part of her arm flapped open, revealing a pocket of yellow fat the fire had not burned away. He held his arm over his mouth to stop from retching and began to pace the room like a penned stallion.

"If you can't handle the sight of this, I'd rather you leave now," Dr. Ambrose said. "I must be allowed to concentrate."

"Why hasn't she woken yet?" Papa asked.

"She's been through a traumatic experience. Her body will need time to start the healing process."

Papa turned, pouncing on his words. "Then you think . . . you think she will heal from this?"

Dr. Ambrose hesitated. "If she is to heal," he amended. He glanced at me with an uneasy expression.

"She's pregnant," Papa blurted out. "We haven't said anything yet, but—do you think that . . . Will the baby be all right?"

The doctor's face grew grave. "Pregnant!"

With a gentle touch, he ran his hand over the soft swell of her stomach. She'd not yet begun to show.

"It's . . . it's hard to say for certain. . . . Do you know how far along she is?"

"Two months, maybe more," I said.

He pressed tenderly about the flushed skin. "It's certainly possible . . . and the absence of bleeding could be a good sign. But I'm afraid this is far beyond my capabilities, Gideon. I've never treated burns so severe."

"What can be done?" Papa asked, his eyes startlingly clear and lucid. "I can't lose her. I can't . . ." A sob welled in his throat, choking any words. Tears fell down his soot-covered cheeks, and when he pushed them aside, he smeared the dark ash. "I'll do anything I can, Doc. Just tell me what needs to be done."

The doctor turned back to his work, spreading a mixture of egg whites and honey over Mama's wounds. Next came the bandages, laid loosely across the burns. Once everything was covered, he pulled a sheet to her chin. A weight seemed to lift from his shoulders once the damage was hidden.

"Doc?"

He turned to Papa. "I hate admitting this to you, Gideon, truly I do, but I don't know what else we can do. Her bandages will need to be changed and cleaned daily, and she'll need something to help control the pain if she wakes—"

"When she wakes," Papa interrupted with fervent hope.

"When," Dr. Ambrose agreed reluctantly. "My supplies are low. I don't have what's needed to properly treat her here."

"I'll go out of the pass, then," Papa said. "Write down a list of what you need—what we'll all need this winter—and I will go and get it."

"Papa, no!" I jumped in. "Those creatures—"

"I will not watch your mother die!" he said, cutting me off.

The doctor gritted his teeth, worrying over his next words. "I doubt it would make much difference, Gideon. She needs better treatment than I can give. Even with her daughters tending to her . . . she needs proper medical attention, especially if . . . she is still with child."

Papa's face darkened. "What are you saying?"

"I'm saying her best chance of survival is to leave Amity Falls. Take her out of God's Grasp, to somewhere with a hospital . . . more medicine . . . a midwife who isn't always half in her cups."

"Will she even be able to make such a journey?" Papa's voice was softer than a whisper. One wrong word could shatter him completely.

Dr. Ambrose rubbed his beard, wincing. "I don't believe she'll make it *without* the journey."

Papa sank to the floor, head buried in his hands.

I swayed back and forth, wanting to comfort my father but unable to leave Mama's side. "But she's fine now. . . . I mean, she's out of the fire and you cleaned out the wounds. . . . And all the honey . . . The honey will heal her. I know it will! Everyone says it's like magic. It can . . . it can . . ."

My chin trembled as I fought back tears. He was wrong. I would stay with Mama, day and night, nursing her back to health. There would be scars, of course, but she would recover. She would be fine. It would all be—

"I . . . I didn't mean to eavesdrop," a voice interrupted from the doorway. Whitaker stood at the threshold, his fingers on the frame. "But I couldn't stand by and not offer my help. May I come in?"

I think I nodded. He carefully shut the door behind himself and crossed the room to where Papa huddled.

"If you decide to take her out of the Falls, sir, I'll accompany you. I've been up and down the mountainsides and I've found a path, a shortcut. . . . It could handle a wagon and a team of horses, I'm certain of it. You can stay in the back with her, and I'll man the front."

"A shortcut?" Papa repeated, daring to look up and meet his gaze. "Where?"

"Do you have an area map? I can show you."

Papa nodded mutely.

"What about the monsters?" I asked. "The wolves or bears or whatever they are. Six men were *killed*. Something is out in those trees."

Whitaker raked his fingers through his hair, pushing it from his smoke-smudged face. "We'll take firearms and lanterns—so many lanterns. We'll be too loud and too bright—no creatures would want to come near all that." He reached out to cup his hand over mine, and rubbed reassuring circles with his thumb. "And, sir," he said, looking back to Papa, "I'm an excellent shot. If anything threatens us . . . anything . . . I promise I'll be able to handle it."

"You don't know how fast they move," Papa muttered. He looked utterly hollowed out, just a shell of my father.

"But you do," Whitaker said. "We'll know what to expect. Together we'll be able to handle them."

Papa laughed, though there was no joy in it. "I'm damned if I go and damned if I stay. How am I to make such a choice?" He pushed himself over to the edge of the bed, reaching out to take Mama's hand, but stopped himself in time. "Sarah, I don't know what to do. I wish you could help me decide." He buried his sobs into the bedding.

I knelt, pressing my side against his. The honey's warm sweetness nearly masked the stench of burnt flesh and singed hair radiating off Mama.

"Papa," I said softly, keeping my voice low so only he could hear me. "Do you remember what you told me about the bees and the hive? How the actions of one affect the whole?"

After a long moment, he nodded.

"And how even when it feels impossible, we need to honor our commitments to each other, for the good of all?"

Another nod.

"We need you. *Both* of you," I said with emphasis. "We need to get Mama out of the Falls."

"We?" he repeated, uncomprehending.

"All of us. We're all going. Sam and Merry, Sadie and I. We'll all be together."

He shook his head. "No. We can't leave the bees. Not for that long." He sat up, and I could see the plan forming in his eyes. When he looked at Whitaker, they were clear and focused. "I'd be in your debt."

Whitaker held out his hand, helping Papa to his feet. "I . . . I don't want to rush anything, but it might be best to start the journey with the sun in our favor?"

Pink rays of morning stained the sky. The flower fields, so lush and verdant only the day before, were now smoldering heaps of ash. Papa's mouth twitched. He hated rushing into decisions and would often stew throughout the night, making scribbled lists to weigh the good and bad before resolutely making up his mind.

"Doc—is she all right to move now?"

Dr. Ambrose fidgeted with a corner of the sheet. "As good as she'll ever be. You'll want to take more of these bandages—and the honey. And take this," he said, pulling a small glass bottle out from his bag. Its paper label had "Chloroform" written in spidery script. "If she starts to stir before you make it to the city, wet a handkerchief with a bit of this and hold it to her nose. It will keep her sedated and she won't feel any of the pain."

Papa took it. "How much do I owe you?"

He waved Papa off. "Pay me when you get back. There's no rush at all, Gideon. I know you're good for it."

They shook hands, and the doctor slipped from the room. I wasn't sure if I imagined hearing his sigh of relief.

"We'll take the cart," Papa decided, then frowned. "But I hate to leave you without either of the horses."

"Take them both. You'll travel faster."

He turned to Whitaker. "How much time you reckon this shortcut will save us?"

"I'd guess we can shave a day or two off the trip, sir."

It normally took a week to get through the pass.

"I'll start packing supplies," I offered. "And Merry and Sadie can fill the wagon with fresh hay. We'll spread a quilt over it. Might make it a little more comfortable for Mama."

Papa reached out and cupped my chin. "Thank you, Ellerie." After one wavering look at Mama, he was out of the bedroom in two strides, bringing Whitaker with him, ready for action. "The map is in the sitting room."

Their voices faded deeper into the house. I knew I should start to prepare for their journey, but I lingered at Mama's side, unwilling to let her out of my sight, even for a moment. When would I see her next? What if something happened to her—or Papa—or both of them—while they were away?

What if—

Hot tears welled up and spilled down my cheeks, just when I'd thought I'd cried every last one out.

"Ellerie?" Merry asked, poking her head in. Sadie was at her heels, her eyes wide with worry and fear. "Is it okay to come in now?"

"Yes, of course," I said, brushing at my eyes to dry them.

Merry had occupied Sadie while Dr. Ambrose had worked. Though their nightdresses were covered in dirt and soot, they'd cleaned their faces and hands, scrubbing the skin raw and pink.

"Is she sleeping?" Sadie whispered as she tiptoed in. I was glad the worst of Mama's burns were covered beneath the sheet.

"It's kind of like that," I said, and pulled her into my lap. She hadn't let me hold her like this in months, and I expected a protest. Instead she pressed her back to me, snuggling in close. "Dr. Ambrose said it's her way of trying to heal. She needs lots of rest."

"Papa and Whitaker are looking at maps," Merry said. She never missed anything.

"They're taking Mama to the city. She needs more medicine than we have here."

"But I don't want Papa to go!" Sadie said, her voice cracking. "What if the fire comes back? Who will protect us?"

A sob worked its way up my throat, and it took every bit of effort I had left to swallow it. I so badly wanted to dissolve into tears, to cry like the little girl I felt I was, but what good would that do? I had to stay strong in front of them. "Sam and I will watch over you. I won't let anything happen to you, I promise. For right now, we have to be very brave. For Papa."

"And Mama," Sadie added.

"And Mama," I agreed, pressing my lips to her hair. It was ash gray and reeked of smoke. But somewhere, beneath all that, I could still smell my little sister. "There's much we need to do before they can leave. Will you help me?"

They nodded, and with a final look at Mama, we left.

"I think that's the last of it," Whitaker said, pushing the final sack into place before hoisting himself onto the seat of the wagon.

The sun rose over the mountains, spilling golden light across the valley. The air was alive with songbirds, chirping and singing to greet the dawn. Other than the smoke still rising from the ruined fields—and the small, motionless figure carefully nestled in the back of the cart—it could have been the start to any other morning.

"I just need . . . I think I left behind . . . I just need a moment," Papa muttered, ducking off toward the hives.

"Where's he going?" Whitaker asked, watching my father.

"Probably letting the bees know he'll be gone for a while."

"Letting the bees know?" he repeated dubiously.

"Papa talks to them, all the time. He lets them know about everything going on around the farm—the weather, announcements, even when there are new chicks. He says it helps them feel like a part of our family."

Whitaker hummed, considering the notion. "Will you be all right while they're gone?"

I lifted my lips in an attempt at bravery. "Take care of them for me, and I'll be just fine."

"I'll get your mama to help as fast as I can. You have my word on that, Ellerie Downing." He held out his hand to shake on his promise.

"Just be safe, all of you," I said, slipping my fingers between his.

Whitaker leaned over, resting his elbows on his knees to whisper at me. "There is one thing I find myself wondering."

I took a step closer to join his conspiratorial tones. "What's that?"

"Who set the fire?"

I blinked, certain I'd misheard him. "What?"

"Fires don't start themselves." He looked over the fields as if expecting to see the culprit still there. "Who lit the match?"

"Mama said it was heat lightning."

He raised one doubtful dark eyebrow. "Did you hear thunder last night?"

"Well . . . no, but that doesn't mean—"

"Just think about it, okay?" He tweaked the curve of my jaw, just below my ear. "Keep your eyes out. Be careful. Stay safe."

"You as well."

His eyes bore down as if trying to impart a thousand thoughts that his lips would not. "Keep that clover close, you hear?"

"I will."

Papa emerged from the house, a tiny quilt thrown over his arm. I recognized it as the swaddling blanket Sadie had used as a baby. I knew he worried they wouldn't return before spring if the snows set in early, but I'd not considered exactly how far away that was. If they all came back—*when* they all came back—there would be three of them, not two. Our family would be seven strong.

I released a deep, shaking breath, sending up a prayer.

Please, God, let us be seven.

"I told the bees everything," Papa said, pulling me to the side. "They're all yours."

"Mine?"

He nodded. "Take good care of them, and they'll take care of you."

I was staggered and stunned that he'd entrusted them to me. "But Sam—"

He held up his hands, stopping me. "Ellerie, they're yours."

He stepped away to tuck the quilt next to Mama, and I caught sight of Sam standing a little ways off, watching us. His eyes were dark and unreadable. I started toward him, but he feinted, pretending to check the harnesses.

With a sigh, Papa gestured for us to gather around him. "We'll be home as soon as we can," he promised. "All of us."

Sadie broke into tears and threw herself at him.

"Oh, I shall miss you," Papa murmured, pressing kisses into our hair.

"You've got the extra honey jars?" I asked, trying to distract his sadness.

All the bottles we'd filled last week had already sold. We'd dipped into Mama's honey cake stash to cover her burns.

"I do."

"And the cash too?"

It had been a struggle at first to have him take the money. He'd wanted to leave most of it with us, knowing it was the only way we'd be able to buy supplies in town. But after I'd pointed out that none of us could guess how long they'd be gone or the cost of medical treatments, Papa had finally relented.

"We'll be fine," I said as reassuringly as I could, making eye contact with all my siblings to get them to agree.

"We'll miss you," Samuel added. "But we'll be fine."

Merry stifled a sob.

"Ready, sir?" Whitaker called out, as if sensing my father's wavering resolve.

I shot him a look of gratitude, and he winked back.

"Ready," Papa said, disentangling himself from us. "Sure you don't want me to take the first spell?"

"Stay with your wife, sir," Whitaker said. "I've got everything taken care of."

⚬⟊⚬

"What do we do now?" Merry dared to ask once the cart carrying Whitaker, Papa, and Mama had turned round the path's bend and we could no longer see them.

We'd climbed onto the porch, trying to secure the best vantage for their send-off. I was about to jokingly suggest a bath—we certainly all needed one—but as I stared across the charred fields, the enormity of the task ahead of us sunk in, and its weight cut off any lightheartedness I'd wanted to muster.

What *were* we to do?

"Well . . . I suppose we ought to . . . We should . . ." My words faltered as my face crumpled and I sank to the steps. I just wanted to close my eyes and cry myself to sleep.

Sam settled in beside me, tentatively patting my heaving shoulders. "It's going to be all right. It . . . it looks like a lot right now—"

"It *is* a lot."

"But we're going to get through this. We just need to outline everything into steps. Little steps that are easy to do, and before you know it, everything will be done." I could see he was faltering as well. "So to start with . . . There's no point in clearing the fields just yet, is there? The harvest is done; the bees have their winter honey. We won't need flowers till next spring, right? There are seeds in the shed and—"

"The shed," we said in unison.

Dread bloomed in the pit of my stomach.

None of us had gone near it since Mama had been pulled free.

"We'll need to go through everything in it and save whatever can be salvaged," I said decisively. "Sam, you and I can pick through the stuff. Merry, we'll need you to make a list. Things that will need replacing."

"What about me?" Sadie asked. "What should I do?"

"We'll set up wash buckets in the yard," Samuel supplied as I drew a blank. "You can rinse the things we pull out, get the soot and ash off. We'll all take turns," he added as he saw her face fall. She always felt she drew the short stick with chores. "See who can scrub them cleanest. It can be a contest!"

"What does the winner get?"

"First bath tonight!" I promised, and Sadie laughed with glee.

Our moment of fun didn't last long.

Pounding hooves raced up the drive. At first I feared it was Papa and Whitaker, already turning back. Something must have happened to Mama, and I wanted to retch up every bit of hot bile roiling in my gut.

But it was one of Cyrus's farmhands, riding up on his stallion. Though the morning was still cool, both man and beast were covered in a sheen of sweat. He must have ridden from town at an absolute breakneck pace.

"Is Gideon still here?" he shouted from the horse, without bothering to dismount.

"They already left," Samuel said, and the worker let out a curse of frustration. "What's the matter, Isaiah? You look as though you're about to keel over."

"You're needed in town, all of you."

"Why?" I asked. "Why all of us?"

"You four are the only witnesses we've got."

Merry frowned. "What are you talking about?"

"The fire last night," the farmhand said, squeezing his thighs as the stallion beneath him pranced with impatience. "Joseph Abernathy and Philemon Dinsmore say they know who started it. But you've got to come to the Gathering House and try to reason with them all. It's gotten out of hand."

"What has?" I asked.

"The whole town is out for blood. Come on!"

The stallion, misinterpreting his rider's command, took off galloping down the path, racing back to town.

Carried by the wind, the last of his cries echoed over the farm. "They're going to hang Cyrus Danforth!"

13

"Rule Number Four: Seek not to harm your fellow men,
for Amity's wrath circles round again."

WE RAN ALL THE WAY INTO TOWN AND ARRIVED OUT-
side the Gathering House, gasping for breath. The hall was
crammed past capacity. Younger children spilled out into the yard
but were still keenly focused on the proceedings at hand. No one
jumped rope. No one played jacks. Everyone stood on tiptoe,
smudging noses against the windowpanes.

"They're here! The Downings are here!" Bonnie Maddin announced, her voice screeching as she spotted us rushing up Potter
Road. "Everybody out of the way; let them through!"

The crowd turned toward us. Their faces—still smudged from
the fire—ranged from sympathetic to furious. My heart swelled as
I remembered how they'd all come to our aid when we'd needed
them most.

We had our house, our farm, our very lives because of these
people.

I opened my mouth, wanting to thank them, but hands pulled
us into the Gathering House. I felt like a salmon fighting up-
stream as we were pushed toward the front of the hall. There
were too many people and too little space. My lungs could hardly
draw breath, and I worried something might snap and we'd all be
crushed in a sea of shaking limbs and angry faces.

"They're here! They're here!"

Voices shouted for the Elders' attention. The three huddled together, conferring and closed off from the rest of the crowd in their tight triad.

We were pushed to the front of the room, pressed against the Founder Tree. There was no Book of Decisions, no bowls of pigment to cast our votes and judgments. I glanced behind us. Most of the children were out in the yard, but I still saw small faces hiding behind their mothers' soot-stained skirts, staring in wide-eyed wonder at the proceedings.

There would be no Deciding today, then.

"Where's Cyrus?" Samuel whispered to me.

"He must be here someplace," I said, searching the crowd for his unpleasant face. Isaiah had made the situation seem completely dire, but the man in question wasn't even present.

A ruckus sounded from outside, breaking up the nervous din that had settled over the crowd, an explosion of obscenities thrown about like grenades.

Cyrus.

He was manhandled into the hall, trussed like a lamb to slaughter. His hands were pinned behind his back, wrapped in thick, prickling hemp rope. The rough cording had worn welts into his skin, which was opened raw in some places, and was stained with blood. His two accusers—Philemon Dinsmore and Joseph Abernathy—shoved him forward, struggling to get the protesting man through the crowd.

"Let me go, you pair of whoresons," he growled, foaming at the mouth. His face was swollen red with indignant rage. As he passed through a dense cluster of people, someone spat on him. It landed on his cheek and stayed there, as wet and unmoving as a fat slug. He contorted into painful angles, tossing his head about to dislodge the slime. "Damnit, let me loose! I swear to God Almighty, when I'm out of these blasted ropes, I'm going to tear you limb from limb, Dinsmore. I'm going to reach down and rip out your ba—"

"You heard it!" Philemon shouted in triumph, drowning out the rest of Cyrus's blustering. "Straight from his own mouth—more threats of murder!"

"I haven't murdered anyone, you son of a bitch! But you'll be the first if someone doesn't get me out of these damned things."

The Elders shifted, forming a dark, solid wall. They all wore long, black cloaks with scarlet embroidery along the edges. My breath hitched as I caught sight of the red thread. It wasn't a pretty pattern, a series of French knots or seed stitches. It was words. The Rules. Suddenly the empty Founder Tree made perfect sense.

This wasn't a Deciding.

It was a Judgment.

Leland Schäfer cleared his throat, casting an uneasy hush over the crowd as they strained to hear his soft tone. "Cyrus Danforth, you are brought before Amity Falls today accused of high crimes against your neighbors and fellow men."

Cyrus lunged at the Elder, only to be stopped by Philemon and Joseph as they pushed him down. His knees hit the floor with a crack so loud, I winced even before he unleashed a firestorm of insults.

Leland paled and held up a bit of paper with shaking fingers. "On the night of September ninth, you were seen at the Buhrmans' tavern in an intoxicated state, and were overheard making threatening remarks against Gideon Downing and his family—"

"There's no crime in that—no crime!" Cyrus interrupted. "Amos, how long are you going to let this charade go on? I told you what Samuel Downing did to my storeroom, and you refused to take action. Suddenly I'm shackled on the hearsay of these two loons? This is a joke."

"Stand down, Danforth," Amos warned, raising one bushy white eyebrow with admonishment.

"I will not be treated like this!"

"And what exactly do you plan to do about it?" Philemon asked, grabbing at the rope and tussling him about.

Matthias stepped forward, stealing the paper from Leland. With a strong, commanding voice, he read the rest of the accusation.

"Shortly after these threats were made, fields outside the Downings' farm were found ablaze, the fire purposefully set. Sarah Downing and her unborn child were gravely injured." He paused, fixing his steely gaze on Cyrus. "You, sir, stand accused of arson and attempted murder."

Cyrus's mouth fell open. "I—what?"

Matthias folded the paper and pocketed it in the deep shadows of his cheerless cloak. "I don't need to remind you that the punishment for disturbing our security and peace is quite high."

"Just one minute—" Cyrus started, struggling to his feet. "I certainly didn't mean for Sarah to be hurt."

"So you did set the fire?" Joseph asked, leaping onto the words Cyrus had left unsaid.

"Of course not! I only meant—"

"We heard you last night," someone near the back of the room said. "Berating and cursing the Downings. The whole tavern heard it."

"If you knew the story—the whole story—you'd understand," Cyrus hollered. "You'd even join in!"

"Tell us, then!" the voice cried out.

Others joined in, shouting for details.

Cyrus looked around the room, his eyes searching the crowd. They lit upon someone in the back and lingered. He popped his jaw to the side, deep in thought.

I knew without looking that it was Rebecca. I braced myself for the ugliness to come. To save himself, he'd expose her secret—Sam's secret—and the crowd's anger would shift. It wouldn't take much to set off a blaze, just a little spark of indignation, and the whole town would be in an uproar. It would be her ruining.

Sweat trickled into his eyes, and Cyrus blinked heavily, but his focus stayed unwaveringly on his daughter. After a moment, he shook his head.

"I wasn't anywhere near those fields," he said, and I dared to let out the breath I'd been holding. Was he truly going to keep silent about Rebecca and the baby?

"I'm not a friend of the Downings, it's true, but I'd never go after another man's land." Cyrus let out a derisive sniff. "Hell, I wouldn't step foot on that property if it held the bridge to Heaven and I heard the angels of the Rapture blowing their horns."

Sam stepped forward, balling a fist. "You barged into our yard, on the day of my sister's birthday, swinging punches."

"In retaliation for—"

"Retaliation?" Samuel grabbed my wrist, pulling me alongside him. He fumbled at my cuff, snapping off buttons in his haste to expose the series of purple fingerprints bruised into the soft flesh of my arm. "What has my sister ever done to you?"

The room, which had fallen into a hush at the volleyed accusations, now broke into outraged chaos. Several men pushed their way to the front of the Gathering House, apparently ready to come to my defense with violence of their own.

Jonas Marjanovic, a young man who'd been a grade ahead of me in school—and hopelessly sweet on me, Sam had teased—reached the front first and slugged his meaty fist into the side of Cyrus's jaw. For the second time in less than a day, teeth flew out of his quavering lips, knocked free by the blow.

Everyone gasped, mania sobering as the very tangible evidence of their anger landed at the feet of the Elders.

After a moment of stunned silence, Cyrus spat blood into Joseph Abernathy's face, and whatever bit of decorum the room had momentarily mustered evaporated.

"Untie these ropes at once and let me defend myself! This isn't a fair fight!"

"Neither is picking on a young lady half your size," Jonas said, getting in a second strike to Cyrus's gut before his brother pulled him away.

"You've got to stop," the younger Marjanovic said, unable to keep his grasp on Jonas. "He's headed for the Gallows anyway. He's not worth the split knuckles."

The Gallows.

I stilled at its mention.

It was a small stage erected in the center of Amity Falls—nothing more than a wooden platform, really—and though it had only ever been used once before, its presence was a daily reminder to us to keep our eyes on God, the good of the Falls, and the Rules.

Decades ago, a skirmish had erupted between two neighbors over property lines. It would have gone on for years as petty bickering, trotted out at church picnics and harvests, had it not been for the vein of gold discovered running right alongside the boundary. Sensible men would have mined it together and split the profits equally, but Cotton Danforth and Elazar Downing had been anything but sensible.

They fought endlessly over that stake of gold pebbles. The first Elders ruled in favor of my great-grandfather, giving the Downings the land on which the vein lay. That night Cotton Danforth snuck into his neighbor's farmhouse, a gleaming scythe at his side. Finding him deep in sleep, Cotton whacked off both of Elazar's hands. Ellerie, my great-grandmother and namesake, woke covered in her husband's blood, and later recounted to the Elders that Cotton had danced a mad jig about the room, rejoicing that his nemesis was no longer capable of collecting the gold himself. She said he wasn't even aware that Elazar was already dead.

As quick as a wink, the Gallows were built and Cotton Danforth was sent out as its first victim. The Elders declared that the Gallows remain as a grave warning to deter others who'd seek to harm their fellow men.

"What did you say?" Cyrus asked, noticeably cowed.

"You stand accused of attempted murder," Matthias Dodson said, voice booming as he attempted to bring order to the room. "Where else would you end up?"

"You can't be serious," Parson Briard scoffed. The crowd shifted, leaving a clear path between him and the Elders.

"You've no say in the matter, Clemency," Amos said, a touch of warning in his voice.

"I should think I do. I should think we all do. A man's life hangs in the balance. Who are you to cast judgment upon him?"

"We've been charged with the power to—"

"Power," the parson sneered. "And what of mercy? What of grace?"

Matthias Dodson shook his head. "Why don't you write a sermon on it and leave us to our work."

"I will not!"

"Don't make us remove you from the Gathering House, Clemency," Leland pleaded.

The parson sputtered, his face red. "I—I never—"

"Get out of here," hollered someone at the side of the room. "He shows no remorse for his crimes!"

"Let him hang!"

Someone else cheered, and Calvin Buhrman helped escort Briard out the back.

"No!" Rebecca screamed, watching as her only ally was tossed unceremoniously from the hall. She pushed her way toward the front of the room, holding her hands out toward the Elders. "You can't hang him! You've no proof."

"He was overheard making threats toward Gideon Downing and later seen carrying a bottle of moonshine and rags."

"He was drunk," Rebecca shouted. "There's no crime in being an old drunk. Send him to the stocks—but not the Gallows!"

"The same bottle was later found at the edge of the Downings' fields," Matthias said, and he withdrew a clear glass jug from a bag propped against his chair. The fire had misshaped it, leaving it half-flattened and bubbled on the edges, but the heat's deformities couldn't mask that it was a Danforth bottle.

Cyrus kept a small still at the back of his property, where he made moonshine with his surplus of corn after the harvest. It was immensely popular with the ranch hands, potent and strong. Cyrus was so proud of his spirits, he made his own bottles for them, giving the glass handle a distinctive, colorful flourish to represent the Danforth *D*.

Rebecca's mouth fell open, and the protest in her eyes died away as she spotted the bottle. After walking to Matthias with stiff steps, she took it from him and examined the shot of color running through the small handle. "I made a batch of these last week," she murmured. "They're a different blue than we used last year. . . . Papa?" she asked, turning to him. Doubt clouded her face, making her look impossibly small.

"So one of my bottles was found. It doesn't mean I was the one who left it there." Cyrus drew his brows together, struggling to make his features hold a look of contrition. "I admit, I was upset with Downing. I still am. One of them"—he pointed at my siblings and me—"destroyed my storeroom. You'll never convince me otherwise. But I wouldn't have burned down a man's farm, no matter how drunk I was. And I'd certainly never go after Sarah. I'd never hurt a woman."

"The bruises on Ellerie say otherwise," Jonas reminded the room.

Cyrus snorted, disregarding the accusation. "I'm telling you, I was nowhere near that shed!"

Joseph Abernathy perked up. "What shed?"

"The supply sh—" Cyrus paused, suddenly aware of the trap.

"We never mentioned anything about a supply shed. Only that Sarah was burned in the fire." Philemon turned his gaze on the Elders. "He's implicated himself. Amos, you must see that!"

"What—no, that's not what—I must have overheard you mentioning it." Cyrus shook his head, edging back, poised to run. "I was not there. I was not—Rebecca!" he cried out as his eyes fell on her, a drowning man grasping on to whatever driftwood he could find. "Rebecca knows I was home all night. She'll tell you! She'll—"

"You were at the tavern late," she reminded him with a shaking voice. Rebecca had always been painfully shy, and I couldn't imagine how she felt now, having this conversation with the entire town listening. "I went to sleep before you returned. Mark did too." She ran her fingers over the blue handle of the melted bottle before looking up with resolute eyes. "I don't know when he came home."

"Then there was—" He stopped short, whirling around to see who else he could call on. "There was that woman . . . at the tavern. I don't—I don't recall her name, but she was there, with me." He frowned as if drudging the memories from a pool of spirits. "Calvin Buhrman—you must know her. New to town." He shook his head. "Why the devil can't I remember her name?"

Calvin looked warily about. He ran one hand over his closely cropped hair, his expression grim. "I don't recall seeing you with any woman last night, Cyrus."

"Of course you do. I bought her drinks—several drinks! Surely you remember all the money I laid down."

"There was quite a bit of that," Calvin agreed. "But it was only you drinking through it all. No one else."

Cyrus's neck turned purple, and I feared he might keel over from a stroke long before the Elders could decide what ought to be done with him. "That's a lie! She was just a slip of a thing, dark hair, silvery eyes. A real beauty. But . . . her hands . . . they were awfully funny, though. Not like . . . not like they were supposed to be." He glanced about the room. "Judd Abrams—you were there. You saw her."

The rancher shook his head, blushing as he was called out. "Don't recall seeing nobody."

Cyrus nearly howled in frustration, jerking to and fro as he searched for allies. "Winthrop Mullins, I know I saw you staring at her! Tell the truth now, boy."

Winthrop scratched at his freckled ears. "I suppose I might've been staring, but it wasn't at any lady. You just cut such a strange picture last night, talking and ranting to yourself."

"Myself?" Cyrus echoed.

Winthrop worked a bit of chewing tobacco to the side of his cheek, looking uneasy. "There just weren't no one with you, sir."

Amos McCleary swayed back and forth on his cane, mulling over the situation. "Do you recall what time Cyrus left the tavern, Calvin?"

"I do. Everyone else left around ten o'clock, but he just kept drinking. At midnight, I finally had to kick him out, told him we were shutting down for the night. The missus wasn't pleased I'd let him linger for so long. Gave me a right earful about it."

"It was that woman!" Cyrus insisted. "She kept asking about the storeroom, wondering who'd done it. She said we needed to make the culprit pay."

The Elders exchanged weighted glances.

"She said we ought to go over and take something from that bastard Downing. Said we ought to . . ." His words tapered away as his eyes rolled into his head. He sounded drunk now, and I wondered if Jonas's final swing had given the man a concussion. He listed forward, like a small child on Sunday morning, fighting sleep in the first pew. Then he snapped back awake. "I went home after the tavern. Thought I might sample some of my new batch. Make sure it was just right." He glanced at the bottle in Rebecca's hands. "Looked so pretty in the moonlight, all that new, blue glass." He laughed, though nothing about this moment was funny. "New, blue."

Merry reached out to me, her face looking as troubled as I felt. What was wrong with him?

"It was as silvery and shiny as that lady. That beautiful, beautiful lady. She said we ought to take a bottle out into the woods. Have some fun . . ." He closed his eyes again, swaying unsteadily and sinking to his knees. "But then we heard the shouting. Heard the crackling. Went to see. Went to watch."

Rebecca frowned, aghast. "Why would you go watch? They needed help; they needed . . ." Realization dawned across her face, and she turned to the Elders. "He didn't set the fire! If he wandered over to watch, someone else started it!"

Cyrus blinked heavily, his head nodding like a fishing bobber out on choppy waves. "She did it. That woman. The one with the silver eyes. It was her. Said she loves a good blaze."

"You saw someone set the fire, and you didn't try to stop them?" Joseph murmured, his face slack with horror. He took a step away from Cyrus, as if physically repulsed by this strange admission.

"There was no one with him," Calvin reiterated, his words weighted with exasperation. "He was at the bar alone. He left alone. Look around—do you see any newcomers to town? There is no woman. He's gone crazy. All that moonshine finally addled his mind."

Prudence Latheton shook her head, on the verge of laughter.

"What is it?" Calvin asked.

"It's just funny. . . . You sell all that devil's brew, and now you're blaming it for this mess."

"That's not what I said at all," Calvin sputtered. "You've been trying to shut my tavern down for years, lording your trumped-up pious sobriety over all of us. Tell me where in the Good Book it says that alcohol is a sin. Christ himself served wine at the Last Supper, or did you just skim that bit?"

"Now, look here—" Prudence said, stepping forward with her finger pointed, as sharp as a dagger.

"Stop it, the both of you!" Amos ordered, his reedy voice carrying with surprising force over the chaos.

Prudence's eyes flashed. "Just seems to me, if he'd not been intoxicated last night, Sarah Downing wouldn't be knocking on death's door this morning."

"Mama's not dying!" Sadie shrieked, bursting into tears. "Why would you say that? Papa is taking her to the city. The doctors will help her! Isn't that right, Merry?"

"Of course it is," Merry said, rubbing Sadie's back as Sadie pressed into Merry's skirts, sobbing. "What is wrong with you?" Merry hissed at Prudence.

"This is why children ought not be in the Gathering House— *ever*," the woman said.

"Children." Cyrus spoke up, as if agreeing with Prudence. "Children are funny things, aren't they?"

"This is all getting out of hand," Leland murmured, touching Amos's elbow. "Perhaps we ought to—"

"You spend their lives trying to keep them, you know? Keep them fed, keep them schooled, keep them safe. But then they're not such children anymore, and suddenly . . ." Cyrus trailed off, listing heavily to the side.

"He needs the doctor," I said, but no one heard me. "Where is Dr. Ambrose?" I tried raising my voice over the melee, but it still didn't carry.

Cyrus tilted his head, staring into the distance. A gleam of light fell into his eyes, a bright circle of sunlight undoubtedly reflecting off something shiny in the room. There were too many people crushing about for me to see where it had come from.

"You!" Cyrus roared, spotting my brother. He swayed back and forth, trying to heave himself from the floor, but he was like a soufflé made too thick and sludgy to rise. "I thought it was you!"

Samuel's eyebrows furrowed with confusion. There was another shout from the middle of the room, and my brother took a step closer to hear.

"Last night, in the shed . . . ," Cyrus was saying. "Didn't know it was Sarah in there. . . ." His tongue licked at the corner of his mouth with a lazy swipe. "I thought . . . I thought it was you."

Philemon grabbed at the ropes, yanking Cyrus toward him. "Say that again, Danforth."

Cyrus let out a garbled growl. "I didn't set fire to the fields. I swear that wasn't me. But when I was watching them burn, I saw . . . I saw a figure moving about inside the shed. I thought it was this bastard, so I struck a match and prayed to God it would go up fast."

My mouth fell open.

"Papa, stop!" Rebecca cried, her words as piercing as a barn owl's call. "You don't know what you're saying!"

"It sounds like he knows exactly what he said, exactly what he did," Philemon said, holding out an arm to keep her from Cyrus.

"You tried to kill me?" Samuel murmured, his eyes impossibly wide. "All because of . . ." His eyes fell to Rebecca, but he had the decency to stop speaking.

She turned, grabbing at Leland's suspenders. Tears of pleading welled in her eyes. "He doesn't know what he's saying. Please—my father is not well. Let me take him home and nurse him. He didn't do it; he couldn't have!"

We were swept from the Gathering House in a crushing press of moving bodies. The crowd marched into the street, and I was like a piece of driftwood tossed about in a storm, utterly helpless in the face of such chaotic momentum.

"Stop!" I shouted as Cyrus Danforth was hauled past the church, past the stocks and hoisted up onto the Gallows. Angry voices cried out for rope. "This isn't right! This isn't how things are supposed to be handled!"

"Ellerie, stop!" Samuel hissed. "He tried to kill me—he admitted it himself."

"Something's wrong with him—can't you see that? When he was punched—he must have a concussion, maybe something worse. He doesn't know what he's saying, doesn't realize what he's doing. He can't be held accountable for that nonsense pouring out of him."

Samuel grabbed my elbow and pulled me toward the outer ring of the mob, then yanked and twisted when I dug my feet down in protest.

"It's not nonsense. Go home if you can't stomach it." His words were laced with sharp callousness. I'd never heard him sound so hardened. "But I'm staying to watch. I want to see the Dan-forths pay."

"You can't truly mean that," I said, grasping at his shoulders, trying with all my might to waylay him. He brushed my hands aside with a look of bitter disappointment. There was a spark of rage and madness flickering in his eyes, burning so intensely, I barely recognized him.

It was not my brother who pushed his way to the Gallows, shov-ing people aside and demanding the best view. It was as though a stranger had taken his place and was doing a poor job imitating him. He looked almost like my brother—but Samuel had never worn such a fearsome expression of hate before. His voice nearly matched my twin—but the words from his lips were strange and twisted, broken and cruel.

The mob grew louder, cheering as Winthrop Mullins raced into the square with a length of rope held triumphantly above his head. My stomach lurched as I took in the leering faces, the bloodthirsty grins. These were our friends and neighbors, people we lived alongside, who were always ready with helping, open arms. They were good people, kind people, not . . .

Not this.

There was no way to stop this, I realized with a sudden clarity, and it propelled me into action. I could not save Cyrus Danforth, but I could spare my little sisters from seeing his murder play out. I had to find Merry and Sadie and get them out of here.

"Ellerie!" Merry sobbed in relief as I pushed my way toward them.

"Come on, we've got to go, we've got to leave," I said, wincing as I heard the sound of the rope smacking over the crossbeam.

"But Mr. Danforth," Sadie said, just on the verge of protest.

"We can't do anything for him now," I said, grabbing her hand and holding on tight.

We took off at a run, racing to get away from the crowd's madness, and didn't stop until we reached the outskirts of the village. Even still, we heard the moment when the dreadful deed took place, as the wind carried with it the roar of cheers and, above all else, the sound of Rebecca wailing.

AUTUMN

14

A WEEK WENT BY.

Then two.

As the third dragged on—days lingering far longer than they had any right to—we kept a watchful eye out for the wagon's return.

We jumped at every sound, certain it would be Papa striding across the yard, carrying Mama in his arms—still recovering but safe and whole, her stomach bumped out in a proud curve.

But it was never them.

At first, our path was a veritable game trail, buggies and wagons riding up at all hours of the day, bringing condolences and baskets of food. Men helped Samuel tear down the ruins of the supply shed and make plans for its replacement. They even scheduled a day to build it, and we knew the work would go much faster with so many helping hands.

Once the crazed madness of Cyrus's death had passed, I suspected that everyone felt uncomfortably remorseful about the role they'd played in it, and sought to assuage their guilt with penitent baking and stalwart neighborly kindness.

But cherry pies and apple preserves couldn't erase the memories I had of that day, the jeers and cheers, the cries for a man's blood. Guilty or not, no one deserved to have their death so loudly celebrated.

I tried to visit Rebecca once, bringing over a poor imitation of Mama's honey cake, a tiny pair of booties I knit, and a fervent wish that we might somehow heal the horrible riff between us.

Once she opened the door, her pale face seemed to float in a sea of dark shadows and even darker mourning garb. She squinted against the bright afternoon light as though it physically pained her. Upon spotting me, she slammed the door shut so hard, I dropped the cake, and spent an agonizing hour cleaning up the broken platter and toppled layers of cake without the aid of a bucket or rags.

Merry's face soured when she saw me return, my skirts encrusted with smears of dried cream and crumbs.

"She could at least have had the decency to smash it in your face first," she said with a scowl, throwing the mess into the laundry basket she'd just hauled from the creek. "All that sugar wasted."

Then, late one afternoon as I was taking bedsheets off the lines, I heard a horse whinny, and looked up to see Whitaker galloping from town. He was riding Luna, and my heart thunked painfully in my chest. No one but Papa ever rode that mare.

Dropping my sheet midfold, I ran out to meet him, nearly losing my shawl in the process. A cold spell had settled over the Falls days before, forcing everyone to bring out sweaters and wraps from attic trunks. Samuel had been chopping cords of wood from sunup till sundown for the past two days, filling our woodshed for the winter to come. We girls picked the garden clean, and the kitchen grew unbearable with steam as we filled and sealed dozens of jars.

"Where are they?" I asked without preamble. "Is Mama okay? Where's Papa? And the wagon? Where's—"

"Whoa there," Whitaker said, raising his gloved hands. Luna assumed the command was for her and came to a prompt halt, breaking some of the tension spreading through my chest as Whitaker cracked a grin.

"They're back! They're back!" I heard Merry exclaim, followed by the slamming of the screen door. She and Sadie came tumbling down the steps. Samuel ran out from the side yard, close at their heels.

"Are they okay?" I asked Whitaker. "Just tell me before the others get here—are they all right?"

He nodded, the wide brim of his leather hat obscuring his eyes. "We got there just fine. I'll tell you everything you want to know, but first"—he stretched one leg over the saddle, dismounting with a groan—"I've been riding nonstop for the last three days. Mind if I rest a bit on your porch? Maybe get something to drink?"

"We've got water or tea. Cider too—Violet Buhrman sent over a bottle of their finest after the fire."

I took Luna's reins so Whitaker might walk unencumbered, and his knuckles brushed against mine. I couldn't tell if it was anything more than an accident.

He was tired. Dark circles rimmed his eyes, and his face was lined with the grime of old sweat and trail dust. His shirt looked and—if I was to be completely honest—smelled like he'd worn it every day for the last three weeks. But none of that mattered. He'd raced up and over an entire mountain range to bring us word of Mama.

Merry reached us first. "Where are they? What happened?"

"Everything is fine," he promised, raising his voice for Sam and Sadie.

"Where are they, then?" Samuel asked, out of breath as he jogged up last.

"Still in the city, at a hospital."

Merry clutched her chest, releasing a sob of relief.

"I tucked the four-leaf clover you gave me into Mama's pocket before she left," Sadie confessed, patting Luna's heaving side. "Think that will help her any?"

Whitaker nodded, ruffling her hair. "I'm certain of it."

After Sam had taken Luna to the barn and given her a rubdown and water, we gathered on the porch, eager to hear everything that had happened. Whitaker sat in Papa's chair, with Sam in Mama's. Merry and Sadie and I clustered along the steps, our shoulders pressed against each other's.

Whitaker downed half the mug of cider in two large swallows, then wiped off his mouth. "We reached the city in just five days."

"And the creatures?" Samuel asked.

He scratched at his jawline. "We didn't run into any trouble in the woods, though we did see quite a bit of bear scat. Your father thought it might be grizzly, but we never saw anything more than a few prints."

"Did Mama ever wake during the journey?" Merry jumped in, showing no patience for talk of bears. We all had leaned in, but she was completely on the edge of the steps, looking as though she might launch herself across the porch if Whitaker didn't pick up his pace.

"She woke up the day after we arrived at the hospital. She doesn't remember much of that night. The burns are . . . not good, obviously, but the doctor cleaned them out and is letting the new skin grow. It will take some time but they're hopeful—"

I hated to further interrupt, but I couldn't wait any longer. "But how is she? Is the baby all right?"

He smiled at me. "The baby is just fine. Three different midwives looked in on her, and they all declared it an absolute miracle. But . . ."

"But?" I repeated, instantly alarmed.

"They warned that further travel could put both her and the little one at risk. That's why only I returned. Your father wanted to stay with her. And with the snows coming . . . the pass will be sealed off with the first big storm of the season. . . . They won't be returning until spring."

He fell silent, letting his words sink in.

Snows didn't usually clear until April.

That meant . . .

"We're on our own," Samuel murmured, saying what we'd all feared.

My eyes shifted, glancing over the fields. The fire was long gone, but its destruction was still an open wound upon our farm. We'd raked through the ashes and debris, praying that, come spring, there would be flowers.

The bees would be fine. Once the air cooled, we wouldn't open the boxes again until the snow melted away. Honeybees survived the winters by huddling together at the center of the hive and shivering. Their buzzing warmed the space, keeping the center—where the queen stayed—comfortable and safe. They worked all winter this way, so that the queen could survive and lay eggs, further populating the hive. It was a marvel to me, the way these little insects could see the bigger picture and strive for the greater good, forsaking their own needs to protect the hive.

"We'll be all right." I sounded far more confident than I felt, but my family needed that, Sadie and Merry especially. "We'll need to be more cognizant of our chores around the house and help fill in the gaps."

"And get ready for the baby," Sadie added.

I nodded, pleased she'd fixated on the good, the hopeful. "We'll have everything ready for them when they all come home."

"If," Samuel said darkly.

"When," I repeated with a heavy firmness.

I blew out a long breath. We needed to stop stewing and picking at each other. We needed to get off the porch and stir into action.

I stood up, brushing off my skirts. "We might as well have an early supper tonight. Whitaker, you'll join us?"

"Think I'll have time for a quick dip in the creek?" Whitaker removed his hat, making a face as he caught his own scent. "I might have a clean shirt left in my pack—I know I'm not at my finest. Certainly not fit to sit in the presence of such pretty ladies," he said with a wink toward Merry and Sadie.

They both reddened and scurried off toward the kitchen.

"Think I'll check on Luna," Sam said, wandering off before anyone could say otherwise.

"Let me get you some soap and a towel," I volunteered, ushering him inside.

When I returned to the sitting room, Whitaker was nowhere to be found. A whoop of delight drew me to the window, and I caught a quick glimpse of him ducking under the water. Little eddies swirled about his bare shoulders.

"I . . . I'm just going to run this out to Whitaker," I called to my sisters before slipping out the door.

My breath surrounded me in wispy puffs as I headed down to the rushing creek. He'd found a deeper channel and was almost completely submerged. Even so, what little I saw of his muscular back had my cheeks burning with embarrassed delight. "Aren't you freezing?"

Whitaker turned with a smile. I tried to focus on it instead of the dark patch of hair covering his chest. "It's invigorating! Fancy joining me?" My mouth fell open, and he laughed in wicked glee. "Oh, Ellerie Downing, I do enjoy seeing you blush. Have you missed me?"

"I brought soap," I said, holding it and the towel up as if to explain my presence.

"You can leave them on the bank, unless you'd rather bring them in. . . . I know which I'd prefer." He raised one eyebrow with open suggestion. Scrunching my nose, I tossed him the bar of soap. He caught it deftly, his eyes remaining steadily on me. "Pity."

I placed the towel on top of his rucksack, left out on a large rock. "I have, you know."

"What's that?" he asked, lathering up the bar of soap. Without his shirt, his green tattoos stood in stark relief, and I found myself inching closer to the edge of the bank to see.

"Missed you." I tucked back strands of hair with a self-consciousness I despised.

His eyes brightened. "Is that so?"

"I'm grateful you accompanied Papa out of the mountains—you've no idea how grateful—but . . ." I brushed off my skirts, using the movement as an excuse to break eye contact with him. A girl could drown in the depth of those eyes. "I'm awfully glad you've returned."

"You should look in the pack," he said, scrubbing the soap into his hair and scratching at his scalp.

"Right now?"

He dunked under the water to rinse off, and came up spraying droplets into the air like a wet dog shaking dry. "Go ahead. The two packages on top."

Lifting the flap, I spied the parcels, each wrapped in brown paper and tied with twine. I unwrapped one and saw a bundle of dark gray tweed.

"For you," he said gallantly. "Your mother mentioned you were in need of a new dress. She asked me to bring fabric back. The shopgirl said something sturdy and practical would be best."

I ran my finger over the soft wool. It would keep me wonderfully warm this winter and was more stylish than anything I owned. Tears sprang to my eyes at Mama's thoughtfulness, her remembering my plight even as she convalesced.

"I picked out the second all on my own." He'd stopped scrubbing to watch my reaction. "It reminded me of your clover crown."

I couldn't help my cry of delight as I opened the second parcel. A beautiful length of blush-pink voile, scattered with embroidered Swiss dots, lay nestled in the wrapping.

"Whitaker, it's the most beautiful cloth I've ever seen—thank you!"

"It's probably too thin for this cold weather, but when I saw it, I couldn't imagine anyone else wearing it." His eyes locked on mine, and I couldn't look away, even as my cheeks heated once more.

"I . . . I love it. Thank you. It's just . . . perfect."

He grinned, clearly pleased that I liked his choice. "Why don't you take them back inside? I'm ready to come out, and I don't need your ogling eyes roving about my naked frame. I'm quite modest, I'll have you know."

With a smile, I turned to go. My heart felt lighter than it had in weeks, and I was already dreaming up patterns for the new fabrics. I pictured wearing the pink voile next spring, sitting in a field of wildflowers with Whitaker. We'd hunt for four-leaf clovers until twilight came and we could no longer see anything but the twinkle of fireflies and a heartbreakingly large crescent moon.

"Oh, Ellerie?" he called after me, interrupting the daydream. His eyes sparkled green and amber as he smiled up at me. "I missed you too."

15

THE SOUND OF HAMMERS FILLED THE CRISP AUTUMN air, their cheerful tapping carrying across the farm. As the men of Amity Falls shouted and laughed outside, framing out the new supply shed, our kitchen was being turned upside down as the wives bustled about, preparing for the noon meal.

Chicken sizzled.

Biscuits rose.

Pies steamed at open windows.

But even these wafting aromas were not enough to overpower the scent of sawdust. It permeated the morning, covering everything outdoors with a fine silky film. Sadie and her friends had been charged with keeping it out of the house, and they ran races with their wide straw brooms, their merriment infectious.

"It was awfully good of you all to come out," I mentioned to Charlotte Dodson as she whipped a bowl of egg whites into lofty peaks. "We'd never be able to rebuild the shed so quickly on our own."

"When neighbors reach for helping hand . . . ," she said with a smile.

"Extend your own, as God commands," the rest of the kitchen spoke up, reciting the last part of the sixth Rule.

"All the same, I'm so very grateful to everyone. All of us are."

I glanced out the window at Samuel. He was looking over a drawing Matthias Dodson had sketched out. The Elder was pointing to some detail, and Sam nodded, an unusual solemnity weighting his face.

"It was a terrible thing that happened to you Downings," Charlotte said, spooning out the meringue over the pie crust I'd labored over. "Terrible. We're just happy we can help in some way."

She stole a quick glance toward the Danforth farm and shook her head. Nearly no one had seen Rebecca or Mark since the Judgment. They'd hidden away in their cabin, cloaked in grief and rage.

"Perhaps we could bring them a plate after the meal," I suggested, and her cheeks colored, as if she was embarrassed to be caught staring.

"The Danforths aren't receiving visitors," she said, then carefully added, "at least not from our group."

"Group?" I echoed, looking about the kitchen.

Martha McCleary and Cora Schäfer worked together ladling beans as Violet Buhrman stirred a simmering pot of dumplings and gravy.

"Founding families," she murmured, dropping her voice. "She blames us for what happened to her pa. Now the only person Rebecca Danforth will let darken her door is the parson and his family. I saw Clemency and Letitia riding up on the buggy earlier today." She shook her head.

"I . . . I'm sure he's a comfort to them in these times," I said, stringing together words that felt far too grown-up to be coming from my lips.

After a pause, Charlotte nodded.

Merry and Bonnie Maddin came in, giggling. We'd set up

a long series of tables in the side yard, and they'd been busy all morning, laying out napkins, plates, and cutlery.

"Mr. Dodson wanted to know what time the meal will be ready," Merry said.

"We're just about ready to start serving up the chicken," Martha called out. "Ellerie, can you get me a serving bowl or two? I'm not sure where your mother keeps them."

I ducked into the larder, and stood on tiptoe to pull down Mama's wedding china. We didn't use it often, but I wanted to show my appreciation for everyone's hard work today, however I could.

A scream sliced through the air, and I nearly dropped the bowl from my hands.

Its high pitch was unmistakably Sadie's.

"What's wrong? What's wrong?" I raced out, praying there'd not been an accident.

The kitchen was empty.

All the women stood on the porch, hands shielding their eyes as they squinted at the commotion in the yard.

A monstrous, hulking *thing* lay in the dirt.

At first, my mind couldn't wrap around what I was seeing. There was fur and feathers. Sharp pointed ears. Sharper teeth. Giant curved talons poking from enormous padded paws.

"What is that?" I dared to whisper, horrified the beast would turn its head toward me and devour us all.

"It's dead," Cora murmured, stepping away from the safety of the porch.

The thing *was* unnervingly still.

All of the yard was.

The men had stopped their work, had dropped their tools where they stood. Saws and hammers littered the ground like confetti. Most of them stared, slack-jawed, at the creature, but Calvin Buhrman studied something beyond the beast.

Someone.

"Ezra?" he asked, his tone incredulous enough to draw the others' attention. "Is that you?"

My gaze drifted toward the tall figure standing beside a cart I only now noticed.

He looked to be around forty, maybe a little younger, though an unlikely pair of gold spectacles balanced precariously on the end of his nose. His hair was as dark as coffee beans, and his skin was sun-kissed and freckled. This was a man used to being outdoors, fighting the elements, and—judging from his well-toned muscles—winning.

Another man was with him, still seated in the wagon. A boy no older than myself. Chocolate-brown eyes gleamed beneath a mop of dark curls. His lips upturned, his smile easy. There was no doubt the two men were related.

"I can't believe it—Ezra Downing—in the flesh?" Matthias asked, stepping toward the stranger.

Ezra Downing?

Papa's long-lost younger brother.

My uncle.

"We all thought you'd died," Martha McCleary said, joining everyone in the yard and peering up at him. "You went into the woods and just disappeared." She circled around him, even going so far as to grab his chin and tilt his face from side to side. "You look just like Gideon."

Did he?

I stared at him critically.

There was a resemblance, I supposed. A bit of familiarity around the eyes. I could make that out even around the glasses.

"A Downing through and through," she declared.

There was a long beat before the stranger, Ezra, my uncle, nodded.

"Yes. Yes. I've finally returned home to Amity Falls." He took off his spectacles and polished the glass on the corner of his vest. Once they were clean, he returned them to the bridge of his nose and looked around the yard, acknowledging everyone there. "It's so good to see you all again."

"Where have you been, Downing? It's been nearly twenty years!" Matthias clutched the man's shoulder, bringing him in for a closer examination.

"Out beyond the pass—in the city. I . . . I wanted to find my way in the world, but . . . I've traveled long enough and just wanted to come back home." The young man sitting at the buckboard of the cart coughed discreetly. "And I've brought my son back with me. Thomas."

Thomas nodded.

"Where is Gideon?" Ezra asked, sweeping his eyes over the gathering.

"He's gone," Amos McCleary said, rubbing his thumb over the miniature Founder Tree at the top of his cane, his cataracts glaring an otherworldly blue in the morning light. "There was an accident."

The man's face paled, and he pressed a hand to his mouth. "No. Is he . . ."

"There was a fire," I said, unable to keep from stepping forward. I wanted to see the man who was my uncle face to face for myself. "His wife was badly burned. They went to the city for her to convalesce."

"And he's—was he all right?"

"As well as can be expected."

"This is Gideon's daughter Ellerie," Matthias filled in. Then he pointed to Merry and Sadie. "His eldest girl."

"My niece," the man said, appraising me with fresh eyes.

"And nephew," Sam said, moving in closer. "Samuel Downing."

"Look at you. Both of you," Ezra said. "You look so much like him."

Sam and I exchanged quick glances. We both had Mama's coloring.

"Uncle Ezra," I said once it was clear that someone would have to speak. I offered my hand. "What an unexpected pleasure to meet you."

His hand clasped around mine lightly, as if he wasn't certain his touch would be welcome. He moved on to Sam, then threw a small wave to Merry and Sadie.

I turned to the cart. "Cousin Thomas."

"Cousin Ellerie. Cousin Samuel," he greeted. For a moment, I thought his voice held a strange melodic cadence to it, an accent unheard in these parts of the world, but as he greeted Merry and Sadie, who'd finally crept forward, it was gone.

"Did you . . . did you bring this . . . creature with you?" I asked, though it was obvious they had.

"We came across it wandering in the forest as we made our journey here."

"In a pack?" Winthrop Mullins asked, his eyes shining with eager interest.

Ezra shook his head. "No . . . this one was on its own. I know it looks positively ferocious, but it was quite disoriented and weak. It only took one well-placed shot to fell it."

He strode over to the monster and pulled its head up, revealing a broken arrow jutting from its neck.

It's a wolf, I realized belatedly. *Mostly.*

"Remarkable," Matthias murmured in seeming admiration. He knelt down beside the misshapen animal and gingerly poked at its talons. "Almost like a harpy, isn't it? And . . . are those feathers?"

"Possibly," Ezra said. "I've never seen anything like it."

"And you said it was all alone?"

He nodded. "Have there been others of its kind around here?"

"No . . . not exactly. There was a stag about a month ago. Elk, I think . . . ghastly thing."

"Malformed?" Ezra asked. "Like this?" He nudged the creature's tail with the tip of his boot. The gray fur was punctuated with long quills that looked dangerous even with the animal dead.

Matthias's eyes raked over the carcass. "Yes."

My uncle scratched at the stubble of his beard thoughtfully. "I wonder if—"

"Perhaps this isn't the best place to discuss this, Father," Thomas said, nodding his head toward the house. "There are ladies present, and we've clearly interrupted some festivities."

"Of course, of course. I only—"

"It's a workday," Matthias said. "We're raising up a new shed for the Downings. The old one burned away with the fire. In fact, we were just about to sit down for a meal. Join us, won't you? I'm sure we'd all love to hear your tales."

"Please." Sam nodded encouragingly. "We'd be honored to have you with us, Uncle Ezra."

Ezra waved off Sam's words. "That's far too formal for me. 'Ezra' is fine. Just fine."

The benches filled quickly as most of the adults vied for a place near the center section, where Matthias sat with Ezra, deep in discussion. Sam had sat across from them, listening in rapt wonder.

Thomas hung back, his ears acutely red as a gaggle of Merry's friends huddled nearby, preening for the object of their whispered giggles. He was undoubtedly handsome, with a sophisticated air unknown in the other boys in town. I couldn't begrudge the girls their admiration, but I did want to set my new cousin at ease.

"Sit with me?" I asked, pointing toward a quiet section.

He nodded gratefully.

At the other end of the tables, Amos raised his hands. We all bowed our heads for his blessing. "For that which we are about to receive, we offer thanks. For the hands that prepared it, we offer gratitude. For the new faces who've joined us, we offer welcome." Prayer done, he sank onto the rickety bench and slapped his knee. "Now, who will pass me one of Martha's biscuits?"

I let Thomas fill up his plate with chicken and dumplings. He tore into the green beans first, clearly ravenous.

"So, Thomas Downing."

He swallowed back a mouthful before responding. "Cousin Ellerie."

"Just 'Ellerie,'" I said, echoing his father. "I've never had a cousin before."

"Nor I," he said, and again I felt as though I wasn't hearing his true voice, but a disguise.

"Have you lived in the city all your life?"

His eyes darted toward Ezra, boisterously laughing over something Leland Schäfer had said. "Yes. Mostly."

"I've never been before," I admitted, and he relaxed into an easy smile.

"It's quite grand."

Perhaps this was just the way people in the city spoke, peppering their speech with unfamiliar "quites" and "grands," so much more affected than I was accustomed to.

"Why on earth would you want to leave all that to come to the Falls?" Bonnie Maddin asked, three spots down. She and Merry were wedged together on a stool truly only big enough for one.

"As Father said—it was time to come home."

"After being gone so long? Everyone thought you were dead." Merry blinked at her mistake. "Well, not you—your pa. Has he ever talked about what happened to him in the woods? People have wondered about it for years."

Thomas's eyebrows rose. "Is it so strange for a boy to go missing in the forest here?"

"There've been many stories about what happened to him," I said, eager to finally hear the truth as well. "Most people assumed he'd died. Others thought he must have run into the creatures in the woods."

"The monsters," Sadie clarified, drawn away from her conversation with Trinity Brewster.

"Monsters? Like—like that?" Thomas asked, pointing to the wolf-thing.

I shook my head. "Different monsters. Older ones."

"How many beasts are those pines meant to keep?" he asked, his eyes bright with mirth.

No one at the table joined his laughter.

"There—there are a lot of stories," I said charitably. "Legends."

"Are you really moving to Amity Falls?" Trinity asked.

He picked up a fried chicken leg, studying its crispy skin, before nodding. "I suppose so. Father is the one with all the plans."

"Where's your mother?" Merry asked. Then she cupped a hand over her mouth, aghast. "That was too prying. I'm sorry."

He shook his head. "Long gone. It's just been Father and me for years."

Bonnie clucked sympathetically. "Where will you stay?"

My eyes darted to the farmhouse.

I wondered if we ought to invite them to stay with us. Papa and Mama's room was empty, and we could try to squeeze another ticked mattress into the loft. They were family, with nowhere to go. It was the right thing to do.

But something held me back from offering such hospitality.

They were family, true, but we didn't know anything about them.

"I . . . I'm not sure," Thomas said, pushing back a wave of hair. "Is there a boardinghouse in town? Somewhere we could let a room or two?"

"The Buhrmans have a room at the tavern," Merry said, pointing out Calvin and Violet. "It's usually kept open for anyone too drunk to ride home, but I'm certain they'd let you stay there."

It was a relief to know she wasn't keen on them staying with us either.

"That man mentioned seeing a stag. . . . Did any of you see it?" Thomas asked, pushing his fork about on the plate, searching for morsels hidden away in the gravy. He looked up, his dark eyes falling on me.

"We were there when the McNallys brought it in. It was . . . so strange-looking. It was like the wolf. . . . Its shape was a stag, but nothing else made sense."

"Have there been others like it?"

I started to shake my head, but Merry stopped me. "The foals at Judd Abrams's ranch."

Bonnie nodded enthusiastically. "Abominations, all of them."

"When it was alive . . ." I looked back toward the fallen body, studying its grotesque appearance. "Did you notice what its eyes were like?"

Thomas tilted his head. "Yes. We could see him tracking us all last night, two bright spots beaming out of the darkness. They were a strange silver. It wasn't until this morning that we saw the . . . full extent of him."

"There's been talk around town about a thing with silver eyes. That must have been it."

"Must have," Thomas said, his own eyes shifting to the beast.

"What could cause a wolf to look like that?"

He shrugged. "Nature can be quite cruel. But there weren't any others with it, at least, thank God. Can you imagine an entire forest full of those things?"

"You were awfully brave to go after it," Bonnie said, propping her elbows on the table to lean closer to him. "If I ever had to venture into those woods, I'd want someone like you at my side." Her lashes fluttered like the wings of a butterfly, and Thomas turned bright red.

"It—it wasn't anything," he stammered.

"Oh, but it was! It was the most—"

"At least that mystery has been solved," I said, interrupting whatever platitudes Bonnie was about to utter. "Over and done with."

16

"Rule Number Two: Tend your land, your beasts, your field,
and prosperous bounties the Falls will yield."

"I JUST DON'T UNDERSTAND," SAID ASHER HEYWORD. The farmer's voice rang through the Gathering House. "It's like half the crops have just . . . vanished."

"You suspect theft?" Amos McCleary asked from his seat at the front. He ran his pointer finger over the carved tree on the top of his cane, considering the room as if he could sniff out the culprit himself. Behind him, through the plate-glass windows, it seemed even the pines leaned in to judge.

The farmer shook his head. "No—the plants are still there, but all the harvest has withered away. Right on the stalk—on the branches themselves. What could do something like that?"

"Disease?" Leland Schäfer suggested, sounding uncertain. The Elder did no farming whatsoever, filling his land with flocks of sheep.

"It's affected all my crops, not just certain strains."

"I've found the same thing, and our farms are miles apart," Roger Schultz said. "All our carrots and potatoes—completely rotten and withered."

"And our apples," Elijah Visser chimed in. "Shriveled and black, just when they ought to be at their peak."

I hated to hear that. The Vissers' orchard bordered the southern edge of our property, and the bees loved foraging through the apple blossoms. Could this rot affect them? I glanced at Sam to see if he was as concerned as I was, but his face was turned from me.

"The cold snap?" Matthias asked.

The farmers shook their heads.

"I've never seen anything like it," Asher added. "I don't know how my family will make it through winter without the harvest. We need to try another supply run."

"Well, with rationing—" Leland began. "We'll all have to tighten our belts a bit."

Asher's eyes narrowed. "I don't think you understand the full scope of the matter. Even a strict ration won't make up for losing half my crops. And it's not just my family who count on that harvest. Folks like you, without fields of their own, depend on us. What will you do come February, Leland Schäfer, when your storeroom is empty and your children are crying? You can't eat boiled wool."

"It's not just food we need to be worried about," Dr. Ambrose said, rising to his feet. "I'm gravely concerned about our medical supplies. They've never been so low."

"Not all of us subscribe to your practices, Doctor," Letitia Briard said, choosing to remain in her seat to hurl her obvious derision at the doctor. "Clemency had that terrible cough last winter, and nothing you gave him helped. I applied a poultice of fried onions, and he was up and about in no time. I see no reason why we need to risk men's lives for more of your snake oils."

Dr. Ambrose's cheek tightened as if he was biting his tongue. "I have a great deal of respect for home cures, Letitia, you know I do. But fried onions and wives' tales will not set a broken femur or assist in a blood transfusion. Medical supplies are necessary for the continuation of this town!"

"Let's not lose our heads here," Parson Briard intervened.

"Perhaps, in light of this new trouble, we ought to rethink a run before winter sets in."

Calvin Buhrman scoffed. "We're weeks away from the first big snow, and you want to talk about a supply train? The pass will be blocked before they can even fill the first wagon."

The parson searched the room, and his gaze landed on us. "Samuel Downing, that new trapper helped your folks out of the pass with a shortcut he found, right? Perhaps he would be willing to guide another party?"

"Haven't seen him in a week or two," Samuel said, rising off the bench. "He's checking traps along the western ridge. Don't know when he's expected back. Ellerie?" he drew out testily, looking down at me.

I folded my arms over my chest. "I don't know anything more than you."

Samuel and I had been butting heads since Whitaker's return. Sam assumed he'd easily slide into Papa's shoes, looking after the farm and hives. Had my brother been remotely competent at either, I'd have been content to let him, but it was as though he'd suddenly stepped foot on a foreign shore, and was completely unaware of how anything worked.

Just that morning I'd caught him whistling his way out to inspect the hives. I lit into him with a fury I'd never known was in me. He could have easily killed off half our bees, opening the boxes with frost on the ground. Even worse, when I asked what he'd been thinking, Sam said he wanted to harvest a bit more honey—he was eager to make some money, since Papa had taken most of the family cash to the city.

After a volley of heated words, Samuel slammed his fist against the new supply shed door and stormed off. He only joined us at lunch to announce that an emergency town meeting had been called and attendance was mandatory.

"This isn't something we can afford to wait around on," Asher said, taking control of the situation. "The snowfall is coming. If we're going to send out a run, we need to do it now."

"Today?" Leland blinked. He was notoriously slow at making decisions.

"Tomorrow morning at the latest." The farmer looked about the room. "We'll need several wagons—who will join me?"

"What about those things in the woods?" Prudence Latheton asked, standing up. "Isn't that why we delayed all this in the first place? There was a Deciding and everything."

Amos held up his hands and spoke, fighting to be heard over the murmurs in the hall. "We have it on good authority that the threat of the creatures has passed. Only days ago, Ezra Downing returned to the Falls, bringing with him the body of one of these . . . aberrations. Ezra?"

I glanced to the front row, where my new uncle and cousin sat. We hadn't seen them since the day they'd arrived, though I'd heard they were staying at the Buhrmans'.

After a beat, he rose reluctantly and faced the town, fidgeting with the hem of his vest. "It's true. We've been traveling throughout the woods for several weeks, and . . . that was the only one of them we crossed."

Prudence's nostrils flared. "But Gideon said—"

"I've no doubt my . . . brother . . . saw what he saw. I've never known him to lie or exaggerate. There well may have been a pack, but you all saw the remains. These mutations weren't meant to be. Animals so badly . . . changed don't usually live long lives." He took off his glasses and polished them earnestly.

"Even still, we will take an abundance of precautions," Asher said. "Torches, firearms. Perhaps we ought to light the Our Ladies tonight to drive back any creatures that might still linger in the area."

"I'll go with you," Jonas Marjanovic volunteered. "I have a cart we can use, and my parents' horses are some of the fastest in town. They'll get us up and over the pass before the snows."

"I'll go as well," said Joseph Abernathy, the store clerk, jumping from his seat. "Asher is right—the store is nearly emptied clean. We won't last a winter without more supplies." He glanced down at his mother, as if seeking permission. After a pause, the older woman nodded.

"Who else?" Asher said, stepping to the front of the room.

"Wait just a minute," Matthias protested, realizing control of the situation had slipped entirely from the Elders' grasps. "Prudence is right—we cast a Deciding against another run, and that vote ought to stand."

"Surely you're not going to let the town of Amity Falls starve over a bit of legalese," Parson Briard challenged, folding his arms over his chest.

"This is a Deciding the town must make as a whole. We need to cast votes. We need—"

Asher let out a groan. "There's no time for all that!"

"We must have decorum," Amos said, struggling to raise his voice as a burst of wet coughs erupted from his chest. He leaned forward, gripping his cane as their force racked through him. As his chest stilled, he pulled out a handkerchief and blotted the spittle from his papery lips, regaining focus. "There is a way things are done. We cannot forsake our very identity as a town for expediency."

In the silence that followed, Briard nudged Asher, spurring him into action.

"People of Amity Falls, I put forth the motion for a supply train, leaving tomorrow at first light. We will bring back enough provisions to help us through the winter. All in favor, raise your hands."

After a moment of uneasiness, the room stirred to action. The Elders' eyes darted about, counting votes.

"And opposed?"

Not a single hand raised.

"There you have it," Asher said. "May we proceed?"

Matthias's jaw tightened. He wasn't used to having his authority ripped out from under him. "You have the floor."

Asher slowly looked about the crowd, making eye contact with everyone before speaking. "We'll need at least one more to accompany us. Who will go?"

The room remained silent. Everyone wanted the benefit of the supplies without the risk.

Matthias stroked his beard. "Parson? Perhaps you'll join them? They'll certainly need every blessing they can get." Though his words seemed friendly, there was a dark undercurrent to them, daring Parson Briard to say no in front of the whole town.

"These old bones wouldn't make it up a mountain under the best conditions," he said, waving aside the challenge. "I'm afraid I'd only slow the younger fellows down."

"Simon, then," the Elder said, undeterred, fixing his eyes on the parson's son.

"Simon can't leave at present." Parson Briard cleared his throat. "I hadn't intended to make this public today—it certainly isn't a moment for celebration—but we'll be having a wedding soon. You're all invited, of course."

"Who's the girl?" someone called out.

The parson clapped his son on the back, giving him the floor.

Simon was as lanky as a beanpole, all arms and legs and angles formed too sharply. He was only a year or two older than me, but I couldn't remember a single thing about him from school. I'd never met anyone so thoroughly unremarkable. From his mop of

179

mousy-brown hair and muddy eyes, to the way he spoke—too soft, and as though on the verge of tripping over his words—everything about him seemed utterly forgettable.

Simon's face somehow both turned ashen and flushed as he mustered the courage to speak. He opened his mouth once, twice, looking for all the world like a trout, too cowed to answer.

"Rebecca Danforth," Parson Briard filled in, ignoring the gasps and looks of confusion.

Beside me, Samuel's hands clenched and unclenched, leaving little half-moon indents pressed into the meat of his palms. "I knew it," he muttered.

"We know it's not the custom for such an event to take place after . . . a death in the family," the parson continued. "But Rebecca and her brother are all alone on that big farm of theirs, and, well . . . young love oughtn't to be stopped."

Young love indeed.

I glanced back to Rebecca, studying her stomach with a critical eye. She'd not yet begun to show but must have been terrified of her secret slipping out before she was safely married away. My heart ached for her for so many reasons. Her eyes were dark and glassy—nearly on the verge of tears—but she smiled wanly and accepted the well-wishes from those surrounding her. When our gazes met, she looked away as though she hadn't seen me.

I wondered if Simon knew about the baby. I couldn't imagine he did. He'd never be able to keep such a secret from his father, and there was little chance the parson would sanction such a union, even with all the land and money Rebecca now brought to the table.

But it wasn't his, no matter what Sam claimed. I was certain of that with a bone-deep conviction.

Rebecca had only ever loved Sam, but when faced with absolute ruin, she'd latched on to whatever option could pull her from it.

Abruptly, Samuel stood. "I'll join you, Asher. I don't have a cart, but I'm a good shot. I know I can be of help."

"Sam, no!" I said, tugging at his hand. He was volunteering out of anger and wounded pride, ready to prove himself capable of service.

"Leave me alone, Ellerie. I'm going," he hissed through the side of his mouth.

"You're sure?" Asher asked skeptically. "Your sisters—"

"Will be just fine," Samuel said, cutting him off. "Ellerie knows how to handle everything on her own. It's remarkable, really. Besides, our uncle is here now." He glanced toward Ezra, who startled into a nod. "I'm sure they'll all get along just fine."

He plunked himself back onto the bench, his decision made.

I covered his hand with mine. "Stay, Sam, please," I whispered. "I'm sorry for the fight, for the things I said."

He shook his head with resolution and tossed my hand aside. Only six inches of space separated us on the bench, but it felt like miles.

"If there's no one else willing to go, I suppose this meeting has come to an end." Asher glanced about the room, clearly hoping more would jump to their feet, but everyone swarmed Rebecca and Simon. "Can those going meet at the front to discuss details? We'll leave at first light."

I woke with a gasp, prodded by the nagging feeling that something was wrong. I lay in bed, wondering what had bothered me. My sisters' even breathing was punctuated with Sadie's occasional soft laughter. She was always happy in her dreams.

What was it?

I didn't hear anything amiss, didn't smell smoke. There wasn't a sound from Samuel's corner of the loft, but with Mama and Papa gone, he'd taken to sleeping in their room, eager to be away from our roomful of girls.

I strained my ears, listening for noises downstairs. Was Samuel up, already packing for the trip? The moon was still low in the sky; it couldn't be past midnight.

I stole across the room and peered out the window, blinking against the darkness. The blackened rows of the barren fields were still, sparkling with frost.

A pale figure stood in the middle of them, palms raised high to the starlight.

Merry must have been out praying again.

In the days after the fire, she'd doubled down on her fervor, slipping out to the fields for meditation whenever she had a spare moment.

I once asked what she was asking for, but she only smiled and said it was between her and God.

But praying in the middle of the night was new.

How had she even snuck from—

A soft murmur from the bed broke my thoughts. Merry rolled over, murmuring in her sleep.

I snapped back to the window. The figure who was definitely not my sister was still there, frozen in such a static pose, I almost convinced myself it was a scarecrow.

But no scarecrows had survived the fire . . .

Then, slowly, as if feeling my gaze upon it, it moved, lowering its arms as it turned toward the house.

I jerked back from the window, feeling sheepish. There was no way it could see me through the tiny, dark windowpane.

Even as I tried to reassure myself of this, the figure lifted one hand, reaching high up into the night sky, and waved at me.

There was something . . . not right with its hand. The fingers were too long and twisted. They reminded me of the stag the McNally brothers had brought into town, its antlers braiding around themselves, spindly and misshapen.

I stilled, remembering Cyrus's jumbled mutterings at the Judgment.

But . . . her hands . . . they were awfully funny, though. Not like . . . not like they were supposed to be.

This was her.

This was Cyrus's silvery woman.

The one he'd seen at the tavern, the night of the fire.

The one only he'd seen.

And now I had too.

In a flash, she cut across the field, moving far too swiftly to be human, like a bit of gauze caught in a sharp wind. When I blinked, trying to focus on her, she was gone, as though she'd never been there at all.

I stared into the dark, willing myself to see her once more.

But the field remained empty.

I rubbed my eyes.

Squinted.

The night stayed still.

"You're tired," I whispered. "It was just a trick of moonlight. An illusion."

Nodding to myself, I joined my sisters back in bed, grateful for the warmth they offered. I settled in and tried to drift to sleep.

But as I closed my eyes, I saw her, saw the longer-than-they-should-be fingers fluttering at me as if I ought to recognize her. As if I knew her. As if we were friends.

I buried deeper into the mattress, a chill descending over me.

"It wasn't real," I muttered into my pillow. "Your mind is playing tricks on you."

But Cyrus had seen her too.

"He was drunk."

But I wasn't. Not now. Not ever.

I froze, remembering the night I'd lit the Our Ladies. A woman in a pale dress had come out of the wheat field. I tried to recall what her hands had looked like, but it had been dark and she'd been so far away.

Who was this mysterious woman, and why hadn't anyone else in town seen her? The Falls wasn't very big, not like the cities out east, where every person you met on the street was a stranger. There was no place here for outsiders to hide.

The wind picked up, racing past the window to rustle through the woods and set the Bells to chiming.

The pines.

Was she out there, hiding in the woods?

For what purpose?

Cyrus had seen her, and the next day he was dead.

Did she mean to harm me as well?

I flipped onto my back, picking faces out of the gnarled wooden knots in the beams above me as I wondered through my options.

I wanted to hope, wanted to believe, that she wasn't real.

But it seemed unlikely, given that Cyrus Danforth had not only seen but engaged with her.

So if she *was* real—and hiding away somewhere in the woods— what was I supposed to do? Ignore her? Confront her?

I wanted to laugh.

The pines went on for miles, spreading across five different mountains—that I knew of. Trying to find anything in that dark and tangled mess would be nigh impossible.

But . . .

Whitaker.

He knew the forest better than I ever would and was far more skilled at tracking.

He could help me, I was certain of it.

I nodded, feeling more settled now that there was a plan.

I closed my eyes again, praying sleep would come.

But something still nagged at me. There was a heaviness at the back of my neck, poking and prodding. I couldn't shake the notion that I was being watched. I rolled over to face the doorway, and a bit of the tightness in my chest lessened when I saw its emptiness.

My gaze fell on Sadie and the rag doll she clutched in the crook of her arm. In all the chaos surrounding her birthday, I'd forgotten about the chocolate cake and Abigail's gift.

Not Abigail, I clarified in the sleepy depths of my mind. *Abigail wasn't real.*

But someone *had* made the horrible little thing and left it for Sadie. Why?

Again, the unbidden image of the woman waving at me entered my mind.

Was *she* behind this?

The dark red stitches seemed to glower in my direction. No matter how much reason screamed that the *X*s were only bits of thread and cotton, I *knew* that the doll was staring at me.

Without thinking, I stole it away from Sadie and tossed it beneath the bed. It landed on the wooden floorboards with surprising heft, making far more of a thunk than any doll ought to, and I sank back into the mattress with caution, certain I was about to hear skittering noises as the monstrous *thing* pulled itself to freedom.

But the noises never came, and when I next opened my eyes, the sun was up. Its golden rays pushed back and discarded the terrors that had consumed my night.

I knew without a doubt that Samuel had left. The house already felt lighter without his stewing presence.

I padded downstairs, then stopped short in the kitchen, staring in horrified confusion at an absolute disaster. It took me a moment to realize what Samuel had done, but when I saw the super frames—the combs cut away unevenly with jagged slashes—it all sank in.

He'd stolen out in the middle of the night and pilfered the bees' winter reserves. I counted the wooden frames, quickly doing the math.

Each hive ought to be left with sixty pounds of honey to last out the cold months.

He'd taken too much.

Far too much.

My chest went numb with dread. I flipped through the supers, searching for their identifying symbols. Papa always branded little markers into each colony's frames to keep them separated in case of disease.

I wasn't sure which scenario would be worse—that he'd robbed one hive of its entire winter supply or that he'd taken an assortment of supers, letting in the cold and killing bees in each box.

I counted three different marks and pictured hordes of dying bees scattered across the frozen yard like macabre confetti.

Stupid.

How could he have been so stupid?

With the flowers burned and the cold settling in, there would be no chance for the bees to create more reserves on their own. We'd have to feed them a supplement as the months wore on, a combination of water and . . .

Sugar.

Laughter burst from my chest, bitter and biting.

We had no sugar.

McClearys had no sugar.

Had this been written into a drama, I would have found it too absurd to believe.

There in the kitchen, in the middle of the mess Samuel had left, I sank to my knees and clasped my hands together, begging

God to ensure that the men would return from their run with sugar. It seemed so inconsequential in the grand scheme of things, I feared they wouldn't think of it.

As I prayed—whispering my pleas over and over again, as if their sheer quantity would somehow convince God to listen more carefully—tears spilled down my cheeks, drowning out the laughter. It was as though a dam had broken, the floodgates smashed wide open, and the river of worry and fear I'd been pushing aside since the night of the fire sprang free, ready to drown me. The sobs' force brought me even lower to the floor, and I pressed my face to the floorboards, letting them cool my scalding abject misery.

I don't know how long I lay like that, but eventually my brain began sorting out next steps.

I had to pull myself together before my sisters woke. Merry and Sadie couldn't see me like this. I was the only adult in their life right now.

I had to be strong.

For them.

Pushing myself up, I wiped my eyes. I counted breaths, slowing them until my heart calmed its painful pounding rhythm. Blinking with unfocused eyes, I gazed over the mess waiting to be cleaned up. The enormity of the situation struck my chest, square on like a battering ram.

A whimper escaped from deep within me, and once again I lost myself weeping.

17

THE BOTTOMS OF THE BROOD BOXES WERE LITTERED with the dead.

We'd scooped out as many of the husks as we could, and were dumping them into a bucket to dispose of away from the hive. Honeybees liked to keep a clean living space and would carry out the dead or dying far from the colony to keep disease from spreading. I couldn't imagine how the undertaker bees would be able to clear out the massacre and wanted to lighten their load, however I could.

If there were any undertakers left.

The damage was far worse than I'd feared. After waiting until the afternoon—the warmest time of the day—Merry, Sadie, and I created a makeshift tent with canvas tarps and lit several lanterns to warm the space before opening the boxes. It was unconventional, but I couldn't think of a better way to check on the hives' health.

What we found made me want to cry. A single hive could hold several tens of thousands of bees. Sam's carelessness had cost us at least half of every box he'd opened. And more deaths would follow if we couldn't somehow supplement their winter honey.

Each of the hives we checked seemed agitated, buzzing irritably at our unwelcome intrusion. I worried they might decide to attack, sacrificing even more of their numbers to protect their queens. We'd brought the smoker with us, but I was scared to use it, uncertain how far the temperature inside the hive would plummet if the bees stopped shivering.

Papa would have known what to do. I felt as though I was making up everything as I went along. In a wretched moment of utter selfishness, I wished he was here instead of at Mama's side. This mess was too big for me to handle on my own.

"We have to get them sugar cakes," I said, putting the lid on the final box with grim resolution and casting aside my treacherous thoughts.

"There truly isn't any sugar left?" Merry asked, sitting down and folding her skirts about her goosefleshed calves. We'd decided to keep the tent up around the hives for a bit after the inspection, hoping it would help warm the boxes once more.

"We bought the only sack left at McClearys. I used the last of that on the cake for Rebecca."

Sadie made an ugly face, picking at blades of dead grass. "And she didn't even taste it."

I pushed aside the memory of all that precious sugar smeared across the Danforths' steps. I couldn't salvage it any more than I could our relationship. Like all that sugar, our friendship seemed utterly lost.

"Has it been long enough, do you think?" Merry asked, leaning her head toward the makeshift tent.

"I don't know. Maybe?"

"I can't remember ever seeing Papa do this. Can you?" Sadie asked, looking up dubiously at the canvas.

"Papa was never in a situation like this," I said through gritted teeth.

"If it's keeping the bees warm, maybe we should just leave it up?" She traced a series of shapes against the cloth.

"Then the bees wouldn't be able to get outside when they need to."

"Why would they want to go out in the cold?"

I wanted to howl with frustration. I felt damned no matter what I did. No one but me would be judged on how we got through this situation. No one would blame Sadie if every single bee starved to death. No one expected Merry to fix it.

I didn't want this responsibility, this horrible and heavy weight pressing into my chest, stabbing its sharp talons around my throat and digging in until I feared I'd suffocate. Looking after my sisters was one thing, but adding the bees and other animals on the farm was too much. It was all too much, and I felt too young to handle it on my own.

Why, why, why had Samuel left me with this mess?

"I think . . . I think it's been long enough." I tried to keep my voice resolute even as my insides floundered. "Why don't we blow out the lanterns and then take down the tarps?"

Merry didn't budge from her seat, clearly not ready to leave the manufactured warmth. "How much sugar will they need?"

I raised my shoulders. "Papa has the recipe for sugar cakes written down in one of his journals. We'll look it up and see for certain, but I think it's about ten pounds per hive."

Merry whistled out a low note through her teeth. "Where are we going to find thirty pounds of sugar?"

"I don't know. I just . . ." Hot acid burbled up from my stomach, scalding my throat and choking my words. "I don't know, Merry."

"We could ask around town, see if people have any they'd be willing to let us buy?"

"With what? Papa took the harvest money with him, and Sam took the honey. We don't have anything to buy or trade with. Certainly not enough for thirty pounds of sugar."

Sadie chewed on her lip. "What about Uncle Ezra? And Thomas? Maybe they have sugar. Or would know what to do."

The thought had crossed my mind. You were supposed to be able to lean on family in times of trial. But Ezra wasn't exactly family. Not yet, at least.

"Maybe," I said half-heartedly. "But we don't know them well. It's best not to count on them for anything yet."

Sadie's eyes were dark with worry. "So . . . what are we going to do, then?"

"I don't know," I repeated, hopelessness casting a bleak shade of gray over everything. I bit my lip, drawing blood, and ground myself into that pain. I would not lose control in front of my sisters. I would stay strong. "I don't know."

Later that night, I lay in bed while my sisters slept, hopefully lost in sweet dreams and heedless of my stumbling plight. I'd been able to hold back the rushing eddies of panic through dinner and cleanup—we'd even read the story of Jonah and the whale before bed, one of Merry's favorites—but the moment I closed my eyes, worry swept over me, dragging me down, down, down into its dark abyss.

I had to get out.

It was too hot.

Too stifling.

I felt as though the house would collapse under the weight of my distress, crushing me into a dismal grave I'd never escape.

I raced out the door and ran into the night, clutching at my chest and gasping for air. My rib cage felt too small by half, squeezing and tightening until I feared I'd snap in two. I drew breaths in as deeply as I could, but they weren't enough. Dark stars spun before my eyes, and some small functioning part of me wondered if I was about to pass out.

The frigid night air was a shock to my system, but even it couldn't stop such unchecked hysteria. I couldn't keep still. My feet itched to be in motion, and carried me out into the burnt fields, where I paced like a madwoman.

Sadie and I had gone through every possible thing of value we could sell or trade, while Merry had gone door-to-door, pleading for sugar. She'd returned home with downcast eyes, misery written across her face.

There wasn't a single sack of sugar to be had in Amity Falls—not at any price.

I sank to the ground now, staining my nightdress with remnants of old ashes and frost.

Our only hope was the supply run.

I'd tried reassuring myself that surely someone would think to bring sugar back with them, but my mind wouldn't leave well enough alone. It wasn't a guarantee. I couldn't assume that would happen and relax. I needed a backup plan. There had to be some way of getting out of this mess. If only the waves of panic would recede long enough for me to be able to think.

I'd run through the absolute worst scenarios that could occur—all three hives starved, leaving us with only two boxes. Two wouldn't produce enough of a honey surplus. Not with all our savings being handed over to a faraway hospital. We needed more bees.

It was possible to lure a swarm of wild bees in, come spring. Papa had certainly done it before, but I didn't have the slightest idea how to go about such a thing. Bees swarmed at the beginning of spring, as flowers burst into bloom and their nectar flowed heavily.

But our fields, usually so tempting to bees, were decimated, our supply of seeds burnt to ashes.

Even if I knew how to catch a swarm, I had no way to draw them to the farm.

I needed to find a way to feed the bees we already had.

"Ellerie?"

The voice came out of the darkness, cutting its way through my haze of despair, almost as if the night itself had spoken to me. When I glanced about the barren fields, it seemed I was alone. I shifted my eyes toward the tree line and the watchful gaze of the ever-present pines. The shadows there shifted, lightening into a form, and for one horrible moment, I feared it was the thing I thought I'd seen racing across the fields the night before.

"What on earth are you doing out here in the cold?" Whitaker asked, stepping free of the forest's grasp. Unlike me, he was dressed for the chilly night, with a heavy wool coat. His rucksack was thrown over both shoulders and stuffed impossibly full, making him look like a turtle moving about.

"I—I don't really even know," I admitted, a shiver slicing through my words. "I just couldn't stay inside the house any longer."

In an instant, the bag was off and he slipped free of his coat and wrapped it around my shoulders. His body heat lingered, warming and surrounding me with his scent—leather and tannins and something green, like freshly cut grass. It was an intoxicating combination, and it wasn't until I took a deep, savoring breath of it that I realized the tightness across my chest was gone. The panic had ebbed away, soothed by his mere presence.

"Thank you," I said, tugging my braid over my shoulder in an attempt to cover the split neckline of my nightdress. I burrowed deeper into the coat's sleeves. "You're traveling awfully late. How was your hunting trip?"

"Awfully early," he corrected me, pointing to the moon's position in the sky. "Birds will be up soon. Couldn't sleep?" he guessed.

"It—it's been quite a whirlwind since you left."

He plopped himself down in the middle of the field, heedless of the dirt, the dark, or the cold. "Is that a fact? Tell me about it."

I explained the emergency town meeting, the poor harvest and black rot, and the necessity for a late-season supply run.

"Sam volunteered to go out with the party," I ended, and his expression grew grave.

"He left you and your sisters all alone?"

"Even worse—he decided to harvest more of the honey before he left. I guess he wanted to try to sell it in the city? He took it from the bees' reserves, and now they won't have enough to get through the winter."

"He's a fool," Whitaker said. "What can be done?"

"If it was a normal year, we'd make sugar cakes and leave them in the hives, but there's no sugar left. Every bit of it is gone. I don't know what I'm going to do."

"Surely they'll bring sugar back with them, won't they?"

I raised my shoulders, shrugging. "Even if they do—we don't have the money to pay for thirty pounds. Papa took everything with him when he left with Mama. And I'm sure whatever Sam gets will be squandered away before he returns home. *If* he returns home."

The dark thought soured my stomach.

What if Samuel didn't come back?

He'd been miserable and petulant for weeks, and now Rebecca was marrying another man. He'd tried acting blasé about the whole affair, but I couldn't forget his reaction at the Gathering House—sharp and visceral and impossible to disguise.

What if he saw this run as his chance to break free of the Falls? He'd be long gone, completely untraceable, by the time our parents returned. With all his ill-gotten money, he'd be able to start a new life elsewhere. It was the perfect setup for him to run.

"Oh God," I whispered, seeing everything with painful clarity. "What if he doesn't return?"

Whitaker pressed a tentative hand on my shoulder. "Then you'll have one less mouth to feed this winter and be better off for it." His eyebrows furrowed together. "That sounds more callous than I intended, but it's still the truth. You don't need dead weight holding you back—or worse, dragging you down."

"But I—I don't know how to manage the farm. Papa taught me a little about the hives, but I feel as though I'm making up everything as I go along. . . . What if I fail?"

"Oh, Ellerie," he said, and cupped my cheek, rubbing his thumb across it. His hand was deliciously warm, and I fought the urge to lean into it, seeking more of his touch. "You won't. You're too smart for that, and you care too much. You'll make mistakes—we all do—but you care enough to keep fighting. That's the truly important part. You care too much to quit."

"I might have to. Without sugar there really is no way to salvage the situation."

Moonlight cast stark highlights down his profile, and it was too dark to accurately read his eyes. "What do you plan to do?"

I shrugged. "I don't know. I'd give up just about anyth—"

He held up a hand, swiftly silencing me. "Be careful what you say in the dark of the night, Ellerie Downing, lest you promise something you might regret."

I tilted my head, not understanding him. "What?"

"You were about to say you'd give up anything for that sugar, weren't you?"

I nodded.

"But you wouldn't, not truly."

"I would," I insisted with fervor.

"Not *anything*. Not your sisters, for example?"

My mouth fell open in horror. "Of course not!"

He raised one eyebrow at me. "Then choose your wording carefully. You never know who might be listening."

He lowered his voice and waved his hands toward the whispering pines with wild theatricality. Though I knew he meant to be teasing me, my blood ran cold, thinking of all the things that could be out there, watching us now.

Things dressed in white, with fingers grown too long.

With all of the morning's chaos, I'd forgotten about seeing it. Seeing her. Seeing whatever it was.

"How much did you say you needed?" he asked. "Thirty pounds?"

"You have sugar?" I asked, a glimmer of hope daring to spark in my chest and pushing back thoughts of the woman for a second time that day. "That much?"

He said nothing, only leaned back on his hands, watching me.

"Whitaker, truly?" I pressed. The tiny glimmer was quickly spiraling into a blaze, racing through me, impossible to check.

This could solve everything.

This could save the bees.

He grinned. "We have sugar, back at camp. Winter rations. Off the top of my head, I don't know exactly how many pounds there are, but—I'm sure Burnish will lend some of his, and any bit ought to help, right?"

"Ought to? Whitaker, this will save us! You've no idea how— This is just—Thank you!" Coherent thought failed me, and I threw my arms around his neck, pulling him into a grateful embrace. He paused for a moment, then folded me to him, his fingers sinking into the base of my braid. I felt a soft pressure at the crown of my head, as though he'd pressed a quick kiss to it, but it happened so fast, I wasn't certain.

"But I can't just take your sugar. I'd need to pay you. And Burnish too," I added, remembering the man with the top hat.

He shook his head. "He owes me a favor."

"You, then," I insisted.

"You have no money," he reminded me with an endearing smile.

"A trade, then."

Whitaker settled back, the space between us suddenly feeling too big and too cold. "There's nothing I want or need," he said gently. "Just take the sugar, Ellerie."

"But that's not right. I can't just—"

"Take it," he insisted. "What am I going to do with that many pounds of sugar?"

"You bought it," I pointed out. "You'll need it for rations, as you said."

He waved his hand, dismissing my concerns. "It was part of the kits we got at our last trading post. There's no way we'd come even close to using all of it. We'll have to carry it out of the valley when we pack up camp. You'd be doing me a favor, honestly."

My stomach twinged at the thought of him leaving in the spring. I'd known he would. It's what all trappers did once their furs were ready. But I'd thought—no, I'd hoped—Whitaker might be different. I'd hoped he might see a reason to stay.

He pressed his lips together, studying me, and for one dreadful heated moment, I worried he'd somehow read my thoughts.

"Do you gamble much?" he asked.

"Gamble?" I repeated, confused at the turn in conversation.

His eyes crinkled in amusement. "I didn't think so. Oftentimes when people are playing cards, making bets, they'll use a marker as a substitute for the actual item being pledged. I might want to bet my horse on a good hand, but I can't exactly pony him up to the table, see?"

I nodded reluctantly, unsure what any of this had to do with our deal.

"Why don't I take a marker from you tonight? You can get the sugar now, but I won't be left without anything."

"That sounds . . . fair," I allowed. "But what am I pledging to give you?"

He shrugged, wholly unconcerned. "We can work that out later—maybe a honey cake, once the bees have survived the winter."

"The harvest won't be ready till summer's end," I worried pragmatically.

Whitaker smiled. "I said 'maybe.' Nothing needs deciding tonight."

"Then what should I give you for a marker?"

He cocked his head, thinking. "There's a kind of oath. It's what most gamblers use—the simplest of all pledges, but the most sincere."

"What kind of oath?"

He took my hand in his, studying it. "Prick your finger and press it to a handkerchief. Say . . . three times? A drop of blood for every ten pounds of sugar." He ran his pointer finger across my palm, following the arc of my heart line and sending ticklish tremors through my core.

"I . . ." I paused, trying to picture what Papa would do, but the image wouldn't form. Papa would never have gotten into a situation where he'd have to borrow anything in the first place. When he needed something, he paid for it outright.

But wasn't that all a marker was? A payment, of sorts?

I looked across the charred fields to the bee boxes. Even in the dark, their white sides could be seen, but just barely. They didn't look like bustling hives of activity and work.

In truth, they looked like tombstones.

"Yes," I agreed definitively, pushing the images of graves and

Papa from my imagination. Papa wasn't here, and Papa didn't have a stupid brother who ruined everything he touched before running away like a coward. I was the one who had to take care of the messes Sam created, and this one was too big for me to handle on my own. I'd be a fool to not accept help where I could.

Whitaker pulled a knife from the back of his belt and before I even knew what was happening, he sliced the silver blade across the pad of my ring finger.

With a cry, I snatched my hand free. Blood welled from the wound, as dark as cursed rubies under the night sky.

He reached inside his coat even as I wore it. I jerked backward as he pulled free a handkerchief from the inner pocket.

"Blot it on that," he said, tossing me the little bit of cotton. Something was embroidered on one corner, but it was too dark for me to make out the monogram.

"You stabbed me!" My voice squeaked too high with indignation. It hadn't truly hurt, but the speed at which he'd done it had taken me by surprise.

"Not deeply," he said, unconcerned. "But you'll want to press the drops in before the blood stops. Otherwise we'll just have to open it back up again."

I blotted the cloth, once, twice, three times, then wrapped it around my finger, staunching the flow. After a moment, I threw the handkerchief at him.

"Thank you," he said, folding it. "Now hold out your hand."

"You can't be serious."

"I swear your fingertips are safe from me." He secreted the knife away as if to prove it.

And then, quite suddenly, there was a bag of sugar between us.

One second, his hand had been empty; the next, he'd held a paper sack, bulging and full. "Take it," he said, offering it out. When I hesitated, he broke the wax seal, opening the top. It was chockful of sugar. In the moonlight, the white granules sparkled like quartz.

"How . . . how did you do that?" I whispered in awe, my indignation instantly forgotten.

"Doesn't matter. It's only about five pounds. I'll make sure the rest is at your house before sunrise. You have my word." He laughed at my bewilderment. "Take it; it's yours. You paid in full. Well, nearly." There was a flash of white and red as he pocketed the handkerchief.

My fingers itched to snatch the bag away, but I waited, uncertain of what was happening. Things didn't appear just because you wanted them. Life was not like the fairy tales we girls had pored over. Magic wasn't real.

Then I saw it.

"Your rucksack," I said, remembering the worn bag, hidden in the shadows. "The sugar was in there all along. You just—" I pantomimed the reveal. I certainly couldn't have pulled off such dexterous sleight of hand, but it didn't mean it couldn't be done. I'd read a book once about a boy who went to a circus and saw magicians do all sorts of impossible trickery. When he stayed after the show, one of the performers explained the tricks to him, showing how wholly pragmatic and logical they were.

Whitaker's eyes twinkled as he studied me. "You caught me, Ellerie Downing." He waggled his fingers playfully. "Magic."

"But . . . I can have it? It's mine?"

He sealed the bag before hefting it in my direction. It fell into my arms, heavy and solid and very, very real.

"All yours," he swore, swiping an *X* across his heart. "Feeling better now?"

My fingers wrapped around the bag, still wary that I was about to wake up and find this had all been a strange and terrible dream. But I took a deep breath and could even *smell* the sugar. Light and altogether too sweet, it played through my nose like a coy spring breeze, there one moment and gone the next.

"I am," I decided.

Whitaker broke into a smile. "Good. Why don't you head back inside, then? It's late, and I'm starting to wish I'd not been so gallant in loaning you my coat." He rubbed his hands up and down his arms, warming himself.

I slipped out of his coat and returned it with already trembling limbs. The temperature must have dropped ten degrees while we'd sat outside. "Thank you. . . . You saved everything."

He pushed aside my words of praise. "Your caring saved those bees. All I did was provide the sugar." He tapped me on the nose. "Get inside before you freeze. I'll have the rest to you by morning."

I wasn't sure how to end the conversation, so I stuck my hand out, like Papa would after working a trade with the farmers in town. Whitaker shook it with an amused smile and nodded toward the house.

After scooping up my precious bag of sugar, I raced across the lawn. When I turned to wave good night, he was already gone.

18

THE MORNING SUN CAST DEEP GOLDEN RAYS THROUGH the sitting room, catching a flurry of dust motes dancing through the air. As I turned the corner, going into the kitchen to start coffee, I fully expected the worktable to be as bare as it had been when I'd gone to bed with Merry and Sadie the night before.

But there the bag of sugar sat, unmistakably real.

I circled the table, staring warily at the sack as if it might contain a poisonous snake, agitated and ready to strike. After a moment, I opened it and examined the crystals, even sampled them. The lingering sweetness confirmed everything for me.

It was sugar.

It hadn't been a dream.

My shawl hung by the back door. I grabbed it and wrapped it around my shoulders before slipping out to the porch. Curiosity burned in my veins.

They sat on the steps, positioned so I couldn't miss them. Five sacks of sugar waiting for me, just as Whitaker had promised.

Five bags of five pounds, plus the sixth from last night.

Thirty pounds of sugar. Exactly what I needed.

I couldn't help but burst into giddy laughter. All of yesterday's worries had vanished with three drops of blood.

Whitaker had saved us.

He'd saved the bees, he'd saved my sanity. I couldn't wait for Merry and Sadie to come down and see our good fortune.

I brought the sacks in and lined them across the kitchen table. Standing back, I inspected my work with a critical eye. They didn't look particularly impressive that way. Maybe if I put them in a basket, like a cornucopia of good fortune?

But that looked wrong too.

Perhaps if I laid out Mama's best tablecloth—it was cause for celebration, after all. But as I knelt beside the basket of linens in the larder, I realized what bothered me about the entire setup.

The sugar *was* precious.

Too precious to lay out.

I couldn't leave it out in the open, I decided. It would be too tempting to steal pinches of it. Pinches would turn to sprinkles, sprinkles to tablespoons, and soon we'd be baking enough cookies and pies to cater to every sweet tooth in the Falls.

The safest course of action was to make the sugar cakes and be done with it, but until we got a hard frost, the cakes would be in danger of drawing ants. They'd invade the hive boxes, and we'd be in an even bigger mess. We'd have to slip the cakes in sometime after the first real snow. I wanted to laugh—or cry—as I pictured us resurrecting those ridiculous canvas tarps.

No. I'd have to hide the sugar.

But where?

I glanced over the shelves of the pantry, but they seemed an obvious choice if someone came looking for sugar.

The supply shed was out of the question. Anyone could access it without our knowledge, and while I didn't want to think poorly of our friends and neighbors, it was impossible to forget that one had so recently set fire to the shed, gravely wounding my mother in the process.

I spotted two tall, empty metal canisters stored at the top of the larder. They'd once held coffee, but the beans were long gone. Mama had liked the cheery red paint and had kept the tins for storage. The six sacks would neatly fit within them, sealing off the sugar and preventing it from contamination.

As I pulled the second one down, standing on tiptoes and stretching my arms, a wave of clarity washed over me.

I was being patently ridiculous.

No one was out to get our sugar.

No one even knew we had it.

No one except Whitaker.

Why was I going to such absurd lengths to keep it safe?

I shook my head, feeling the last bit of possessive concern dissipate. I would leave the sugar right where it was and wait for Merry and Sadie to wake. We'd take the afternoon off to celebrate. No chores, no work. I might even pack us a picnic lunch. We could go down to the big rocks near the waterfalls—the sun warmed them like an oven even on the chilliest days—and we could skip rocks into the Greenswold.

It would be the perfect day.

Through the open doorway I spotted a dappled shape perched on the kitchen table.

Buttons.

He was poised near the sugar sacks, batting at the last one in line with his outstretched paw, wholly intent on knocking it over.

"Buttons, no," I whispered, then dove for the bag as he pushed it off the table. I imagined it striking the ground and bursting open. The sugar would explode everywhere, like dynamite in the mines. Five pounds lost in an instant.

The coffee canisters clattered to the ground as I dropped them. My only concern was saving the sugar. I lunged in time to catch the sack.

Buttons sauntered away with an extra swish of his tail, as if pleased to see me in such an undignified posture.

I cradled the sugar bag in my arms like a baby.

I *wasn't* being overly protective.

The sugar *did* need safeguarding.

It needed to be kept somewhere out of the way and hidden. Someplace where no one could find it, neither roving neighbor nor malicious pet. I'd need to think through it carefully, choose the right and perfect spot.

The sugar was too precious for anything else.

Picking up the coffee tins, I went to work.

19

BESSIE'S MILK HIT THE SIDE OF THE EMPTY PAIL WITH A hiss, steaming in the frigid morning air. Her udders were warm in my hands, full but pliant, and she snorted softly as I worked, as if pleased to have me there.

After three pulls, I paused and leaned backward, looking out the stall.

The two canisters were in the center of a makeshift table in the middle of the barn.

It was just an hour or so before sunrise, truly too early to be up and working, but I'd not been able to fall asleep. I'd spent half the night jumping out of and back into bed, checking on the canisters, moving them around the house to safer locations, certain Buttons was on the prowl, ready to destroy them.

When I could slip into shallow rest, my sleep was plagued with nightmares of Cyrus Danforth's mystery woman, a shift of white always lurking in the corner of my vision, eyes glowing an eerie silver, elongated fingers stretching out for me.

My restlessness finally woke Merry, who'd snapped irritably before covering her head with a pillow. After a moment's indecision, I'd grabbed the tins and spent the rest of the night pacing the sitting room, jumping at every sound, certain the woman had come out of my dreams and was now stalking about the house.

When the grandfather clock had chimed four, I'd thrown on Papa's work coat and knit hat.

Making my way to the barn, the clouds had seemed low enough to touch. I'd whispered a prayer for snow before ducking inside.

Today we'd boil down the sugar and make the bees' cakes.

We had to.

I felt as if I was going mad.

Bessie shifted impatiently from foot to foot, bumping against me with her round side to win back my attention. Dragging my eyes from the sugar, I turned to the cow and the task before me.

And the bucket full of blood.

I slipped off the low milking stool, landed hard, and nearly knocked over the tainted pail. Bessie swung her head around, mildly concerned at the crash. She was working on a mouthful of cud and chewed it thoughtfully as she regarded me with docile brown eyes.

"What happened, girl?" I asked, righting the stool and running a hand along her side. She shivered under the ministration, and a heavy worry pressed into me. Was she getting sick?

It wasn't wholly unusual to get a little blood in the milk—udders could grow raw and chafe—but I'd never seen so much of it in one bucket before. This wasn't a soft pink hue that Papa would overlook and Sadie would refuse to drink. It was a dark red, harsh and angry in the soft predawn light.

I took an udder, inspecting it with a critical eye. There wasn't any damage to it, nor on any of the others. The skin was as pink and smooth as ever.

"Then how—"

Cringing, I tilted the lip of the bucket toward me. Pale liquid sloshed along the bottom, frothed with bubbles from the force of Bessie's stream. I blinked heavily, trying to clear my eyes.

It was just milk.

Nothing more, nothing less.

I seized hold of the udders once more and gave them an experimental pull. More milk hissed out, every bit as white as it ought to be.

I kept working, slowly allowing my head to rest against her side. The rhythmic motion of my hands and the steady beats of the milk into the bucket lulled me into a hazy trance. My eyelids fluttered shut, once, twice as I struggled to keep them open. My sleepless nights were catching up to me, making me see things that weren't there.

We would make the sugar cakes this morning, as soon as we were done with breakfast. I'd tell Merry and Sadie everything and finally be able to rest once more. My forehead pressed into Bessie, a dead weight, unable to hold itself up. I felt my mouth fall slack, and my breath deepened.

In the far corner of the barn, something stirred, and my eyes shot open. My neck creaked, stiff and sore, as though I'd spent the entire morning propped at that awkward angle. But the stalls were still dark and the bucket not even half-full. I couldn't have been out for longer than a minute or two.

"Merry?" She must have come after me when she realized I wasn't in the house.

There was no answer.

"Sadie?" I tried, though it was wholly unlikely my littlest sister would have come all the way down to the barn by herself at this hour.

I cocked my head, trying to pick out what noise had drawn my attention, but I couldn't hear anything over Bessie's even breaths. Picking up the lantern, I left the stall, straining my ears against the quiet. I held out the little beacon of light to cast back the darkness, but it only deepened the shadows in the corners, allowing them to fester while my imagination ran wild.

The silvery woman had learned of the sugar and had come to take it. She'd waited until my defenses were down, my mind sluggish from lack of sleep. She was real and she was here to steal it, and like a fool, I'd left it out in the middle of the room.

A series of soft whispers came from just over my shoulder, and I whipped around, ready to catch the thief. Thieves. It was probably a whole team of smugglers. An army of women in pale dresses with long, taloned fingers.

But there was no one, only Bessie.

The whispers came again, now from the far wall where Papa kept the pitchforks and scythes. Each one hung properly on its peg, shining with dull splendor in the feeble lighting. I crossed over to them, certain the intruders were hiding behind the half wall bordering the birthing stall, but there were only bales of hay, stacked high into columns. The birthing stall wouldn't be used until spring. Papa was fanatical about keeping everything as neat and tidy as he could.

The whispers persisted, growing loud enough for me to nearly make out actual words, and they all seemed to be coming from the hay.

"Who's hiding there?" I cried out. "I can hear you—show yourself!"

"Shhh!" someone hissed, and the murmuring cut off with an abrupt halt.

Exchanging the lantern for one of the smaller pitchforks hanging on the wall, I paused on the threshold. The wall of hay loomed in front of me, dominating the small space like a tangled hedge grown wild and unkempt. For the life of me, I couldn't figure out how the woman had wedged herself within the bales, but I knew

I'd heard her hiding there. Brandishing the wickedly pointed tines, I stepped into the stall. "I know you're in there," I said, trying to force the trembles from my voice. "Show yourselves."

The silence dragged by as I waited for a response. My entire body felt taut, like a cord wound too tight and about to snap. When a rustle sounded, soft and low to the ground, I sprang into action without thinking. I ran toward the bales with the pitchfork raised high, then brought it down again and again, stabbing at the straw with as much force as I could muster.

I knew I was being illogical.

I knew there couldn't truly be people hiding inside such tightly packed hay.

But I didn't care.

I was tired of the worrying. Tired of the fretting. I was sick of waking every morning in fear and dread.

It felt good to stab that hay, physically attacking the anxieties and doubts that had haunted me since the fire. I remembered how Mama had said she did the same when making dough, and I redoubled my efforts, flinging chunks of straw about the stall without care. Every bit of me felt like it was screaming itself raw, and the only way to make it stop was to raise that pitchfork again and again.

Then, I struck something decidedly not hay.

The pitchfork jabbed into an object within the straw. There was a moment of resistance before the points sank in, finding their mark. Instantly I let go of the handle, but it remained in place, stuck within the hidden obstruction.

My mind raced, trying to imagine what could possibly be stored within the bales. I'd not gone deep enough to encounter the wall, and I couldn't remember a post being in the stall. Had Papa squirreled away some extra stock of rations here, saving away sacks of flour or cornmeal for a rainy day?

Pressing my lips together in a grim line, I wrapped my fingers around the wooden handle and gave it a tug. With a wet squelch, the pitchfork came free. It fell to the ground with a clatter as I caught sight of its bloodied tines.

Slowly my eyes lifted to the wall of hay. Blood trickled out from the section I'd destroyed. First one rivulet wet the dry stalks, then another, and another. I opened my mouth to let out a cry, but the only sounds I could make were choked gasps for air, like a fish pulled from water and left to die on a wooden dock.

With trembling hands I began to pull down the remainder of the bale. Hot blood coated my fingers, smudging and staining Papa's heavy coat. The front of my nightdress was soiled beyond repair. Whatever I'd struck was bleeding out fast.

I pulled down chunk after chunk of straw, but still the blood flowed, creeping down the hay to be sucked into the dry ground.

Where was it? Surely I couldn't have struck so deep, not even in my wildest fury. And why was it so unnaturally quiet? The wounded creature—animal or human—hadn't uttered a sound. Not when struck. Not now in what must be an agonizing death. Why wasn't it crying out in pain or shock? Shouldn't it have shown itself?

Behind me the lantern flickered, casting long, wavering shadows across the birthing stall, as if the flame was being pushed about by an unfelt draft. I turned just in time to see the wick blow out, plunging me into darkness.

"Oh," I whispered, finding my voice once more.

I reached into the pockets of Papa's coat, fumbled about with sticky fingers before finding the little box of matches he kept there. Blindly I opened the lantern's door, struck a match, and fed it the oiled wick.

The lantern sparked to life, lighting the room once more. I moved the lantern out of the draft and turned to the gruesome task at hand.

But the stall was clean.

The hay bale was still in ruined shreds—piles of discarded straw littered the ground—but there was no blood.

Anywhere.

Not seeped into the dirt. Not oozing from the stacks. Not even on me.

I pawed at Papa's coat, checking deep into its folds and creases. It had been horribly stained just moments before but was now clean. The pitchfork looked pristine. There was nothing to suggest I'd ever stabbed anything.

"I don't . . ." I wiped my fingers over my face, certain I would blink once and the massacre would return. "I don't understand. . . ."

Twice this morning I'd seen things one moment that were gone the next. I wanted to believe—I had to believe—the sleepless nights were to blame. Once the cakes were made, I wouldn't have to worry over the sugar any longer and things could return to normal.

"Please, God, let them return to normal," I whispered, clutching my fingers together so tightly, the tips turned white and tingly.

An unwelcome memory stirred in the back of my mind, like a thin cotton curtain caught in the draft of an open window. Just a wisp of a remembrance, truly. It wasn't even my story to remember, only something I'd heard Papa speak of once, when he hadn't known that Samuel and I were in the adjacent room, listening in.

A few harvests ago, Levi Barton—one of our neighbors to the south—had become convinced there was gold to be found in the caves along the Greenswold. He wandered off to search, leaving his wife, the farm, and the harvest. Days turned into weeks. The wife was beside herself, certain he'd fallen into a crevice. Search parties were sent out, but no one knew exactly where to look. After a week of scouring the caves, the people of the Falls gave up and declared him dead.

But then, one morning, Levi sat down for breakfast as though he'd only been gone for hours. His wife told other ladies in town that there was something peculiarly off about him. He was always muttering to himself, responding to questions no one had asked, staring into empty corners and nodding as if listening to someone who wasn't there. Her friends told her not to worry—the caves must have been stressful, full of echoes and dark shadows. An overworked, overstimulated mind was apt to imagine all sorts of unusual things. Once rested, he'd be fine, they promised.

A week later her friends came visiting for tea and found the wife at the dining room table, a pickaxe lodged deep in her skull. Levi had slaughtered all their animals too, quick slits across the neck, and had left their bodies in stalls and out in the fields, festering with flies. Before the farmer had taken his own life, he'd left a message scrawled across the side of his barn, written in blood.

"THEY HAVE WATCHED AND I HAVE SEEN AND NOW I WILL SEE NO MORE."

That phrase had haunted me, eliciting chilled shivers on even the hottest summer nights when it had inevitably popped into my head, always as I was on the cusp of sleep.

What had he seen?

Had Levi seen blood too?

The rustling noise came once more, snapping me from my thoughts. It sounded as if someone was crossing the loft above, stealthily on tiptoe. I grabbed the lantern and raced into the open area, keeping the light as high as I could.

It caught a dark form slipping between the posts, keeping to the shadows.

I hesitated for only a moment before climbing the ladder to the loft. If it was a hallucination, I had nothing to fear, and if someone was truly in our barn, they needed to be caught.

"Show yourself," I called out, searching for movement. "I have a gun," I lied. "Come out now and I won't shoot."

"Ellerie, don't!" The voice came from behind a stack of old wooden crates not far from me. Though it was distorted and too highly pitched, I'd have recognized it anywhere.

"Sam?" I hissed. "What are you doing here? You're supposed to be on the supply run. You—" I stopped, coughing against the horrible, raw odor filling the loft. It smelled like the Kinnards' pig farm on slaughtering day, coppery and biting and so terribly, terribly *wet*. Covering my mouth and nose did nothing to help mask it. "What *is* that?"

All I could make of Samuel were his eyes, reflecting the lantern's glow and shining brightly even in the midst of the barn's shadows. They looked too large for his head, panicked and stretched open wide. "They're dead," he whispered, and my heart plummeted into my gut.

I wanted to move, wanted to step forward and take Samuel's hands in mine, but I was frozen with fear. It was Mama, I was sure of it. Though the idea was utterly preposterous—Sam couldn't have made it all the way to the city and back in just a week's time—in that moment, I was certain my mother was dead. "Who is?"

"All of them."

Tears pricked at my eyes, blurring my vision. I'd never felt so impossibly small. "Papa too?"

"What? No!"

"I thought you meant . . . What *did* you mean? Who's dead?"

"I—I'll come out now and explain everything, but . . . please don't scream, Ellerie. Just . . . please."

I squinted around the glow of the lantern, trying to make sense of what I saw, trying to find my brother within the monstrous shape that crept forward.

"Oh, Sam," I whispered, fighting the urge to flee.

The smell, that blackened, foul odor, was coming from him. From the viscera coating his clothing, his arms and chest. He was covered in it.

My eyes flickered over the streaks of red that had trickled down his face and dried there, unnoticed and unwiped. It couldn't be his, not all of it. There was no way he'd be standing before me if he'd lost so much . . .

Blood.

"You're not really here," I said, clarity dawning on me. I shook my head, trying to force his image to disappear. "You're not real."

His eyebrows furrowed together, his hurt evident. "Why would you say that?"

I shut my eyes tight, certain he'd be gone when I opened them.

He wasn't.

"You're not Sam, you're not Sam, you're not Sam," I whispered as he stepped closer. My thigh bumped against the ladder. I had nowhere to run.

"Ellerie, I'm right here," he said, tears welling up in his words. "Aren't I?" His voice broke, so soft, I almost didn't catch it. "Am I still in the pines? Oh God, let me out of the pines, please, *please*." His entreaties morphed into giant sobs racking his body. He fell to his knees, his chest heaving.

I rubbed my eyes, but still he would not disappear. With shaking fingers I dared to reach out and touch his shoulder.

"Sam?" I whispered. My hand came away stained dark red.

This *felt* real.

But so had the other visions.

He uncurled from his fetal position and gazed up at me with such hope that my heart hurt. "Can you see me, Ellerie?"

I knelt beside him. "Of course I can. Of course I— What is

that?" I dared to ask, rubbing my fingers together to get rid of the sticky, stinking paste coating them.

"The supply run," he said dully, glancing down at his ruined clothing. "What's left of them."

"The supply run," I repeated, piecing together his sentences. "They're dead."

"Every last man." He pushed one hand across his cheek, flicking aside a piece of . . . something best not dwelt upon . . . and sniffed. "Everyone but me."

It was incomprehensible. We'd seen them just days before. "Asher? And Jonas? They can't be—you're saying they're . . ."

His back teeth ground together and his mouth wrinkled into a sneer. "If they went on the supply run, they're gone. Dead. Dead and gone and gone and dead and what about that phrase don't you understand?"

"How?" The word escaped my lips, even as I cringed from his grip on my shoulders.

"The monsters. They're back. Or . . . they've been here all along. . . . I don't know how Papa and Whitaker made it through without encountering them."

"Did you . . . did you actually see them?"

He nodded grimly. "We heard them following us for the first two days, making a horrible clicking noise and laughing. . . . They waited until the third night to attack. It was . . ." He let out a strangled noise, burying his face in his bloodied hands as he remembered. "They're not wolves, Ellerie. They're something far, far worse."

"A bear?" I hoped, even as my mind recalled images of that misshapen stag.

"No bear could scoop Jonas Marjanovic into the air." His throat constricted. "He was the first to go. I still hear his screams. His blood showered down on us like a hot summer rain. They took Asher next." The memory of whatever had happened to the poor man brought up a wave of bile Samuel was helpless to fight. He turned his head, emptying out his stomach with a shuddered cry.

I knew I should ask what had happened to Joseph, but I didn't truly want to know.

"Did you hurt any of them?"

He frowned as if my words were incomprehensible.

"Sam—there were guns. Were you able to shoot any of them?"

"Them." His eyes were glassy and unfocused.

"The creatures."

"There . . . there were no guns."

"None of the men took guns?" Disbelief colored my voice.

"They weren't there. Not when we needed them. Even my pocketknife was gone." He patted his pants, feeling for it. It was one of his most treasured possessions. Papa had given it to him on our sixteenth birthday, and Sam was never without it. "Am I really here now?" he asked quietly, laying his head against my side. Tears pooled in the corners of his eyes and spilled down his cheeks, running red. "When I was lost in the pines . . . sometimes I thought I was back at home, back with you and Merry and Sadie. Mama and Papa too. I was so certain I was there . . . here," he corrected me. "But then I'd wake up and I was even farther from home."

"You're here now," I promised. "You're home and you're safe."

"You said that before, but I always woke up in the woods," he whimpered. Then he let out a long sigh. "I've messed up, Ellerie. I've messed up so many things. When I was out there, with those *things* talking to me, laughing at me, they said . . . they knew . . ."

"Enough," I said firmly. He was spiraling and it needed to be stopped. His eyes faded into and out of focus, blinking heavily. I knew I ought to offer some comfort, but I couldn't bring myself to touch whatever it was of Jonas Marjanovic that had turned Samuel's blond locks umber. "We need to get you out of the loft, get you cleaned up. Sadie and Merry can't see you like this."

"They're going to hate me."

"They won't do anything of the sort." I hauled him to his feet, choking back a gag as the stench clogged my throat.

"You do," he said, grabbing my chin and forcing me to look at him. "I see it in your eyes. I made too many mistakes, and now you hate me."

"I don't hate you." The honesty in my answer surprised me. "You messed up, as you said. You've made mistakes—colossally big and stupid mistakes—and I don't understand why . . . but . . . you're the other half of me, Sam. I would never hate myself."

He pressed his lips together, but a sob still broke free. "It's surprisingly easy to do."

"You're going to have to tell the Elders what happened," I said, jumping to next steps, planning and preparing. I already knew the sugar cakes would not be made today.

Samuel shook his head. "I can't. I can't relive that again. Please, Ellerie, don't make me go to them."

"They can come here," I reasoned. "But first, you've got to get all this off you."

After a moment of consideration, Samuel let me help him out of the loft.

The Elders came. The Elders went. The Elders returned with more men to listen to Samuel's story, and it was finally decided upon.

There would be no further attempts at a supply run.

Amity Falls would hunker down for winter, ration our supplies, and pray to God for temperance and a bountiful spring.

Any talk of retrieving the wagons and ammunitions left behind was firmly squelched. Parson Briard made a half-hearted suggestion that they ought to at least go after the bodies so the poor souls could be laid to rest in a church grave, but Samuel swiftly pointed out that the creatures had left no bodies to bury.

The Elders and the other men left after that.

Samuel fell asleep and didn't wake for three days.

We made the sugar cakes and resurrected our silly tent.

We fed the bees and sparingly fed ourselves, and the days passed much in the ways they always had.

We missed Mama. We missed Papa. We missed the fullness and life they'd brought to the house.

But the weeks carried on and the snow began to fall, covering our grief, covering our farm, and covering the Falls.

WINTER

20

A PERSISTENT TAPPING SOUNDED AT THE WINDOWS, drawing my attention from Parson Briard's admonishments that his son and Rebecca Danforth love, honor, and obey one another till death should part them.

It grew louder, like a giant insect skittering over the panes of glass. I drew my shawl closer, imagining hundreds of raspy legs rubbing against themselves as they cavorted and squirmed.

"What *is* that?"

Judd Abrams's voice rang out, interrupting the service. Up at the altar, Rebecca's head snapped toward him. If you could ignore the daggers burning in her eyes, I'd never seen her look lovelier.

Letitia Briard had gifted her new daughter-to-be a length of cloth from her stash of fine fabrics specially ordered from the city. Though the pale blue checks brought out the creamy glow of Rebecca's cheeks, she'd crafted the pattern with an unfashionably high waist and had selected a long organdy veil to help cover the small bump.

Surprisingly, it appeared the ruse was working. Not a single person in town had whispered a word against the hasty betrothal. Rebecca appeared to have grown up overnight. I barely recognized my best friend in the woman standing before us all.

Former best friend, I supposed, watching her eyes skirt mine.

Parson Briard frowned at the interruption but cocked his head toward the windows, finally noticing the sound himself.

"You uh—you may now kiss the bride," he stammered, and after a quick peck on the lips, the ceremony came to an end.

Merry, Sadie, and I stood up with everyone to clap as Simon and Rebecca walked down the aisle together, hands joined in a tight fist. Samuel had opted to stay home, citing exhaustion, but I guessed he was nursing a broken heart.

Simon grinned widely, as happy as I'd ever known him to be. Rebecca's lips were lifted in a smile, but it looked too stiff, as though she was wearing a mask. Simon opened the doors at the back of the sanctuary with a gallant swing and gestured for his new bride to leave first.

Rebecca stopped short before stepping into the dark afternoon. "It's hailing!" she exclaimed, turning back to the congregation. "That's what the tapping noise was. Hail."

"In December?" the parson asked, his eyebrows furrowed with confusion.

Murmurs rose, and several people made their way to the open door to see for themselves.

Outside, the wind shifted, growing into a high-pitched howl, and a shower of icy pellets flew into the church, thudding onto the floorboards with unsettling heft.

"She's right," Calvin Buhrman said, picking one up. It was nearly the size of his palm and had a strange bluish tint to it. "Hail."

"Shut the doors, shut the doors!" Rebecca cried as a small boulder struck her shoulder.

Simon and Calvin worked together, fighting against the wind's sudden swell, as a terrific crash of thunder broke directly above the church, pounding its fury into our sternums. Sadie screamed, and several pews over, the Visser baby began to cry.

"Sorry," Sadie whimpered, pressing herself against my side.

"It's all right," I promised, giving her a side hug. She was notoriously scared of lightning storms. I'd never thought it was something we'd have to worry over once the snows had set in.

Parson Briard peered out a window into the darkness. He raised one hand to grab hold of our attention again.

"I know my family had planned to host a small reception at the Gathering House following this afternoon's nuptials, but I think perhaps it's most prudent for us to hunker down here and wait out this storm."

Amos McCleary joined the parson at the window, leaning on his cane. His breathing seemed to require too much effort these days. A heavy wetness rattled at the end of every gasp for air, devolving into bouts of coughing that nearly shook him apart.

"Amos, sit, sit," his wife, Martha, insisted, gently pulling the Elder back to a pew. "You need to rest. This has been too much for you today."

Across the aisle from us, I noticed Matthias Dodson and Leland Schäfer exchange worried glances. The group of Elders was composed of men from the Falls's founding families, passing their cloaks from father to son. With Jebediah dead, there would be no one to take Amos's place should this cough kill him.

A council would have to be formed to elect his replacement. There were only three families who would be eligible. The Buhrmans, the Lathetons, and us. With Papa gone . . .

I shuddered to think of Samuel wearing Elder black.

One of the farmers who lived near the north ridge, Thaddeus McComb, approached the two Elders, nervously running his hands over one another, his jaw tight.

"Thaddeus." Leland greeted him, signaling to Matthias to pause their conversation. "You look worried. Is there something we can help you with?"

Outside, the wind picked up, rattling the church doors in their frames and causing the group of children playing near them to titter with anxious glee.

"I—uh—I didn't want to bring this up today, not at a wedding and certainly not in a church. But since we're all stuck here for a bit . . ."

Matthias waved his hand, gesturing for the farmer to speed up the delivery of his tale.

"I want to report an . . . uh . . . incident."

"Incident?" Matthias repeated.

"Of vandalism . . . I think."

"You think?"

Thaddeus licked his lips. "It's only . . . I've never seen anything like it before. I'm not even sure what to call it . . . not really."

"Go on."

"With all the black rot that's plaguing the other farms around me, I decided to plant a crop of winter wheat this year. It sprouts quickly and it would be ready to harvest in the spring. I know . . . things could get bad this winter, and I just wanted to have something to hope for." He paused, scratching at his scraggly blond beard. "And . . . and it was growing. Really growing. Too fast, maybe."

"Too fast?" I echoed, so drawn into his story, I'd forgotten I wasn't supposed to be listening in.

"Don't you know better than to eavesdrop on other people's business?" Matthias folded his arms over his chest, peering across the aisle with disappointment.

"I'm sorry. I couldn't help but overhear."

Thaddeus waved off their concern. "Winter wheat should only

get so high before the snows set in, you know?" He pantomimed several inches between his fingers. "But this wheat . . . it's waist-high now. Or . . . it was." He swallowed, aware others nearby had also begun to listen in. "It started turning yellow, like it was almost ready for harvest. And the heads . . . I've never seen such large ones in all my seasons. There wasn't just one on each stalk either. Some of the straw had two, three, even four heads apiece. It was a miracle, I thought. This could help everyone through the winter. I was going to harvest it and mill it down to flour. I would have had enough to feed the Falls. But then this morning . . ."

His voice caught.

Edmund Latheton leaned in. The carpenter was captivated. "What happened?" he asked, his voice hushed.

"Nearly all of the wheat was . . . gone. Stripped bare."

Leland's eyebrows shot up. "Someone else harvested it?"

The farmer shook his head. "Sections of the fields were . . . flattened. Whole areas just . . ." He swiped his hand out.

"We have had unusual weather of late," Matthias reasoned, glancing to the hail still pelting the windows with chinks and clinks. It was a wonder any of the stained glass was still whole. "Perhaps a wind—"

"No, no, sir," Thaddeus disagreed. "It wasn't an even sweep through the fields. There was a pattern to it." His lips twisted with dismay. "There're . . . pictures drawn in the wheat."

A wave of uneasy murmurs stirred.

"Sets of circles, side by side. They're dotting over the whole field. Like a tornado came down but went back up to try again. There're hundreds of them."

Edmund's eyebrows furrowed into a worried line. "How big would you say they were?"

"Not very. Maybe six, eight feet wide, each of them."

Edmund let out a sigh. "I know what did it."

Simon and Rebecca had drifted over to the group and were standing in the aisle. Rebecca's hand flittered toward her stomach, but she caught herself in time and opted to sit down in an empty pew.

Simon leaned against its side. "What do you mean, Latheton?"

"A couple of days ago, I noticed that some of my lumber had gone missing. Several boards were gone and some lengths of rope. I didn't think much of it at the time—figured someone needed it and would come back with payment when they could spare it."

Beside him, Prudence let out a sharp huff. It was no secret that she kept a fanatical eye on accounts.

"Now I wonder if it weren't some children up to a bit of mischief."

As if we were all puppets pulled by strings, our heads turned to the group of young boys playing in the back of the sanctuary.

Thaddeus shook his head. "I can't see how children could create such—"

Edmund cut him off. "It's not hard. You set a pic point in the field with a tether for a mule. The board goes on the ground behind the mule. Two people balance on either end of the wood, holding onto the harness. And then, just give the beast a whack and let it run."

Thaddeus looked stricken. "Why would someone do that? With winter upon us and supplies so low? I looked through the flattened wheat. It's all spent, the heads stripped clean and the seeds scattered."

Matthias's nostrils flared. "The better question is *who*? Have you had any disagreements with anyone of late, McComb? Anyone looking to settle a score?"

"No. No one."

"Has your wife? Your children?"

Thaddeus glanced about the sanctuary as if looking for someone to pin the blame on. "I can't think of anyone."

Leland clicked his tongue. "I can. The newcomers. Ezra and
his boy. I don't see them here today. Could it be they're sleeping off
their exhaustion after a night of sabotage?"

Matthias frowned at the other Elder. "What are you suggesting? It's Ezra Downing," he reminded everyone. "A member of
this town. Of the founding families. He's hardly a stranger."

Leland pursed his lips.

I'd never seen the Elders so openly in disagreement.

"He disappeared when he was—what? Fifteen years old? He
wasn't even part of the Gathering yet. And now suddenly he returns. How are we meant to know anything about them?"

Several townspeople turned, glancing back toward our pew, con-
taminating us by association. Sadie pressed herself close against
my side.

"I think . . ." Matthias's gray eyes drifted to look above our
heads, unfocused as if watching something play out, far in the future. "He was horribly wrong about the wolves being gone. I'll give
you that, but that could have been any of us—"

Leland shook his head, not backing down. "I think they ought
to be cut off from town. Shunned."

"Shunned?" From the back of the room, Parson Briard stood.
"We've not had cause to shun anyone in the Falls in years. Decades, even."

Leland's eyes narrowed. "This is for all of our safety."

"Safety?" Briard snorted. "I'm certain we can handle any threat
those two men might pose."

"Two came into town," Leland allowed. "But we don't know
how many others there might be left in the forest, waiting for
a signal."

"Hiding in the forest? After all these months? You sound absurd."

Amos rose on creaky legs, holding on to Martha for support. "With so many strange events, I think it best to exercise caution. I don't want to cast blame, but . . . Leland is right. It's been many years since we last saw Ezra Downing. We don't know what sort of man he turned out to be. Vigilance is prudent." He offered a tentative smile across the sanctuary. "We'll pull through this as we always do in Amity Falls—together."

It sounded like a strong statement, meant to unite and comfort, but after he uttered it, a terrible bout of coughs erupted, causing him to crash back into the pew.

"Doctor!" Martha called out. "Dr. Ambrose!" She scanned the room, panicked. "Where is he?"

Prudence Latheton stepped forward. "He was on his way to Cora Schäfer's house earlier today. Heard she's taken ill with a terrible fever."

Parson Briard watched carefully, tilting his head toward Gran Fowler and muttering earnestly.

Martha looked around helplessly. "We can't . . . Amos can't stay here. He needs to be home." Her eyes fell on Matthias. "Help us, please."

It was the "please," impossibly frail and broken, that stirred the other Elders to action. They carefully hoisted Amos from the pew and made their way from the sanctuary, using their heavy cloaks as covering from the hail.

"Get through it together," Briard muttered with a snort of derision. "As though we're all truly working as one. We've had strange events for months, and there were no strangers to blame then. There's a darkness in the Falls that can't be explained away by outsiders."

"He's right." Elijah Visser nodded. "Back in July, someone

dragged the scythes from my shed and stood them on end in the wife's garden, like scarecrows." He shuddered, remembering. "Those men weren't here then. How do you explain that?"

"Ain't nothing been right in this town since . . . ," Gran began, his eyes quickly sweeping toward the pew where Rebecca sat with her new mother-in-law. "Well, since Cyrus got himself killed like that."

"My father didn't get himself killed," Rebecca snapped, with more backbone than I'd ever have given her credit for. "He was murdered. Hung in the town square, with everyone in the Falls cheering it on. Perhaps you remember that?" She stared him down, mettle flickering like flint in her eyes.

He wiped the back of his hand over his mouth, hiding his discomfort. "All the same. Nothing's been right."

"The only thing my father's death did was expose the ugly underside of this town. Every single person here has his blood on their hands, but they were stained long before Papa and that stupid, stupid fire. Neighbors arguing with neighbors. Fights and slights and so much pettiness. We all smile and wish each other Good Blessings, but I'd wager there's not one family in the whole of God's Grasp that doesn't have it out for another. And you all know I'm right."

Heedless of the raging weather, Rebecca stormed out, slamming the sanctuary doors behind her.

Her words lingered like an echo around us, hitting too close to home.

"Well now," Calvin Buhrman said slowly, his voice so low, I could barely hear him. "I don't choose to believe that . . . but, with everything that's happened this year, I can understand how the Danforths would."

The parson cleared his throat. "But she isn't a Danforth any longer. She's a Briard."

Calvin stopped just short of rolling his eyes. "For all of five minutes."

As the room fell into stirred murmurs, Letitia laid a hand down on her husband's. "Perhaps we ought to go after Rebecca . . . make sure she's all right? Right, Simon?"

The bridegroom nodded, clearly reluctant to go out into the hailstorm.

"You're right, my love." Parson Briard stood, readying to leave. "Good Blessings to you all . . ." He trailed off as Rebecca's words rang sharply in our ears, and he rushed from the church before anyone could return the sentiment.

21

"WHAT DAY IS IT?" MERRY ASKED, LOOKING UP FROM her basket of mending.

We were situated around the fireplace, our sewing projects covering our laps as a fierce wind blew outside, howling over the valley.

I stabbed my needle into the wool that Whitaker had brought from the city. I'd finished making the dress weeks before but was already forced to add pin tucks to the bodice. It hung large around my thinning frame, gaping and catching. Our larder was still full, but I knew it wouldn't always be and had taken to cutting my share of meals by half. I was always hungry but couldn't bear the thought that my sisters might be. "Sunday, I think."

"No, what *day?*"

I thought back.

Rebecca had married Simon on Tuesday.

"The wedding was on the eighteenth," I remembered, and counted from there. "So today is—"

A sharp knock on the front door broke our conversation. I glanced at the grandfather clock, worry edging into my chest. It was just after four, but twilight already blanketed the Falls. With the weather as fickle as it had been, it was rare to receive visitors so late in the day.

I set aside my sewing and approached the door. "Who's there?" I could make out a large silhouette framed in the window of the door, but Mama's eyelet curtains obscured all features.

"Gran Fowler."

I frowned. The Fowlers lived clear across the valley, their ranch pressed as close to the western border as the pines would allow.

"I know it's awful late, but Alice wanted to make sure you all got one."

With a twinge of reservation, I removed the iron bolt and opened the door, peering into the inky light.

"A Christmas blessing," he said, holding out a wrapped bundle.

He seemed just as reluctant to cross our threshold as I was to invite him in.

"Christmas! Today is Christmas?" Sadie's surprise behind me echoed my own. How had we forgotten Christmas?

This was usually my favorite time of year—we decorated the house with swags of pine boughs and holly berries. Mama made a punch with cinnamon tea and oranges and cloves, and we'd stay up late as Papa read the story of the first Christmas from our family Bible. There was popping corn and sleigh rides, a dance held in the Gathering House, caroling and ghost stories told in giddy whispers around a single tapered flame.

But with Mama and Papa gone, I'd forgotten about the holiday entirely, and it seemed most of the town had as well. Cheer and merriment were hard commodities to come by in the Falls these days.

"Not just yet. It's the twenty-third today."

"Tomorrow is Christmas Eve," Merry whispered, and she cast a sharp glance at the calendar as though it had betrayed her. "Christmas Eve and we've done nothing to prepare."

Sadie dropped her embroidery sampler. "What does that mean? No Christmas? We have to have Christmas!" Her eyes shifted toward an empty corner of the room. "I can't believe you didn't say anything, Abigail!"

"Of course we will," I said, skirting over the mention of her imaginary friend. My mind raced with how to come up with an approximation of what Mama would do. "I'm so sorry, Mr. Fowler," I said, drawing my attention back to the large rancher filling our doorway. "You've caught us a bit off guard. Please, come in. Would you like some tea?"

He shuffled his feet before stepping inside. "I can't stay. Need to get back to Alice before supper. Just wanted to deliver this." He held out the parcel again.

I peeked beneath the wrapping. "A chicken!"

We'd not had chicken on our plates in weeks. Once the Elders had declared there would be no further attempts for supplies, Merry and I had drawn up a list of every bit of food in our possession and created a rationing plan. We'd decided it was more prudent to keep the laying hens alive, however much grain they might eat themselves.

He wordlessly pushed the plucked bird into my hands.

"This is far too generous. . . . I'm afraid we don't have anything to offer in return."

"Not asking for anything. . . . We decided—in light of the holiday and all—we ought to share our . . . abundance." His eyes shifted away, not meeting mine.

"Is everything all right, Mr. Fowler?" He looked ashen and miserable.

"We're fine," he started. Then he pressed his hands together, nearly squirming. "There . . . there was a bit of an incident at the ranch. Alice went out for eggs this morning and, well . . . all the chickens had been slaughtered."

"Slaughtered," Sadie said, pressing herself against my side with rapt attention.

"Every last one of them."

I tried to not envision the massacre but couldn't help but imagine it, the yard festooned with bursts of white feathers and sprays of arterial red. "The coop is near the forest edge, isn't it?" I'd been to the ranch once before. "Do you think the creatures came through the Bells?"

Sadie's fingers dug into my thigh, pressing hard enough to leave bruises.

Gran Fowler shook his head. "Wasn't the creatures."

"How do you know?" Merry asked, her voice hushed with horror.

"Whoever did it left behind a message of sorts." He swallowed once and ran his fingers through his hair as if casting back the memory. "A picture, really. Drawn out on the side of the chicken coop with . . . with all the blood."

I leaned in. "What was it?"

He looked up, directly meeting my gaze for the first time that afternoon. "An eye. A big watching eye."

My mouth fell open. Once my mind had added the gruesome detail to my imagining, I couldn't unsee it. Even when I blinked, it remained, imprinted upon my eyelids, shocking and ghastly.

He scratched at his beard with a helpless shrug. "We alerted the Elders, but it's not as though they can truly do anything. Alice suggested we share the birds before they started to turn. She . . . she wanted to make sure you all got one. We know what a difficulty it must be, not having your ma and pa around."

"That's very kind of you—"

"Best be on my way. Don't want to be traveling after dark." He paused before stepping off the porch. "Merry Christmas to you all."

"Merry Christmas," we repeated perfunctorily. Our voices held no cheer.

"That'll need to go into the ice chest," Merry said, scooping the parcel from me after I shut the door.

Buttons raced into the room, knocking my sewing project off the settee. It landed perilously close to the fireplace.

"Get that cat out of here," I said, scooping up the dress. Sadie chased after him, and the two bounded up the stairs to the loft.

"Was that Gran Fowler I saw riding off?" Sam asked, coming in. He'd been out in the supply shed, refilling the oil lanterns.

"He came by to give us a chicken for Christmas."

Sam blinked with surprise. He too had forgotten the approaching holiday.

"Apparently someone slaughtered their entire coop last night." I folded up my dress, keeping the needle and thread safely stored away within its tucks. I'd have to work on it later that evening. Supper needed starting.

Sam's eyebrows furrowed. "Who would do such a horrible thing?"

"No one knows."

"Bet it was Judd Abrams," Sam said, trailing after me into the kitchen. "Gran borrowed his auger a few weeks back—he was installing some new posts along one of his property lines—and Judd said he returned it with a broken bit. Cracked the point entirely in half but didn't say anything. No apologies, nothing."

A piece of broken farming equipment hardly seemed reason to murder an entire coop of chickens, but I didn't say so.

"Christmas is in two days," Sadie announced, bursting back into the kitchen. "Two days! We almost missed it!"

"We wouldn't have forgotten Christmas," I said, grabbing the cast-iron skillet from the hook on the wall. I drummed my fingers along the edge of the worktable, willing inspiration to come to me, but I couldn't think of anything but fried chicken.

"We might have," Samuel told her with a wink.

"What should we make for dinner?" I raised my voice over Sadie's cry of outrage.

Samuel let out a snort. "Why ask? You know it's just going to be beans and corn bread again."

"It's all we've had for weeks," Sadie agreed. "And you don't even put the bacon or onions in it like Mama does."

"We don't have any bacon," I reminded her, releasing a sigh. Our meals *had* grown staggeringly stale. "Why don't we do something special for Christmas? A big family dinner, just like Mama would make." I paused, guilt tugging at me. There was more family in the Falls this year than we were accustomed to. "We could invite Ezra and Thomas. We'll roast the chicken and fry up some of the potatoes."

"That would be lovely," Merry said, coming in from the cold and rubbing her arms. "I'm sure they're sick of Violet Buhrman's cooking by now. And there are still a couple of apples in the back bin."

"And cinnamon!" I added. "I'll bake them, and we'll have a real feast."

Sam's lips twisted. "I suppose I could ride out tomorrow afternoon and invite them."

"We'll need a tree!" Sadie exclaimed. "Papa always got a big tree for the sitting room. We could do that, right? Trees aren't being rationed."

"Tomorrow morning," I promised. "We'll cut one down and start decorating."

∽✦∾

"Just remember, the farther we go out looking for a tree," Samuel grunted as we trudged through the snowbanks, "the farther we have to pull it back."

We'd had to all but drag him from the house. He'd woken in a grumpy mood, sour and snapping at everyone. Dark circles smudged his eyes, and I wondered if he was coming down with a cold.

Sadie paid no attention, her gaze fixed in the distance as she searched for the perfect tree. She pulled along a sled, ready to bring our prize home.

"What about that one?" Merry asked. She'd lingered back from the group as if taking Samuel's words to heart. She hated using snowshoes.

Samuel looked at the one she pointed to. Shaking his head, he followed after Sadie's exuberant steps. "Too tall."

"This one?" I asked, gesturing to a smaller tree. It didn't look like it would be too heavy if all four of us helped.

"Too small!" Sadie giggled at her rhyme.

We shuffled on through the snow, Merry muttering behind us as the tips of her snowshoes crossed and she toppled over once again.

"That one!" Sadie exclaimed, pointing deep into the woods.

Situated among the underbrush, the tree's branches were thick and lush with verdant needles. It was just the right height and almost perfectly symmetrical. A shaft of weak gray sunlight struck it just so, as if even the sky knew this tree was special.

"Isn't it beautiful?" Sadie asked with a hushed, reverent tone.

"It's lovely," Merry agreed.

"It would fill the sitting room perfectly." I envisioned it swagged with strands of red string and popcorn. We could even use old scrap paper to make snowflakes.

"No," Samuel said, putting an end to the magical moment.

Sadie's head snapped toward him. "What? Why not? Abigail thinks it's pretty too!"

"Then she can wander out and get it," he grumbled. "It's beyond the Bells. I'm not going that deep into the forest for a tree, when there are others that will do just as fine."

"But that's our tree! That's the one we want," Sadie said, pawing at him.

"I said no," he replied with a sudden harshness, using the firm tone to mask the quaver undercutting his words. It only took a glance at his face to understand what was going on.

Sam wasn't sick.

He was terrified of stepping foot into the woods again.

Sweat beaded his upper lip, and his skin was pale with a sickly sheen. He breathed out of his mouth, almost panting, his pupils shrunk to tiny pinpricks.

Our days were so often spent bustling about, tending to the animals, keeping the house clean, ourselves clothed, and our larders stocked. I didn't mean to ignore Sam's trauma, but it was easy to forget what he'd been through, with other concerns piling up around us. But it was clear to me now, as I studied his trembling form, that he wasn't as fine as I'd assumed he was.

Dark shadows limned his eyes—was he not sleeping through the nights?—and his frame seemed so much *less* than it used to be.

"Why don't I take the hatchet?" I offered, wanting to spare him embarrassment. "I . . . I've never gotten to cut down the Christmas tree before—Papa always does it. It might be fun."

"We should find another—"

"Just give me the axe, Sam," I said, holding out my hand. "You all wait back here, until the tree is cut, all right?"

Merry nodded. Sadie handed me the sled's rope. Samuel

remained motionless, eyes fixed on the pines as though an army of monsters were there, lurking in the shadows.

When I turned, there *were* eyes.

Dozens of them.

Round and full, with enormous irises, staring wide, staring at *me*, all-knowing and unblinking, a horde of eldritch creatures come to claim me.

I nearly cried out in surprise and alarm before realizing they were marks on the trees, whorls in the trunks where limbs had fallen off, leaving the impression of human eyes in the wood.

Or almost human, I thought ruefully, staring at one with an uncomfortably malformed pupil.

Were these Sam's monsters? I wanted to laugh. They were nothing but knots and felled branches.

Then I remembered the blood that had covered him, running like a macabre river down his arms and face, staining his clothes with fetid rust.

Pines and firs had not done that.

So I hesitated at the tree line, giving the moment when my foot first stepped into the woods a strange importance I normally would never have noticed. One moment I was with my family, a part of the Falls, and the next, I belonged to the pines.

It was darker in the woods, the evergreens' full branches blocking out most of the morning's light. Quieter too. All the soft background noises I was used to hearing—the wind pushing across the valley, the rustling of the winter wheat, waves slapping on the Greenswold—they were all swallowed up as I crossed the invisible boundary.

The Bells jingled uneasily, each clinking note sharp with discord. There was no melody, no pattern, just noise. Being in the midst of the Bells, I understood why our forefathers had thought the little chimes would hold back strange animals. The pitches grated on my nerves until even I wanted to flee them.

The Christmas tree was farther in than I'd thought. I picked my way through the thick undergrowth, pulling free my skirt as it snagged on thorny brambles. When I finally reached the edge of the Bells, the axe felt heavy in my hand, and a flicker of irritation swept through me as I noticed how weathered the wooden handle was.

Samuel must have left it out on the splitting stump after finishing the last cord of firewood. How many weeks ago had that been? The head was dulled gray, with bits of rust sprinkling the blade. When Papa had left, this hatchet had looked brand-new, the wood oiled, the metal polished and clean.

Anger sparked in my chest, kindling a firestorm of fury, and I suddenly had the sharp and terrible urge to hurl the axe at Sam. I pictured it thwacking into his face, cleaving those smug, thin lips into two jagged halves. I'd never have to see that arrogant, selfish smirk of his again.

God, what a relief that would be.

The shock of the thought startled me, and I nearly dropped the hatchet. What—what was I thinking?

I glanced back at my brother, alarmed he might somehow guess my thoughts. His eyes were worried. He wasn't fretting over my wicked thoughts but my safety.

I blinked hard, clearing my head before raising the axe for the first strike. It bit into the trunk with a mighty crack, but I only heard a wet squelch, as if I'd struck flesh instead.

"Everything all right, Ellerie?" Samuel called out after a moment went by. "It can be easier if you build up more of swing, really get some momentum into it."

I narrowed my eyes. "The blade is dull. Someone must have left it outside too long." My voice was flinty, making sure there was no doubt who I held responsible.

"Looked just fine to me," he said, unconcerned.

In response, I swung it again, letting anger guide my aim. I struck the tree over and over, dark bitterness seizing hold of my limbs, clinging fast like thorned ivy. My blood simmered, hot with rage and troubling thoughts. They curdled my insides until all I felt, all I saw, was a ferocious and biting slash of red. Again and again, I whacked the trunk. Chips of bark flew through the air, as mad as buzzing hornets.

My breath hung in a dense fog around me as I gasped for air and my dress clung uncomfortably against my skin, soaked with sweat even in the chilled morning. With a final blow, the trunk gave way, splitting under the tree's weight. I had the presence of mind to shove Sadie's sled out, and the tree crashed onto it with a resounding thud, shaking the ground.

Out in the open, away from all the shadows and trees, my sisters let out cheers, jumping in victory.

Deep within the forest's gloom, I eyed the fallen giant in silence. If Samuel were to actually help, we'd be able to carry it out in no time at all, but as I watched him toe the tree line, I knew there was little chance of it. My fingers tightened on the axe's handle, hatred unfurling across my chest like the opening leaves of a fern.

"I thought all loggers were meant to call out 'Timber!'"

I turned to see Whitaker standing behind me, leaning against a tree as though he'd been watching me for quite some time.

"You could have killed me," he chastised lightly.

"Hardly."

"Oh yes," he continued, the corner of his lips raised in an endearing quirk. "If there'd been just a wee more breeze blowing this way rather than that, I'd be as flat as a flapjack." He held up a wet finger as if proving his claim. "But luck was on my side today. And yours too, I suppose. I see you require some assistance with that?"

"I can handle it," I said, surprised how sharp my words sounded.

What was wrong with me? I certainly couldn't pick the tree up on my own, and Whitaker had done nothing to earn my ire.

Not like Sam. The coward.

I didn't mean that.

At least, I didn't think I did.

Since I'd stepped into the woods, the very worst facets of my being had suddenly sprung to the forefront—impatience, short-temperedness, and above all, a burning, primal rage—and I was helpless to push them back.

"I've no doubt you could, Ellerie Downing," he said, ignoring my barbed tone and stepping forward to help. "But if you have four hands, why use two?" He reached down and easily hoisted one end of the tree. "I'll pull if you steer?"

I nodded, not trusting myself to voice an assent. Who knew what would come out?

As we set off, I felt a shift inside me, layers of blushing reds and crimsons falling over the black, angry rage. My skin throbbed, my nerves were raw, and a sudden ache reached out from the center of my core, down my arms, and into my fingers until they itched to move in its bidding. My heart panged, overcome with a physical yearning, a hunger, a need.

My breath felt impossibly heavy, and my chest heaved as if I'd run a sprinted race.

When Whitaker turned back to offer an encouraging smile, all of the strange sensations came together to a sharp edge.

Desire.

Lust.

I wanted him.

I wanted to march right up and kiss him. I wanted to taste his lips, to rip open his shirt and feel his pounding heartbeat beneath my touch. I wanted his hands on me, pressed against my bare flesh, gripping and grasping. I wanted to feel the edge of his teeth rake down my neck, wanted to feel him suck at the hollow of my throat before moving lower, then lower still. It would be so easy to lose control in this forest, to give in to temptation, to bask and bathe in it.

To drown.

The sliver of me acknowledging how absurd these wild thoughts were felt very distant, as if it were watching through a spyglass, miles away and utterly powerless to extend reason.

The sensation grew worse as we approached the tree line, as if the depraved thoughts overriding me knew we only had a short time to act. They rose up, droning in my mind until all I could hear was their horrible buzz, baiting and urging me on. Part of me wanted to reach out and caress Whitaker; the other wanted to take the axe and hurl it into his back.

He'd never see it coming.

As I pictured the split skin, the raw wound, the blood—so much blood—that tiny distant part of me, the *real* me, rushed back and slammed into the dark rage with all the force of a rockslide. The wickedness did not give up easily, shrieking its displeasure so loudly, it wasn't until we'd stepped free of the pines' shadows that I could even begin to pick up what was happening around me.

I could tell from the looks of expectation on Sadie's and Merry's faces that someone had asked a question, but I'd been too wrapped in the struggle in my head to respond.

"If it's not too much trouble, I'd be honored to join your celebrations tomorrow," Whitaker said, covering my moment of blankness. He blinked curiously at me, sensing that something was amiss.

Tomorrow.

Christmas.

The girls had invited him for Christmas.

With the sudden departure of the darkness, I felt hollowed,

too thin, a mere shell of my usual self. Even trying to figure out the last of the conversation had taxed me to the point of exhaustion.

"Yes, please," I said, forcing a smile when one didn't automatically form. "We'd love to have you for supper . . . if you've not made other plans already."

His eyes were warm and amber, happy and wholly unaware of all the exquisitely horrible things I'd dreamed up for him in the woods. "None whatsoever."

22

"SADIE, CAN YOU GRAB THE BUTTER FOR ME?" I CALLED, flipping over the potatoes. Their sizzling filled the cast-iron skillet with a happy sound, and my stomach rumbled in anticipation of the meal to come.

"Whitaker's here!" my little sister cried, racing down the stairs. Her pounding footsteps thundered through the house, and I hoped Ezra and Thomas—chatting with Samuel in the sitting room—didn't think to compare Whitaker's arrival with their own luke-warm reception.

I pushed at a wayward lock of hair with the back of my hand. "That doesn't . . . That's not an answer."

"It's not," a warm voice agreed with me.

I turned to see Whitaker leaning against the doorframe, the pot of butter in his hands.

"Merry Christmas, Ellerie Downing." His eyes trailed over me. "You look lovely."

"I look a mess," I said, accepting the butter and turning to scoop some into the skillet. "I truly don't know how Mama pulled these dinners off. She always had everything ready at the same time and would sit down with all of us to eat, not a hair out of place."

"An impressive feat, to be sure."

He leaned in from behind me to inspect the potatoes with an appreciative sniff. My shoulder blades brushed his chest, and a delicious thrill danced through me. It was such a wonderfully intimate, familiar gesture. I'd seen Papa do it many times before, and it always ended with a kiss pressed into the crook of Mama's neck.

I glanced at him. He was so close, our faces brushed against each other's, and I caught the scent of him. It was intoxicating, drawing me closer still, and I was certain this was it.

My first kiss.

I couldn't think of a better Christmas gift.

He smiled as our eyes met, and my chest hitched, too happy to draw full breath.

"Whitaker, I didn't hear you come in." Sam greeted him from the hallway, breaking the moment. "Come meet our uncle and cousin."

"Samuel," Whitaker said, pulling away from me. "Merry Christmas."

"To you as well." Sam gestured back to the sitting room. "Coming?"

"Do you need any help in here?" Whitaker asked me.

"I'm sure Ellerie has everything all covered. And look, there's Merry," Sam said as Merry ducked inside, carrying a basket full of kindling. "I was just about to tell Ezra and Thomas about my trek into the woods. Join us," he beckoned.

Whitaker tapped my nose, a playful twinkle in his eye. "To be continued later," he promised.

"What a marvelous feast!" Ezra exclaimed, clutching the chair in front of him and staring down at the table in wonder.

"Have a seat, please," I said, setting the roasted chicken down with a flourish.

Pride was a sin, but I couldn't help but be pleased with the meal Merry and I had prepared. Mama might have been away, but it felt as though she were here, looking down the length of the table. We'd made all the Christmas favorites—roasted chicken, fried potatoes, green beans salted with butter and little onions. Biscuits and gravy. Cranberry sauce and stewed plums.

My mouth watered as everyone gathered around the table and we bowed our heads for the blessing.

Both Sam and Ezra started to speak at once, neither aware that the other felt the delivery belonged to them.

"A thousand apologies," Ezra said, ceding quickly. "I didn't mean to step on your toes."

Sam's lips twisted into a scowl, and he rushed through a terse and somewhat bland Christmas prayer.

"Amen," we echoed as he finished.

"So tell me, Mr. Price," Ezra began, breaking the quiet that had descended over the table as we'd all begun filling our plates and passing the dishes and bowls. "Ellerie says you're a trapper."

Whitaker finished spooning a drizzle of gravy across his chicken before glancing to my uncle. His eyebrows rose, as if waiting for a question to answer.

"I'd be interested in seeing some of your pelts. I've a mind to make a new coat for myself."

"Is there anything in particular you're interested in?" Whitaker asked, passing a tray of biscuits to Merry, at his left.

"Fox, if you've got any at reasonable prices. I'll need something warm for the collar. I plan to be spending a good amount of time out in the woods soon."

"Doing what, exactly?"

I studied my uncle, curious myself. He had no homestead of

his own to tend and no discernable trade. I wasn't sure what he or Thomas did all day at the Buhrmans'. It seemed odd to not know, but odder still to come out and ask. I hadn't wanted him to think we were busybodies.

"Ah. I intend to write a book," he declared, proudly adjusting his glasses.

"A book?" Sam echoed. "On what?"

"Amity Falls, of course! I've been fortunate enough to travel quite a bit throughout the West and always admired the field guides of the coast. They're chockful of information on plants and animals native to the region. Watercolor illustrations and such. But there's nothing like that for this area of the world. I thought I'd try my hand at creating one."

"You're an artist, then?" I asked, slicing into a sliver of potato. He beamed.

"And you?" Merry glanced at Thomas. "Do you like to paint as well?"

"I mostly carry the supplies," he said with a dry chuckle.

"I even plan to include a few pages on the mutated animals. The wolf we came across. The stags. Frogs and fish. We've heard all sorts of stories around town. Mr. Fowler caught a pike ice fishing last week. It had two tails and a little set of legs between them. Curious, isn't it?" He reached for the pepper shaker. "Have you seen any oddities in your travels, Mr. Price?"

"Just 'Whitaker,'" he corrected Thomas around a mouthful of beans. He swallowed. "I can't say I have. I am awfully grateful to you and your son for taking out that wolf. I wouldn't have wanted him to stumble across my campsite."

Ezra and Thomas nodded, diving into their meals.

"There are more of them out there, though," Sam said. "Wolves, or whatever they truly are."

My sisters and I exchanged looks with each other. We needed to turn the direction of the conversation, or Sam would spend all night brooding on the supply run.

"Tell us more about your book, Uncle Ezra," Sadie said. "And pass the beans?"

Thomas obliged her, and we continued eating.

"Are you sure you want to head back into town now?" Samuel asked as Ezra wrapped a navy scarf about his neck.

"So early?" Merry added.

We'd just cleared away the dessert plates.

"We promised Calvin and Violet to be back in time for a Christmas toast," Ezra explained. "But thank you all, so much, for this lovely evening. Being with family on this day has . . . has truly meant the world."

Thomas nodded. "Happy Christmas, everyone."

After a round of hugs, they headed out to their wagon and disappeared into the purple twilight.

"Happy Christmas?" Sadie repeated.

"Some people say that," I allowed, although I too had noted the peculiar phrasing.

"The tree looks splendid," Whitaker said as we stepped into the sitting room, and the matter was forgotten.

He spun around, taking in the entire picture as his eyes sparkled with appreciation. Paper snowflakes twirled in midair, caught in tangles of baker's string, and swags of holly branches—dark verdant leaves and glistening red berries—decorated the room.

"The whole house does. You ladies truly pulled off a Christmas miracle."

"Sam hung all of that," Sadie offered, throwing a loyal look to him as she pointed to the ivy. He'd been quiet all evening, seemingly cowed by the other men's bold and boisterous presence. "None of us were tall enough."

Samuel waved aside her praise. "But it was your idea to string all the berries on the tree with the popcorn."

"If only we could have made gingerbread ornaments," Merry said, squinting at the tree as if dreaming them into existence. "They make the house smell so good, and Mama always lets us pick them off the tree to eat whenever we want."

"They sound delicious, but it's been the perfect day," Whitaker reassured her. "I can't imagine anything improving it."

"Presents," said Sadie wistfully.

"The baked apples Ellerie made *were* our presents," Merry reminded her. "She used the last of the cinnamon on them."

"And they *were* very good," my little sister allowed. "But it wasn't as though we could stick them under the tree and unwrap them. Not like real presents."

"Sadie," I said with a warning note. Her lower lip was poking dangerously close to a pout. "We talked about that. Not this year."

"I know. I just—"

"Why don't you go and look underneath the tree?" Whitaker cut off her whine. "You never know what you might find!"

Dubiously Sadie knelt beside the pine and lifted a heavily needled branch. With a squeal, she removed a small parcel. It was wrapped in plain brown paper and twine, but Whitaker had stuck a sprig of ivy between the cording for a festive touch. An elaborate *M* was scrawled across the paper.

"Merry, this is for you," Sadie said, handing out the present with such authority that one would have thought she'd wrapped it herself.

She dove back under the tree and retrieved two more gifts,

each with an *S*. Sadie held them up to Whitaker, her eyebrows question marks.

"The smaller one is Samuel's; the bigger one is yours," he said with a wink.

Pleased, she gave Sam his gift, then turned back to the tree.

"Actually, that's all there is," Whitaker said, catching her before she could scramble beneath the branches. "Time ran short, and I couldn't wrap anything for Ellerie." His eyes flickered over to mine. "I am sorry."

"You joining us for Christmas is all the gift I need."

He'd added a breath of life to the house today, keeping us from missing Mama and Papa too much.

Even so, he smiled apologetically before turning to the rest of the group. "Well, what are you waiting for?"

With whoops of delight, Sadie and Sam tore into the paper coverings, ripping the string in two when the knots didn't give way. Merry opened hers with a weighted thoughtfulness, carefully folding the wrapping and curling up the twine, undoubtedly to save for later use. I wanted to hug her for her resourcefulness.

"Oh, pretty!" Sadie exclaimed, drawing my attention. She twirled a little wooden figure between her fingers. "It's a princess!"

"A fairy princess," Whitaker corrected her. "See the wings?"

"They're maple seeds! Look, Ellerie!"

She foisted the carved figure into my hands. The fairy's full-skirted dress had a surprising amount of detail carved into it. Shooting stars fell around the hem, and she held a bouquet of tiny four-leaf clovers.

"Did you carve this yourself?" I asked, glancing up at Whitaker. He nodded. "It's lovely."

We turned to see Merry, inspecting her gift curiously. It was a horseshoe, brand-new, without a trace of wear.

"For luck," Whitaker clarified.

"It's beautiful. I've never seen one so shiny before." She looked up with a shy smile. "Thank you."

"Oh," Samuel murmured. We all leaned in to see what it was.

"A pocketknife," Sadie announced, and immediately lost interest. She took her gift back to the tree and created a game where the figure had to traverse the branches, hopping up higher and higher each time.

"It's *my* pocketknife," Sam said carefully. He held it out to me. "See the little initials on the body? Papa carved those in."

"I remember," I said, examining the knife.

"I lost it . . . during the supply run," Sam continued, glancing up at Whitaker.

"Ellerie mentioned that when she told me what happened. I was checking traps a few days ago and came across it on the forest floor. Thought you'd want it back."

"I . . . yes, thank you."

My twin stared at Whitaker for a long moment, his gaze dark and terrible.

"We didn't get you anything," Sadie realized, her brow furrowing. Her bright tone pushed aside the strange tension threatening the room.

"Are you in jest?" he asked, gallantly sweeping his arm about. "Look at everything you've done. If it wasn't for the Downing family, I'd be spending a cold and lonely night back at my camp. This has been a wonderful evening. I can't remember a better Christmas!"

"Really?" Sadie asked, glancing about the room with suspicion. "But if you could have any Christmas wish—anything at all— what would you want?"

Whitaker's gaze fell on me, and my cheeks flushed under the warmth of his stare. Ever since our intimate moment in the kitchen, there'd been a charge between us. Every stare seemed weighted with an anticipation I wasn't sure how to meet.

"Is that a piano in the corner?" he asked, his eyes never leaving mine.

Merry nodded and pulled off the heavy tapestry cover that Mama had made for the upright. It was one of only three pianos in the Falls, and she was fanatical about keeping dust from it. Reuben Downing, pockets heavy with the gold pebbles his father had been murdered over, bought it as a wedding gift for my parents. It had been shipped in pieces across the mountain pass and reassembled in the sitting room. Whenever Mama had a spare moment, she'd sit on the little tufted stool and run her fingers up and down the polished ivory keys, singing old church hymns or folk songs in her rich alto. Though she'd taught all three of her daughters how to play, none of us were as gifted as her.

"A dance," Whitaker decided. "I think if I could have any Christmas wish, I'd want a dance."

"I'll dance with you!" Sadie exclaimed, easily grabbing his hand and pulling him into the center of the room. "Merry can play something. She's the best of all of us."

"I'd be honored," Whitaker said, sweeping into a bow as Merry began to pick out a careful string of notes, testing the keys.

The piano was a bit out of tune—no one had touched it since the fire—but it was still serviceable, and the carol Merry started filled the house with a warm cheer the holiday had been lacking, despite our best efforts. Even Sam's disinterest seemed to melt away and he grabbed my hand, happily drawing me into a spin.

Sadie shrieked with laughter as she tried mimicking Whitaker's footsteps. He stomped his feet and clapped his hands in a complex pattern she was hopeless to follow, missing half the steps through her giggles.

When the song ended, I took over for Merry so she could have a turn dancing. We sang and stomped till the grandfather clock chimed midnight and Sadie huddled in an exhausted heap at the end of the settee.

"What a perfect evening," Whitaker said over the final stroke of the clock. "But I've trespassed too long on your hospitality. It's time I made my way back to camp."

"All alone? In the dark?" Samuel asked. He'd just picked up Sadie, and her long limbs spilled over his arms.

"I have a lantern and I know the way well."

"Even still . . . there are things in those pines. Dangerous things. You'd be welcome to stay overnight."

"I could make up the couch down here." As I pictured Whitaker sleeping beneath our roof, just rooms away from me, I flushed. "We've plenty of quilts and . . ." I trailed off as the memory of him bathing in the river consumed my thoughts. The thought of one of my quilts covering his naked, slumbering form killed any hope of me finishing that sentence.

If he sensed my thoughts, he did not show it. "I couldn't impose. Truly, I'll be just fine."

I wasn't sure if I was more relieved or disappointed by his insistence.

Whitaker called out a soft goodnight as Samuel carried Sadie's prostrate form up the stairs.

"I ought to help him," Merry said, shooting me a surreptitious wink. "You know she's a bear to change once she's drifted off. Good night, Whitaker. Thank you again for the horseshoe."

"You should hang it above the door you pass through most," he suggested. "That's what they say, anyway."

"I'll make sure to do that." She nodded. "Merry Christmas."

"Merry Christmas, Merry," he echoed. "That was neatly executed," he said once her footsteps had reached the loft. "Did you orchestrate that?"

"What? No! I—"

He laughed. "I know. I did," he admitted in a stage whisper. "I mentioned to Merry what a shame it was you were at the piano all night long."

"I didn't mind."

"Well, I did," he confided. "I hoped I'd get the chance to dance with you."

Pleasure flooded through me, warming my chest. "You did?"

"It was my greatest Christmas wish." He reached out but did not touch me. Instead his hand hung in midair as if waiting for permission. "Could I tempt you into one now?"

I stared at his fingers, admiring the way the candlelight high-lighted their long lines. They were beguiling and hypnotic in their beauty. "There's no one to play for us."

"We don't need a piano." His hand sprang into action then, wrapping around mine and drawing me onto the porch.

The night air was frigid, but I didn't notice. I couldn't feel any-thing beyond the warmth of his fingers, the brush of his arm at my side.

"Do you hear the music?"

I stared into the night, listening. Everything was still as a new snow fell, dampening and muffling the world. "I don't hear any-thing."

"Try harder," he insisted. "Close your eyes and really listen. Do you hear that gentle push of the wind?"

Eyes shut, I nodded.

"The orchestra is warming up."

"A whole orchestra?" I asked, a smile tugging on my lips as his free hand settled at my waist, gently pulling me close against him. This wouldn't be a rowdy country reel.

"And hear the snowflakes as they fall, landing on branches and limbs? There's our downbeat."

His lips were close to my temple, skirting my skin as he whispered, and eliciting a thrill of anticipation.

Whitaker hummed a soft tune, one I was not familiar with, and he began to sway back and forth, pulling me along with the slow shuffle of his feet. When I opened my eyes, his were on mine, as dark as resin.

He slowly turned me into a spin, and I let my hand linger on his arm with far more confidence than I actually felt.

"What a magical night." The snow clouds striated across the sky, and twinkling stars peeked between their lines. "Look, you can even see Cassiopeia."

Whitaker's face shifted into a disbelieving grin. "Who?"

"The constellation." I pulled him down the steps and out into the yard, and pointed at the zigzag of light. "See that cluster of five stars there?"

"Of course."

"That's Cassiopeia, named after a terribly vain queen. To punish her impertinence, the gods made her constellation hang upside down for half the year."

His laughter was light and easy.

"No, see how the *W* is faced?" I traced the pattern into the air above us.

"I see it just fine, Ellerie Downing. It's only . . ."

"What?"

His dimples winked. "Even the stars have to have names?"

I raised my shoulders, shrugging. "It's not as though I christened them myself."

His eyes fell upon me, surprisingly serious, given the grin on his face. "But you know their names? Their stories? All of them?"

"Don't you? Papa used to tell us their stories as we fell asleep when we were little. And there was a book in our schoolroom— I loved reading that."

He shrugged. "It just seems silly to me, I guess, naming something so very far away. Those stars don't know our myths. Why would they want to be named after heroes and legends they've never heard of?"

"I think they'd be happy to know they're so often thought of," I reasoned. "Their names give them importance. Otherwise they're just a scattering of light up in that big, vast void."

He tipped his face up, admiring the night. "It is awfully big and vast." He pointed to a cluster of stars. "What about those ones? They look as though they're important. They must have a story. And I know you'll know it."

"The Harp," I said without hesitation.

He laughed. "Why would there be a harp in the sky?"

"It's Orpheus's." He looked at me blankly. "He was a musician. When the love of his life died, he followed after her into the underworld. Using his music, he persuaded Hades to return her soul to earth, so they could be together forever. Hades relented, saying she would follow the musician out, but Orpheus was not to turn around to mark her progress. He made it through trials and torments, but just before he reached the mouth of the river separating the underworld from the realm of men, he faltered and looked back."

"What happened to the girl?"

"She was dragged back into hell."

Whitaker looked horrified. "And he gets his harp immortalized forever? All because he failed?"

I glanced up to the little diamond-shaped constellation. "I never thought about it like that. It is rather terrible, isn't it?"

Our shoulders brushed as we leaned against each other with a cozy familiarity.

"Would you follow me to the underworld?" he asked. His voice was deep and low, tinged with suggestion.

A smile blossomed across my lips. "If I did, you know I wouldn't look back."

The wind shifted, sending a scattering of snow over us. The flakes danced across my cheeks and caught in my lashes like tiny cold kisses. When Whitaker brushed them aside, I nudged my cheek against his fingers, wanting to feel more of their warmth, wanting to feel more of him.

"You never told me your Christmas wish, Ellerie Downing," he murmured, drawing the pad of his thumb down the curve of my jaw.

I could not answer. My breath was caught in my throat, every fiber of my being waiting for his lips to descend upon mine. I wasn't sure what to do, how to initiate it, where my hands should be. I wanted to pull him down to me then and there but worried he'd think me too brazen, too bold.

But oh, I wanted him.

Before I could throw my caution aside, a gust of wind picked up, blowing past us with a spray of snowflakes. The cold broke us, and the moment, apart as we raced for the cover of the porch, laughing.

"Too cold for dancing, I suppose," Whitaker said ruefully.

"It was a lovely thought," I allowed, aching to rekindle the intensity we'd just shared. He'd wanted to kiss me, I was certain of it. "Come back inside? I can make you a cup of tea—warm you up before you go?"

"A tempting offer."

Disappointment crashed through me as he went inside to retrieve his heavy coat. As he stood at the threshold, tucking the ends of his scarf deep into the collar of his sweater, he glanced up and spotted a sprig of mistletoe. Sadie had hung it earlier while decorating, though I was certain Samuel had taken it down before Whitaker arrived.

But there it dangled now, poised like a promise.

"Very tempting."

"Is it?" I asked, stepping forward, twisting my fingers in knots. It wasn't the cold of the night that sent shivers down my spine.

"Ellerie, I . . ." Whitaker leaned in, nudging my forehead with his, brushing knuckles across my cheek, his touch softer than the snowfall. I tilted my chin, encouraging him to close the little space remaining between us. Our breath fogged gently about us, mingling together like the kiss about to come.

But a flurry of movement drew our attention.

Sam was back, dousing candles.

Instantly Whitaker stepped away from the mistletoe and grabbed his lantern before fleeing into the yard. Another gust of wind blew by, making the distance between us feel like miles. He turned back, a rueful smile playing at his lips.

I leaned against the nearest porch rail, bewildered by his sudden departure. I'd never yearned so badly for something in all my life, and he'd walked away from it today with utter ease. Three times. My stomach churned, embarrassment and vulnerability mingling together into an unpleasant combination.

"Safe travels," I offered, knowing that goodbye must be somehow said. Empty platitudes seemed the easiest way to go.

"I . . . There's something I need to tell you."

"There is?" I hated the rising hope ringing in my words.

Whitaker rolled his tongue over the front of his teeth. "There's not an easy way to say this, but . . . Sam's supply run . . . I'll admit, it's gotten under my skin. I'm always looking over my shoulder, letting our campfires grow brighter and higher than ever."

"I'm glad you're being cautious."

He twisted his fingers together. "It's just . . . have you ever wondered what really happened that night?"

"What do you mean? Sam said—"

"Sam said how terrible the attack was. All its horrifying aftermath. And . . . I saw the remains; it *was* awful. So . . . how did he escape?"

"Well, he said. . . ." I stilled, thinking over Sam's account.

Whitaker raised his pointer finger. "He said the animals were fast. He didn't have a horse. They scattered when the things struck." A second finger popped up. "He said the animals were ferocious. He didn't have a weapon." His eyebrows furrowed together unhappily. "How is he still alive?"

Silence fell between us as I struggled to form an answer. I'd envisioned my brother running through the woods, hiding behind fallen trees, sheltering in a hollowed log. But that was my imagination. What had truly happened? "Maybe he . . . He could have . . ." I shrugged helplessly. "Dumb luck?"

If anyone were to believe in the power of luck, it was Whitaker.

He nodded reluctantly. "Maybe."

"You don't sound convinced."

Whitaker cast out a deep sigh. "Ellerie—there was no sign of creatures attacking that camp. When I came across it, I found . . . a lot of dried blood and some bones and . . . other *things* . . . but it didn't look as though animals had attacked those men."

"What *did* it look like?" I whispered. I rubbed my arms, uncertain if my chill was from the wind or his words.

"Like the men had been killed . . . murdered," he whispered.

I drew a quick breath, horrified. "You can't possibly mean Sam—"

"I didn't say that!" he clarified, his hands raised in defense. "I'm not suggesting that, at all. . . . I don't think. Only that it was a man who did it. Men, maybe. I don't know."

"That sounds crazy."

"Crazier than an entire pack of those mutated wolves?"

"No one in Amity Falls would kill those men."

"Maybe the men didn't come from the Falls."

We startled at a sharp tap on the window. Samuel waved once. "Good night, Whitaker. Merry Christmas again."

He nodded, and we watched him go in silence.

"But Sam saw the wolves . . . ," I persisted, watching my twin retreat deeper into the house.

Whitaker cleared his throat, making a soft sound of concession. "A traumatized mind can see an awful lot of things, but I'm telling you, Ellerie Downing, there are no monsters in those pines."

"What should I tell Sam?"

"Nothing. Do . . . do you feel safe with him? Do you think he'd ever hurt you—or your sisters?"

"Of course not!" I exclaimed, horrified.

"Of course not," he echoed with less certainty. "Just . . . be vigilant. Be safe."

Whitaker glanced back to the empty window before stepping in and pressing a fervent kiss to my forehead. I wanted to savor its tender warmth, but in truth I barely felt it.

"I'll check in on you all in a few days," he promised, before disappearing into a swirl of snow.

23

SAMUEL'S FORK DRAGGED ACROSS THE PLATE, PICKING up every last crumb of the oatcakes I'd made for breakfast. Without sugar, syrup, or cinnamon, they were nearly inedible, but Sam didn't seem to notice or care. He licked the corner of his mouth, savoring every bit of the tasteless cake, finishing his before I'd even served the others.

Sadie made a face as I dropped a cake onto her plate. "Again?"

"Again," I confirmed.

"Is there any . . ." She trailed off, unable to think of a single thing that would salvage breakfast.

"I'll eat it if you won't," Sam said, claiming the cake by reaching across the table to stab his fork into it the second we'd finished saying our morning prayer.

"Sam!" I cried as Sadie let out a painfully loud screech.

"What? She said she didn't want it." He'd popped nearly half the oatcake into his mouth and was chewing around his words.

"No, I didn't!" Sadie wailed.

"Have it, then," he said, foisting the remains back onto her plate. She pushed it back at him. "I don't want it now!"

"Take mine," I said, shoving my plate over to stop the shrieking.

I'd woken up with a dull pressure pounding across my forehead, and their squabbling sharpened it into a truly horrific migraine. I pressed the pads of my fingers into my forehead, but nothing helped.

"There's that last bit of ginger root in the pantry," Merry said, noticing my discomfort. "I'll make you some tea."

Sadie perked up. "I want tea!"

"Then come help. You can shave the ginger. I'll get the water."

Sadie pointed a warning finger at Sam. "Don't eat Ellerie's. That's mine!"

They left for the kitchen, and the room fell into blissful silence. Sam poked at the last of Sadie's oatcake, taking his time finishing it off.

"Bad night?" he asked.

Whitaker's parting words had circled round and round, clouding my mind with shades of doubt and dread, and spinning outlandish and horrific possibilities. I hadn't fallen asleep until the early hours of the morning, and even then, my dreams had been distorted with nightmares.

Tall pines leering over a campsite destroyed.

Cries of terror.

A pair of bright dots I'd thought were the creature's silver eyes.

But when I'd focused on them, I'd realized it was moonlight reflecting off the blood spattering my brother's face.

And the knife in his hand.

Whitaker was mistaken; he had to be. There was no other explanation. What he'd guessed—that the men had not been killed but murdered—made no sense. It couldn't be true. No man was capable of—

My temples tightened.

I didn't know what had happened on that supply run. No one

did, except Sam. His account was the only one we'd heard. The only one that could be accepted. Everyone had been too afraid of the wolves to investigate further.

Wolves that Whitaker insisted were no longer there.

"Ellerie?" Sam prompted, still waiting for my answer.

"I'm sorry, my mind was elsewhere."

"It has been all morning." Was his tone laced with accusation, or was that my worried imagination?

"I didn't sleep well."

"Maybe we shouldn't let Whitaker stay so late the next time he comes visiting. It took me an age to go down once he'd left."

I twisted my lips, uncertain if I should say what was truly on my mind or let it lie dormant. "It was good of him to return your pocketknife," I said, landing somewhere in the middle. "I'm sure it's a relief to have it back."

Sam hummed his acknowledgment before his face turned sour. "I don't understand him. Living in the woods like that, when he knows those *things* are out there. And then to go poking around that site . . ." He shook his head.

"I don't think Whitaker was poking around. He was just checking traps."

He sniffed. "So he says."

"Why should you care, anyway?" It was like pressing at a loose tooth, gently pushing and prodding to see how much give it had before it finally broke free. No good would come of it, but I couldn't stop myself.

"Just don't like it. He shouldn't be nosing into things that don't concern him. He's not a part of the town. He didn't know those men." I must have made a noise he didn't care for. "What? State your piece, Ellerie. I can see you've got something all worked up in your mind. Just spit it out."

"It just . . . I don't understand why it bothers you so much—him being near the campsite. . . . Is there something there you didn't want him to see?"

Sam's eyes narrowed. "Meaning what?"

I ran my fingers over the tabletop, glancing into the kitchen to see if our sisters were listening in. Merry stood beside Sadie, showing her how to get the thinnest slices from the ginger root. "I don't know. You're just acting as though you've something to hide."

"Something to hide? Like what?"

"What really happened, Sam? How did you get away from those creatures, all on your own? I don't . . . I don't see how you escaped. Without protection. Without even your knife."

He blinked in surprise. "I told you what happened."

"You did. Mostly."

"Mostly?" Sam bristled. "What else do you want to hear? Do you want to know what it sounded like when Joseph Abernathy's chest ripped open? The color of his innards? The way he screamed for his mother?"

I turned away, wincing as the images flooded my mind. "No! Of course not."

"Then what, Ellerie? What do you want to know?" He leaned over the table.

"Only . . ."

"What?"

I squirmed. "It's terrible."

"Tell me," he growled.

"If the attack was that devastating, that fast and awful—how are you here right now? You didn't have a gun. You didn't have arrows. You didn't even have your pocketknife. So how are you alive right now?"

He opened his mouth, but no words came out.

"I'm so glad you are . . . obviously . . . but it just doesn't make any sense to me."

"I ran," he admitted quietly. "It was a cowardly thing to do, but I ran."

"How could you outrun those wolves? You said how fast they were. How there were so many of them."

A flicker of irritation lit his face. "Why aren't you believing me? What did he say?" Sam asked, his voice turning dark and sharp. "What else did Whitaker tell you?"

"He said . . ." I squirmed in my seat. "He said it was an absolute massacre. A bloodbath. No one could have survived it. But . . ."

"What?" he demanded.

"He didn't see any traces of animals at the site."

Sam's mouth fell open. "What? That's absurd. What else could have . . ." He trailed off, putting the pieces together. "He thinks I . . . ?"

"He didn't say that! He doesn't think that at all!" I raced to amend.

"Then who does he think did it?"

I shrugged helplessly.

"Answer me!" Sam struck the table with startling force.

"Is everything all right?" Merry asked, peeking in from the doorway.

"Go upstairs," Sam ordered. "Both of you!"

Merry's face clouded with confusion. "But what about—"

"Now!" Sam snapped.

We listened to their footsteps shuffle up the staircase, then linger on the landing.

"Shut the door too!"

"Sam," I tried.

"You think I murdered those men?" He leaned over the table, glaring daggers into my eyes.

"No, of course not! I—"

"But he does! He told you I did!"

"He didn't say that. He said he didn't see any evidence of wolves—of the creatures you saw."

"The creatures that were there," he corrected me.

"Yes."

"You believe me, don't you?"

I hesitated, and immediately saw it was the wrong choice to make.

He shoved backward, nearly knocking his chair over. "I can't believe you, Ellerie. I can't . . ." He raked his fingers through his hair. "I can't be here. Not right now. Not anymore."

"Sam—"

"Save it." He sprung into motion, racing to Mama and Papa's bedroom and slamming the door shut. I heard motion inside, drawers yanked open, things tossed about, but I didn't dare approach. He'd come out when he was ready, when he'd cooled off, spouting contrition.

I was exhausted just picturing it.

My sisters' uneaten oatcakes were growing cold on their plates. I pushed myself from the table and took quiet treads toward the staircase. But before I could call them back down, the bedroom door whipped open and Sam stepped out, a rucksack slung over his shoulder.

His eyes fell on me without recognition, and then he looked away. He stalked into the kitchen, and I heard him rummage about the shelves.

At the top of the stairs, Merry peeked around the corner, scouting to see if it was safe to come down. I shook my head at her, and she slipped back into the loft with an audible sigh.

I heard the porch door open and swing shut, then silence.

I paused, listening closely.

Was he still in the house?

When I dared to check the kitchen, I spotted him through the window, his form dark against the new snow.

He'd left.

Again.

A flicker of irritation kindled within me, and I was out the door in a matter of heartbeats, throwing my wool cloak over my shoulders.

"Sam!" My voice echoed strangely off the falling snow.

Thick flakes danced down from the clouds, heavy and wet. We'd have another two feet on the ground before twilight fell. Only an absolute fool would try to travel in such weather.

Only Sam.

"Go back home, Ellerie," he ordered.

I floundered after him, drifts calf-high and freezing. At least he'd had the sense to strap on his snowshoes before he'd left.

"What are you doing?"

He stopped, back to me, his sigh steeped in a deep plume of white breath. "What does it look like?"

"Like you're about to get yourself lost in a blizzard."

"I'm sure that'd please you."

"Sam."

He remained motionless. "It was hard enough living in that house with you, Ellerie, stomping about as if you were the head of everything, as if you know *everything*. You've no idea how much it hurt when Papa left the bees to you."

"I didn't ask him to. I—"

He whirled around, finally looking at me. "They were supposed to be mine!" He swung his arm out, gesturing toward the farm. "All of this was supposed to have been *mine*! I'm the oldest! I'm the son! What right do you have bossing me about, as if I'm stupid, as if I'm in need of your almighty guidance?"

"What right?" I repeated, feeling the barrage of his words hit like bullets. But rather than shredding and stinging, they sparked, incinerating a scolding fury within me. "I'm the only reason the hives are still here. You nearly killed them all, trying to get those extra bottles of honey! How could you have been so thoughtless, Sam?"

A cloud of breath flooded from his mouth, as though I'd pummeled him. "I had to—I needed—you wouldn't even begin to understand."

"You're right. I don't understand. I won't. Ever. It was too cold. It was too late in the season. And I can't decide which is worse—that you were too stupid or you just didn't care!"

He shook his head. "I guess Papa was right, then. Maybe I am the weaker one, the lesser twin. Maybe I'm supposed to stick to the background while you reign supreme over your little hives. But I will not stay in that house while you accuse me of murder! While you believe another man's word over mine." His lips trembled, rage and sorrow whipping together into a tidal wave of misery.

I faltered in the face of his pain, casting my anger aside. "Sam, I didn't—I haven't!"

"I won't!" He snapped and trudged off, leaving me behind once more.

"Where are you going?" I called after him.

"I don't know and it doesn't matter. I'd rather live in the forests, fighting off those damned monsters, than spend another second under that roof with you!"

He disappeared in a curtain of snowfall before I could stop him. But even if he hadn't, I don't think I would have tried.

"I can't believe Sam really left," Sadie said, settling back into her seat, our cold breakfast laid before us. She stared at the empty chair with morose regard. "Do you think he'll come back when Mama and Papa do?"

I doubted it and didn't feel poorly for saying so. My blood boiled, remembering his accusations.

"Won't he want to see the baby? And . . . me?"

"I'm sure he'll come visit," Merry promised. "Cheer up, little love. You'll see him soon enough."

"But why did he have to go? Is he mad at us?" A quick flick of her eyes in my direction made it clear who she truly meant by "us."

I bustled back to the kitchen and unhooked the kettle from the hearth. After grabbing the tea, I returned to the dining room. "I don't think so . . . certainly not at you. This was bound to happen. Sam's growing up. He wasn't going to stay here forever. Remember when he hung the curtain in the loft? It's like that—he just needs his own place. Space to become himself."

"But you're twins," she observed. "You won't leave us too, will you?" Her eyes were as round as an owl's, pleading and dark with worry.

Sinking into the chair next to her, I grabbed her hand and pressed a fervent kiss to its back. "Of course not. I'd never leave my sisters." Sadie twisted her fingers through mine, still miserable, and I gestured for Merry to join us. "Let's say the blessing before the food gets any colder."

The three of us joined hands and closed our eyes. Before I could find the right words, there was a brisk knock on the front door.

"Sam?" Sadie guessed, her eyes flashing open.

"He wouldn't knock," I said, standing up.

"Or use the front door," Merry added.

I pushed myself from the table as another flurry of knocks sounded. Across the lace curtains a silhouette swayed from foot to foot.

"Ezra. Hello," I said in greeting, opening the door, surprise in my voice. "Thomas," I acknowledged, seeing my cousin standing behind him.

"We're terribly sorry to call at such an early hour—" Ezra began.

"Did you forget something last night?" I swept my eyes over the sitting room, but nothing looked out of place.

"No, no . . . nothing like that."

"My sisters and I were just settling down for breakfast. Would you care for some tea?"

"We didn't mean to interrupt," Ezra said. He pushed his gold wire spectacles up his nose, looking lost. "We can come back another time . . ."

Thomas placed a hand on his father's back, bolstering him up. "We're already this far." My cousin turned to me. "We were attacked last night."

"Attacked?" Merry echoed. She'd wandered in from the dining room, fingers at her throat. "Are you all right? What happened?"

His mouth opened as if to smile, but it contained no joy. "We're fine, mostly. Calvin woke us in the middle of the night. Our wagon was being ransacked. Our supplies cast out and set on fire. It was too dark to make out faces, but we saw at least three shadows fleeing the scene. And the oxen . . ."

"They eviscerated them," Ezra filled in when Thomas could not.

I took in a sharp breath, unable to keep from imagining the blood slashed across the newly fallen snow. Last night had been Christmas. Who would do something so horrific on such a holy night?

My stomach ached as I remembered Rebecca's wedding.

The Elders had accused Ezra and Thomas of being behind all the strange events in town. Too many people had stood by, nodding in silent agreement. Any one of them—buoyed by a bit of holiday spirits—could have decided to take justice into their hands.

"That's terrible." An obvious understatement, but I couldn't think of anything else to say.

Ezra's face was grave. "My notes and journals can be salvaged—it will take some time to put everything back in order—but the oxen . . . I'm afraid we're stranded now. We won't be able to leave the Falls without them, however much some may wish it."

"Leave the Falls?" Merry repeated with alarm. "In the middle of winter? Oh, Uncle Ezra, you can't!"

I placed a gentle hand on her forearm. "Why don't you and Sadie start up some more oatcakes?" My fingertips worried over my thumbnail, tallying up exactly how many scoops of flour remained in the larder. I turned back to the men. "It's freezing out here. Please, please come inside."

After they were ushered inside, I glanced about the yard before shutting the door. They'd walked here, through the snowbanks, carrying the last of their possessions with them. It must have taken hours. Four large packs, stuffed to overflowing, were on the porch, a small wooden trunk nestled between them.

Of all the days for Sam to have stormed off.

Thomas followed after Merry, leaning forward to attentively answer her flood of questions. Ezra hung back in the sitting room and gestured that I do the same.

"You'll stay with us, of course," I said, jumping over whatever preamble he'd worked up in his mind.

"Oh, I—we—"

"You're family," I said firmly, settling the decision. "Family helps each other out. Always."

He squinted through his glasses. "I appreciate this kindness, Ellerie, you've no idea how much. We'd never dare to presume—but if you have space in your barn? Or an outbuilding?" He released a soft laugh. "Even a spot in an open field would be preferable to staying in town."

His thick eyebrows raised together with such hope, I felt powerless to say no. "Mama and Papa's room is open," I heard myself say.

It was true enough. Sam had taken all of his possessions from it.

He took a deep breath, relief evident on his face. "Oh, how good of you."

"There's just the one bed, but . . . Sam stormed off this morning. I don't know when he'll be back. Thomas can use his bed in the loft till then. We'll work out something after if we need to."

He fidgeted with the spectacles, clearly flustered. "Oh, no. No. No, he couldn't possibly. He can stay down here. He's got a sleeping roll and we'll clean it up each morning." Ezra nodded, glancing about the open floor of the room.

"Nonsense. He needs a bed, and it'll be far warmer up there. Besides," I said, forcing a smile. "We're all cousins, right?"

After our meager breakfast, I escorted Ezra and Thomas down to the barn and showed them an empty stall where they could store their packs.

"I suppose we ought to start going through everything, see what is truly left," Ezra said, throwing one of the rucksacks onto the worktable with a sigh.

He looked exhausted.

"Is there anything I can do to help?" I wandered over to where they'd piled their supplies at the barn door. The packs were bigger than me, but I picked up the small crate easily. "Pretty lid," I said.

Intricate patterns had been carved along the border with surprising detail.

"Oh, let me take that," Ezra said, swiping the box from me. "It's so heavy."

"I don't mind."

"Nonsense, you've already helped us so much." He whisked it away to the stall before I could study it further.

"Thank you again, Ellerie," Thomas said, opening up a sack and removing a roll of canvas. He laid it out on the ground and began unfurling its length.

"It's no trouble at all." I knelt down to help, flipping over the folds until the full expanse of the tent lay spread out. "Oh."

My mouth fell open as I caught sight of the picture crudely drawn on the tent's side.

It was a large, lidless eye. The paint—I refused to think of it as blood—had been heavily applied and streaked down from the drawing in eerie rivulets. Even more disconcerting was the eye's pupil. Someone had dipped their hand in the blood—no, paint—and pressed it to the oilcloth. It seemed to see nothing and yet everything all at once.

"I have seen," I said, reading the words painted beneath the lurid rendering.

I froze, my breath caught painfully tight in the hollow of my throat as I recognized the familiar phrase. It was a snippet of what Levi Barton had scrawled across his barn after murdering his wife and livestock.

Why would someone copy it here?

Thomas came around to my side of the tent and stared at the dripping words. "It's rather curious."

I nodded uneasily. "A few years ago, one of our neighbors painted something similar across their barn."

His eyebrows rose sharply. "Really? Perhaps he was the one behind the vandalism last night."

"Not likely. He killed himself." I told him the whole story, and Thomas shuddered.

"Ah, admiring our new mural, Ellerie?" Ezra asked, coming

out of the stall. He brushed his fingers over his palms, job done. "Ghastly, isn't it?"

"Ellerie was just telling me the most ghoulish story. All sorts of murder and mayhem. There was a giant eye involved in it as well." Thomas stared at his father as though imparting a deeper meaning than I could discern.

"We have bleach," I offered, my eyes drawn back to the hand-print pupil. It was smaller than I'd have expected it to be, as if a child had created the macabre image. "Up at the house."

"That would be very helpful," Ezra said. "Would you mind getting it now? I'd hate for this horrible thing to set in any longer than it already has."

"Of course."

I could hear Ezra's low murmuring as I left the barn, but couldn't make out exactly what was said.

Outside, movement near the pines caught my attention, and I spotted Whitaker at the edge of the forest. He was paused along the tree line, half in weak sunlight, half in shadows, watching the barn with a strange expression of concern on his face.

Before I could call out a greeting, he slipped back into the darkness, eyebrows furrowed and his lips drawn into a worried line.

24

THE EARTH WAS WARM AND DAMP AS I STEPPED INTO the flower field, as if it had just rained. I could feel the black soil smudge my feet, working its way between my toes.

I was barefoot.

The flowers rustled around me, their blooms wide and glowing an eerie blue beneath the full moon.

Papa told me once that the moon pulled at waves here on earth, drawing the water across wide oceans and bringing them to their intended shores.

This moon hung so low, I could feel its persistence working on me, tugging me through the heady blossoms and urging me toward town.

I was in my nightdress, long and white, but it didn't matter.

I had no lantern to see by, but that didn't matter either.

The only thing that did was putting one foot in front of the other, following the moon's insistence.

"Ellerie Downing."

Whitaker had come out of the forest, out of the night, out of the sky and stars themselves, it seemed. Was he too pulled along by the glowing moon? Had she intentionally brought us together?

"What are you doing out here?" I asked.

"Couldn't sleep," he admitted. "You?"

"I think I am sleeping," I decided. It certainly felt possible.

He smiled, the tips of his teeth winking. "Are you saying you dream of me?"

"All the time," I said in a teasing manner, light and flirtatious even though it was true.

"What do we do in these dreams of yours?"

"I think . . . I think we ought to walk."

He offered his arm with a cavalier charm.

We rambled down country lanes, covered by bowers of tree limbs and fragrant ivy. We cut through lush meadows where the dew dotting the long grasses caught the moonlight from overhead, forming an entire galaxy of sparkling stars around us. We walked on and on until we made our way into town.

I don't remember speaking as we traveled, but I memorized the pressure of his fingers on my forearm, the sweep they made across the small of my back as he helped me over a bit of rocky terrain. Words were not needed. I felt safe, secure, and—as he tucked a brilliant red poppy behind my ear—cherished.

All around us, Amity Falls slept, houses shuttered and dark.

"I feel like we're the only people left in the world, don't you?" I'd never seen the town so quiet and still.

"It does seem rather abandoned," he agreed. "We could do anything we wanted, and no one would ever know."

We came to a stop outside the schoolhouse, its white clapboard at odds with the heavy black window frames.

"I've always wanted to ring that," I said, peering up at the bell housed in a jutting gable. "All those years of school, and I never once got to."

"You could, right now," he suggested. "But that would wake everyone in town and we'd lose our chance."

"Our chance for what?"

The world felt impossibly slow and dreamy as he pulled me toward him, bringing his hands to my face and gently cupping my cheeks. His thumbs traced down my jaw, ran over my mouth.

An unfamiliar sensation woke within me as he brushed my lips, his own so close, I could feel the heat of his breath warming me. There was a heaviness in my belly, a thrilling prickle of awareness racing across my skin. My fingers danced to its pulse, aching to reach out and touch him.

"This," he murmured, lowering his lips. They moved over mine, like a whisper, a song of reverence and praise, a prayer. "This is how I should have kissed you at Christmas—this is how I've always wanted to kiss you."

And then his fingers were tangled in my hair, drawing me closer until I answered back with kisses of my own, soft at first, but then so much more. When I parted my mouth, daring to flick my tongue against his lips, he let out a strangled gasp of surprise. His arms wrapped around my back, confidently pressing me flush against his body. It was so warm and unfamiliar, so wholly different from mine. Where I was soft, he was hard. Where I curved, he flexed. We were like little wooden puzzle pieces at McCleary's store. Just little bits of colorful chaos on their own, but once they were snapped into place, you could see they were meant to be together all along.

When his long fingers traced their way from the nape of my neck down my spine, I felt a wave of delicious shivers race through me, shimmering with need and demanding more. More touching, more kisses, more *him*.

"Whitaker," I tried to whisper, but his mouth was on mine, swallowing my words. I felt him groan, the vibrations ringing against my lips, my skin, down into my very bones, and my fingers curved reflexively, sinking into the soft skin at the back of his neck, desperate to draw him closer still.

He responded in kind, his fingertips running over my arms,

down my side, tracing the curve of my hips. His worked his way lower, kissing the column of my neck, the hollow of my throat. He could feel my heart pulsing there, I was certain of it. It pounded, racing faster and faster. Every beat felt like a drum snap, spelling out his name, until my entire body throbbed with its cadence.

The pads of his fingers brushed my skin as he toyed with the buttons of my nightdress, and a sound rose, so completely foreign and primal that at first I didn't recognize it as myself. It was dark and full of wanting and desire and absolute need.

"This is madness," I murmured, blood sizzling through me, setting my nerve endings ablaze. I couldn't think, couldn't reason. I just wanted to feel.

"Madness," he echoed. Then he paused, his lips only a breath away from my bared skin. Every bit of me was hung aloft in anticipation, yearning for the moment when he'd descend.

When he stepped back, stepped away, turning his attention toward the forest, I felt his absence as keenly as a cold slap. My chest heaved, wholly aware he'd been against it and was then suddenly not. I reached for him, but my hand fell short. He was too far away to touch, too attuned to whatever he sensed in the woods.

Realization stabbed at me, sharp and swift. Something was out there, watching us. I followed his gaze. There was nothing but moonlight on the dew, sparkling and shining dots of silver.

Then something shifted, stirring pine needles, a shadow darker than the other shadows, sneaking and sly.

The silver dots danced with subtle movement, as if breathing.

Panting.

They blinked.

And Whitaker took a step forward, drawn to this living, breathing entity, a moth to flame.

"Stop."

We had nothing to protect ourselves with.

He took another step and another.

"Don't!"

He was getting too close. Much too close. I could no longer distinguish his dark jacket from the forest.

One moment he was there, and the next, it was only those silver eyes.

Staring and studying.

Watching us.

Watching *me*.

Then they too were gone, leaving me alone in the empty town. A breeze whispered through the branches, and swirled around me with a sharp, acrid bite.

It smelled like fire.

Like ashes and cinders.

"She loves a good blaze," said a voice rising out of the darkness, a specter slithering forth from a tomb.

I turned to see Cyrus Danforth on the steps of the school-house.

He blinked at me, eyes radiant with an otherworldly shine.

A glow of moonlight and madness.

Silver.

"You're dead," I whispered, my throat drying up and closing in on me.

This was a dream.

This was only a dream.

"You're about to wake up," I whispered to myself. "You're about to wake up in bed, next to Merry. And Sadie. None of this is real."

But he looked real.

The purpling bruises that circled his broken neck looked real.

And the handkerchief he held in his hand, dangling between his unusually long fingers, also looked very, very real.

"Have you forgotten about this?" he asked.

The little square of cotton fluttered in the wind, my three drops of blood standing out in stark relief.

"How did you get—that's not yours!"

"Isn't it?" He wrapped it around his pointer finger, turning it over and over. "Finders keepers, I suppose."

The way the fabric wound round his finger was mesmerizing, beguiling. I couldn't have looked away if I'd tried.

I did not try.

"Why . . . why do your fingers look like that?" My voice sounded as distant as a dream.

This *was* a dream.

Cyrus opened his mouth, but the laugh that came out was not his. It was high and light, seeped with feminine charm.

"Why, the better to beckon you with."

She laughed again, this creature who was not Cyrus Danforth.

"I need you to do something for me, Ellerie Downing."

"How do you know my name?"

I felt drugged, caught in a stupor where the world moved too slowly and the shadows grew too dark.

"I've been watching you. I've been watching you for a very long while."

I blinked heavily, trying to clear my head, but the daze persisted, turning the world bleary.

For a flash of a moment, Cyrus morphed into something else—a slip of a figure sporting a white eyelet dress and dark curls.

I blinked again and saw only Rebecca's father, so terribly, terribly dead.

"Why?"

"You're special, don't you know? So very special."

I shook my head. "I'm not. I'm just—"

"I wasn't finished," she reprimanded, her fingers balling into quick fists.

Someone with such a lovely voice shouldn't have fingers like that.

My thoughts listed, like wilting flowers. There was a strange presence within my mind, another entity warring for space.

"As I was saying . . . I need you to do something for me."

I shook my head. I didn't know who or what this thing was, but I wouldn't go along with anything she suggested. The real Cyrus's shouts from the Gallows echoed through my thoughts.

This Cyrus held up the handkerchief again. "I have your pledge. I hold your blood. And I need you to do this one small favor for me."

In a flash, the figure skittered toward me, moving with such a ferocious speed, I felt sick. My eyes struggled, finding it impossible to focus on the new form the creature took. She was too close, pressed against me with an unrelenting insistence. I could only understand pieces of the whole. A brilliant smile. An arched brow. Misshapen knuckles, as bulging and bulbous as knots on a tree.

"What that drunk old bastard said was true," she murmured, drawing one grotesque finger down my cheek. "I do love a blaze. The bigger, the better, I always say. If I could watch the entire world burn down, I would with a cheerful heart. So I need you to take this, Ellerie. I need you to take this and use it."

She pressed something into the palm of my hand.

It was a match.

Such an unassuming little bit of wood and sulfur.

Thoroughly innocuous when dormant.

"Wake up, Ellerie," I said to myself. This dream, this nightmare, was getting too strange, feeling too real.

"You need to take it and use it," she instructed, closing my fingers around it.

"Wake up."

"Take it and light it."

"Wake up now."

"I have your pledge, I have your blood, you must do as I say," she hissed, pressing her lips close to my ear, her voice invading my mind. "Take it. Use it. Burn it all down."

Against my will, my hands moved, acting of their own accord.

I swiped the match against the side of the schoolhouse, sparking it to life.

The flame flared brightly, a little flash lighting up the night, biting and burning.

The creature released a sigh, relief whistling through her rotting teeth.

Just as I dropped the match, letting it fall carelessly to the ground, I came to, startling awake with a gasp for air.

When I woke up, I was alone in the loft. Merry and Sadie must have let me sleep in, taking on my morning chores themselves.

For a moment, I allowed myself to sink back into bed, relishing the warmth of the quilts against the bitter cold. Frost covered the windows, but it reassured me.

It had been spring in my dream. In my nightmare.

Not like this.

This was real.

That was not.

Part of me longed to stay in bed, whiling away the morning in a dozy, dreamy nap. But there were things to do, and I couldn't remain here while my sisters handled everything. With a groan, I kicked the blankets from me, hoisting my legs to the floor.

I paused, staring down at my feet, unable to comprehend what I saw.

Usually I bundled up in several layers of Papa's wool socks to stave off the night's chill, but the socks were gone now. My toes were darkened with a crust of dirt, as if I'd spent the night walking through the Falls with bare feet.

25

DAYS SLIPPED BY WITHOUT WORD FROM SAM.

The snow continued to fall, piling past Sadie's knees, then Merry's, then mine.

My dreams returned to normal, without heated visions of Whitaker or terrifying encounters with the creature in the pale dress.

My feet stayed in their socks.

Then came an unexpected knock at our front door one morning.

It sounded once, then twice. The third rap was louder. Our guest was clearly vexed no one had answered.

"Merry!" I was elbow-deep in the washtub, and the front of my apron was soaked.

Buttons had bounded through the kitchen, knocking a stack of tin plates into the soapy water before falling in himself. I could still hear him yowling in the loft as Sadie tried to dry him.

"Merry!" I tried again after the third set of knocks.

"She's in the barn," Sadie announced, coming down the stairs, carrying a murderous Buttons in a towel.

"Can you answer the door while I change?"

Her mouth fell open. "You want *me* to answer the door? I never get to answer the door." Another set of raps spurred her into action. "Coming!" she shouted, her feet clattering loudly through the house.

I tossed the sodden apron onto the worktable and did a quick check in the little plate-glass mirror Mama kept in the kitchen for moments such as these. Wispy flyaways framed my face, but there was no time to fix them. I grabbed a clean pinafore off the hook and made my way to the front.

"What are you doing here?" I heard Sadie ask as she opened the door.

I inwardly groaned. Mama would have given her an earful if she'd heard her.

"Manners, Sadie," I said, coming around the corner. When I saw the visitors, I stopped short. "Oh."

Simon and Rebecca Briard stood in the middle of our sitting room wearing a set of matching scowls.

"Good Blessings," I said, recovering.

"Good Blessings." Only Simon echoed my sentiment.

An uncomfortable silence filled the room, making it clear neither of the Briards would speak first. "We've not seen you since the wedding. You look well."

"Yes, my Rebecca is quite the picture of radiance these days, don't you think?" Simon smiled at her fondly before letting his eyes drift to her belly.

She must have finally let him in on the happy news.

"Would you care for a cup of tea?" Even as I offered, I prayed they'd say no. We were down to our last tin.

Simon's eyes lit hopefully, but Rebecca shook her head with a curt snap.

"We won't be staying long."

"What brings you by, then, neighbor?" I asked, adjusting my tone to match her clipped cadence.

"Coming home from town two days ago, we saw a troubling sight," Simon jumped in as his wife nudged him in the ribs. "It appears your new relatives have come for a visit."

"They were out chopping wood," Rebecca added.

I said nothing, waiting for them to come to their point.

"Well?" Simon asked as the moment ran long. "Are they?"

"Are they . . . chopping wood?"

"Living here," Rebecca hissed.

"Their wagon was vandalized on Christmas night," I said. "Their oxen killed and—"

"We've heard," Simon interrupted.

"We invited them to stay with us. At least until the worst of winter passes."

His face fell, growing grave. "And you didn't think to warn us?"

"Warn you? Of what?"

"Their presence. Near my—our property."

The corner of Rebecca's mouth tightened at his mistake, but she said nothing.

"Simon, you sound ridiculous. They're my family. It's not as though I'm harboring criminals."

"I told you," Rebecca muttered, tugging at his sleeve. "We ought to leave."

"Well, actually," he began. "There's another reason for our visit. We weren't sure if you'd heard the news yet."

"What news?" Alarm knit in my throat. Parson Briard kept a falcon to send and deliver messages to and from the bishop in the city. Had Papa been able to send word? I braced for the worst.

"There was a fire. A few nights ago."

"Oh." Misplaced relief rose over me like a swell at sea. "What burned?"

"The schoolhouse."

I inhaled sharply, certain I'd misheard. "The school?"

Simon nodded. "It's completely destroyed, burnt to cinders."

"I . . . that's terrible."

"It is."

"What . . . what happened?" I asked carefully, uncertain if my interest might be perceived as a guilty conscience.

It was a coincidence. It had to be.

"No one knows for sure. It happened late in the evening. No one noticed until it was too late to save anything."

I frowned, trying to look sympathetic. "When did it happen? There was that strange thunderstorm two nights back. Could it . . . could it have been lightning?"

Simon shook his head. "It burned the night before. On Wednesday."

I thought hard, counting back my evenings. The schoolhouse had burned down the night I'd dreamed I'd set fire to it.

Coincidence.

A strange one, admittedly.

But a coincidence.

Nothing more.

"We thought you should know. . . . There are rumors going around about who set it," Rebecca said, arching one eyebrow at me.

Bile slushed about in my stomach, hot and acidic. It didn't matter how deserted the town had appeared. Someone had seen me. Someone had watched me strike that damned match.

My mind raced. What would the penalty be for such a crime? They'd hung Cyrus for burning down our shed, but Mama had been seriously hurt. If no one had been injured, would my sentencing be more merciful?

Pull yourself together.

It had been a dream.

A terrible, nightmarish coincidence of a dream, but a dream all the same.

It had been warm. I'd been barefoot.

In reality, there were feet of snow outside on the ground.

Impossible.

There was a long moment of silence, and I realized I'd missed hearing something Simon had said.

"What?"

"It just . . . The timing feels awfully suspicious, don't you think?"

"Timing?" I repeated.

"I mean . . . it happened shortly after their wagon was vandalized."

The missing piece clinked into place for me. "You think my uncle burned down the schoolhouse? That's preposterous!"

"Is it? After his oxen were slaughtered?"

"What does that have to do with the school?" I felt as though I was in a hazy nightmare. I could understand individual words, but when they were strung together, nothing seemed to make sense.

"Alice Fowler teaches there." Rebecca let out an exasperated sigh, taking in my blank face. "The Fowlers wanted revenge for their chickens."

I blinked, struggling to put together the logic. "So you think Ezra and Thomas were responsible for the chicken massacre *and* burning the school? They don't even know the Fowlers. None of this adds up."

Rebecca and Simon glanced at one another, considering my statement.

"I know who killed all those chickens," Sadie said. I'd nearly forgotten she was standing beside me. "Abigail told me."

"Abigail?" Rebecca repeated. "Abigail who?"

"Not now, Sadie," I hissed through my teeth.

"Who's Abigail?" Rebecca pressed.

"My friend—"

"Her imaginary friend," I corrected Sadie, overriding her. "She's not real."

"She is too!" Sadie screeched. "She's just as real as you or me. Stop saying she's not real!" And with that, she tore out of the room.

"I'm sorry about that," I tried, knowing I needed to fill the silence. "It's a phase she's going through and—"

"You know what the good Lord says about false idols," Simon said, falling into a poor imitation of his father.

"No, Simon, I don't," I said testily. "Remind me."

"He said . . . he said you shouldn't have any," he sputtered, quickly losing the steam of his conviction.

Rebecca's eyes fluttered shut, and she took a deep steadying breath before daring to look at me. "Are you going to send them away?"

"Of course not."

"They're arsonists."

"There's no proof against them. I would have thought that you of all people would need proof of guilt."

Her tongue clicked against the roof of her mouth. "You're being stubborn, Ellerie. You've always been stubborn."

"And you're letting gossip and speculation sway your reason, Rebecca. You say the fire took place Wednesday? When?"

Her eyes darted to Simon. "Clemency said the commotion woke him around midnight. . . ."

"Then it couldn't have been Ezra who set it," I said triumphantly. "Both he and Thomas stayed up late that evening, to see in the New Year."

Relief flooded through me as the full understanding of my words hit home.

I couldn't have been sleepwalking into town, seeing strange women and setting fires at midnight. I'd been awake then too, wearing a silly paper crown Sadie had made.

A coincidence.

Nothing more.

Her nostrils flared. "I don't suppose anyone else could corroborate your story?"

"Merry and Sadie, of course."

"Not Sam?"

It slipped from her, softer than she'd intended, and her face quickly hardened into an unreadable mask.

"Samuel Downing is at Abrams's now, working at the ranch," Simon supplied, blissfully unaware of his wife's slip. "I thought I'd told you that."

Wordlessly she shook her head.

Sam at Judd Abrams's. I couldn't imagine him as a ranch hand but stored away the information to deal with later.

"All the more reason why I'm uncomfortable with those men staying here, Ellerie," Simon continued, turning back to me. "You and your sisters are all alone. What if something . . . untoward should happen?"

"I appreciate your concern, Simon. Both of your concerns," I added, casting a look toward Rebecca. She didn't meet my gaze. "But Ezra and Thomas are both fine men—they've been helping with quite a lot of work around the farm, and, as I've now clarified, they couldn't have had anything to do with the fire. I'm terribly sorry it happened, it's an awful tragedy, but they didn't set it."

"Well . . ." Simon seemed at a loss for how to continue. "I suppose we ought to be on our way, then. Good Blessings."

"Rebecca, would you like to stay for a bit?" I said, keeping my voice low with hope. "We dyed a few skeins of yarn from the Schäfers' flock yesterday—I'd love to show it to you."

I could see exactly how it would play out. Simon would kiss her goodbye and promise to return with a sled so she wouldn't face the cold walk home alone. There would be an awkward moment of silence before we both tripped over ourselves to apologize at the same time. I'd show her the yarn—it wasn't just a ruse to get Simon to leave—and we'd spend the afternoon knitting tiny hats and blanket squares and laughing, our friendship solidified once more.

But when her eyes met mine, they were as fierce as a rattlesnake before the strike. "No." Simon glanced at her curiously, and she added, "Thank you." She pulled her cloak about her, preparing to leave. She paused at the door, fingers tracing down the wood grain. "Actually, Simon, could you ready the horses and give us a moment? I won't be long."

He nodded and ducked out. Rebecca kept her back to me, looking out the window.

"I could make some tea if you'd like—"

"Stop it, Ellerie. Just stop."

"I only—"

She spun around, eyes flashing and cheeks heated. "You only what? What could you possibly want from me?"

"Could . . . could we talk?" I asked, treading cautiously.

"Talk? As though we're friends?"

Staring down her sudden rage made my insides squirm.

"We *are* friends," I said firmly.

"We were," she corrected me. "But that ended the second my father was strung up at the Gallows."

I dropped back, as if slapped. "I had nothing to do with that!"

"Your brother did. If he didn't—if he hadn't—" Her eyes darted out toward the side yard, where Simon fussed with a harness. "It doesn't matter. I'm done—with all of you."

"You don't mean that."

The line of her jaw was hard and unforgiving. "I do. I lament the day I ever befriended you. The Downings have brought nothing but misery to my family, and I only wish Papa's fire had finished you all off."

The force of her words bit into me like a hatchet striking its mark. I wanted to believe she didn't mean it, wanted to excuse it as nothing more than the fevered uprising of grief, but I couldn't. Some things ought never to be said. Some words were too cruel to forgive.

I turned away from her without a guilty conscience.

She said she wanted me out of her life.

I could happily oblige.

She stepped out into the cold without another word.

26

"Rule Number Six: When neighbors reach for helping hand, extend your own, as God commands."

"LIMA BEANS," I REPEATED, PASSING THE LARDER AGAIN.

It was my third time by.

Merry tapped her chin as she examined our dwindling supplies.

"It's what we have the most of," I added, turning for another loop of pacing.

"It's what everyone has the most of," she said, a deep scowl marring her features. "Remember market last month? I've never seen so many beans in all my life. Green beans, butter beans, navy beans, kidney—"

"Lots of beans," I interrupted, hating that she was right.

"I never want to see another bean again as long as I live," she muttered, shifting the glass containers.

I stopped pacing to watch her. "They're keeping us fed."

Merry hummed in response and pulled out the second-to-last jar of onions. "We could get something good for these."

"Not if everyone else is bringing beans," I pointed out.

The corner of her lips twisted with reluctant agreement, but she made no motion to pick up the jar.

"Merry?"

She let out a sigh. "No. You're right." She grabbed the beans and brushed past me. "You're always, always right."

It was said under her breath, so low, I almost missed it.

"What?"

She turned to look at me, her face a placid mask, eyebrows arched. "What?"

"What did you just say?"

Merry cocked her head. "Nothing. Only, you're right about the beans. . . . Maybe we can trade these for green beans. Sadie loves them so."

I studied her closely. This wasn't the first time I'd thought I heard her muttering little snide remarks, but I'd never been able to quite catch their full meaning. Merry was the one person I usually got along with—I never butted heads with her like I did with Sam, and she never bickered like Sadie.

But now . . .

She seemed quicker to anger and less prone to confide her thoughts.

The winter had changed her.

But it had also changed me, forcing me into a position I wasn't quite ready for. I was trying to fit roles I couldn't hope to properly fill. I felt far older than my eighteen years, and the weight of my new worries warped and stretched, leaving me too thin, saddled with too many burdens.

Who would ever want to be around someone like that?

"We should probably leave soon, if we want to get any good deals," Merry called over her shoulder before leaving me in the hallway alone with my thoughts.

❦

The Gathering House wasn't as full as it usually was.

A dozen families, maybe fewer, wandered about the hall,

critically eyeing their neighbors' wares, judging and determining how they could best profit. Dark circles lined hungry eyes. Dresses gaped too large. Belts were notched too many holes deep.

The Elders had arranged for market days, spread out to once a month, as a way to help Amity Falls make it through the long, uncertain winter. People brought whatever items they had in surplus, to barter or trade with. Some people promised away their first bounties of spring. Others offered to help with farming or repairs.

The markets had started out as a success—everyone smiling and eager to be of assistance—but as the snow piled higher and higher, anxiety lined the faces of those present. Worry hung so heavily, you could taste it in the air, a coppery bite, potent and bitter. The same goods seemed to be brought every month.

Beans.

Eggs.

Never the flour or meat we all so desperately hoped for.

But still we came.

"Mama canned these just at the peak of summer," Merry said, offering our jar to Cora Schäfer. "Would you want to trade?"

The older woman had brought the prized item of today's market—a large canister of cherry preserves—and everyone circled about her like vultures.

"I've got all the limas I could ever want, Merry Downing."

We stepped back, allowing for other people to try their luck, but Cora grabbed Merry's upper arm, detaining us.

"I think you girls have done a kind deed, allowing your uncle and cousin to stay with you. Don't let others tell you anything otherwise."

Merry frowned, unaware of the conversation I'd had with Rebecca and Simon. "What do you mean?"

Cora's eyes darted about the room. "There are some who think we ought to cut ties with them. That they ought to be shunned."

"Some?" Merry asked. "You mean Amos?"

"Leland," I added pointedly.

Cora had the grace to redden as her husband's name was mentioned. "They're all becoming a bit unreasonable these days. All three of them. It's the strain of the situation. They're only trying to take care of the town, however they can. Trying to keep the balance of powers steady."

"Balance of powers?"

"From Briard, of course. Haven't you noticed he's not here? That several of the more . . . fervent members of his congregation aren't either?"

I glanced about the room, noting the Lathetons' and Fowlers' absences. Simon and Rebecca weren't present either. "Perhaps they didn't have anything to trade."

"Perhaps they're at the church now, plotting ways to seize control." Her eyes shone with a glassy heat, and I noticed her hands were trembling.

"Cora, when was the last time you had something to eat?"

I'd begun skipping a meal here and there, trying to make our supplies stretch a little further. My head always swam on those days, feeling too light and easily befuddled. I wondered how much of her accusation was fueled by hunger pangs.

"It's fine. I'm fine," she insisted. As her gaze fell to the cherry preserves, I heard her stomach rumble.

Though I hoped Cora's comments were all fevered conjecture, I couldn't help but wonder why Briard's biggest supporters were missing today.

"Come on, Ellerie," Merry said, tugging on my cloak as the Elder's wife waved off my concern.

"Good Blessings, Cora Schäfer," I said.

"What was that about?" Merry hissed once we were out of earshot. "She sounds crazed."

"I think she only—"

"Ooh, lima beans!" Bonnie Maddin called out as we went by. She sat on a bench, drowning in a cloak now two sizes too big for her. Her hair, usually full of curls and luster, was pulled back in a limp braid, roots greasy. She raised her lips in a hopeful smile, revealing two missing teeth. "Mama would adore those!"

Merry narrowed her eyes, searching for Bonnie's contribution. "What have you got?"

Her terseness surprised me. She'd not seen her friend since the last market day, nearly a month before. Too many storms had prevented the rebuilding of the schoolhouse, so classes had been suspended, forcing the children of Amity Falls to remain at home.

Wordlessly Bonnie pulled out two lengths of ribbon. They were lovely shades of blue and purple, and I longed to run my fingers over their grosgrain edges.

"What would I do with those?" Merry asked, her tone as sharp as nails.

"They'd be pretty on a bonnet," Bonnie suggested, foisting them closer to us.

"I can't eat a bonnet," my sister snapped. Then she turned and set off to find someone else to trade with.

Bonnie's face scrunched with tears. "Mama told me if I didn't bring food home, she wouldn't let me in at all."

"They're beautiful ribbons, Bonnie," I said half-heartedly. "I know someone will want them."

Her watery eyes fell heavily on me. "Ellerie, please."

"I . . . I'm so sorry," I said, hurrying away.

"Martha McCleary has peas," Merry murmured as I joined her.

The Elder's wife had just entered the Gathering House, shaking snowflakes from her heavy shawl. Amos staggered in after her, pressing a handkerchief over rattling coughs. His dark skin was unusually ashen, and his milky eyes watered. Flecks of red stained the cloth, and I shook my head.

"Better not, just to be safe."

"Why isn't he at home?" Merry wondered. "He looks like he ought to be in his deathbed."

Unkind, but true.

Matthias joined them, offering an arm to Martha and looking Amos over with a sharp eye. As they spoke in tones too low to hear, Leland drifted closer. In public, the Elders were always drawn to one another, much like geese pulled south in the autumn and back north as spring dawned.

"Potatoes?" Roger Schultz stepped in front of us, his burlap sack raised high.

Merry peeked inside and immediately wrinkled her nose.

"They don't look the most appetizing," he admitted. "But you can cut away that black rot. There's still plenty of edible bits."

There was a whine of desperation to his voice.

The Schultz farm had been decimated by the strange black rot spreading throughout the Falls. Nearly all of their harvest had been tainted. Knowing he had five small children at home—and another on the way—made me ache to simply hand over our jar of beans, but I swallowed back such charitable thoughts.

Compassion would not keep our bellies full.

Another volley of coughs rose from Amos, harsh, raspy barks that sounded as though his lungs would burst free and splatter upon the wall, oozing and utterly spent.

Martha struck at his back, as if dislodging a stubborn bit of phlegm.

"Let it alone, woman, let it alone," he hollered. He waved his cane at her with warning.

"Amos, old friend, you need to rest," Matthias said. "Why don't you let me take you home? Leland can escort Martha safely back once she's finished here."

The old man swatted the offer away, his bushy white eyebrows drawn into a solid line of anger.

Martha shook her head and stalked off.

"I just don't know what to do," she confided too loudly to Cora. "Every day I go to sleep thinking this will be his last night on earth, but every morning the sun rises and he's still here, even worse than before."

"I'm sure he'll recover soon," Cora said. "Men like Amos are stubborn. One little cold won't take him down."

"And the doctor is no help at all," Martha continued as if she hadn't heard Cora. "Says there's no medicine." She snarled. "He's a doctor. Of course he has medicine. He just wants to keep it all to himself."

Across the room, Dr. Ambrose's jaw tightened.

"You know that's not true, Martha," Cora said, trying to placate her.

"All I know is that I would do anything to make Amos well again. Anything," she repeated.

"Come now," Matthias said, calling out to the doctor. "There must be some medicine you can offer him. You always have something squirreled away in that black bag of yours."

Dr. Ambrose shook his head. "I told you back in the summer that I was running low on stock. What makes you think any of that has changed?"

"He's an Elder," Leland tried. "Surely that ought to mean something."

"I don't care if he's Christ himself. I have nothing!"

"Not here, perhaps," Matthias allowed, noticing how the room's attention had fallen upon them. "But at your cabin, surely. No one would blame you for having a little stash tucked away for a rainy day."

The doctor's sigh was sharp with impatience. "This is getting out of hand." He turned toward the door, but Leland stepped in front of him, blocking his escape.

"Just give him the medicine."

"I have food. I have money," Martha said. She crossed in toward the doctor, pawing at his wool coat. "Please."

"Let me by," Dr. Ambrose said, skirting away to avoid her touch.

Matthias came forward, arms crossed over his chest. The blacksmith made an imposing wall.

The doctor's mouth fell open. "You're not letting me leave?"

"She's been entirely reasonable. We all have. Just give up the medicine."

"I would, if there was any left. What about that don't you understand?"

"Where are you keeping it?"

Dr. Ambrose's arms went up, trying to keep the Elder back as Matthias stepped toward him. "Nowhere. There's none. I swear!"

There was a terrible wrenching sound outside, like the sky ripping open to herald the start of Armageddon, and we all turned to watch in horror as one of the giant pines bordering the Falls fell over. The remaining trunk was a mess of jagged spikes reaching out like grasping fingers.

The doctor used the moment's distraction to hurry away. Once out, he raced down the road as fast as his arthritic limbs would carry him. Wind howled through the open door, and the walls of the Gathering House shuddered.

"Storm's getting real bad," Calvin Buhrman said, peering out the window. "Saw three trees down on our way in. Think it's best if we head home." Beside him, Violet nodded.

"Maybe we ought to stay here," Leland countered, his gaze fixed on the stump. "It sounds as if it's getting worse." As if on cue, the wind altered pitch, screaming like a banshee over the icy roads. "We have firewood—some," he said, checking the pile near the stove. "And supplies. . . . We certainly won't go hungry with all these beans."

There should have been a gentle laugh.

There was not.

Amos coughed. Bonnie sniffled.

I glanced around the room, truly looking at everyone there and seeing all the little details I'd missed before. The fevered glassiness of their eyes. The pallor of their skin. Hand trembles and noses red from wiping. Exhaustion and aches.

Everyone seemed on the verge of sickness.

I turned to Merry. "I . . . I think we need to leave."

"We can't make it home in that," she said, gesturing to the gales of snow pelting the windows.

"We can't stay here. Look at everyone. They're sick. They're sick and afraid."

Had the tree not fallen over, I shuddered to imagine what might have happened to Dr. Ambrose. Desperation was changing the Falls, making people lash out for themselves. Not for the whole of the community.

Unconsciously I grabbed our jar of beans and tucked it beneath my cloak to keep it from view.

Amos sank to a bench, fighting for breath. He hacked once, twice, too exhausted to bother with his handkerchief.

I could almost feel the drops of spittle land on me. Repulsed, I wiped at the phantom spray, but my skin still itched. I pictured the sickness burrowing within me, like a colony of ants spreading out through the ground. I scratched, leaving red welts across the tops of my hands, but that only further fanned the flames of irritation.

My shoulder blades chafed; the backs of my knees twitched. Things crawled in my hair, but they were impossible to find, no matter how I raked my fingers through it.

Still the Elder gasped and wheezed.

Matthias's countenance turned grim, his thoughts written upon his face. "Calvin is right. We all need to get home before the storm gets any worse. In fact . . . I think we all ought to stay home for a while. Until the danger has passed."

"What are you saying?" Cora asked.

I squirmed, trying to relieve the prickle of unease creeping down my spine. Merry grabbed my hand, stilling me.

"With resources so low, I think it prudent to keep to ourselves. Hunker down and make do. Spring will come and this will all be over. But we need to stay safe until then."

Murmurs filled the hall.

"Until the thaw, this will be the last time we're all together," Matthias said decisively. Leland's mouth dropped open, and Amos raised a hand in weak protest, but they did not deter him. "Good Blessings to you—to all the Falls—till then."

27

TAP, TAP, TAP.

Tap, tap.

Rubbing away the film of sleep from my bleary eyes, I stared at the rafters above, wondering what had woken me. The faces I picked out of the wooden whorls in the beams were leering and cruel. Their clarity was blurred by the fog of my breath in the air. I sank into the bedsheets wishing I could slip back into slumber, hunkered beneath the mountain of quilts heated by my sisters.

It was the only time I ever felt warm enough.

Tap, tap.

Tap, tap, tap.

What was that?

I rolled over and peered out the window at the enormous elm growing nearby. Papa had trimmed back the branches last year, worried that summer storms might toss the limbs too near to the house. Perhaps they were in need of another pruning. It *was* March.

But the naked, gnarled twigs were still. Not even a hint of a breeze moved throughout the branches.

With a sigh, I forced myself from the cozy nest. My feet jerked as they touched the chilled floorboards, even encased in a pair of

Papa's thick socks. After pulling a wool sweater over my night-gown, I made my way downstairs, rubbing my arms. Mama had knit me the sweater just last year, but it hung too large on my frame now, as baggy as a tent.

Stepping into the sitting room, I let out a hiss.

It was even colder here.

I set to work, ignoring the way my hands trembled as I scooped the ashes from the hearth. The shakes were from either the cold or my constant hunger—but I'd stopped being able to tell the difference weeks ago. I lit a bit of kindling and slowly added sticks to the fireplace, letting the flame grow and feed.

Tap, tap.

Tap, tap, tap.

Muscle memory prodded me toward the side door, instinctively on my way to milk Bessie. I'd slipped on Papa's work coat and boots before remembering that the poor beast had died the day before, ribs sticking from her sides as sharply as scythes.

My hand remained paused on the doorknob, as I wondered what I ought to do instead.

The room spun for a moment as I considered my options. My head was too light, a dry leaf caught in a brisk wind and powerless to do anything but dance.

Breakfast. I needed breakfast.

After shuffling to the larder, I checked the barren shelves, hoping that—against all logic and better judgment—a miracle had taken place overnight and they'd be more stocked than when I'd inventoried them the day before.

It had not.

They were not.

I lingered in the doorway, swaying as my center of gravity wobbled. Finally I grabbed a tin of dried mint leaves—Sadie had discovered a patch just before the snows had set in, and we'd plundered it bare—and returned to the fire.

I set the kettle on its hook and waited for the water to boil.

Tap, tap, tap.

Tap, tap.

"Sam?" I called out, confusion clouding my senses. My throat felt raw, creaking with uncertainty.

No response.

No, there wouldn't be. Sam had been gone for months.

Months? That's can't be right.

"You know that, Ellerie," I muttered, trying to ground myself in the present.

It was the tree, it had to be. Once I'd had my tea, I'd walk around the outside of the house and find where the branches scraped. Perhaps I could coax Ezra and Thomas to help me get the ladder from the barn and chop down the offending limbs.

I nodded as the kettle began to whistle.

Yes. Good. That would be what we could do today.

Tap.

Tap.

Tap, tap.

"What *is* that?" Merry asked, coming into the room.

I hadn't heard her footsteps on the stairs, but in truth, I wasn't hearing much of anything over the persistent *tap-tap-tapping.* Focusing on more than one task at a time felt impossible these days.

"Tree branch, I think. Water is on." I took a sip, letting the weak brew warm my insides. It would almost be enough to trick my stomach into thinking it was truly full.

"It woke me up," she said, busying herself with a cup.

I hummed in agreement, oddly pleased she'd heard it too. As the winter had progressed and our supplies had dwindled, I'd often wondered if my hunger had caused me to see or hear things that weren't truly there. I'd wake from dreams so vividly real that actual life felt dimmer by comparison.

Just last week, I'd dreamed Mama and Papa had returned. I'd spotted their wagon approaching, out the little diamond window in the loft, and raced down to greet them. In the dream, Mama had been healed whole, no trace of burns or scars marring her skin. Papa was smiling and happy and so, so eager for us to meet our new baby brother, tightly wrapped in Sadie's blanket. But when he pulled back the quilt, a horrible creature lay within the cozy folds.

The baby's head was bulbous and misshapen, grown too big for his tiny body. He looked too soft, as if his bones had never formed and his skin struggled to hold back the weight of his insides. Strange bumps protruded along his face, like teeth sprouting from the round curve of his baby cheeks. But worst of all, our brother had stared out at the world with burning silver eyes.

"I'm hungry," Sadie called out, her voice echoing down the stairwell.

"Come have some tea."

She stomped into the room. "I'm sick of tea." Sadie had pulled one of the quilts off the bed and wrapped herself into a cotton cocoon. I could barely see her eyes winking from the dark folds. It was enough like my nightmare to send a flurry of shivers down my spine.

"You can have my share of the oatmeal this morning, love," Merry offered generously.

"That's just as watery as the tea," Sadie grumbled, plopping herself in front of the flames. "I'm sick of winter."

"Keep the quilt from the hearth," I said. "The last thing we need is another fire."

Sadie repositioned the blanket and begrudgingly accepted a cup of tea. "Can we go into town today?"

I briefly pictured us waddling across the icy fields. The path had long been buried under steep drifts of snow. Every time we left the house, I worried we'd lose our bearings and wind up freezing to death, caught in an endless sea of blinding white. "What for?"

"We haven't seen anyone in ages. I miss my friends."

It did seem forever ago that the Elders decided to close the church and Gathering House, thinking it would be easier to tuck ourselves securely into the safety of our homes.

Easier in theory, at least.

After two months of isolation, we were all feeling the stirrings of cabin fever.

Tap, tap, tap.

Tap, tap.

Tap.

Sadie rubbed at her face. "Ugh, that noise again! What is it?"

"Ellerie thinks there's a branch hitting the house," Merry said, polishing off the last of her tea. She stared longingly at the tin of mint before firmly setting the cup aside. "It'll be good to replenish the firewood, I suppose."

I nodded grimly.

We'd been far too liberal with our woodpile at the beginning of winter, and now the log shed stood nearly as empty as the larder. Eventually we'd have to wander into the pines in search of felled trees, but biting storms had kept us squirreled away in the farmhouse.

It seemed like this winter would never end.

Tap, tap, tap.

The soft strikes were echoed by louder booms as footsteps sounded across the porch outside.

Merry shot up in alarm. "Who's there?"

My eyes automatically swept to the mantel, but Papa had

taken the rifle with him. At the time it had made sense, but after so many months of being unable to hunt for game or protect ourselves, my nerves frayed anxiously, jumping at every unknown.

The door swung open, and a figure stepped inside, immediately choking the room with the stench of offal and the bite of iron. Three shrieks split the air. Ezra raised his hands to calm us, but they were stained dark red, covered in blood.

"What happened to you?" I managed to gasp.

"Dealing with Bessie," he said, removing his coat. He glanced down the front of his shirt with a frown, spotting a splatter of blood.

Sadie paled.

"That's right. Thank you," I said, suddenly recalling his offer of assistance yesterday. I shook my head to bring focus to my thoughts. I was forgetting too many things lately. "Beef for supper tonight, at least, I suppose." My stomach rumbled, and I guiltily pushed aside memories of our milk cow's docile stare.

Merry busied herself making our uncle a cup of tea.

Tap, tap.

Tap, tap, tap.

"There's a limb hitting the house," I said, feeling as though I was repeating myself.

"Is there?" he asked, taking too big a sip and wincing as the hot water burned him.

"Don't you hear that?"

Tap, tap.

Tap, tap, tap.

Ezra cocked his head, listening intently to the steady rhythm permeating the house. His eyes crinkled and he began to laugh.

"What's so funny?" Sadie asked. Her eyebrows were set in one sharp line across her face.

"That's no tree. Haven't you silly geese looked outside this morning?"

Like a slow-moving herd, we wandered onto the porch, clutching at blankets and coat flaps.

"See?" he asked.

I peered into the yard. Morning's light cast weak silvery beams across the covered fields. The yard sparkled, pretty until I caught sight of Ezra's bloody footprints marring its purity.

"I don't see anything," I admitted.

"There," he said, pointing to the porch's overhang.

Tap, tap.

Tap, tap, tap.

Ezra was right.

It wasn't a branch.

It wasn't the wind.

Drops of water trickled off the jagged teeth of icicles hanging from the roof. They fell to the wooden planks below with metronomic persistence.

Hope leapt high in my throat.

Tap, tap, tap.

"The snow is melting," Ezra said needlessly. "It's finally spring."

SPRING

28

"EASY NOW," I CAUTIONED. I COULD BARELY MAKE OUT Merry's profile beneath the enormous brim of Papa's hat. The veil shrouded her frame with such excess that not even the bright afternoon sunlight could penetrate its folds.

"I don't think I'm doing this right." Her voice was thin and reedy; she was clearly unhappy with the situation. "Can't we wait a few more days?"

"It's finally warm enough to open the boxes. We need to see if the queens made it through the winter."

I'd been hunting for eggs in the chicken coop that morning when a honeybee had landed on the lawn of my sleeve, preening its wings as if to say hello. It was the first bee I'd seen since snowfall, and I took it as a sign the hives were ready for inspection. After breakfast, I'd enlisted Merry, even letting her choose which duty she'd prefer—the smoker or handling the hive frames.

"I can't pick the frames up myself," she'd protested.

"Then the smoker is all yours."

I'd been so certain we'd be able to handle the job ourselves, but as she struggled with the metal can and bellows, I wondered if I ought to have asked Ezra or Thomas.

Surprisingly, neither of them had shown much interest in the bees. Ezra claimed they were both terribly allergic to the stings. When I'd asked how he'd managed to grow up in a house of apiarists, he'd laughed.

"Very carefully."

"Just a little more smoke along the bottom board," I instructed now, trying to sound confident. I slowly counted to twenty—just as I remembered seeing Papa do—and lifted the inner cover.

A mass of bees greeted us, swarming around the last of the winter sugar cakes. Only a few chunks remained, and my heart swelled. This hive had not only survived the winter but—from the initial inspection—it had thrived. Using the chisel, I freed several of the super frames, sweeping my eyes over them. Most of the combs were a pale yellow, filled with honey created by the sugar that the bees had ingested over the winter. There was a smattering of dark orange cells—combs full of pollen and bee bread. It was strange to see so few of them, but it had been a hard, long winter and the bees were only now beginning to venture into the world again. Though our fields remained barren, flowers were blooming all over the valley. They'd be able to store more pollen soon, I was sure of it.

"Let's check the brood box before we clean the bottom boards," I said, removing the top layer, my arms trembling.

Merry doused the lower region, and I checked the brood frames, cheered to see capped cells along the outer edges. This hive's queen was alive and busy laying eggs. Several queen caps stuck out from the comb, like metastasizing toadstools, but there was no royal jelly in them or larvae—nothing to signal a problem with the current queen. The last traces of my anxiety slipped away.

With a grunt, I hoisted the brood box free of the base board and set it to the side as gently as I could manage. The box had to weigh at least a hundred pounds.

"Oh," Merry said, peering across the floor of the hive. It was littered with dead bees.

"It's okay," I said, reassuring her as much as myself. "Not every bee was going to survive the winter, and it was too cold for the undertakers to remove the bodies. We'll clean out the bottom, then put everything back together."

Wax caps dotted the floor, and there was a blue hue in one corner. It wasn't unusual for mold to form in the winter months, when the hive was less ventilated, trapping the excess humidity inside. It wasn't a good sight to see, but I was grateful it was only here, where condensation must have pooled, and not within the upper frames.

We set to work, shaking out the dead and scraping off the mold. Once the first hive was restored, we moved on to the next one, and the one after that, and the one after, until all five colonies had been inspected. The sun was beginning to dip behind the mountains as I covered the final hive with a contented sigh.

Grabbing Merry in a playful hug, I pressed a quick kiss to the top of her hat. "We did it," I breathed with relief. "We got the bees through winter."

"Long day's work, ladies?" a voice called out across the side yard.

Merry pulled up the edge of her veil to better see the tall figure leaning against a cottonwood tree. "Whitaker!" she exclaimed, and my stomach plummeted joyfully into my boots.

We hadn't seen him since Christmas. Deep snows and wicked blizzard winds had kept him away. I'd agonized over our separation. What the poets wrote was true: absence did make the heart grow fonder. Fonder and fanciful and wholly prone to fits of yearning and anguish.

But he was here now. Finally.

"Is it safe to approach?" he asked as we gathered our tools. "I didn't want to agitate the bees."

"The covers are on—you're just fine," I said, reaching under my veil to push away an errant lock of hair. I'd daydreamed countless variations of our reunion, but I'd never been wearing a bee hat in any of them. "You'll be fine," I amended, heat flooding my cheeks as I tried tempering my grin. Every fiber in me ached to throw my arms around him, but Merry's presence held me in check.

Just barely.

Though Whitaker smiled, something seemed off. His eyes were cautious, considering, as if he was assessing a situation that could turn dangerous. His hesitation gave me pause, and worries rose like a flock of startled birds within me.

"You made it through the winter," Merry said. "How are you?"

"Fine, just fine," he said swaying back and forth on his heels and studiously avoiding my stare. "And how are the Downings?"

"We're fine," I said, uncomfortably aware of how often we'd repeated that word. "We all made it through the winter, mostly. . . . Bessie died. Our cow. And a few of the chickens."

He dragged his gaze away from Merry. "I'm sorry to hear that. It was certainly a rough winter on everyone . . . but you're both looking well."

His lie rang hollowly in the spring air.

We weren't, and we knew it. Hip bones jutted uncomfortably through the gathers of our skirts, and shadows rimmed our eyes. After so many months cooped up in the farmhouse, my skin was sallow, tinged with a yellow hue that would take more than an afternoon of hive inspections to correct.

A dark burr worried me as I took stock of my flaws. Had he truly cared so much about my outer appearance?

"Merry!"

We turned to see Sadie standing on the porch, peering over the fields with her hand shielding her eyes from the sun.

"Are you done with the bees? I need help!"

With the schoolhouse still closed, Merry oversaw Sadie's class-work, often leaving her tasks quickly scrawled on bits of paper throughout the house. Though it brought neither of them delight, both Sadie's penmanship and math skills had been improving.

With a heavy sigh, Merry foisted the smoker into my arms and muttered goodbye to Whitaker. The screen door slammed shut behind her with a listless thunk.

"Here, I can take those," Whitaker said, scooping the chisels and smoker from me.

Hands free, I took off my hat and shook out my braid. It felt damp and heavy at the back of my neck. We stared at each other for a long moment. I opened my mouth, but words failed to form.

"How are they?" he finally asked, gesturing to the boxes.

I grinned around my discomfort. "Every hive made it through the winter. It was all because of your sugar. . . . If you hadn't—"

"If *you* hadn't," he corrected me, and for a moment the tension—tightening between us like a thread pulled taut by a spindle—snapped.

"It's . . . it's good to see you again," I said, stepping into the shed. I set down my hat and gathered the netted veil into its center to keep it safe from snags.

"Yes." He arranged the chisels along the table, from smallest to biggest, and straightened their line with soft, short adjustments.

"I . . . I missed you," I admitted, careful to keep my voice neutral.

His smile neither faded nor deepened. "Ellerie," he started, and my sternum ached at his tone. His feelings had changed. Or I'd read too much into them in the first place, wistfully dreaming up things that were not mine to dream.

I crossed toward the door, intent on fleeing my embarrassment and shame.

"I've not been fair to you," he called out, stalling me. I didn't shift but could sense his approach. I had the distinct impression that he reached out, nearly touching the sharp curve of my shoulder blade, before having second thoughts. "I had a lot of time to think this winter, and . . . I won't be in Amity Falls forever. You know that, right?"

I nodded. "You've got the furs to sell . . . but you'll return when they have, won't you?" When I looked back, he seemed taller somehow, as if he'd spent the season growing fuller and wiser, while I'd shrunk smaller, tired and hollowed from the inside out. "Before fall?" I persisted. "Jean Garreau always did. He'd come back to set his traps and ready his camp and—"

Whitaker cupped my cheek, silencing me. "I don't know. The others . . . I don't have much say in it." He mustered a small laugh. "I'm making such a mess of this. . . . I came here to let you know that the winter drifts have finally thawed. The pass is open again."

"So you'll be leaving soon," I murmured, feeling my heart sink.

He nodded. "And I want you to come with me."

"What?"

He took my hands in his, the press of his fingers against mine pleading and fervent. "Let's leave this place. Leave the Falls. We could go anywhere, do anything. Sleep under the stars or stay at the finest hotels. There's so much of the world beyond God's Grasp. Let's go find it. Together."

His words painted such an alluring daydream, I was dizzy with the possibilities. I pictured promenading down a street in a far-off city, clutching Whitaker's arm as we marveled at the wonders in the shop windows, dressed in stylish clothes and laughing gaily. I imagined nights spent in a shared tent, falling asleep as we listened to spring peepers and each other's heartbeats, warm and safe in the security we'd created.

But when I glanced around the work shed, those thoughts faded away as reality came into sharper focus.

I smiled sadly. "That sounds lovely."

"But?" he guessed, feeling my words to come.

"What about Sadie? Merry? Who would look after them?"

"Your parents will be back soon. With the pass open, they could arrive any day now."

"With a new brother or sister," I said, praying that was true. "They'll need me here, especially with Sam gone." I took a deep swallow, wanting to cry. "I couldn't leave them like that."

He sighed, his gaze falling to the tight pledge our hands formed. "No, I suppose not."

I leaned into him, breathing his scent. "But . . . you could stay here. There's always work that needs to be done, and when Papa comes back . . . I know he values you. And he'd give us his blessing if . . ."

I stopped before I could pour out the tangled hopes I'd wished for all winter.

Whitaker taking my hand in his.

A pretty dress and a pair of rings.

A cabin of our own where we'd wake each morning, even more in love than the day before.

His gaze weighed heavily on me, but I couldn't bear to meet it lest he somehow read those tender, private thoughts flooding through me.

"I wish it was that easy."

"Why couldn't it be?"

"There are things I have to do—"

"Things?" I echoed.

He squirmed. "Debts that must be repaid."

"Debts?" I persisted stubbornly. I'd thought we were past his vague answers and half-formed explanations. I'd thought he'd finally begun to open more of himself up to me. I'd thought—

I'd thought a lot of things.

He raked his fingers through his hair, releasing a growl of frustration. "There are some things I can't share with you."

"Why?"

"Because I like you!" The words exploded from his chest like cannon fire. "Because I find myself falling in love with you, and I can't bear the thought that I'd say something to cause you to think less of me."

"You couldn't."

"I *could*. So easily. And I don't want to." His eyes closed as he grabbed at the bridge of his nose, warding off a headache.

"Why do you always do this?" I heard myself ask before I was even aware the words wanted to come out. "You can be so light and charming, but whenever something real comes up, whenever you have to admit a truth about yourself, you run away and hide behind these responses that don't mean anything. It's infuriating. I feel like I don't know anything about you, Whitaker," I said, keenly aware of the irony. "Not anything real. Not anything of substance."

"Come with me," he tried again. "Bring Sadie. Bring Merry. Hell, bring the bees if you can. Just come with me. I'll tell you everything you want to know. Later. I promise. Please, Ellerie."

"No. No later. Tell me now. Tell me one true thing, right now."

His eyes darted about, as if he was fighting a rising current and searching for anything to grab on to for help.

"I can't," he finally mumbled. "I can't."

"Of course." I pushed back a lock of hair, my hands trembling. What a waste.

What a stupid, stupid waste.

All of the fantasies and dreams I'd yearned for. All of the hopes I'd pinned upon him. Upon us. Upon a future together. I wanted to set fire to them all, burn out every idiotic notion that had ever dared to unfurl within me.

Shame flushed my cheeks, staining them hot.

Why couldn't I have seen through his charm? How could I have overlooked such glaring faults, allowing his evasions to seem mysterious and romantic when they were nothing more than a ruse to cover up a past I would never get to know? You couldn't get close to a person like that. You couldn't build a life on half-truths and artifice.

Every affectionate thought I'd ever had for him filled me with deep regret.

I'd been such a lovesick fool.

"When will you leave?" I asked, mustering as stoic a mask as I could. Better to end this conversation quickly, stamp out whatever was left of our friendship like a campfire left to smolder too long.

He looked disappointed, as though I'd asked a different question than the one he'd wanted to answer. "Soon, I imagine. If . . . if you change your mind . . ." He let out a sigh. "Please change your mind."

"I won't."

Stepping outside, I hoped I'd be able to breathe easily once more, but the wide expanse of sky seemed to press in, crushing me with its insistent blue.

Ezra strode across the yard, heading to the barn. He waved as he saw us but continued on his way. I was grateful he didn't stop to chat.

"Are you . . . Do you feel comfortable having them in the house?" Whitaker asked, watching Ezra pull open the barn doors with a wide swing.

"Do I—what?"

"Something has never set right with me about him."

"Why don't you go on and forget all about it, then?" I snapped. I couldn't bear to have a conversation with him now, acting as if everything was normal, acting as though he still cared.

"Ellerie." His tone was too warm, too familiar.

"Don't."

He sighed. "I just . . . What's he doing out there?"

"What does it matter?"

He shrugged. "You said the cow was dead, so he's not milking. Your garden looks planted, so he doesn't need any tools. What's he doing?"

"He keeps their supplies there. What was left after their wagon was ransacked."

"Like what?" he persisted. "What's out there that couldn't stay in the house?"

"It doesn't matter. You're just using Uncle Ezra to get out of talking about us."

"*Uncle* Ezra," he echoed with a strange inflection.

I turned to face him.

There was a moment when I thought he was going to reach out and take me in his arms. I'd almost welcome it. We'd embrace and I'd change my mind and the whole mess would be put behind us.

But he stayed still, feet rooted to the ground beneath him, his eyes impossibly sad.

"Goodbye, Ellerie Downing."

He didn't wait for my response; he trekked toward the pines and slipped into their dark grasp without a word from me.

I turned on shaky legs and let them carry me back to the farmhouse. I made it up the front steps before sinking into sobs.

29

"WE GATHER HERE TODAY TO MOURN THE PASSING OF Ruth Anne Mullins and to formally commit her remains to the earth," Parson Briard intoned, looking over the congregation with woeful, watery eyes. "Though her sudden departure saddens us, we rejoice in knowing her spirit has been freed of its terrestrial shackles and reunited with her beloved Stewart in the Kingdom of Heaven, where they shall worship before our Lord and Savior forevermore."

Throughout the church, noses sniffed and tears were pressed into beautifully decorated handkerchiefs—most of them embroidered by Old Widow Mullins herself. She'd had the loveliest needlework in all the Falls, having spent most of her days hunched over a wooden hoop. Her crooked fingers would dance through her supplies, taking obvious pleasure in the creations. The skeins of collected thread were so colorful and dazzling, her kit resembled more a treasure chest than a sewing box.

I wondered who would inherit it, now that she was gone.

Winthrop, probably, though I couldn't picture him knowing what to do with it.

I had often tagged along with Sam when he'd play at the Mullinses' house. Winthrop's parents had died young, leaving him to his grandmother's care. He'd had little patience for her gentler arts, and she, well into her seventies, hadn't had the energy to race after children. Their house had always been full of laughter and too many neighborhood boys, drawn to Winthrop and his endless supply of mischief.

There was a soft rustle across the aisle, and Simon and Rebecca Briard slipped into the pew, eyebrows drawn with contrition.

"Forevermore," the parson repeated, his train of thought momentarily derailed as he frowned admonishingly at his tardy son and daughter-in-law. "Let us pray."

Everyone's heads bowed as Parson Briard launched into his invocation, imploring God to grant mercy on Old Widow Mullins's soul and accept her into the Heavenly hereafter. To my left, Sadie squirmed uncomfortably, and I pressed her hands together in an attitude of prayer. My eyes darted over to Rebecca before I could stop myself.

I hadn't seen her in months, not since the morning she and Simon had come over, brimming with accusations. Judging from the curious looks of those surrounding her, no one else had seen her either. Her hands were spread wide over the outrageous curve of her belly, as if trying to somehow press it into a less conspicuous shape. The weight of the prying stares must have been unbearable.

At least Samuel wasn't here to add to her discomfort. Half a dozen of Judd Abrams's heifers had gone into labor, and the promised money was apparently too great an allurement for my twin. Merry had marched over to the ranch that morning and begged for him to come to the funeral with us. Old Widow Mullins had always been fond of Samuel, giving him one of her most prized handkerchiefs on his sixteenth birthday—yellow daffodils surrounding his initials. He'd snorted with derision when Merry had suggested he step away from the ranch on this one day to honor her.

After a short sermon, the parson invited anyone wishing to

share a memory to come to the front. Several of the older members of the Falls came forward, telling stories that best exemplified the widow's kindness and surprisingly wicked sense of humor.

"You should go up," I murmured to Ezra. He sat on the other side of me, shifting back and forth as if his collar was too tight.

"I wouldn't know what to say." He took off his spectacles and polished them as Cora Schäfer headed up.

"Papa and you were at her house all the time as boys," I said, recalling stories my father had told of afternoons spent running the then-not-widow ragged. "You used to play so many pranks on the poor woman, but she always laughed it off. Like the time you brought her that pie."

Ezra's lips rose, remembering.

"But it was just a tin of bees, covered in a cloth." I paused. "Papa said you were stung so many times."

He nodded. "What clowns we believed we were."

"Only . . ." I thought hard, a burr of importance prodding at me. The way Papa had told the story, Ezra had been stung so much on his backside, he could hardly sit the next day. "You're allergic to bees, though, aren't you?"

Ezra stilled, and though he kept his smile, a bit of wariness crept into his eyes.

"Well . . . after being stung that much, people develop allergies. It's a wonder I made it out alive, really."

Whitaker's concern washed over me. He'd insisted something was off with Ezra and Thomas. I'd thought he was only deflecting our conversation, but now I wondered if there wasn't more to it. Uneasiness pooled uncomfortably in the pit of my stomach.

"Well . . . if you don't want to talk about the pranks . . . why don't you say something about the quilt she made for you?" I said carefully, thinking of all the embroidery Widow Mullins had done for the Falls. It was a running joke that despite her pristine stitches,

ERIN A. CRAIG

she was a terrible quilter, never having the patience to create something so large and time-consuming. "Papa said she worked on it for months, trying to get the poppies just right."

"I could, I suppose," he said, but he remained planted in the pew. "It *was* a lovely quilt. Nice and warm on even the coldest nights."

I looked back to the front of the sanctuary, my heart galloping in my chest.

It was possible to develop an allergy later on in life, and I probably couldn't remember every gift ever given to me in childhood.

But why not come out and admit it?

Ezra's lies didn't prove anything exactly, but it also didn't look good.

I decided to try one last thing.

"What about the time when you and her daughter Betsy got caught out by the Greenswold? What was it she said to you?"

"Ellerie, my memories of her are from so long ago. I'd rather listen to those who knew her better."

"Well . . . we should at least give Betsy our condolences after the service," I pressed, waiting for him to guess my game.

"Absolutely." He nodded and turned his attention back to the front, unaware of my discomfort.

Old Widow Mullins had never had a daughter.

She'd had one son, Winthrop's father. Christopher. He and Ezra had been especially close before my uncle had disappeared.

It was possible to forget all sorts of things, but remembering a girl instead of your best friend seemed unlikely.

As Cora returned to her seat, Violet Buhrman slipped up the steps. She adjusted the collar of her dark shirtwaist with fidgety hands.

I tapped my foot unconsciously, hoping Violet would say her

piece quickly. I couldn't wrap my mind around everything, with so much noise going on around me. The stories, the sniffles. I needed somewhere quiet to think through why Ezra would lie.

Not Ezra, a tiny voice in my head whispered. *He's not Ezra.*

"Widow Mullins was a dear old soul, and she will be greatly missed," Violet began. "She was always kind to me and Calvin . . . and I think everyone knows Amity Falls will be a little less without her presence."

"Of that we can all agree," Parson Briard said, sensing the crowd's attention was beginning to flag.

"A true Christian woman," Violet continued. "Never putting others down, never judging—and she certainly wasn't too high and mighty to come have dinner or a drink at the tavern. Not like some."

Several people around me shifted in their seats, sneaking surreptitious glances at Prudence and Edmund Latheton. It was no secret the Lathetons were teetotalers and often butted heads with the tavern keepers.

I snuck a glance at Ezra, examining him with fresh eyes.

Martha McCleary had said he was the spitting image of my father, a Downing through and through, but as I studied his jawline and the curve of his cheekbones, even the shade of his hair, it was all wrong. A close approximation, but not quite right.

Violet's eyes burned brightly with anger, her fingers digging into the sides of the lectern. "Not like some," she repeated, "who would dare to take and destroy things that aren't theirs, who would hurt and maim defenseless animals."

"Animals?" The parson's echo was laced with confusion.

"That shrew murdered my nanny goat!" she screamed, sending a shock wave across the congregation. All my thoughts of Ezra disappeared as Violet struck her palm against the pulpit.

"My wife would never do such a thing!" Edmund Latheton said, jumping to his feet half a beat after Prudence prodded him in the ribs.

Parson Briard held up his hands. "Can you tell us what happened, Violet? I'm sure we can get to the bottom of this."

Her nose flared. "No need to get to the bottom of anything. I know who did it and I want retribution! The Elders need to—" She stopped short, looking about the sanctuary. "Where *are* the Elders?"

We looked about, noticing their absence.

"Amos said he'd be here soon," Martha McCleary answered. "Said something needed tending to."

The Elder had not been seen since the market day in February, and a dark conspiracy was whispered among some that Amos had died and the other Elders were covering it up, giving them time to plan for his successor.

"*We* have things that need tending to," Violet said, jumping onto the older woman's words. "Calvin—tell them!"

Her husband stood up, peering anxiously about the congregation. "It's true—someone did slaughter our goat in the night. When Violet went out to milk her this morning . . ." He swallowed deeply, unable to continue.

"I opened the door and was greeted by her head on a spike. Nearly scared me to death! Just like she wanted," Violet hissed, glowering at Prudence.

"That's an unfortunate situation—" Parson Briard began.

"'Unfortunate' doesn't even begin to cover it, Preacherman," Violet snapped.

"But you can't make accusations on conjecture and hearsay," the parson continued.

"I know it was them. Tell them about the hammer, Calvin! Tell them!"

He scratched at the back of his head. "The weapons were left behind. A handsaw and a strange little wooden hammer. Looks an awful lot like a carpentry mallet." He glanced meaningfully at Edmund.

"Those tools were stolen from my workshop weeks ago!" Edmund roared. "I haven't been able to finish any of my projects!"

Prudence narrowed her eyes. "I wouldn't be surprised if those two stole them, then killed the goat in the middle of a drunken escapade."

"Now, look you here—" Violet started, launching herself down the steps. Parson Briard caught her before she reached Prudence, and lashed his arm about her waist as she struggled. "Unhand me, Preacher! This isn't none of your concern!"

"By accusing Prudence Latheton in front of all of Amity Falls, you've made it my concern," he said, wincing as she threw a bony elbow into his gut. "Now, calm down and we'll discuss this like rational adults."

"There's nothing to discuss. I didn't do a damn thing!" Prudence insisted, fighting her way into the aisle. She charged up, pointing her finger like a dagger at the tavern mistress.

"Enough!" Parson Briard's voice boomed into the rafters. "Accusations and curses hurled in the house of the Lord! I will not tolerate it! Stand down before I throw both of you out myself!" He wiped a trembling hand over his ruddy cheeks. "This is no way to behave, not here, not ever. May I remind you you're at a funeral? What would Ruth Anne say if she could see what's going on?"

Violet pressed her lips together, looking almost remorseful.

Prudence folded her arms across her chest, clearly unwilling to let the matter die away. "She'd be appalled," she quipped. "Just as I am. I came here to mourn the passing of my good friend—"

Winthrop let out a soft snort. The Mullinses and the Lathetons had openly squabbled over minor annoyances for years.

"My very good friend," Prudence insisted, more loudly on her second attempt. "And this is how I'm treated? I won't stand for it."

She turned on a sharp heel and stormed out of the church without a backward glance. After a moment's pause, Edmund excused himself from the pew and trailed silently after his wife. The door closed behind him with a dull thud that settled over us all as we uncomfortably waited to see what would happen next.

Parson Briard trudged to the pulpit. Running fingers over the open Bible, he took one deep breath, then another, as if struggling to recall what he was meant to be doing.

"I know . . . ," he began, then cleared his throat. "I know tensions, and nerves, have been . . . frayed as of late." He smiled at his understatement. "We've all suffered unimaginable hardships this winter. Lack of supplies, failed crops." He let out a small, humorless laugh. "There was certainly no shortage of trials. Which is why . . ." He paused, thinking. "Which is why my family and I would like to host a social, this Saturday, on the town green, to celebrate the resilience of the Falls. We will roast chickens and a pig and . . . invite anyone able to bring their favorite dish to pass and share." He brightened. "Thaddeus McComb—will you lend us your fiddle?"

The farmer nodded.

"Excellent. There will be songs and dancing, a true celebration of God's unfailing abundance." His face was radiant with inspiration. Then he faltered a step, looking out over the sea of black mourning clothes. "If no one else has any other words . . . we will now adjourn to the burial site."

⚜

Mounds of freshly turned dirt dotted the sacred ground of the church cemetery, reminders of all the townsfolk who had not made it through the winter. The earth had been too frozen for the bodies to be buried, so they'd been kept in a little shed farther down on church property, waiting for spring.

So many people had been buried in the last month, there had been no coffins ready when Widow Mullins had died, and hers had had to be hastily assembled. The wood was so green, it still bled sap as the four pallbearers carried it to the site. Corey Pursimon tried to wipe the sticky residue from his hands after they'd lowered the box into the gaping maw, and ruined his best dress pants.

"We shall all receive the due reward of our deeds," Parson Briard said, casting a gimlet eye over all who'd gathered. It landed and lingered on Violet Buhrman, appraising her thoughtfully.

Winthrop Mullins, eyes red and wet, was the first to throw in a handful of dirt.

It landed on the pine box with a thud as loud as cannon fire, signaling the start of the burial. We all came forward to say one final prayer at the foot of the widow, then scooped up a handful of rich black earth and dropped it into the depths. With quick work, the coffin was covered, and most of the townspeople headed to the Gathering House for a shared luncheon, leaving the heavier work for Simon Briard to finish.

"Let's go home," Merry said, watching the crowd wander away. "I'm exhausted, and now we've got to make something for a picnic, tomorrow? Doesn't the parson know no one has anything to make?"

"We can think about it on the way home," I said, privately agreeing with her.

"Oh," Ezra murmured, waylaying us as we slipped out of the graveyard. "Ellerie, you wanted to speak with Betsy Mullins, didn't you?"

"Who?" Sadie asked, cocking her head curiously at him.

Ezra's expression faltered for a quick second, and as our eyes met, recognition flickered over his face.

He knew I knew.

But *what* was it that I knew?

Ezra had lied about so many things. Things he should have known.

Things he should have known if he was . . .

If he was Ezra.

"It's fine," I said with a forced smile. "I'm sure I'll see her at the social."

The man who was not my uncle nodded and stepped through the gate, heading back toward our farmhouse.

He said something to Merry to make her laugh, and as I watched them go, a dark bloom of dread unfurled within my chest.

If he was not the man we'd assumed he was, if he was not Ezra, not my uncle, not a Downing, then who the devil was he?

30

"LUNCH?" SADIE ASKED HOPEFULLY THE MOMENT WE returned home.

I started toward the kitchen, then stopped. I ought to change out of my black dress first.

I turned for the loft but stopped again.

I didn't want to be here. I didn't want to be around anyone. I needed a moment to myself, but the house felt fuller than ever.

Ezra wasn't who he claimed to be.

Which meant Thomas wasn't either.

"Is there anything we can do to help, Ellerie?" my not-uncle asked, standing in the middle of the doorway, appraising me.

Neither of them were who they said they were, and I—an absolute fool—had welcomed them into our home with open arms.

I shook my head and changed my mind again, going into the kitchen. I backed into Thomas and nearly jumped out of my skin.

They were everywhere, impossible to escape.

"How about scrambled eggs?" Merry offered, giving me a strange look.

She was worried.

Good.

"With the mushrooms I found yesterday," Sadie suggested.

Merry shook her head. "I threw them out this morning. They were already black with rot."

Her face fell.

"I know," I began, my voice sounding octaves too high. "I think I saw a couple of jars of Mama's bean soup in the barn. Where Papa was storing the extra stock. I'll grab one."

Merry had to have known I was lying. We'd scoured every inch of the farm looking for supplies when we'd drawn up our first inventory. The barn had been empty of food.

I hated to speak falsely, but I couldn't stand to be trapped in the house any longer. I needed to think. Needed to plan.

How would I get these men out of our home?

"Why don't you come with me?" I asked, trying to steady my tone. I was certain Ezra knew something was wrong. "It would be good to have you hold the ladder, Merry." I froze, realizing this left Sadie with the strangers, all on her own. "And, Sadie . . . the hens need their lunch. Will you check for eggs while you're out there too?"

With a heavy sigh, she swanned out of the room, snatching her basket as she left.

"We'll be right back," I promised, giving Ezra my best smile.

"There's no soup out here," Merry said as I swung the barn door shut behind us. "What are you doing?"

"There's a trunk in here someplace." I raced over to where Ezra and Thomas had stacked their supplies.

The curious little crate Ezra had swiped away from me was gone.

"Ellerie, we can't look through their things!" Merry hissed.

"Keep an eye out, will you?" I tore open one of the rucksacks. Then another. Perhaps they'd stored it there, out of sight. "Do you remember seeing that small crate Ezra was so possessive of when they first arrived? The one with all the things carved into its top?"

"I—I don't." She looked away from the window. "Ellerie, stop—just tell me what's going on."

"We need to find it," I said, upending the last bag. Clothing and boots fell out, but no box.

"Why?"

I let out a strangled howl. It wasn't here.

"Ellerie, please!" She left her post and grabbed my elbow, forcing me to look at her.

"That's not Uncle Ezra," I said, deflating as every ounce of fight fled. "Or Cousin Thomas. I don't . . . I don't think we have a cousin. Or an uncle, for that matter."

Her eyebrows furrowed together. "Of course we do. Papa has talked about Ezra for—"

"But that's not Ezra. He lied, Merry. He's lying now."

"But . . . if he's not our uncle . . . then who is he?"

"I don't know. I was so certain the trunk would tell us. The way he grabbed it from me. . . . There must be something important inside."

Her eyes slid from mine, and she drifted from me. My chest burned with a spike of fear. She was about to run back to the house and tell of my treacherous ideas. What would they do to us when their secret was exposed?

"You mean . . . that crate?"

She pointed up to the loft, where a bit of the box's corner peeked out from a pile of straw.

There it was, irrefutable proof. Ezra had left all his other things out in the open but had taken pains to hide that. That crate had to hold something damning.

We went up the ladder and rustled through the hay until I felt the trunk. I tugged it free, bringing it out into a ray of sunlight beaming through a hole in the roof I'd clearly need to patch before the spring rains set in.

If the spring rains ever set in.

"E-E-F," I said, reading the initials carved on the trunk's lid. "He might be an Ezra, but he's certainly not a Downing."

Merry stared uneasily at the box. "That could belong to someone else. . . . Perhaps he bought it secondhand—or is borrowing it from a relative."

"We're supposed to be his relatives," I reminded her.

I ran my fingers over a set of carvings done just above the latches.

Two lanterns.

The one on the left was dark and still, but the one on the right had been lit and was casting its light into the world.

"Should we open it?" I asked, suddenly hesitant.

What if I was wrong? So he'd hidden the box? He didn't know us any more than we knew him. Perhaps this held his money or important documents. Things you wouldn't want to leave about in a house full of nieces.

Opening this could shatter any trust we had between us.

But he lied, I reminded myself. *He didn't know things he should have, and rather than admit that, he lied.*

With a burst of confidence, I flipped the latches. Before I could open the lid, a hand fell heavily onto my shoulder, and the fingers curved around my collarbone as if to hold me back.

As Ezra peered down at me, I knew exactly how a squirming mouse felt, caught in the sight of a great horned owl. I wanted to run, but there was no way to leave. The only path into and out of the loft was the ladder he stood in front of.

"I—we—" I glanced at Merry. Her mouth hung open and her eyes were wide with fear.

"Just know," he said, his voice low and even, "I will explain everything."

He wasn't angry. If anything, his eyes looked sorrowful, deep with repentance. That sent a wave of trepidation over me that settled just under my skin, persistent and chilling. My fingertips danced over the symbols. "What are these?"

"Lanterns," Thomas said, stepping out of the shadows. They must have climbed the ladder while we were looking for the box, too intent on our quest to hear their footfalls. "To help light the darkness."

I knew without a trace of doubt that he meant something beyond an absence of sunlight.

A cold sweat prickled at my neck. "What's inside the box, Ezra?"

He didn't blink. He didn't move. I couldn't even see him breathing, so frozen were we in this awful, horrible moment. "Open it and find out."

At first it looked like nothing more than a simple medicine crate. The bottom was divided into sections, and every square held a corked glass bottle. Folded papers and a few thin journals were tucked into the top bands of the lid. Ink had bled through the backs of the pages, but the handwriting was too spidery to read. Along the side of the box was a deep compartment, crammed with an assortment of silver. Chains and medallions, crosses and bells. There were even a few stray bullets. They all nestled together in a twisted tangle, glimmering with dull luster.

"What is all this?" I pulled a vial free, watching as a silvery liquid danced against its confinement. The last bit of a faded label clung valiantly to its side, showing a hasty rendering of three crosses. "Holy water?"

Ezra shook his head. "It's a bit more special than that. And much more potent. There's a hidden catch on the side of the crate. If you press it . . ." He fidgeted with his glasses. "Everything you need to see is in there."

After a moment of fumbling, I released the hidden compartment running along the bottom. It was full of papers and notebooks, a series of sketches, and journal entries.

Flipping through them, I took in a sharp breath.

Shadowy figures with wide-brimmed hats smudged the pages, their eye sockets left empty so that the blank paper seemed to glow with an eerie sheen.

"What . . . what are those things?" I whispered, scanning more pages. The notes were in a jumbled combination of English and Latin, too complex for me to make sense of, but I understood the pictures.

Mostly.

Beasts of myths and lore were rendered with a startling, lifelike quality, every bit as detailed as the drawings in Papa's field guides—as if these things had been scientifically studied and catalogued with a meticulous hand. Water snakes with fangs and flared nostrils swam alongside boats whose crews were dwarfed by the serpentine monsters. Angry elfin men, with hooked nails and webbed fingers, leered off the page, their barbed tails nearly hidden in a haze of smoky pencil lead. A cloaked figure, too tall to be human, lurked in a forest glade, a glowering antlered skull for its face.

There was a small set of initials in the picture's corner.

EEF, dated only months before.

"Is this . . . What is . . . I don't understand." Rational words failed me. I wanted to justify these away as the wild imagination of a skilled scientist, as doodled daydreams gone horribly wrong. They were the ideas for a story, for a book, for *something.* They could not be real.

These *things* were not real.

"What are they? What do they do?" I paused uneasily, feeling as if I was asking the wrong questions. "What are *you*?"

He let out a sigh, a slow hiss like the release of steam on canning day. "I'm sure you've figured it out by now, but I am not your uncle. My name is not 'Ezra.'" He tapped at the initials on the crate. "My name is Ephraim Ealy Fairhope. And I'm from England." His voice changed, altering into a more melodic cadence. One I'd heard before.

I turned toward Thomas. "And you?"

"My name *is* Thomas," he said, dropping his trumped-up accent. "That much is true. And Ephraim is my father. I'm just not your cousin."

"We've been sent here on a research expedition. When we stumbled across your farm, that day with the wolf, and Martha McCleary mistook me for Ezra . . . it seemed like the perfect chance to become part of the town, learn all we could. Usually when we arrive somewhere new—strangers in a strange land, as it were—it can be harder to find out what we need to know."

My muscles ached as I listened to him, frozen in a strange motionless state, yet poised to fly if an escape attempt proved necessary. "What . . . what exactly is it that you need to know?"

"Strange occurrences about town, in the forests. Unusual crops, unusual weather. Mutations in livestock. Unexplained mysteries."

"Amity Falls has had all of those things."

He nodded. "We know."

Merry shifted. "Do you think . . . is there something that's causing it?"

He nodded again and stepped forward, then flipped the sketchbook back to the dark shadows with the hollowed eyes.

Eyes like Prudence Latheton claimed to have seen.

Eyes like Cyrus Danforth had shouted about all the way to the Gallows.

Eyes like those that haunted my brother.

Eyes that I had seen myself.

That was a dream, insisted the tiny voice within me.

I turned the page, trying to read the notes scrawled along the edges of the drawings. "The . . . Dark Watchers?" Ephraim didn't move a muscle, but the look on his face told me I'd translated it correctly. "What are they?"

"Creatures that look like you and me—most of the time—but they can assume other forms when needed. They're fast. They're cunning. Their very presence in an area can change the world around them. Morphing it, altering it. Things that should be pure and good become twisted and wrong."

"The stag," I said, remembering the misshapen creature the McNally boys had killed. "It had too many horns, too many hooves."

"Exactly." He took my hand, pressing it between his, his face worried and earnest. "Thomas and I . . . we belong to the Brotherhood of the Light. Those lanterns are our sigil. For centuries, the Brotherhood has sought to hold back the darkness of the world with knowledge. We study these creatures—and others—to learn how to stop them."

"Stop them? From what?"

"Destroying this town," Thomas said softly.

Ephraim peered through his glasses, squinting as if a smudge bothered him. To his credit, he left them on. "Dark Watchers thrive on discord. They've often been linked to terrible events around the world. For many years it was thought they could sense a tragedy before it occurred and were drawn to it—like ships to a beacon."

"But now?" I pressed.

"We think they actually instigate the events leading up to the disasters."

"Instigate?" Merry echoed. "How?"

"When they first arrive, Dark Watchers ingratiate themselves into the life of their new town, watching, learning all they can, to set up . . . well . . . a game for themselves. It always starts small, with little harmless pranks. You might have a hairbrush go missing, tools found in a different place than you left them."

I wrinkled my nose. "That sounds so childish." I held up the sketch skeptically. "These creatures are really out there moving things around in houses?"

Thomas shook his head. "No. No. *They* don't do anything. They have others carry out the acts. People in town."

I shook my head. It made no sense. "Why would anyone go along with that?"

"It's all part of a trade. The person gets something they want, something they desire, and the Dark Watchers have a new pawn."

"I don't see the fun in it for them."

"The pranks are efficiently designed. Frustrations build. Accusations are cast upon innocent people. Disagreements turn to arguments. Arguments into fights. And soon the whole village is tearing at the seams."

"Why would anyone want to watch that?" Merry asked.

Ezra—Ephraim—shook his head helplessly. "It's just their nature."

I closed the journal, eager to get rid of the disquieting pictures. "What are we to do?"

"*We* are doing nothing," Ephraim said. "Thomas and I are keeping a close watch on the town. This is the first time we've been able to watch one of their games unfold. We've always been a step or two behind, always coming across the aftermath. To see them in action, at work . . . this could prove very useful for the Brotherhood."

"And you're going to stop them," Merry supplied, filling in what he hadn't said. "Right?"

There was a sliver of hesitation before he answered. "Yes, of course."

My sister and I shared a worried look.

"How?" Merry asked. "You've never even seen them before, but you—"

"That's true, but—"

"I have," I said. "I thought it was a dream, but I'm starting to worry it was a great deal more than that."

Ephraim frowned. "What do you mean? Who did you see?"

"It was a woman, dressed all in white. She had long dark hair and horrible silvery eyes. And her hands—"

He sucked in a sharp breath. "The Queen."

"Queen?" Merry repeated.

"They're a hive, of sorts. Just like your bees. They take their orders from one head, doing everything they can to serve the good of their group." He turned back to me. "You must tell me exactly what happened."

I recounted the dream, backtracking to explain who Cyrus had been, what he'd claimed to have seen before his Judgment. I told them of the times when I'd seen the wisp of white walking through the fields, lighting an Our Lady. I even confessed my fears that I'd had something to do with the schoolhouse fire, however impossible it seemed.

Ephraim's face was grave as I finished my tale. "You well might have. But . . ." He took off his glasses and wiped at his eyes before returning them. "When you saw her, before this dream, did she ever speak to you?"

I shook my head. "She was always so far away."

He sighed. "You never spoke to her? Never struck up a trade?"

"No."

"It . . . it *could* have been a dream, Father," Thomas allowed.

"With so many awful things going on throughout the valley, I shouldn't wonder their sleep has been affected."

"But the school *did* burn," Ephraim insisted. "That's an awfully large coincidence. . . . Someone had to have lit that match."

My stomach sloshed with guilt that I wasn't sure I'd earned.

"We need to do more research," he decided. "Clemency announced the social for tomorrow?"

Merry nodded.

"I propose we all attend, keeping up the Ezra Downing charade. With so many townspeople gathered together, I'm certain the Dark Watchers will be nearby. But," he added, raising a sharp finger of warning, "neither of you should mention this to anyone outside this barn."

I frowned, glancing out the small loft window to the chicken coop below. "We have to tell Sadie. We can't leave her in the dark about something so—"

"That's exactly why we need to stay silent. We can't afford to tip our hand. The only advantage we have against these fiends is our element of surprise. They don't know we know," Ephraim said firmly. "We need to keep it that way. For tomorrow at least." He looked toward Merry, then Thomas. "Shall we all swear to it?"

They nodded readily, but I remained still.

"What's your plan for tomorrow? We go to the social and . . . what, exactly?"

"We watch. We glean every scrap of information we can. See what disputes break out. See where the frictions are. I'm positive everything will lead us directly to the Dark Watchers."

"And then we . . . we kill them?" I hazarded to guess.

Ephraim looked queasy at the prospect. "You see now the necessity of keeping the matter quiet, don't you?"

I didn't like not telling Sadie. She needed to know, needed

to be warned. It felt as though I was somehow lying to her. A lie of omission.

But I could also understand Ephraim's reticence. She was eight. All it would take was a whisper of her prized secret to Trinity Brewster, and suddenly the entire town would be abuzz with the story.

After a moment, I agreed.

"Excellent. It's settled, then." Ephraim shifted his voice back to Ezra's accent. "Tomorrow the Downings shall be front and center at the Falls's social."

31

ONE SACK OF FLOUR.

A bowl of eggs, gathered fresh from the henhouse that morning.

Two apples so shriveled, they hardly deserved the title.

A few spices, nearly petrified and probably without flavor.

I drummed my fingers on the kitchen table, eyeing each ingredient with disdain. We were due to leave for the social in a few hours, and I couldn't come up with a single idea for a dish to bring.

Mama always brought a honey cake, but I had no honey, no cream, and certainly no sugar.

If everything had been normal, I would have sliced up green beans, simmered them with little white onions and fat cuts of bacon, but without the usual spring rains, our seedlings had withered and shriveled.

A custard, perhaps, I thought, staring at all those eggs. It wasn't a dish anyone would ever expect to see at a picnic, but it truly was all we could spare.

But what would I flavor it with?

I pushed the jars of spices about, eyeing the mustard seeds.

Deviled eggs it would be.

I set to work, boiling the eggs.

"You're not wearing that, are you?" Merry asked, coming up behind me.

"I'll change before we leave." From the corner of my eye, I caught a swish of her blue check skirt. It was her best dress and only came out for the most special of occasions. "Pretty."

"Does it look all right?" she asked. "I thought I'd done well, but Sadie said I look like a clown."

I turned. Bright circles of pink dotted her peach complexion. "Oh. What did you use?" I asked, drawing her over to the wash-basin. After dampening a handkerchief with water, I removed half the offending color from her cheeks, leaving behind a more subtle blush.

"There's a cluster of thimbleberries down by the creek—they're not ripe enough to eat yet," she added quickly, seeing my hopes rise. "But I thought I could use one or two for today. I just remember how Papa would tell stories about when he fell in love with Mama. . . ." She pushed back a ringlet of hair framing her face, uncomfortably self-conscious. I studied the new curls with pained understanding. She must have spent nearly an hour at the hearth, bullying her stick-straight hair into this softer style with Mama's old curling rods.

"The Schäfers' wedding reception. He spotted her across the churchyard, through a haze of fabric banners."

"And even though he'd grown up alongside her his whole life," Merry jumped in, taking on Papa's familiar cadence.

"He was still surprised to see the pretty girl with the pink cheeks and the sparkling eyes," we finished together.

She smiled shyly, toying with the curls again. "I miss them."

"Me too," I admitted.

"I thought they'd be home by now. It's nearly summer."

I agreed but didn't want to say it out loud. Each day that went by without their arrival soured my stomach. Where were they?

Had something happened to Mama? Or to their wagon as they returned? I tried to not picture it, but as I lay in bed at night, just on the cusp of sleep, horrible images would fill my mind.

Papa, wandering alone and bereft in a city too big and busy for his grief . . . Mama trapped beneath the heavy axle of a torn-apart wagon, unable to reach our little brother, his cries filling the surrounding woods, the pines red with sprays of blood.

And now . . . knowing there were monsters—real, actual monsters—in the trees . . .

Had the Dark Watchers gotten our parents?

"Is there someone whose eye you're hoping to catch today?" I asked, forcing away my gruesome reverie. I longed to return to a time when our biggest problem of the day was Sadie upsetting Merry's tender feelings.

"Of course not," she lied, flustered. "There are far bigger things to worry about today than boys."

"Merry."

"Thomas," she disclosed quickly, a flush rising to her cheeks, burning even more brightly than the thimbleberries. "I know— *I know*," she protested, even as I said nothing. "He was our cousin up until yesterday. But . . . even before that, I'd catch him staring at me, and I wondered . . . There was just something not very cousin-like in those stares, you know? But it's stupid to be thinking of that." Her gaze flickered to outside, toward the pines, and I knew she was trying to spot a Dark Watcher. "I just thought . . . it would be nice to be ready . . . in case anyone decides to notice me."

"Oh, Merry," I murmured, pulling her into a hug. I kissed the top of her blond head. "I'm certain there will be a whole lot of young men noticing you today. And if Thomas doesn't see how special you are, he's a fool."

"You should go get ready," she said, flushed but pleased. "I'll finish up in here . . ." She paused, studying the ingredients, then sighed. "Really? Deviled eggs?"

I ran my hand over the bodice of my dress, smoothing the pin tucks and adjusting the ruffled collar. It was my first time wearing the blush-colored voile Whitaker had brought back from the city. The dress had turned out even better than I'd dreamed it would. I took a practice spin. The long lengths of dotted Swiss swirled about my ankles in a delightful froth.

I only wished Whitaker was here to see it. When I imagined dancing with a young man at the social, it was his arms I was in.

No.

I cast such foolish thoughts away as quickly as jerking a hand from a sizzling skillet. Memories of him burned just as hot but with far more destruction.

Footsteps echoed up the stairwell.

"Merry?" I called out. "I can't get the last button clasped. Can you help me?"

She didn't respond.

"Sadie?" I tried. "It's almost time to leave. Did you change into your calico?"

The footsteps paused.

"I can come back later if you . . . Oh, Ellerie Downing."

I froze, every hair on my arms rising to attention as I recognized that voice. I looked in the mirror, and there he was, standing behind me as though my thoughts had summoned him.

"Whitaker?" It came out as soft as a breath.

"You are so, so beautiful."

I turned.

He looked . . . longer somehow. Weeks of traveling had worn him down. He was tired, leaner.

He was still the most perfect boy I'd ever seen.

"What are you doing here?"

"I couldn't miss seeing you in your new dress," he said, a ghost of a smile lighting his face. "I was right. That is the perfect shade for you."

A charming deflection.

Of course.

He pressed his lips into a sober line, as if sensing my thoughts. "I . . . I realized I made a mistake."

I fought the urge to cross my arms over my chest. "Really?"

He nodded reluctantly. "I should have been more open with you. Should have told you . . . I should have told you so many things. I . . . I wanted to come back and set things right, El-lerie."

It was everything I'd wanted to hear. Everything I hoped for, in the dark of night when I found myself unable to sleep, remembering our last conversation and wishing I'd said so many things differently.

Even still, I hesitated to believe him.

"Then start with something simple," I challenged. "What's your name?"

He sighed. "I don't want to talk about my name right now."

"You don't want to talk about anything ever," I reminded him, irritation flaring in my throat. "If you thought coming back would be such a grand gesture that I'd forget everything else, you were mistaken."

My heart ached even as it knew I spoke the truth.

"That . . . that wasn't all. I wanted to tell you . . ."

"What?" I snapped. I took a step forward, showing him—showing myself—I could be in his presence without running into his arms.

Whitaker scratched his neck. "I . . ."

"What, Whitaker? Tell me this one thing. No excuses. No tactics. Just answer me."

"I . . ." He jangled his fingers in a flurry of suppressed motion. "I realized . . . I care about you, Ellerie. Deeply. Maddeningly. And I . . . I don't know what to do and I'm obviously getting it completely wrong, but I couldn't bear the thought of leaving you, of leaving you here, not knowing how much I love . . ."

My heart stilled even as Whitaker trailed off with a sigh.

"So I came back, and now I don't . . . I don't know what I'm doing." He looked up to the ceiling. "I've made a giant mess of this all, but I know . . . I would rather be here, with you hating me, than anywhere else in the world."

His open confession stunned me. It wasn't the truth I'd expected from him, but it was a start.

It was a good start.

"I don't . . . I don't hate you," I murmured carefully.

"You don't?"

"I couldn't."

He frowned, fighting hope. "Why?"

I wanted to bridge the distance between us, but my feet were planted to the floorboards, roots deep and unyielding. "I . . . I care about you too much to ever hate you."

He let out a breath. "You do?"

"Deeply. Maddeningly, even." His words tasted bittersweet on my tongue. "But that doesn't mean I'm ready to forget everything."

"Oh."

I'd wounded him.

"I . . . This is a lot to think over."

He lowered his eyes. "Of course."

"I'll need some time."

And time was something I had very little of at present.

"I . . . I don't suppose you'll have thought everything over by the social?" He swallowed uncomfortably as his attempt at light-heartedness fell flat.

"You shouldn't go to that." I tried keeping my voice even but firm. It pained me to keep secrets from Whitaker, but it wasn't as if he was ever entirely forthcoming with me. This leveled out the field a bit.

After a beat, he nodded, amber eyes full of sorrow. "If that's what you want."

It wasn't. Not really. Inside my chest, my heart screamed out his name so loudly, he must have heard it. But I bobbed my head. "I think it best. For now."

"I should get going, then. Let you finish . . ." He gestured toward the mirror. "All that."

He turned to leave but then changed directions, striding across the room in the blink of an eye. Surprised, I stepped backward, catching my foot on the corner of the bedpost.

He caught my elbow, steadying me, and for the longest second, we gazed into each other's eyes.

"I mean it, Ellerie. You look so terribly beautiful."

He reached out with tentative fingers, cupping my cheek, his touch lighter than a warm summer rain.

I should have pushed him away, righting myself. Should have stormed off to sort out my confusion far, far away from the alluring glint of his eyes.

But he was so warm.

He was warm and solid and so impossibly strong. I grasped his shoulders, our faces close enough for me to feel the soft caress of his breath. His fingers curved at the nape of my neck, sinking into the curls, and a maddening need seized me, aching to forget the fight, forget my anger, forget everything that had gone wrong between us.

Before I could do any of those things, Whitaker was off, pressing a tender kiss to my forehead and disappearing down the stairwell.

32

THE SUN STREAMED DOWN, BRIGHT AND SPARKLING AS we made our way to the town square. Soaring oak trees bordered its edge, providing ample shade, and colorful pennants hung swagged throughout their branches, forming a festive bower. Beneath their zenith, Thaddeus McComb and his sons tuned their fiddles, preparing for the dancing to come, and all around us, people were laughing and happy. I couldn't remember the last time I'd seen so many smiling faces in town.

The star of the day turned slowly on a spit, and the mouthwatering scent of roasted pork made my stomach growl with anticipation.

It couldn't have been a more perfect day.

The potluck was laid out across two tables dressed with Letitia Briard's best tablecloths. I ran an appreciative finger across one of the floral batistes. Though I knew it was wicked of me, I envied her collection.

Merry snuck our plate of deviled eggs between offerings of custards and quiches with an amused smirk.

"God bless the fine hens of Amity Falls," Parson Briard proclaimed, coming over to inspect the feast. His laughter boomed over the town square. It faded as he caught sight of the Fairhopes, hanging back from the tables and keenly aware of the many eyes upon them. "Ezra, Thomas. Good to see you both." He shook their hands before turning to us. "And, ladies, how well you all look."

Pleased to have her new hand-me-down dress noticed, Sadie spun in a circle, showing off the full skirts with a giggle. Merry smiled up at the parson, taming back a strand of hair.

"Is that a new frock I spy, Miss Ellerie?" he asked.

"It is. I made it myself over the winter."

"What a unique color. Lovely, lovely," he repeated, distracted as more families arrived. "Enjoy the social."

"You made that?" Thomas asked. "All those little . . . what are those called?" he asked, gesturing to my bodice.

"Pin tucks."

"Pin tucks." He pronounced it carefully, tasting the sound of it. "I like knowing the proper names for things. The world truly seems more ordered when you know what to call everything, doesn't it?"

"It does," I admitted.

Sadie ran off, giggling and screeching with glee, the second she saw Trinity and Pardon. I helped Merry spread our quilt over a sun-dappled patch of grass. My heart twinged as I traced over the tiny lines of Mama's stitches.

"Oh, you've got something caught in your hair," Merry said, gently tousling my locks as she worked to free the squirming intruder. "There." A ladybug crawled over her hand, twining round and round her fingers.

Thomas leaned in to see. "Coccinellidae. Seven spots too." He smiled at me. "You've been touched by luck—feel any different?"

"I'll let you know if I do."

"You really can never have too much luck, you know," Ephraim mentioned, settling into a comfortable spot. He took the ladybug from Merry. "I always keep a four-leaf clover on me—just to be safe."

"So, Ezra . . . Ephraim . . ." I still was uncertain what I was supposed to call him. "What exactly are we looking for today?"

He raised his finger, letting the ladybug fly away, then squinted around the square. "We're observing. Looking for things out of the ordinary. You know this town better than us. You're more likely to see where things look different, look wrong." He paused, waiting until Bonnie Maddin and her circle of friends crossed by. "And of course . . . if you happen to see that woman, you let me know."

Hushed murmurs rose around us, growing in strength as everyone turned to see Amos and Martha McCleary making their way up the hill to join the picnic.

"He's better," someone whispered.

"He's . . . *alive*." I turned to see Alice Fowler, her jaw slack with wonder.

Amos nearly danced up the hill, smiling and waving and moving like a man twenty years his junior. He still relied on his cane, but his free arm assisted Martha with the climb. His skin had lost its sickly pallor and glowed with robust heartiness.

"Amos, Martha," Parson Briard greeted, crossing to the couple. "We're so happy you could join us."

"Wouldn't miss it for the world, Preacherman." Amos's voice was strong and clear, without a trace of wheeziness. "You can smell that hog all the way across town!"

"You're looking much improved," Briard started carefully.

"I feel like a new man!" Amos said, giving the parson a cheerful smack on the back. He took a deep breath, boisterously filling his chest as if to prove he could.

"Excellent, excellent."

"Martha brought a custard," Amos continued. "Where should we put it?"

The parson ushered them toward the buffet tables. We watched with interest until a shadow fell across our quilt.

"Ellerie Downing. I can't believe your gall."

Letitia Briard stood at the edge of our blanket, her hands pressed to her hips and a dangerous glint sparkling in her eyes. "I knew the thief would show themselves eventually, but I never would have dreamed it would be you!"

"Thief?" I echoed in confusion. "What are you talk—"

"That's my dress!" she snapped. Her nostrils flared, making her narrow nose look even more pinched than before.

"It's not," I protested, though her accusation caught me so off guard, I had to glance down to be certain. "I made this. This winter. My sisters saw me design and cut it myself."

"With cloth you stole from me!"

I shook my head, acutely aware of the attention her outburst was drawing. Prudence Latheton and her circle of friends stared with rapt attention. "You're mistaken, Mrs. Briard. This voile came from the city."

"It did! It came back with Jeb McCleary's spring run. Specially ordered. I was going to make curtains with it last summer, but when I went to bring it in off the wash lines, it was gone." Her voice cracked. "Clemency said the wind must have carried it off. But I knew—*I knew*—it was stolen."

I raised my shoulders helplessly. "I don't know what to tell you. It was a gift. Whitaker brought it back after he helped Mama and Papa get to town."

"Lies!"

Ephraim held up his hand, trying to defuse her anger. "I'm sure there must be an explanation for all of this. Ellerie says she was given it, and I've never known her to lie. Perhaps we ought to be asking Whitaker where he acquired it?"

The parson's wife scoffed. "As if we'd get the truth from a trapper."

In a flash, Parson Briard was at her side, fingers circling her elbow. "Is everything quite all right here?"

"I found her, Clemency!" she hissed, picking at the fullness of my skirt and swishing the fabric about. "I found the thief!"

He glanced at my dress. "Can you prove with absolute certainty that it's yours?" he asked his wife.

Her mouth set into an unhappy line. "Well, no, but—"

"Then let it alone, Letitia. We will deal with this later."

"But—"

"Not now," he hissed. "Have you forgotten there's a social going on?"

With a final glower toward me, she turned on her heel and marched past her husband, heading for the parsonage.

"Perhaps I ought to make sure she's all right," Prudence volunteered. Her skirts kicked up a cloud of dust behind her.

"I'm terribly sorry for that," Parson Briard said, fixing his attention on me. "The strain of the winter has taken its toll on Letitia. I'm certain she meant no harm. It was a simple mistake." He nodded, more for his benefit than mine. "Her fabric was a darker pink. Yes, I'm sure it was."

"Are you all right?" Ephraim asked once the parson had left and was loudly greeting Matthias Dodson with a laugh so boisterous, it rang false.

"I'm fine. It's fine." Though it was balmy out, I rubbed at my arms, chilled by the encounter. I couldn't forget the look of contempt in Letitia's eyes, the glint of scorn and hatred. "That . . . all of that . . . felt wrong."

He glanced toward the pines.

"Do you think they're there now? Watching?" I asked, following his gaze.

"I'm certain they are. Somewhere."

❧

"Good Blessings, Amity Falls," Parson Briard called out from the makeshift stage, hushing the merriment.

"What a wonderful day, full of the Lord's bounty." He pulled out a small Bible and flipped it to its ribbon marker. "I thought, perhaps, we might spend a bit of time with the Word before the feast begins."

He launched into his sermon without another comment, reading from Matthew, holding his Bible aloft and jabbing his finger to the page as he enunciated each syllable.

"'And the King shall answer and say unto them, Verily I say unto you, Inasmuch as ye have done it unto one of the least of these my brethren, ye have done it unto me.'" With a heavy thud, Parson Briard snapped the Bible shut, his gaze steely, his jaw resolute. "And what do you say, Amity Falls? Have you heard the calls of your fellow men? Have you seen the hungry, the tired, the sick? I've lived in the Falls for all my adult life and have never seen a lack of Good Samaritans here. The founders of this town so cared about helping their fellow men, they even included it within the Rules."

Townsfolk nodded, and I saw several chests puff with pride.

"I feel honored to call the Falls my home. And yet," he said, his eyes darkening with the message's turn. "And yet, we've failed to be the good shepherds God calls us to be, tending and caring for his flock as he has for us. We allowed division and hatred to reign in our hearts, ruling our thoughts, and governing our hands. Prejudice supplanted compassion. Animosity overcame grace."

The afternoon had grown warm, spring teetering into the

dangerous heat of summer. A line of perspiration dotted the parson's brow, and he removed a handkerchief, embellished with one of Widow Mullins's designs.

"I am not here today to take confessions—God will judge those who commit despicable and cowardly acts. He sees all, he watches all—but I am here to condemn them. Amity Falls will not abide discord. We cannot allow our community to harbor enmity and strife."

He tucked the Bible back into his pocket and clapped his hands, changing tones.

"Will you do me a favor? Can we stand, right here and now, and reach out to a neighbor? Look them in the eye, take their hand. Come on now, let's all join together."

We stood and shuffled about to form a circle across the town green, each of us a link in the chain that made up Amity Falls.

Across the circle, I noticed Sam, chuckling with Winthrop Mullins as they pretended to not want to hold each other's hands. When he glanced up, our eyes met. I tried offering a little smile, but he looked away with indifference.

When we were smaller, we'd clung to each other with an unbreakable fierceness. Seeing his detachment now made me want to cry. Where had we gone so wrong?

Parson Briard stepped onto a bench, raising himself over the giant circle. His smile beamed, showing off even the very last of his molars.

"This is Amity Falls," he cried. "United by God. United with friendship. United together!"

Briard broke into applause, and everyone else followed suit, hugging their neighbors, offering pats on the back and smiles as wide as the parson's. Winthrop Mullins was the first to leave the circle, stumbling his way to the parson.

He greeted the boy with a hearty handshake. "Happy to see you today, Mullins. We've missed you at services."

Winthrop ran stubby fingers through his hair. It was badly in need of a trim. Old Widow Mullins had always kept her grandson's red hair cut short and neat, but he seemed utterly lost without her now. This was the first time I'd seen him since her funeral.

"Interesting sermon today, real interesting."

Parson Briard's eyes lit up. "Indeed? I'm glad to hear you enjoyed it."

"Don't know how much I agree with a lot of it," Winthrop confessed. "You say we ought to be like a shepherd, right?"

"Well, it's not just me saying that. You'll find references to shepherds and their flocks all over the Good Book."

"Now, see, that's where I have the problem. I only know one shepherd"—Winthrop glanced at Leland Schäfer, who stood under an elm tree, laughing at something Cora had said—"and he doesn't do any of the things you said he ought to. My grandmother died because of him, Parson. Starved to death. What crops weren't taken by the black rot were pillaged by that man's sheep!" He pointed an angry finger at the Elder. "So if being a shepherd is allowing your fences to rot away and fall apart—if it's letting your flock wreak havoc on another man's land—I don't know that I want anything to do with it."

"What the devil are you talking about, Mullins?" Leland asked, striding across the lawn, his black Elder cloak trailing like thunderclouds.

Cheerful conversations died away as everyone watched this new drama unfold.

"Is he going on about those fences again? I've told you a thousand times, the southern field is yours to keep up. My flock would have never gotten loose if you'd tended your posts better."

"Now, look you here"—Winthrop grabbed the Elder's shirt, yanking Leland to his toes—"it's not our fence to tend! Our corn isn't going to get loose and eat every damn thing in its path."

"Leland—Winthrop, son . . ." Briard placed a calming hand on each of their backs. "Surely we can talk through this—away from the crowds?" His eyes drifted across the green. Most of the town watched on with horrified fascination, the moment of united peace gone.

"Sometimes words aren't enough!" Winthrop snarled, and his fist flew through the air and caught the side of Leland's jaw with a meaty smack.

Matthias was across the yard in a flash, pulling the boy off the other Elder. He caught a wayward elbow to the stomach in the process and threw Winthrop to the ground.

"Gentlemen—gentlemen!" The parson struggled to grab at Leland but was decked himself as Matthias's punch missed its mark. Briard grabbed at his eye and whirled back, searching for something to stop the madness. "Thaddeus McComb—play something. Play anything. For God's sake, just play!"

The farmer immediately launched into a song, though most of the crowd lingered at the edge of the fight, enraptured.

"Dance, please," the parson instructed, holding Winthrop back from the melee. "We'll handle this and—Dodson!" he snapped as Leland charged at them. Matthias grabbed the other Elder. They all but dragged Winthrop and Leland down the hill toward the church.

"They're here. They have to be," Ephraim said, suddenly at my side, scanning the crowd. "They'd never miss something like this."

I glanced around the gathering. "I don't see her. I don't see anything that looks like those drawings."

"They won't always appear like that," Ephraim muttered, his dark gaze flickering across the crowd. "Look around, Ellerie. Look hard. Who's here who shouldn't be? Someone new. Someone un-known. Someone—"

"Whitaker," I said, catching him wandering through the square. When he spotted me, his eyes brightened. "I told him not to come. Let me . . . I'll be right back, I promise."

"Keep your wits about you," he warned. "This town is primed like a powder keg. It won't take much to set it off."

"Did I miss the picnic?" Whitaker asked as I joined him.

"What are you doing here?"

"I know you said I shouldn't come. I know. But . . . I was down at the creek's edge and I heard the music starting, and . . . I just really hoped you'd forgiven me enough by now."

"Enough? Enough for what?"

"A dance?" he asked earnestly. He held out his hand, hope written across his face.

"I . . ." I glanced back to where Ephraim had been, but he was gone.

Thaddeus McComb began a new song, a sweeping and sad ballad that pulled every strain of angst from his fiddle. Without the spectacle to watch, couples came together now, eager for the intimacy of the forlorn waltz.

After a moment of hesitation, I took his hand and our fingers laced together. Whitaker's other hand rested at the small of my back as we began to sway to the song's tempo.

"That dress truly is the perfect shade on you," he said, gently turning me out into a spin. "I've never seen you look lovelier."

"It nearly got me in trouble." His eyebrows rose. "The parson's wife accused me of stealing the fabric off her clothesline last sum-mer."

His smile froze. "Oh?"

"Right here, in the middle of the social. Can you believe it?"

"How strange."

"It's become increasingly strange around here since you left."

"Really?"

"Things haven't been right, and . . ."

I caught sight of Ephraim once more. He'd made his way over to Thomas and was listening to something his son said, eyebrows furrowed into a thick line. Merry joined them, shaking her head, her eyes wild and cheeks bright.

I stopped dancing.

Something was wrong.

Something was terribly wrong.

"What is it?" Whitaker asked, turning to see what I stared at.

"I need to—"

Before I could offer an excuse, Merry burst into tears.

I was at my sister's side before I even realized I'd left Whitaker behind.

"What is it? What is it, Merry?" I asked, grabbing hold of her shoulders. A bolt of fear stabbed at my chest, cracking it open wide.

Merry broke into fresh sobs, horrible and keening. "She's gone, Ellerie. Sadie is gone!"

33

MERRY'S CRIES GREW LOUDER, DRAWING A GATHERING around us and even stopping Thaddeus McComb's song.

"What is it now?" Matthias asked, struggling to run back up the hill from the church. His shirt was soaked in sweat, the rolled cuffs and collar yellow. The afternoon sun baked down in an unrelenting layer of heat.

"The little girl, she's gone missing," Ephraim explained, changing his voice to sound like Ezra's once more.

"Sadie Downing?" the Elder guessed, staring down at me as I held Merry.

Her fingers sank painfully into my arms as she rocked back and forth in her grief.

"Why such hysterics? She probably wandered home or down to the general store." Matthias scanned the group for other young girls. "Trinity, Pardon—do you know where Sadie Downing has gone?"

"Last time I saw her, she was over there," Trinity said, pointing to the pines.

Merry doubled over in a fresh set of tears. "Those things got her. I know they did. The creatures!"

Matthias knelt beside us, awkwardly patting at my sister's

shoulder. Matthias wasn't known for compassionate comforting. "I'm sure those wolves are long gone, Merry Downing. When did you notice her missing? She can't have gotten far."

"It hasn't been long," I said, grabbing on to that sliver of comfort.

"Not the wolves. The other—" Merry started, but a swift shake of the head from Ephraim silenced her.

Matthias stood, raising his hands to quiet the group. "We need to assemble search parties for Sadie Downing. Trinity Brewster says she was last near the pines, but she could have also wandered into town. We need to divide up and look for her."

"Thomas and I will take the woods around the square," Ephraim volunteered quickly, stepping forward before anyone else could.

"Surely you don't believe she'd go into the forest." Matthias chuckled as if to lighten the situation. No one joined him. "I know grown men who won't wander into the pines. A little girl would never—"

"I'll search there too," I said.

Matthias looked uneasy. "Perhaps you could help Merry back home? She's in no condition to search, and Sadie might have returned there."

"I'm going after my sister," I said, a flint of determination steeling my voice.

"I can take Merry back," Bonnie Maddin said, working free of the crowd.

"Thank you," I said as we pulled Merry to her feet. "I'll find Sadie," I whispered, bringing Merry into a tight embrace. "I promise."

Matthias scanned the crowd. "Cora and Charlotte, why don't you form a party to check the north side of town? Violet and Alice, you ladies take a group to the south. Calvin, take some men to search the western fields near the Our Ladies. Edmund, Thaddeus—the lakeshore. Gran and I will take the east. Everyone else, join a group and let's get to work."

I gave Merry a final hug before joining Ephraim and Thomas. They'd already edged away from the rest of the group, planning in private.

Ephraim squeezed my upper arm. "Ellerie, there's no shame in searching the town."

"You know that's not where she is."

"Then . . . if you're going to do this . . . you need to arm yourself."

I bit my lip. "Papa took our rifle with him."

"Not with bullets." He reached into his leather satchel and pulled out a stash of . . . things.

"I don't . . . I don't understand."

Rabbits' feet and four-leaf clovers—some pressed between small panes of glass, others encased in resin. Vials of ladybugs and monarch butterflies. Rosaries with silver crucifixes. Spinner rings with prayer wheels. Horseshoes. Pennies. Sets of dice, and so many animal figurines.

"Luck," Ephraim said, as though the word ought to clarify everything. "Dark Watchers feed off fear, despair. Items of luck bring people hope and comfort. They can repel them."

He pressed a handful of the trinkets into my palm.

"I've never seen anything like all this before," I said, toying with an elephant charm. The soft fur of a rabbit's foot brushed against my fingers, and I suddenly realized I *had* seen such a collection. And it belonged to the one person who would need it most, living out in the woods, surrounded by the very monsters he'd claimed not to see.

Whitaker.

I froze, hearing his footsteps behind me, as if he'd been drawn by my thoughts.

He reached out and trailed a gentle finger down my shoulder blade. "Ellerie, I'm coming with you."

◦⚮◦

The woods were darker than I'd thought they would be.

Much darker.

Hundreds of branches, laden with long pine needles and dozens of Bells, blocked even the boldest sunbeams and cast the forest into an eerie, murky gloom.

Years of fallen needles softened our footsteps, deadening them to the point of silence.

I'd expected to be attacked the moment we set foot on the forest trail, eviscerated by sharp claws and barbed teeth, but there'd been nothing. No monsters, no shadowy figures. Not even a bird or squirrel scampered through the canopy overhead.

It was only us and the pines.

And the Bells.

I stood at their edge now, staring into the dark, silver-less void before us. The Bells did not taper to an end, simply trailing off where our forefathers had run out of trinkets. There was an unmistakable boundary dividing the areas as sharply as a line of ink upon a map.

Here there was protection.

Here there was not.

I took a deep breath, clutching at my silver locket for reassurance. Months before, I'd tucked away Whitaker's four-leaf clover within it and had been unknowingly protected against the Dark Watchers ever since.

"Sadie! Sadie Downing!" Whitaker called out, cupping his

hands around his mouth to make his voice carry deeper into the woods.

We paused, listening to the air around us, but all I could hear were the cries of others searching for my sister.

For the first time since the social, I turned to face Whitaker, truly looking him in the eye. I'd expected him to look different somehow, as if his betrayal would cast a tangible mark across his face.

But he was as he'd ever been.

Just Whitaker.

"We can cover more ground if we split up," I said.

"And we have already," he said. "Ezra and Thomas went east."

"I mean—"

"I know what you mean, and no. It's better to stick with someone—"

"But—"

"Especially when one of the team members doesn't know the lay of the land."

"Especially when the lay of that land is full of monsters." The accusation burst from me like shrapnel.

He sighed. "There are no—"

I grabbed every piece of Ephraim's luck from my pockets and hurled them at his feet. "I know they're real."

He looked at the scattered trinkets, confusion growing across his face. "What is all . . . How did you—" His eyes met mine with swift understanding. "Ezra."

"Ephraim," I corrected him. "Why did you lie to me? You said there was nothing out in the woods. You said everyone was imagining the monsters. You said there was—"

"I wanted to keep you safe."

"By lying?"

"To protect you!" His voice was firm, resolute, but after a moment he pushed at his sleeves, fidgeting uncomfortably as if his tattoos itched. "Then . . . he lied as well. He's not Ezra Downing."

"He's not."

"Not your uncle."

"No."

"And that's all right with you?"

I dragged my gaze up from the green bands. "I never said it was."

He raked his fingers through his hair. "So . . . he knows about them. About the—"

"Dark Watchers."

"Dark Watchers," he agreed unhappily. "And you obviously know about the luck."

I glanced at the scattered pieces that lay between us.

"Then you must see I've been trying to keep you safe, from the moment we met—the four-leaf clovers, the silver horseshoe for Merry at Christmas."

"You knew they were out there, that they were watching us, and you didn't say a thing!"

He whirled away from me with a groan, swiping at a nearby tree branch. "I couldn't! If you knew about them, what they are, you'd know to fear them, and that's what they want. That's what they're drawn to. Fear and chaos." He turned, eyes full of remorse. "I couldn't bear that for you. Not you, so full of light and cheer. I wanted to keep that . . . to keep *you* . . . safe."

I wanted to hold on to my anger, but he slipped his hands over mine, ran his thumbs along the ridges of my knuckles. Like a bolt of cloth, I felt my indignation unspool under the weight of his beseeching stare.

It wasn't how I would have handled this situation, but I could see his side of it.

I could understand his reason.

I could forgive.

"I'm sorry," he said. "I'm sorry about lying and misleading you. I'm sorry for keeping you in the dark. I'm sorry . . . for so many things. And I will spend the rest of my life apologizing if you want, but right now, we need to be searching for Sadie. If they went after her . . ."

"Do you think they would do that?" I asked, giving voice to my darkest fear.

"I don't . . . I don't know." He swallowed. "But if they did, we don't have much time."

I nodded.

"Now think," he began, and bent over to pick up the scattered pieces of luck. "Is there any spot she might have wandered off to? Somewhere she likes to play at? A creek bed or an old hollow tree?"

"Sadie has never gone into the woods. Not that I know of. And she'd certainly never have gone past the Bells." I glanced uneasily at the dark trees before us.

He gripped my fingers tightly. "We're together, Ellerie Downing. I won't let anything happen to you. You have my word."

But still my hands trembled as we took the first step over the boundary.

We followed a small game trail, hollering Sadie's name again and again. We pushed through knotted copses of saplings, young birches that would never gather enough sunlight to grow any larger. If they'd been within the protection of the Bells, they might have become kindling for the Our Ladies, but here, out in this vast and untamed wilderness, they'd waste and wane, eventually toppling over to rot and ruin.

The farther in we traveled, the more doubts crept into my mind. Little tendrils of unease grew grasping roots, sinking their grip into my ribs until it felt like my chest would crack in two.

"Sadie? Sadie, where are you?" I called out, shaky and desperate, hoping, praying, believing she would somehow hear me, but only my own voice ricocheted back.

A flicker of irritation kindled in the pit of my stomach, then licked higher and higher, burning at my throat.

Where was she?

The farther we wandered, the more my anger grew.

How could she have done something so thoughtless?

She knew the Rules. She knew that the pines were dangerous.

What had she been thinking?

A snarl ripped from my throat, leaving me breathless and seething. I'd never felt so enraged, teetering on the verge of a fury so encompassing, it threatened to consume my very being.

She hadn't been thinking.

I wanted to pull out my own hair. I wanted to scream and strike. Hurt and howl my indignities, set the world on fire so that I wasn't the only one feeling this . . .

Darkness.

Just like Ephraim warned me of.

It was as palpable as a shadow across the sun on a hot day. I felt its wrath like a tangible presence inside me, a separate entity forced to share too close a space. It squirmed and flexed, furiously seeking to take control. With every step I took deeper into these woods, its glowering blanket covered me, heavy and twisting and impossible to escape.

Escape.

I had to escape.

"Whitaker, I think we should—"

I stopped short.

Somehow, suddenly, I was by myself, alone in the woods.

I whirled around, trying to spot him.

His hand had been firmly within mine. I could still feel the phantom brush of it against my skin.

"Whitaker?" I tried, feeling foolish. Where could he have gone?

Turning in a broad circle, I tried discerning which direction would take me back toward Amity Falls. But the path was gone. The forest surrounded me, unwavering and deep. It would not give me up so easily. Clouds passed over the sun, creating a false night and making it impossible to straighten my bearings.

I picked a direction and continued on, determined to break free of the oppressing trees. Though I knew it wasn't possible, they seemed to be creeping in closer, squeezing me in a claustrophobic embrace. At the far edge of my vision, something moved through the trees. Squinting, I could almost make out a darker shape lingering there.

"Just an animal. Just a deer," I whispered.

But it didn't move like an animal. It was too wispy, too insubstantial. It slid about with a fluid grace, even seeming to swoop into the air. It darted out in front of me, then shot into the canopy. I glanced up, trying to keep track of its assent, and screamed.

Large eyes peered down at me, black and unblinking.

I could just make out the pale face of a barn owl. It was the largest one I'd ever seen. Twelve talons wrapped around its perch, far longer and more deadly than any owl had a right to possess.

Even creatures of the air weren't immune to the Dark Watchers' contamination.

A bit of lacerated meat dangled from its forked and bloody beak, the last remnants of a vole or rabbit supper, no doubt. His head turned suddenly, his large eyes peering into the darkness, and his meal landed at my feet. When I looked up again, the owl was gone.

A strange warble sounded, snapping my attention back to the

pines. "Is . . . is anyone out there?" I raised my voice far more than I was comfortable with. "Sadie? Whitaker?"

A noise drew my attention farther toward the direction I was heading. It was soft and could have easily been a pinecone falling to the forest floor. Or it might have been . . .

I heard it again.

And again.

And again in a familiar regularity.

Footsteps.

"Whitaker? Is that you?"

Though I could see absolutely nothing but trees before me, I knew without question that something was headed this way.

Before it could catch me, I turned and raced deeper into the pines.

I struggled through twisting briar patches, the thorns sinking into my sleeves, trying in vain to hold me back, but I couldn't stop. The clouds parted, and a sharp ray of sun burst through the canopy, beaming directly into my eyes. For a moment, I saw nothing but blinding white light. As my vision returned, degree by painstaking degree, glowing dots danced before everything I saw.

Or were they eyes?

A set of dots, impossibly bright and low to the ground, stayed stationary, refusing to move as the other sun spots did.

The mutated wolves.

Sam's monsters.

Ephraim's Dark Watchers.

I couldn't make out the figure's shape, just the eyes, silver and hypnotic, enticing and entreating me to come to them. I felt pulled forward even as my mind rebelled against my feet's treachery.

And then suddenly the eyes were moving, directly toward me, and it didn't matter what creature they belonged to. I bolted away, leaping over tree roots poking from the ground like gnarled hands, reaching for me and seeking to do harm.

I could hear the creature's breath, panting with bloodlust, eager to rip and tear. It spurred me on, on when I wanted to stop, when my legs were on fire and every gulp of air seemed tinged with acid and the coppery taste of blood.

I kept running, panic choking my throat, burning a stitch into my side, until I spied a break in the trees, a clearing ahead, and then him.

Whitaker.

He was there.

I'd found him!

"Ellerie?" he shouted out, searching for me. I raced across the clearing as he turned, and I pressed myself into his safety.

Without hesitation, his arms opened and closed around me, holding me close, stilling my ragged gasps. His palms were warm at the side of my neck, and his fingers curved into my mess of a braid. His chin rested on the top of my head, and I could feel his heartbeat pulsing in the hollow of his throat.

"Where did you go?" he murmured, tightening his embrace. "You were right beside me, and then—"

I wanted to stay there, buried away in the security of his chest, but I forced myself to look over my shoulder. "We have to run."

"From what?"

The creature should have burst into the clearing by now. It had not been far behind me.

But there was nothing. No monster. No silver eyes. Just weak sunlight illuminating the tree break, slipping behind the mountains as twilight stole over the land.

"It was . . . it was right there."

"A Dark Watcher?"

"I don't know." I took deep breaths, my sternum aching. "It must have been. It was so fast."

He traced his fingers down my braid appraisingly. "Are you all right? Where were you?"

"Me?" I blinked. "You were the one who left."

Whitaker shook his head. "I've been here all along. I heard something behind us, and then you were just . . . gone."

I glanced around the clearing, noting its peculiarities. It did seem familiar. Had I really just run in an enormous circle, and ended up right where I'd started?

"How is that possible?"

Behind us came a snap. A twig breaking.

"It's back." I shuddered. I could almost see its unnatural shadows prowling low in the undergrowth.

Whitaker shifted, keeping himself between me and the thing.

"Who's there?" he shouted, his voice booming with power. He puffed his chest and threw his arms out, making himself look as formidable as possible, like he was facing down a bear. "Who's there?"

Pine needles quivered as a shape rustled through them.

But it was not a monster that emerged from the wood's grasp.

It was something much smaller.

A flash of calico.

Blond braids.

"Sadie!" I exclaimed, racing forward to catch my little sister as she swooned out of consciousness.

34

"ELLERIE?" SADIE'S EYES FLUTTERED OPEN AND STARED blearily at the ceiling as they struggled to focus. "Where am I?"

"It's all right," I promised, stroking the soft curve of her cheek. On the other side of her, Merry snuggled close. "We're home. You're out of the pines. You're safe."

She tried pushing herself from the bed but fell back into the mattress, pressing a hand to her head. "I don't feel very good."

"You gave everyone quite a fright." Matthias Dodson watched from the doorway of the loft. The Elders and Parson Briard had been at the farm since our return, along with Dr. Ambrose. He'd treated Sadie's injuries—mostly light scratches, but one along her arm had been deep enough to warrant stitches.

"How did I get here? We were at the picnic, and then . . ." She trailed off. "I don't . . . I don't remember. . . . Could I have some water, please?"

I sprang into motion, pouring a glass from the pitcher at the washbasin.

Merry helped shift Sadie into a more comfortable position before holding the cup to her lips. "Ellerie and Whitaker found you."

"You found us, actually," I said. "We brought you back."

It had been a hellish journey. Whitaker had carried Sadie's

prostrate form over his shoulder while I'd navigated us around boulders and brambles, feeling everything with my hands. Though Sadie had remained mostly unconscious, her sleep had occasionally been punctuated by panicked nightmares so strong that she'd kick and lash out, striking Whitaker.

I wasn't sure if it was our collection of luck or my whispered prayers for protection, but the Dark Watchers had stayed away while we'd stumbled through the pines. Once, I thought I saw the telltale glimmer of their silver eyes high above us, but it had only been starlight tangled through the trees. Twilight had come and gone while we were in the darkened forest.

Just as I had begun to fear that we were staggering about in circles, an orange glow had grown through the forest, warming the night and showing us the path home.

The Our Ladies had been lit.

We'd gone toward them, drawn to their flickering flames. I understood now why our town's founders had built the towering structures as protection against the dark creatures of the woods. Seen through the maze of trees, the burning beacons were terrifying.

By the time we'd broken free of the pines, falling into the arms of Amity Falls, I'd been sobbing with relief.

"Do you remember anything?" Leland asked Sadie now. "Anything from the woods?"

"No. I was playing with Trinity and Abigail, and then . . ." She blinked. "I'm so tired."

"We should let her rest," Dr. Ambrose said.

"Yes," Ephraim agreed. "There's much to talk about—perhaps we should go downstairs and let her sleep."

"Don't leave me alone!" Sadie cried, her eyes flashing wide open.

"I'll stay with you," Merry promised.

"And Ellerie?" she pleaded, grabbing at my hand as if to pin me in place.

"I'll check on you soon, all right?" I pressed a kiss to her forehead and ushered the men downstairs.

Before joining everyone in the sitting room, I poked my head out onto the porch, where Whitaker had collapsed in an exhausted stupor. He'd propped his feet along the railing, and his mouth hung slightly open, his eyelids fluttering in dreams.

My fingertips danced above his hands and I wondered if I ought to wake him. He needed to hear everything Ephraim was about to say, but I couldn't bear to disturb his peace. I wished I could join him, pressed against his side, deep in dreams of a happier future, instead of being in the current present.

"Ellerie?" Thomas said, standing in the doorway with uncertainty. "Father wants to get started."

He wasn't trying to conceal his accent any longer.

Reluctantly I trailed after him.

"Where's Dr. Ambrose?" I asked, stepping into the sitting room.

Dining table chairs crowded the area, brought in to create enough seating for the three Elders, the parson, Thomas, and me. Ephraim stood in front of the fireplace, nervously adjusting his spectacles.

"Gone already," said Parson Briard. "With Rebecca's . . . confinement period so near, he thought it best to check on her since he was already out by the farm."

There was an empty chair next to him, but I hesitated at the threshold, my hands restless. "Can I get anyone something to drink? Water or . . . water?"

"Dear girl, we ought to be tending to you, after your harrowing ordeal," Leland said, gesturing to the seat. "Are you all right?"

"Now that Sadie is back, yes."

"Sit, Ellerie. Please," Ephraim requested, offering me a pained smile. He cleared his throat, acknowledging the others. "I'm afraid Thomas and I have something to confess." He furrowed his brow. "Quite a lot of somethings, actually."

Matthias frowned. "Why are you talking like that, Ezra?"

"See, that's just the thing . . . I'm not Ezra. I'm not a Downing. And as much as I'd love to lay claim to such a set of nieces, Ellerie and her sisters are not related to me."

"I knew it!" Leland exclaimed. He turned to Matthias, cuffing him across the shoulder. "I told you something was wrong with them!"

Ephraim fidgeted with the edge of his sleeve. "Thomas is my son; that much is true. But we're the Fairhopes. My name is 'Ephraim.'"

"We belong to the Brotherhood of the Light." Thomas sprang to his feet, unable to remain still.

The Elders exchanged glances with one another.

Ephraim's gaze shifted about the room, taking their reactions in. "An old order of scientists. Researchers. Archivists. We investigate the things of myth and legend, lore and folktales."

"Creatures," Thomas interjected.

"Monsters," Ephraim clarified. "Things of darkness and ill desire. We find them and we bring them into the light." He cleared his throat once again. "Thomas and I were sent to America to track down a certain sect of them—the Dark Watchers. One of our society's founders first encountered them centuries ago. He studied them for years, learning their habits, their rhythms, but when it came time to eradicate them, they fled on a ship sailing for the colonies. They've been causing chaos here ever since."

"What—what are they?" Matthias asked.

"At first glance, they look no different from you or me—human, mostly. But they can move with unmatched speed and dexterity.

They can blend into their surroundings so thoroughly, you'd never notice one, even as it stands beside you. And their eyes, of course."

Leland's own were enormous. "What about their eyes?"

"Dark Watchers are voyeurs, delighting in the creation of discord wherever they go, so that they may . . . watch. They have powerfully strong eyes, able to see the smallest details from great distances, able to hunt and watch their prey, even in the dark of night. They shine silver."

"Silver?" Amos echoed. "Like the creatures in our woods."

"Exactly like them," Thomas confirmed.

"We believe that a family of Dark Watchers has taken interest in this area. Thomas and I have followed their progress, recording the stories of their mayhem, reporting back to the Brotherhood."

"What sort of mayhem are you talking about?" Matthias asked.

"The complete and total destruction of your world," Ephraim said simply.

"Father."

"It is, isn't it? Didn't we see that at Ormbark? At Willow Pass and Blackburn? At the Fairfoot colony? The Dark Watchers are here in Amity Falls. There is no time to temper the reality of the situation."

"I've heard stories of what happened at that pass," Leland said. "Old Jean Garreau, he had the most ghastly tales . . . but wasn't that just circumstance? Bad luck?"

The trinkets in my pocket burned.

"The Dark Watchers spend time getting to know a place before they act. I wouldn't be surprised if they've been in your community for years without you being aware of their presence. There are always signs, but you need to know where—how—to look for them."

"What signs?" Amos asked.

"Animals in the woods that are suddenly wrong. Frogs with

multiple heads. Stags with too many horns or not enough legs. Squirrels and possums too small. Wolves grown too large. Does any of this sound familiar to you?"

The Elders nodded reluctantly. In a darkened corner of the room, Parson Briard pursed his lips, listening with unusual silence.

"And here, inside the town . . . you've had a rash of curious births in your farm animals? Mutations, deformations? Your crops have begun to rot before their intended harvests?"

"The foals at the Brysons' ranch," I murmured. "The Vissers' orchards."

"Everyone's crops," Amos added. "Yes."

"And the weather," Ephraim continued. "Hail and thunder in winter, an unbearably hot spring. Drought and desiccation just as everything should be bursting forth, fresh and new."

Leland frowned. "Surely that's not because of—"

"Even among yourselves—have there been more arguments? More acts of violence? Or vandalism? All signs of the Dark Watchers. They . . . their presence is so insidious, so black, it tarnishes everything around them. Nothing is left unaffected . . . and then . . . and then the tricks begin."

Thomas drew his fingers along the mantel. "Once they've ingratiated themselves into a community, Dark Watchers determine people's dearest desires and offer to fulfill them. They'll propose a trade—it starts out small, a simple prank, a rumor spread. But over time the favors grow larger, more dangerous. And then the creatures watch as the community eats itself alive."

The room fell into an uncomfortable silence, and my stomach roiled with queasiness.

"Cyrus," I finally dared to whisper. "He said that woman—the woman at the tavern had urged him to set the fire."

"There was no woman. There's never been any woman like that here," the parson disagreed, shaking his head.

"There has. There is. I've seen her myself."

"He said she had silvery eyes," Leland murmured, as if recalling something from a long-ago dream. He turned to Ephraim. "I didn't understand what he meant, but you say they have silver—"

"None of us understood anything he meant," Briard snapped. "He was a madman. None of this—none of any of this is real. I'll admit, Amity Falls has had far more than its share of troubles in the last year, but not because of fantastical creatures in the woods." He shook his head, gaining fervor. "I *do* believe a darkness has fallen across our community, but it's festered in the hearts of men, not monsters."

"But what if these things *have* come to the Falls?" Matthias stroked his beard. "*They* are the root of this darkness. They've brought the misfortune upon us."

"I don't believe that for a second, Matthias Dodson, and neither should any God-fearing servant of the Lord."

Amos's clouded eyes fell to the Founder Tree adorning his walking stick. "I think I would rather believe in the Dark Watchers' thrall than imagine that anyone in Amity Falls would willingly seek to harm their fellow friends and neighbors, wouldn't you, Clemency?"

Parson Briard crossed his arms over his chest. "Only the Lord knows what wickedness is kept in the hearts of men."

I leaned forward, aware that none of these men would welcome the input of a teenage girl, but it needed to be said all the same. "I can assure you, the Dark Watchers—those creatures—are real. They chased me in the woods. I heard them. I saw them."

"A guilty conscience is capable of seeing most anything." Briard turned a gimlet eye toward me. "What sins of yours need confessing, Ellerie Downing?"

My mouth fell open. "What? I've done nothing. . . . I'm not the only one who's seen them either. Whitaker has—"

The parson's eyebrow raised. "Ah. Yes. The trapper in the woods. And you and he were alone in these same woods today, were you not?"

My face colored as his implication struck.

"Leave Ellerie be," Amos said, interceding.

"Sins are meant to be confessed." Briard stared at me for a long moment before mercifully looking away. "Perhaps that's what Amity needs now more than anything else." He nodded as his idea formed. "Yes, yes, of course."

"What are you talking about?" Matthias asked.

"A revival . . . We unite as a community, confess and repent our sins, ask for the forgiveness of both the Lord and our fellow men. That is what will save the Falls—not any pagan nonsense from those two." He waved a dismissive hand at the Fairhopes. "Tomorrow morning. You three must get the word out—everyone in town will need to be there—and I must spend tonight in prayer."

Matthias narrowed his eyes. "I don't think this—"

"It's not your place to think, Elder," Briard snapped. "You and yours had your chance to save us. You tried your worldly ways. This town doesn't need Decidings or Judgments. What it needs is a Reckoning. And as the spiritual authority, that is mine and mine alone."

"And God's," Matthias said, his jaw hardened. "Presumably."

The parson didn't answer. His eyes closed as he mouthed a silent intercession. "Yes. A revival. Tomorrow. Every trace of evil shall be stamped from God's Grasp." He opened his eyes and stared hard at Ephraim. "Starting with you."

35

THE NEXT MORNING DAWNED HOT, AND BY THE TIME we made our way into Amity Falls, the air blanketed us with a wet, heavy stillness. Drawing breath felt impossible, and it took us nearly twice as long to make the three-mile walk.

"I wish I had stayed with Sadie," Merry muttered, fanning herself with pained listlessness. Attempting to stir this humidity was like trying to pull a fishing net through mud. "We shouldn't have left her all alone."

"She's not alone. Whitaker is with her."

"One of us ought to have stayed behind. At least."

I agreed, but it was the only solution I'd been able to think of. "The parson said he wanted every member of the town present."

"And he specifically said he wanted us there as well," Ephraim gasped. Even hidden under the shade of his wide-brimmed hat, he was red. He took a sip from his canteen, then offered it to the rest of us.

I patted a handkerchief over my neck, a useless gesture. The lace of my collar was already sodden with sweat.

All around us was a sea of yellow. Dead grass. Dead fields. Dying pines. Without the spring rains, everything in God's Grasp looked on the verge of igniting.

We turned the corner and spotted the church.

A large canvas tent had been erected on the lawn. Its flaps were pulled open, and I could see rows of wooden chairs, mismatched but laid out with a fanatical order that suggested Letitia Briard had been up since dawn arranging them.

Merry eyed the enclosure dubiously. "We have to sit in that?"

"Apparently," I said. "Look, the sides are open. I'm sure there will be a breeze."

I tried sounding hopeful, but so many people milled about the lawn, vying for spots of shade, that I didn't truly believe my words. Merry didn't either. I had to all but shove her into motion.

"We should have stayed at home," she repeated. "Whitaker shouldn't have to look after Sadie all by himself."

"They'll be fine. Come on. Let's get seats along the back."

Stepping into that tent felt as if we'd entered one of the hellish landscapes Briard was always threatening sinners with from the top of his pulpit. My cotton voile was uncomfortably damp, clinging to my frame in a claustrophobic embrace. I took a steadying breath and nearly gagged. The air was rank with perspiration. The foul taste lingered at the back of my throat, bringing tears to my eyes. I turned to flee but ran straight into the parson.

"Ellerie!" He greeted me with a hearty pat on my back, stalling my escape.

I stared with fascinated horror at his long white robes and heavily stitched stole. His face was already as dark as a beet, and he'd not even begun his sermon.

"Take a seat, take a seat. We'll be beginning soon . . ."

I stepped closer to Merry, slipping from the added heat of his hand, and he turned toward the Fairhopes. He looked boisterous.

"Ah. Ezra. No, no, what was it? Don't tell me. . . ."

"Ephraim," he said, showing no inclination to play the parson's game.

"Ephraim." Parson Briard shrugged, as if that was of no consequence. "I'm so glad you could join us. I want you to see this. See and understand. Amity Falls is full of good, righteous people. I know that when we come together in prayer, God will smite this wickedness from us."

His eyes shone with such a delirious fervency, I wondered if he was suffering from heatstroke.

"I'm certain he will," Ephraim said as I scanned the crowd for Dr. Ambrose.

The parson grinned before leaving. "Good Blessings to you—to all of you."

"Good Blessings," we repeated.

Matthias Dodson sidled down the line of chairs. "Ephraim, Thomas," he said, offering a nod to Merry and me. "This ought to be a . . . diverting spectacle." He gazed to Briard, who was cajoling families to sit closer to the makeshift altar. "Amos, Leland, and I would like to speak with you both. We need to have a plan to put in place once . . . all this . . . is over with. Join us, won't you?"

There were only two empty chairs near the other Elders.

"Go on," I assured Ephraim. "Merry and I will be fine back here."

"Keep an eye out," he warned before they left.

"This is going to take all afternoon, isn't it?" Merry asked as we sank into our seats. "I don't see Sam yet, do you? I'll save him a place . . . just in case."

Her fervent belief in Sam's return shamed me. In truth, I'd hardly given my brother a moment's thought since he'd left. There were too many other matters taking up space in my mind, each more pressing than the next. Sam would come back if Sam decided to.

"Good Blessings, Downing girls," said a voice, as sharp as a razor.

Letitia Briard made her way into the tent. Her silvering hair was pulled into a severe bun, making the center of her eyebrows point in perpetual disbelief.

"I'm so glad you all could be here. I simply can't wait to hear what you'll be confessing, Ellerie." Her eyes ran over my wilted pink dress before she turned to greet the other families slinking reluctantly inside.

"You didn't really take that fabric, did you?" Merry asked once the parson's wife was out of earshot.

Her doubt stung. "Of course not. You were there when Whitaker brought it back."

"I know. I know that," she said, and wiped at her forehead. "It's just . . . it's just so hot."

We fell into silence, wretchedly waiting for the revival to begin. Merry kept watch for our brother, certain he'd arrive with the last of the stragglers, but Briard made his way to the front, and the seat beside her remained open.

"Good Blessings to you all on this fine morning," Parson Briard called out, starting the gathering. "I've brought you here today because I believe a serious threat faces Amity Falls. No one can be unaware of the recent string of vandalism and violence plaguing our town. There are some here . . ."

He turned his focus pointedly to the Elders and the Fairhopes. Matthias sat with his arms crossed over his chest, listening with incredulity, and Leland's head listed to the side. Amos appeared to have fallen asleep, his mouth open and panting.

"There are some here who would have you believe that outside forces are to blame. That an army of mysterious monsters"—he waggled his fingers in theatrical disbelief—"have come to the Falls with the sole purpose of disrupting our lives. They would believe in boogeymen rather than taking a good, long look within themselves."

"Are you talking about the creatures in the woods?" Prudence

Latheton asked, standing up. "The ones with the silver eyes? Those aren't figments of our imagination. I've seen them. Edmund has." She looked around at her neighbors. Several nodded in support. "Many of us have."

"Have you seen actual fiends of flesh and blood, or is it perhaps the work of a guilty mind, playing tricks on you?"

"I've seen *them*," she insisted.

"You've seen lots of things, haven't you, Prudence?" Parson Briard said, leveling his full attention upon her. "In fact, I'd say you're known as one of the biggest busybodies in all of God's Grasp."

Someone behind her tittered, and she whirled around with narrowed eyes.

"In Paul's letter to the Romans, he wrote 'wherein thou judgest another, thou condemnest thyself; for thou that judgest doest the same things.' None of us should be so quick to throw stones, for there's not a single person here who is without fault."

Briard withdrew a handkerchief and patted at his face.

"But we can come together, in a spirit of unity and contrition, to confess our misdeeds and ask for forgiveness. I believe this is the only thing that will eradicate the wickedness upon our valley. *We* are to blame. *We* must seek to atone. In fact . . . Prudence, please, come join me at the front."

She made a shallow sound of confusion.

"There's no need for anxiety. You are among friends. Family even, for we are all brothers and sisters in the Gathering. Please."

When she reached the front, he positioned her so they both faced the crowd, and he placed steady hands on her shoulders. I suppose it was meant to show a sign of accord, but his fingers dug into her thin shoulders, keeping her from bolting.

"Why don't you be the first among us to confess your sins? We shall do it publicly, like lancing a boil before its poison can spread. Once our misdeeds—*all* of our misdeeds," he added, glancing across his flock, "have been spoken and cleared, the healing process can begin." He beamed, pleased at his phrasing. "I think even Dr. Ambrose would agree, that was a rather well-worded metaphor."

At his seat, the doctor remained still, his face grave.

"Go on, Prudence," the parson urged. "Confess."

She blew a long breath through her lips. Her eyes were wide and pleading, darting about the tent for help or escape. As much as I didn't care for her, I ached at her embarrassment. Before I was even aware of it, I stood.

"I'll do it," I volunteered with more confidence than I felt. "I'll confess my sins."

Briard's eyebrows rose with surprise, but he released Prudence. She stumbled back to her seat, relieved by her temporary reprieve. Letitia Briard beamed with malicious anticipation as I made my way to the front. I felt Merry's eyes on my back, but when I turned to face the town, I couldn't see her within the stifling shadows.

"How should I begin?" I asked, pushing a damp lock of hair behind my ear. My head was light, though I wasn't sure if it was from the heat or the enormity of what I was about to do. "Should I—should I kneel?"

The parson nodded darkly. "Yes. Kneel before God. Kneel before the Falls. Kneel before the weight of your sins."

Slowly, keeping my eyes on the wash of faces before me, I sank to my knees. "I'm Ellerie Downing." My voice quaked and sounded three pitches too high. "And I . . . I have come forward to confess . . ." I paused, racking my mind as unwelcome tears pricked, threatening to spill free. "To confess . . ."

I caught sight of Ephraim, leaning forward with concern. His anxious face strengthened my spine.

"I've come forward to confess that . . . the parson is wrong."

Gasps of surprise flew across the tent.

"There *are* things in the woods. Twisted wolves and strange mutations, yes, but there's also a group of . . . others. They've come to Amity Falls and have been . . . pitting us against one another. It's a terrible, elaborate game to them. They—"

"Stop this. Stop this all right now," a voice called out. Gran Fowler stood, shaking his head. "This girl hasn't done anything to warrant a public confession. These theatrics are cruel and useless. Listen to her—she's scared witless. She doesn't know what she's saying."

I shook my head. "But I do, Mr. Fowler. Ephraim will tell you—"

"Ephraim?" Gran looked out over the crowd. "There's no Ephraim here."

"Ezra. My uncle—only he's not. Not truly. He and Thomas are Fairhopes, not Downings." I could hear myself not making sense. It was too hot to string together reasonable explanations.

Ephraim started to stand, but Matthias pulled him back into his seat, whispering furiously.

"They're here to help. They're here to stop the creatures."

"Get up, Ellerie. The heat has you muddled." Gran pulled me to my feet. "Get back to your sister. Get some water."

Parson Briard tugged my elbow, casting me to the side of the tent. He looked like a wheel spun too fast, struggling to regain control of the situation. "I can't believe my ears. Cruel and useless theatrics?"

Gran nodded.

"What has happened to you, Gran? You've always been one of my most faithful parishioners."

"I have. But I can't sit by and watch this play out. This isn't the work of the Lord you're doing here, Clemency. No one should compel another to air their sins. Contrition means nothing if it's forced."

The parson bristled. "You think yourself above confession?"

"Certainly not. I've made many mistakes in my life, but I pray to the Lord every night for grace, as he intended. I see no reason to parade it out before the town, when I know I've already been forgiven."

"Forgiven by God perhaps, but not your neighbors."

Everyone turned, trying to see who had called from the darkness of the tent. Someone stood, their silhouette crisp against the open flaps of the tent.

Gran squinted at him. "God's mercy is all the forgiveness I need."

Judd Abrams stepped forward, filling the aisle like a great barge coming down a channel to dock. With his closely shaved hair and smashed nose—broken years before in a fight at the Buhrmans' tavern—he reminded me of one of Matthias Dodson's anvils. His left cheek bulged with a wad of chewing tobacco pocketed within it.

"Ellerie, get out of here." Gran nudged me, but there was no way to leave without passing Judd, and the fury radiating from him seemed too formidable to approach.

"You may have your forgiveness, but I still have a broken auger and no way to fix it. Think God will show some mercy on me?"

"The auger I borrowed last fall? I didn't break that."

"The bit had completely snapped off when I went to use it."

Gran shook his head. "I cleaned every inch of it myself before returning it. I would have noticed any damage."

"He's lying!" Judd snapped. A vein in his temple throbbed, a rattlesnake about to strike. "In front of all of you—and the parson—he persists in his lies!"

I edged toward the side of the tent, pressing against a swag of canvas, and wished for a way to escape this brutal confrontation. Even though the words were not directed at me, I felt their force like a swift punch to the gut.

"Papa?" a voice called out, small and uncertain.

Judd whipped around as his youngest daughter rose on trembling legs, urged by her mother. "It . . . it was me. I broke the auger."

"What?" he roared.

"We were . . . we were playing in the barn—I know you've told me not to, but . . . I bumped into some of your tools. They fell and then . . ." The girl made a motion of something breaking into two.

"That's not possible. That auger weighs more than you. How could you possibly—"

"It just did," the girl cried, her blue eyes filling with tears. "I was going to tell you, I swear I was, but she said how mad you'd get, how you'd beat me bloody. She said I should bury the broken part—make it look like it had always been like that."

"Who?" Judd took a dangerous step toward the shivering child. "Who is this 'she'?"

"My friend. Abigail."

However impossible within the suffocating confines of the revival tent, my blood ran cold.

Judd's wife swatted at the child. "I've told you to stop talking about this Abigail. She's not real!"

"She is!" the girl shouted, before racing out of the tent.

Judd started after her with balled fists, but paused, unable to continue with the weight of everyone's judgment and disapproval.

"See?" Parson Briard crowed. "Confessions help clear the soul. They free the truth. Who will come forward next? Judd—perhaps you've something to say?"

"I—I suppose I owe Mr. Fowler an apology. . . . I'm sorry I accused you just now . . . and I'm sorry I ever mentioned it to Edmund Latheton."

The farmer's gaze darted to Edmund. "What does he mean?"

Every trace of color drained away from the carpenter's face. "I was only helping you out, Judd!" He turned his attention to Gran, utterly stricken. "I—I'm sorry. Judd was so angry and kept saying you needed to be made to pay. . . ."

Gran sucked in a breath. "My chickens. That was you?"

"Abrams helped. And . . . that other man."

Judd snorted. "What other man?"

"The tall one, with the funny hat. I'd never seen him before. I thought he was one of your ranch hands."

"It was you and me in that coop. No one else."

"He was big, almost as tall as you, and . . ." Edmund's brow furrowed as he struggled to remember. "He had a silver coin, I think. A silver . . . something. It kept flashing in my eyes. . . ." His fingers scrubbed over his face, nails raking red slashes down his cheeks. "I'm so, so terribly sorry, Gran. I don't . . . I still don't know why I did it . . . what came over me . . ."

"Wickedness," Parson Briard said. "Your heart was full of wickedness. Repent now and be forgiven."

"I do," Edmund said, pushing his way to the aisle. He knelt at Gran's feet, clutching the farmer's calves. "I want to apologize. To atone. Most earnestly."

The parson nodded gravely. "Your repentance is seen. Your sins are forgiven."

"God can forgive you all he wants. I won't," Gran muttered, kicking Edmund away before he stalked off. When Judd tried to step into his path, the farmer shoved the giant man aside without a second's pause. "Come on, Alice. I've had enough of this nonsense."

The schoolteacher remained in her seat. "I . . . I want to stay."

"You can't be serious."

She cast an uncertain eye over the group. It fell on Bonnie Maddin and lingered warily. "No, I'm staying. Someone here burned down my schoolhouse, and I want to know who it was."

I sucked in a swift breath, my gaze falling to my feet.

I hadn't done it.

It had been a dream.

I hadn't burned down the school.

I didn't think.

Gran studied her for a long moment before shaking his head and walking off.

Parson Briard raised his arms in a welcoming gesture. "Who will clear their conscience next? Come, come all, and be set free!"

The tent came alive with whispers as people urged their friends, their spouses, their family forward.

"I saw Martha leaving the Buhrmans' yard early on the morning of Ruth Anne Mullins's funeral," Molly McCleary declared, her eyes glassy and bright as she pointed at her mother-in-law. "She was muttering to herself, and her dress was splattered with blood."

Prudence leapt to her feet with vindication. "I *told* you I didn't kill that goat!"

Violet turned toward the Elder's wife, aghast. "Martha, is it true?"

The older woman burst into tears.

Near the front, Cora Schäfer rose. "I heard Mark Danforth bragging to his friends about busting up Cypress Bell's fence!"

"That was you?" Cypress exclaimed, and grabbed Rebecca's brother by the front of his shirt.

Rebecca's brother let out a snicker of laughter, even as he tried to squirm free.

At the far side of the tent, an argument broke out between

Alice Fowler and Bonnie Maddin. Without warning, Alice struck her, and left behind a blood-red handprint.

"It wasn't me, I swear!" Bonnie wailed.

"I'll get your confession even if I have to beat it out of you!" the schoolmarm snarled, launching herself at the girl.

Martha's sobs were nearly drowned out in the sea of angry voices and accusations. She fell before Violet, grasping at her skirts and shaking with penitence. "She said she could give me the medicine Amos needed, but I had to do what she said. He was dying! How could I say no?"

"Who?" Violet demanded, trying to shake Martha from her. "Who would want to hurt me?" Her eyes flashed back to the Lathetons. "It was that bitch, wasn't it?"

"Get this cow off me!" Bonnie howled.

Martha's response was lost as a brawl erupted behind her. Corey Pursimon rammed his neighbor Roger Schultz so hard, the farmer fell, knocking Martha over in the process.

"You lying bastard, you ruined my fields!"

"Unhand my wife!" Amos cried as Martha struggled to right herself.

I lost sight of the Elder as he forced his way into the crowd, but suddenly his walking stick swung free and smacked Winthrop Mullins on the side of his head. Red rivulets raced down the boy's face, and he released a string of curses, diving after Amos.

"You have to stop this," I said, whirling around to the parson. He'd made his way to behind the lectern, watching in horror at the chaos he'd created. I grabbed his arm, shaking him. "Parson Briard—we have to stop this! People are getting hurt!"

"Sometimes you have to burn a field black before new roots can grow," he murmured. Slowly his eyes drifted back to me. They were vaguely out of focus, as if he wasn't truly seeing me beside him. "You said it was going to be tumultuous, but I had no idea it would be so beautiful."

His words rang wrong, like a guitar out of tune. "I didn't say that. I didn't say anything like . . ."

I let out a sharp breath, air knocked from my lungs.

I needed to turn. I needed to look. But my body froze with sudden fear and the absolute certainty there was someone behind me. Someone who should not have been there. Someone who had orchestrated this entire revival so they could watch with twisted curiosity as it played out.

"Parson . . . who are you speaking to?"

His eyes fell squarely on me. "Look at her, Ellerie. Isn't she magnificent? An angel of vengeance, come to purify the Falls. You don't know how hard I've prayed for her."

A shiver raced over me, my body cold and trembling. I could feel evil wafting off the creature, malicious and irresistible. It called out to that dark, hidden place within me, where every angry impulse I'd had and shoved aside was buried. It reached out, wanting to sort through them all, find the worst and stoke its rage.

I strained my eyes, looking as far to my periphery as I could. There was a slender form bedecked in white eyelet, and my mind raced back to that night when Papa and Samuel had emerged from the pines. The night I had lit the Our Ladies. The night I had seen a woman in a pale dress step out from the wheat field.

The night I'd lit the schoolhouse on fire.

No.

"What do you want?" I hissed, unable to turn and face her. "Why are you doing this to us?"

She said nothing, but I felt the weight of her gaze shift as she considered me. A hand stirred, impossibly long and bulbous fingers reaching out to brush the weave of my braid. I wanted to cringe from her touch, but was trapped, caged, a butterfly pinned on a mounting board, to be studied and stared at.

"Me?" she murmured, her voice soft and alluring. "I haven't lifted a finger in any of this. Look. This is all them." She made a soft sound of consideration. "All you, honey-haired girl."

"This is madness! We have to stop! We have to stop right now!" Rebecca Danforth shouted, drawing my attention.

She'd pulled herself onto a chair in the middle of the tent and was struggling for her voice to carry over the indignant roar. Someone knocked into her, and she clutched at her belly, altering her balance to avoid toppling over.

"Stop!" I cried, running toward Rebecca and leaving the creature behind.

No matter what unkind words had passed between us, I could not stand back and watch something terrible befall her.

"Stop! Stop this!" I shouted, pushing my way through the melee. Someone swiped their nails across my face, and I had to duck to keep from being hit as Mark Danforth charged into my path, but I finally made it to Rebecca. I held out my hands, trying to steady her. "Are you all right? This is out of control!"

She nodded and pushed aside my assistance. From her pocket, she withdrew a pistol, and before I could scream, she fired a warning shot into the air, ripping open a hole in the canvas above her.

"Enough!" she cried, and the crowd fell into an uneasy silence.

There was a small burst of laughter from the corner where Parson Briard now cowered, but when I looked, the Dark Watcher was gone.

Rebecca dragged her hand over her face. "Look at yourselves! Look at what is going on. Our town is tearing apart. Again. Something is terribly, terribly wrong here." She turned her focus on me. "Isn't it?"

"It is," I said. "And I know why."

Everyone had stopped their struggles, turning to face us. Not a single person looked unaffected by the fighting. Everywhere I looked there were broken noses, broken lips. Torn clothing and swollen fists.

I scanned their rapt faces, turning until I came to the parson. With a trembling hand, I pointed to him. "There are things that man knows and has not told you. There are dark forces at work, causing the troubles in Amity Falls. The drought, the bad harvests, the strange mutations. All of . . . *this,*" I said, gesturing to the destruction throughout the tent. "The suspicions and violence. All because of these things in the woods. The Dark Watchers. I don't know what exactly they are—creatures or monsters, old gods or supernatural . . . *things*. But they're here, and this . . . all of this . . . is because of them."

Alice Fowler—with her silver hair now ripped free of its usual tidy bun, and a sleeve hanging off her bodice, torn ragged—glanced back at the parson. "Is this true, Clemency?"

"I . . ." The parson adjusted his collar, his face dripping sweat.

I pressed ahead. "The Fairhopes told the Elders—they told Briard—and rather than go out and fight these things, the parson wanted to hold this ridiculous revival. And all along, they've been here, using him the entire time. That wasn't an angel of vengeance, Parson. It was a Dark Watcher. Laughing at you, laughing at all of us for falling into her trap."

He shook his head. "That's absurd. That was no—"

"Matthias," I said, whipping around to find the Elder. "Amos, Leland. You were there last night. You heard Ephraim speak. Tell them what he said."

"No. No. It doesn't matter what was said." Simon Briard spoke up, coming out of the crowd. He helped Rebecca from the chair, snatching the pistol away. "It doesn't matter what any of them say. They say to unite the town—be it supply runs or revivals,

Decidings and Judgments. But you can't unite what has already rotted away to the core." He took a deep breath. "Ellerie speaks of strange creatures. Of monsters. Harbingers of evil and doom." He turned on me, eyes blazing. "Call them what they really are—devils."

Voices rumbled throughout the crowd, murmuring and hissing.

"And devils don't come unbidden. Someone in Amity Falls wanted those things here. Someone brought them to us. On purpose. To corrupt and twist. To destroy us all."

I shook my head, trying to stop him, but Simon pressed forward, fingers tightening on the gun.

"I was out along my property line this morning when I stumbled across . . . something. It was a circle of stones and trinkets, strange markings in the dirt. It looked a few months old, probably made before the snows set in. Someone came onto my land and summoned this evil. And I know who did it!"

He held a small square of fabric above his head.

"What is it?" Amos McCleary called out, squinting through a black eye.

"A handkerchief. One of Old Widow Mullins's designs. See here the monogram she stitched into it? *S-E-D*."

My throat tightened as he read off the initials. I knew what he was about to say.

"Samuel Elazar Downing," he proclaimed. "He summoned these devils. He brought this darkness upon our town. And look—here is where he sealed the unholy bargain with his own blood. Three drops exactly."

Three drops of blood.

Three drops of blood on a handkerchief.

I'd pressed my bleeding finger to a handkerchief three times, and given it away.

To Whitaker.

I remembered that night's cool darkness. There hadn't been enough starlight for me to make out the pattern embroidered on the corner of the cloth, but I had felt the textured threads. Something had been stitched into Whitaker's handkerchief. Had it been Sam's initials?

And if so, how had that handkerchief made its way to Rebecca's farm? Into a summoning circle? Into Simon Briard's hand?

I broke away from the group, my head spinning and knees buckling, before sinking to the parched earth. My stomach lurched, bringing up a hot splash of bile, and I had to press a hand to my lips to hold it back.

Blood was needed to seal a bargain. I had thought I was pledging a marker to Whitaker alone, but he had used it for a far darker purpose.

My blood had been used to bring these creatures to the Falls.

This was all my fault.

His fault. He summoned them.

Every death, every misfortune these things had wrought was because of me.

Because of him.

I'd . . .

He'd.

Who was he?

The vomit came then, fetid and as thin as gruel. I'd had nothing of substance to eat since the afternoon before, and it felt like knives razing my throat as it fought free.

The stagnant air pressed upon me like stones. My temples pounded and I couldn't stop my limbs from shaking. Thoroughly hollowed out, I curled in on myself, wanting to die.

No one noticed my plight.

I listened in a listless daze as Simon continued his recriminations. The parson joined in. A search was to be organized. They would root through every nook and cranny of Amity Falls until Sam was found and brought forth to stand trial.

"No," I gasped, struggling to push myself up. I remembered with far too much clarity what had happened at the last trial held in Amity Falls. I could not let my twin pay for my mistakes. I'd brought these things to our town.

But even if I was to confess my crime in front of everyone, here and now, I was not certain it would save Sam. This crowd was far too riled to listen to reason's appeal.

I needed to go to the source of the discontent. I needed to find the Dark Watchers and make them stop this. It was my brother's only chance.

I stood on trembling legs, stumbled to the back of the tent, and grabbed at Merry. "We have to get out of here. We have to get to the farm—now!"

As if he heard me, Parson Briard cast his gaze toward us with a fiery fury. Hot spots of righteous indignation burned across his cheeks. For just a second our eyes met, and his nose wrinkled into a feral snarl. "The Devil has come to Amity Falls. And Samuel Downing has brought him here."

⁂

"She was there; she was right there in the tent with us," I cried as Merry, the Fairhopes, and I fled town, racing home. "What are we going to do?"

"We need to get the little girl and get all of you out of town," Ephraim said.

I stumbled to a stop. "Leave? That's your big plan? I thought you said you were here to fight them? To stop them. If we leave—"

"We survive." Ephraim cut me off with a weighted finality. "We survive to fight again another day."

"But . . . what about everyone else? The town, they—"

"They're all able to make their own decisions. You owe them nothing, Ellerie."

"We can't leave without Sam—they're going after him. They think he summoned the Dark Watchers here."

Ephraim shook his head in disgust. "They're not demons waiting to be called upon. That's not how they work. They just . . . *exist* here, in our world. Like water-hounds and krakens, ahools and thunderbirds, shucks and tatzelwurms. Dark Watchers aren't things to be manipulated or controlled." He paused, considering. "Unless, of course . . ."

"What?" I asked, leaping onto his uncertainty.

"Unless he somehow knew their names . . ."

"Sam didn't bring them here. He couldn't have," I insisted.

Ephraim nodded. "Of course not. Judging by how far their darkness has spread—to the forest's creatures, the farm animals, even all of you—they've been here for years, watching, waiting."

Merry frowned. "You really think they've been here that long? Simon said the summoning circle was only a few months old. And the handkerchief—"

A roar of recognition filled my ears, and I didn't hear the rest of what Merry said. I'd made that marker in October, long after the men in Jeb McCleary's supply run had been killed. The wolves, or whatever animal they had begun as, had been tainted well before my bargain with Whitaker.

Out of the stifling, suffocating haze of the revival tent, I could see that now.

This was not my fault.

My blood had not unwittingly brought the Dark Watchers to our town.

I wanted to sink to the ground as relief poured through me and hollowed out all the places where dread had been. "How . . . how many of them are there?"

"According to our records, two made the initial crossing from England, but they've increased in number. The Queen. A young girl—"

"Abigail," I said unhappily.

"An older woman and two men."

"Five Dark Watchers?" I gasped, tallying them on my fingers.

A sweat broke across Merry's brow that had nothing to do with the heat of the day. "There are Dark Watchers who are men?"

Ephraim nodded as though that should have been obvious.

"Are you . . . are you all right, Merry?" Thomas stepped forward to place a hand gently on her back.

"I thought . . . You only ever spoke of the Queen—the woman Ellerie and Cyrus saw. And then Judd's daughter at the revival, she saw the little girl that Sadie has. . . . I just thought they were all women."

Thomas and Ephraim exchanged concerned glances.

"Merry?" I asked.

"You said . . . you said they offer to give people things, right?"

Ephraim waited a beat before responding. "Whatever you want, whatever you long for most."

She lowered her head. "Like . . . a chocolate cake?" Merry murmured, so quiet, I almost didn't catch it.

I turned to her, stunned. "Sadie's birthday. That was you?"

"He told me there was chocolate powder in Mr. Danforth's storage room. . . ."

I placed my hand on her shoulder. "Who did?"

She squirmed away from my touch. "God."

Her morning prayers in the middle of the flower field.

I remembered her arms outstretched, palms up, reverent and beseeching.

She'd been alone then, I was sure of it.

But I'd also thought Abigail was nothing more than pretend.

Her lips trembled. "I just . . . I need you to know . . . I didn't know. I didn't . . . I truly thought . . ."

"Merry." I kept my voice gentle. "What did you . . . what did you think you were praying for?"

Her lashes were thick with tears. "At first, all my prayers were for good things—a strong harvest, that Papa wouldn't be stung, that our garden would do well. . . . I was surprised when he answered back, when I could actually hear him, but the Bible is full of moments when God talks to people. I didn't think to question it. And . . . he listened to me. He really did. . . . But then . . . Sadie wanted that cake so badly . . . That night when I went out to pray . . . it just sort of fell out."

"You asked for the cake."

She nodded, miserable.

"What did God—what did *he* say you needed to do?"

She looked away, guilt clouding her face.

"You trashed Cyrus's supply room?"

"I was only supposed to knock over some of the canisters. But . . . it was kind of fun, spilling flour and watching all the molasses run everywhere. I didn't know Mr. Danforth would get so angry—or hurt Mama." Merry blanched, looking as if she might throw up.

I wanted to comfort her, wanted to tell her that everything was going to turn out all right, but I couldn't. There were too many unknowns, too many uncertainties. The world seemed poised on the brink of burning out in madness. I couldn't guarantee otherwise.

"We'll think of how to fix this. Somehow. After we help Sam," I promised, pressing a kiss into her hair. "Wherever he is."

"It's absurd that the townspeople think that boy is somehow controlling the Dark Watchers," Ephraim said, bringing us back to the problem at hand.

"But someone could be, right? You said something about

the Dark Watchers' names," I murmured. "What—what did you mean?"

Thomas jumped in. "It's one of Father's theories. . . . The creatures the Brotherhood hunts are very much flesh and blood, but over time they've taken on almost a supernatural status. Stories and songs are written about them, myths and legends. Even children's fairy tales, warning of what lurks in the night—"

"Every story contains some fragment of truth," Ephraim cut in. "You need to glean it from the inflated hyperbole." He fumbled for his glasses but didn't remove them. "Across Europe, folktales are littered with entities able to grant the dearest wishes of people's hearts, in exchange for a little favor. When the bargains inevitably go wrong, the heroes must learn the creatures' names to break them. That's the grain of truth. Their true names hold great sway. If you know it, you control them."

"But you do, don't you? Know the Dark Watchers' names?" I glanced between the two men. "Right?"

Thomas shrugged helplessly. "They've had many monikers over the years. The All-Seeing, the Unblinking. The name 'Dark Watchers' is just something Father and I made up."

I froze as his words washed over me. Realization sparked, a bit of steel striking flint. The sparks grew, kindling into a fire and driving back the darkness in my mind until I could see everything, so clearly.

"Because things . . . important things . . . have names," I whispered, balling my hands into fists as the world spun.

I'd said that to Whitaker before.

There's a power in names, don't you think? Once your name is given away, you can't help but be pulled along by those who have it.

My throat clenched, suddenly too dry, too thick.

Whitaker hadn't brought the Dark Watchers to Amity Falls.

Whitaker *was* a Dark Watcher.

I wanted to sink to my knees, the truth hitting me like a battering ram.

He was one of those things. One of the monsters.

It wasn't possible.

He was Whitaker.

My Whitaker.

The boy I'd come to trust and care for.

The boy I'd fallen in love with.

But deep inside, I *knew*.

There were too many moments that didn't make sense. Too many times he'd evaded telling me the whole story.

Because the full truth would have damned him.

"Sadie," I murmured.

She was back at the house, all alone, with *him*.

"We . . . we have to get going. Right now."

I turned and raced down the road. The others followed, gasping, but I couldn't slow down for them. I had to get to my little sister.

Dust kicked up behind me. It was so hot. So dry. Our land was dying, tainted by the presence of the Dark Watchers. Tainted by him. Whitaker. His betrayal stung worse than a rattler's bite.

How could he have lied so easily?

How could I not have guessed?

As I rounded the bend and our farmhouse came into view, I wanted to cry in relief.

Sadie was there, sitting on the porch and lazily kicking herself back and forth in a rocking chair.

Whitaker sat on the steps nearby, fanning his face with his hat.

He stood as he saw our return, but froze as he caught sight of me. Recognition flooded over his face, and without wasting a moment, he turned and disappeared around the side of house, heading for the forest even as Sadie protested.

I looked back. "Ephraim, you must have some idea—what are their names?"

"Their names?" he panted, face red and breath wheezy. "I don't truly know. We'd hoped to learn more here—we'd hoped. . . . There's still time to leave all this. . . . We can start again elsewhere."

I shook my head, my mind made up. "I'm not running from them. This has to end. Now."

"Ellerie, you can't possibly mean to—"

"Merry, watch after Sadie. Stay here and make sure all the windows and doors are shut and barred tight. If anyone from town comes looking for Sam . . ." I couldn't complete that horrible thought. "Ephraim, Thomas . . . keep them safe. I'll be back as soon as I can."

"Ellerie, wait!" Merry cried after me, but I was already gone.

36

*"Rule Number Seven: Enter not the forest deep.
Beyond the Bells, the dark fiends keep."*

WITHOUT A TRACE OF LIGHT OR LUCK, I PLUNGED INTO the pines.

He would find me; I was certain of it.

Through the trees, through the Bells. Their pealing chimes filled the air, marking my passage, as telling as a stain of ink across a page.

And suddenly he was there before me, in the middle of a small clearing at the edge of the Bells.

Whitaker.

Not Whitaker.

Not even the person I'd assumed was Whitaker.

Not even a person, truly.

Was he?

Despite everything I knew, I wanted to race to him.

He didn't *look* like I'd thought they would. He had no claws or sharp teeth. His eyes were warm and kind and most decidedly not silver. Doubt curled through my limbs as they sought to betray me.

What if I was wrong?

As the pine trees gave way to tall grasses and wild brambles, I paused.

"Ellerie."

His tone was too casual. Too practiced. He knew I knew. His voice betrayed everything.

He ran his tongue over the edge of his teeth, his eyes sharp and appraising. "You know." I nodded. He pressed his lips together, his expression flat. "What gave it away?"

"The summoning circle at the Danforths' farm."

Every fiber inside me screamed for him to deny it. But he remained still.

"That wasn't anything more than a campfire."

I swayed back and forth. "It was enough to panic everyone in town."

"Then it served its purpose, I suppose."

"That was my marker, wasn't it?"

His head dipped once.

"How did you get Sam's handkerchief?"

He shrugged. "It wasn't hard. Just a small favor from Trinity Brewster while she visited Sadie. She wanted a new set of jacks." He brushed his thumb over the pads of his fingers, a small twitch, like the tail of a cat. "If it makes a difference to you, I had it long before we ever met."

"It doesn't."

His lips twisted. "No. I suppose not."

"How . . . how could you?" He said nothing. "The whole town is after Sam. They think he brought you here—summoned the devil to make all these terrible things happen."

His eyes stayed steadily on mine, motionless.

"They'll take him to the Gallows. Is that what you want?"

"I want . . ." His gaze faltered. "What I want is complicated." He took an agitated step forward as if the distance between us pained him. "I did come to this valley wanting . . ." He looked away, guilt ingrained in his face. "But now . . . I'd never hurt you. Or your family."

My family.

I pictured Sadie and Merry at the farm, keeping watch at the windows.

I pictured Sam hiding in a barn, or a shed, or a cave by the Greenswold, and prayed no one had found him yet.

I pictured . . .

My shoulders stiffened as a startling chill flooded me.

"Mama and Papa."

Their names escaped in a soft, breathless hiss. Fear stabbed at my core, gutting me with ruthless efficiency as I pictured the last moment I'd seen them, tucked away in the back of the wagon together, Whitaker at the reins. He'd taken them into the forest and then . . . what?

"They're dead, aren't they? You didn't really take them to the city. You never left the Falls."

He reached out, stopping himself before he touched me. "You know I did."

"I don't."

"I brought them there. I brought you that fabric."

"Fabric you stole from Letitia Briard. Or had some other stupid fool steal for you. For a favor," I spat.

He drew his eyebrows together, wounded. "What? No. Ellerie. No. How could you ever—"

"What else am I to think? You ferried them up the side of the mountain out of the goodness of your heart?"

"I did it because I lo—"

"Don't say it!" I snapped, cutting him off. "Don't ever say that again."

"But it's true."

"It can't be. You're lying. To me or to yourself. It doesn't matter. I'm through believing anything you say."

I looked away, fighting the sudden urge to cry. This was too much. This was all too much.

He took the last step, closing the gap between us, and grabbed my elbows. He twisted his grip, trying to force me to meet his gaze.

"I didn't kill your parents. Look at me! Am I lying now?"

I struggled against his grasp. "I don't know."

"You do," he growled, tipping my chin up.

My treacherous fingers ached to curl around his shoulders, sink into their security, and pull him down to my lips. I dropped my hands to my sides before they could carry out their betrayal. I didn't want to look at him. I didn't want to look and see the face I knew so well, the face I'd grown to care for, worn like a mask over the blank vacancy of a stranger.

But his insistence was heavy, his hold firm. I resisted as long as I could but finally gave in. When he stared down at me, his face open and clear, it was Whitaker I saw. Not a monster, just a man.

"You're not lying."

He loosened his grip, running his fingers down my arms. They touched my wrists gently, pleading.

"Good. That's good."

"But it doesn't change anything," I added hastily, dashing any chance he might have had for hope. "You . . . you're one of them."

"I am."

"You lied about that."

"I didn't lie. I just never said the truth. There's a difference in that."

"Is there?"

His eyes fell. I'd hurt him, and I knew I needed to act fast, act

now, while guilt twisted at him, curling and coiling like a poisonous snake.

"I need your help."

"I can get you out of the Falls," he promised, spots of color
burning his cheeks earnestly. "Your sisters too. Before . . . before
everything falls apart."

"Everything *has* fallen apart. But I think I know how to stop
it." I touched his cheek. "Tell me her name."

His face fell into studied confusion. "Whose?"

"You know who I'm talking about. The woman. Your leader,
your Queen. Whatever you call her . . . I need her name."

"I can't give that to you, Ellerie."

"You can."

He shook his head. "I want to help you—you've no idea how
much I want to, especially . . ." He swallowed. "It's my fault we're
here in the first place. If I hadn't . . . If I hadn't seen you . . . none
of this would have happened."

"What do you mean?"

He stepped away, wandering deeper into the glade, shame
weighing down his every footstep. "We don't always stay together,
the Kindred. If there's not a game afoot, we wander the land on our
own, looking for diversions, looking for the next hunt." He twisted
his fingers, balling them into fists. "Two years ago, maybe three, I
came across this range. At first I didn't think much of it. . . . It's so
isolated, so wild. But then I heard the Bells. Everywhere I went,
there were more and more of them, their chimes pulling me in,
drawing me out of the mountains, down to this valley. I saw the
lake and I saw the village. And then I saw you. . . ."

His eyes shifted, meeting mine with pained remorse.

"I saw a girl—this beautiful, radiant girl, with honey-colored
hair—standing at the edge of the forest. It was almost as if she was

making up her mind about something. Indecision was written all over her face; her eyes were raw with yearning. One foot was in the fields, solidly planted in her world, but the other foot trembled over the tree line, wanting to take to the woods, to learn its mysteries, to come find me—even if she didn't know it at the time." He flicked his fingers as if picking something from his nail. "I couldn't get her out of my mind, no matter how I tried. She was always there, just on the edge of everything, waiting. Wanting. I wanted to be there when she was brave enough to take that next step."

"I don't remember."

It wasn't quite a lie.

Though I wasn't sure of the exact day in question, I'd always felt a certain watchfulness standing before the pines. I'd thought it was the trees themselves, holding their breaths, waiting for something to happen.

Had they been waiting on Whitaker all along? Waiting and watching him watch me?

Goose bumps rose along my arms, pebbled against the stifling humidity.

"I kept watch from the woods, kept returning season after season to watch her. Her honey-colored hair became the loveliest strands of gold," he whispered, gesturing with spindle-thin fingers. Breath caught in the hollow of my throat as though he'd actually touched me. The thought of him stroking my hair set my teeth on edge with a strange, aching pleasure.

Though he remained motionless, I could feel him reaching toward me, beckoning, begging for me to come forward. I wanted to, wanted to move, to step toward him until there was no longer any space between us, but my feet stayed resolutely in place, anchored to the forest floor, unmoving and still.

"What happened then?"

"The others found their way back to me. We never can stay apart for long. They came and they watched. And then *she* decided it was time to be seen."

"Levi Barton," I guessed. "The farmer who . . ." I couldn't bear to finish the thought.

He nodded, weary. "He wasn't well. Such a broken soul, longing for so much more than he already had. She gave him fistfuls of gold, just as he'd wanted. He was supposed to—I don't even remember now—but he grew paranoid, fearful his newfound wealth would be stolen. He didn't trust his neighbors, his own wife."

I remembered the burning, desperate suspicion that had come over me once I'd been given the sugar. I understood with perfect, horrible clarity how such a gift could be corrupted by fear. Tainted and twisted. Taken over by the darkness. We truly were no different from the animals in the forest, our very nature grown distorted and perverse in the presence of the Dark Watchers.

"Then . . . she decided to stay. Amity Falls seemed like the perfect place for a new game." He shook his head. "I'm sorry for that. I'm sorry I ever stumbled across this place. If I could take it back . . ." He sighed. "I want to say I would, but . . ." He paced, drawing closer. "You're the only person who's ever known I lied about my name."

His voice echoed strangely in the glade, a trick that made it seem as if he was directly behind me, heating the air around my ear with his breath, his lips brushing the hairs of my skin.

"You look at me in a way I've never seen before." He brushed his fingertips across the softness of my cheek, looking at me as if I was the wonder. "Others see me as a means to an end . . . but to you, I was only ever a man."

He cupped my face, tilting it toward his. His eyes shone, dark and haunted.

"I would give everything I have to be that man for you," he whispered. "But I never will be. I . . . I can't. I don't remember how and . . . I can't change who I've been, what I've done." He let out a short bark of a laugh. "You've no idea of the things I've done."

"Why don't you just leave? You could walk away, leave them all, and never look back. You could . . ." I ran fingers over his shoulders, recalling every silly, sentimental thought I'd ever dared to dream about him. "You could stay with me. I don't care about your past. We're here, right now, in this moment. Your past can't touch this. It can't define your future. *Our* future," I added firmly.

"These," he said, holding up his wrists, displaying the encircling green tattoos. Some of the bands were thick, with circles of un-inked skin perforating them like moon phases. Others were impossibly thin, stacked on one another like layers of Mama's honey cakes. "Every new place, new village, new town . . . every time I watch . . . another band is added. I don't know how; they just appear when the job is done."

I stared at the emerald ink with a sick fascination. There were so many lines. Dozens of them. How many lives had he watched fall apart? How many towns had been destroyed? Families devastated?

"The others see them as trophies, marking victories well won, but they're nothing more than shackles, reminders of the things, the *awful* things, I've done. They're on me forever, never letting me forget. I tried to go—to leave the Kindred—earlier this spring, but they pulled me back anyway. I can't escape my past, Ellerie. There's no point in trying."

I fell to my knees, grasping at his hands, desperate to change his mind. Hot tears streamed down my face. "You *can*. Just tell me her name. Whitaker, *please*."

He shook his head. "I wish I could."

"Then do it! Just say it," I pleaded.

His eyebrows furrowed together. "She won't let me. It's impossible." He opened his mouth, and his lips pursed as if to form a word, but nothing came out.

I tangled my fingers through his. They'd always felt so strong and sure before. Now they hung between mine, wavering and complacent.

"There must be something . . ." I trailed off as a bit of movement caught my attention. A white dress flickered in and out of the trees, always on the edge of my vision. Silver eyes, there one moment and gone the next. It was like trying to focus on heat waves in the dog days of summer.

I'd almost convinced myself the movement was a figment of my imagination, but then Whitaker froze, confirming her presence. His face hardened, growing distant. The edges of his eyes flickered like a predator's at night.

Not the boy I knew and loved.

The creature.

"There's nothing. Not even for the girl who can name every flower. The girl who thinks she can name the stars. The girl who thought she could name me."

His voice rang cold, his tone barbed and cruel. Was he acting for her benefit, or did her presence simply reveal him as he'd always been?

"Whitaker, I—"

He pulled me to my feet, swift and strong. And then his lips were on mine, moving with thorough deliberateness. He swept me against him, his hands curved at the back of my neck, loosening my braid. Silky strands whispered across his fingers.

It was a kiss goodbye, I realized too late, tasting of salt and regret.

When he broke away, he trailed his thumb over my lips,

memorizing their lines before pushing me backward, causing me to stumble from him.

"Whitaker!" I gasped, stunned.

He turned, unable to meet my gaze. "Go back, Ellerie. Go back and get out of Amity Falls. Go now before you can't."

"I can't leave Samuel to die."

He bared his teeth once before fading into the woods' embrace. "He would you."

37

I STARED AFTER HIS RETREATING FORM, BLINKING WITH incoherence. He'd left me. He'd admitted to all the terrible things his twisted family had planned—the terrible things he'd already done himself—and then he'd left me.

Alone.

With her.

I spun back to where I'd last seen the almost-not-quite suggestion of her form, but there was nothing but pines now, dark and unyielding.

Then, a shift behind me.

Her.

I whirled around.

She was smaller than I'd imagined, clothed in a fine dress of white eyelet lace. An afternoon dress, as if she was civil enough to be on her way to a tea.

Her hair was as dark as a midnight sky, worn half up, with the loose ringlets curled so perfectly, they looked like a porcelain doll's. Her cheeks held a rosy hue, just shy of a blush. Thick lashes framed her eyes, which were an impossibly vivid shade of green, though they reflected light like a feral animal's as they shifted directions, giving off quick flashes of silver.

"Ellerie Downing," she drawled, soft and sweet. "We finally meet, face to face."

"I'm not accustomed to not knowing my companion's name," I called out, my bravado ringing false in my ears.

Her full lips curved into a smile, and she waggled one finger back and forth as if I was a naughty child. It was too long. Much too long, with painfully gnarled knuckles and a talon-like claw for a nail.

"You've caused quite a stir among my Kindred," she said. "Your name rings hot on all our lips."

"I can't imagine why."

Her carefully composed expression twisted into a smirk. "In all our years, we've never encountered someone with the audacity to name one of us. What was the ridiculous moniker you came up with? Whitten? Whitehead?"

"Whitaker," I said, taking the bait.

Another smirk. "Whitaker. He's grown quite fond of you. Too fond, really. It's actually rather a nuisance."

I called upon every bit of mettle within me to not tremble before her. "Am I meant to apologize?"

She shrugged lightly. "It doesn't matter in any case. Even without Whitaker's help, the die has been cast."

"Without his help? He brought you here in the first place!"

She nodded. "For what it's worth, I suppose that's true. It really was quite the idyllic spot for a hunt. I certainly didn't expect the game to take such a turn. It's been fascinating to watch. And of course, you've added such a delightful twist to the play." She grinned, flashing the sharp barbs of her teeth.

"Me?" I blinked, hoping it was a trick of light, but no. Her teeth fanged into points, strange and translucent. They reminded me of the pike Papa often caught in the Greenswold, with rows and rows of teeth, waiting to sink and tear.

"Oh yes. It's why I wanted to meet you. I've come to make you an offer, you see."

"What on earth could you possibly have to offer me?"

Her head tilted, cocking to the side and spilling her lustrous hair down one shoulder. "I would have thought that was obvious."

"What?"

"Why, the safety of your family, of course. Merry and . . . who's the little one? Sadie!"

Hearing my sisters' names on her lips made my stomach ache, feeling oily and sick. "Stay away from them." Warning laced my words, however futilely. If she decided to harm them, how was I to stop her?

Her laughter rang out, as bright as tinkling glass, silver spoons chiming against fine crystal. It almost dazzled me into forgetting the parts of her that were so terribly wrong. "If you were to do something for me, I can guarantee your sisters will make it through alive and well." She leaned closer, and I could smell her perfume, floral and coy. "I will keep them safe."

"Just them?" I asked. "What about Sam?"

"Oh . . . Sam has already seen fit to take care of himself. Don't spend a moment's worry on him."

My mouth felt dry and sour. "What do you mean?"

"He'll be fine, Ellerie. Just fine. But your sisters . . ."

"What . . . what would I have to do?"

She beamed and made a small gesture out to the trees. "Join us."

A stream of figures emerged from the forest. A tall man, his skin dark and gleaming, took off his top hat, doffing it in my direction. He wore buckskin breeches, fringed and beaded.

Whitaker's Burnish, I thought, before shoving the thought aside. That wasn't his name. It had never been his name.

There was an older woman wearing a plain black dress, accented only by a wide white yoke and cuffs. Her graying hair was parted severely down the center, neatly covered by an outdated bonnet.

And a little girl—the so-called Abigail—a blur of motion, danced about the meadow, spinning in a dress of dazzling blue satin, trimmed with lace so intricate, she resembled more a child of days gone by, a fairy-tale princess or a bedecked infanta. Her wrists were so decorated with green marks, they nearly reached her elbows. She skipped gaily about, ignoring us all.

Whitaker was noticeably absent.

"Join you?" I repeated.

"Become like us. Become one of us. We've been wanting to add to our Kindred for years, but the right someone had eluded us." She smiled again. "Until now."

"Become like you—you mean you're not . . . you've not always been . . ." My mouth dried, realizing what she implied.

"They were human once too," the Queen said, putting words to my struggles of the idea. "Before."

"Whitaker was human," I said slowly, letting the idea sink in.

It shouldn't have changed anything.

It didn't, not truly.

But it felt like it could.

She nodded.

I glanced at the others dotting the meadow. "And you . . . you all chose this? You knew the destruction she causes, and you—"

"I saved my daughter," said the woman in the plain dress. "My Sally. We were new to this land. Struggling every day just to get by. No food. Little water. Supplies raided. Children taken right out from their tents in the dead of night. Our colony was on the brink of madness. None of us would have made it out alive." She paused. "And none of us did—except for her. Sally. I traded my life—as I'd known it—for hers."

The man nodded, eyes flashing and beguiling. "My brother."

It was said with such simple stoicism, I ached.

The little girl who wasn't Abigail stopped dancing. "My *maman* and *papa*." Her voice had a musical lilt, like the old fur trapper Jean Garreau's. "The Great Sickness swept through our town. Our servants brought it to the manor, dying right and left, sweating and stinking." Her nose crinkled as she remembered. "*Papa* caught it first, then me. *Maman* never left our side, looking after us even as she fell ill." She paused, offering a grateful smile to her Queen. "They're long dead now, but I have a new *maman*."

"And Whitaker?" I turned back to the Queen, seeking her answer.

Her lips pressed into a thin line. "A sister. Such a sickly thing, if I remember right." She raised her shoulders in a delicate shrug. "It's been decades."

I thought back to Sadie's birthday and the flower crowns he and I had woven alongside the lake. He'd spoken of a sister then.

Amelia.

"Where is he now?" I asked, glancing around the meadow. "They're all here. Where is he?"

"I didn't need him interfering. Not while we have this little chat, you and I."

I remembered his abrupt change once he'd spotted her among the trees, and understanding rippled through me. "You . . . you can control them?"

She glanced toward the other Dark Watchers. Without a flicker of effort from her, they began to walk backward, moving in perfectly eerie unison, their faces as blank as poppets, their silver eyes as flat as beaten nickels. Abigail's legs had to stretch into impossibly long strides to keep pace with the two adults. They all stopped at the same moment and stood, frozen and waiting to be of use.

My mouth hung open, astonished. "How did you do that?"

"How does the moon hold sway over the waves? How do your queens rule their hives? It's just our nature."

"But Whitaker . . . I've never seen him look like . . . look like that." My eyes darted to Burnish's expressionless eyes, and then snapped away. It was uncomfortable to witness such complete servitude.

She frowned. "No. He's proved to be less malleable than the others."

"The luck," I whispered, thinking of his endless supply of trinkets. "It holds back the darkness."

"Holds back *me,*" she corrected me. She tilted her head as if it was inconsequential. "It's not enough to truly override my desires, but it's enough to grant him the illusion of control."

"He chose . . . this . . . to save his sister," I murmured, piecing everything together.

His reluctance to speak of his past.

Mentions of a debt to be paid.

She nodded. "To save her from certain death. Just as you can save yours. If . . ." She left the word hanging in midair, silvery and slippery with potential.

"If I join you."

Her face remained placid, as if it didn't matter to her which path I chose, but I noticed a burning edge in her eyes. She wanted me to say yes. Badly.

"But I don't want to save only my sisters. I want to free the whole town."

She raised one eyebrow with amusement. "That's not what I offered."

"You wouldn't have to offer it—not if I know your name. Your true name," I clarified, cutting off whatever pithy remark she'd undoubtedly planned to counter with.

Her smile was sly and biting. "You're welcome to test your luck. We can even change the terms of the deal, if you like. I'll give you three chances to guess my name."

I felt myself begin to nod, lulled into complacency.

"If you don't guess correctly," she continued, raising that one horrifically malformed finger. "You join us."

"But if I do?" I asked, wanting the terms to be said aloud.

"Then whatever you want is yours, if it's within my power."

My heart thunked painfully in my chest, and I tried to arrange my face into a bland expression. This was what I wanted. This was my chance to save everyone, to save the Falls.

But now that I was here, in this moment, I was terrified to reveal that she'd called my bluff. I didn't know her name. I didn't have a clue as to what it could be.

Or did I?

Whitaker's strange farewell still rang through my head, ripples of a rock dropped into a still pond. His words lingered, twisting over one another into a puzzle. I was certain they meant more than their first impression.

If I could piece them together, would I come up with the Queen's name?

Think. Think, Ellerie. What had he said? Exactly?

The girl who can name every flower.

I recalled that afternoon in the meadow, alongside the Greenswold, the sun's rays long and warm at our backs. We'd picked clovers and I'd made Sadie her birthday crown. I'd pressed him to admit his name. There'd been a flower. . . . What was it?

I closed my eyes, trying to remember.

We'd been walking, and there had been little bursts of yellow and orange—like fireworks exploding in the midst of all that green.

Field marigolds—but I'd called them by their species name,

their true name. There'd been surprise in his eyes when he'd learned that I knew the Latin. Surprise . . . and maybe a touch of worry?

The girl who thinks she can name the stars.

Christmas night. Dancing in the snow. And spotting a constellation. He'd said it was ridiculous to christen something so far away . . . but he'd asked if I knew more of the myths.

The girl who thought she could name me.

Here I stilled, my theories stalling. The name "Whitaker" hadn't been taken from a myth or a dead language. There were no heroes, no legends. It had been the most pragmatic of choices. A name inspired by him.

A name that meant something.

I glanced back at the Queen. She was still waiting for my answer. If I did this, if I did this wholly stupid and unthinkable thing, I could save Amity Falls. If I succeeded, I could save everyone I knew and loved.

Or.

Or I could fail and become one of the Dark Watchers. My skinned crawled, just thinking about it, and my stomach flipped with revulsion. But if the worst should happen, my sisters would be safe. . . .

Sometimes we have to overlook our own desires for the betterment of the hive as a whole.

Papa's words returned to me, floating up out of a memory and ringing with importance. He was right. The good of the hive was more important than the life of one little bee.

"Yes," I decided. "I'll accept your offer."

Her smile was quick and altogether too lovely.

"Excellent."

"Should we . . . should we start now?"

I felt the weight of her silver eyes heavily upon me. "It's strange."

"What is?"

"I would have expected twins to be more alike," she mused thoughtfully. "But you're an altogether other sort. Two garments cut from very different cloth." She blinked, as if working out a trying puzzle before her.

"What do you mean?"

"I met your shadow in the woods once."

"Sam? Sam isn't a shadow."

"Isn't he? A lesser copy of the original? He'd found himself in a bit of a predicament, a nasty little moment with a pack of wolves."

"The supply run," I guessed, and my breath caught as it finally dawned on me. "You saved him. You're the reason he survived that attack."

Her smile deepened. "It wasn't terribly difficult. Not for me. But he was grateful. So grateful, he offered up your life in exchange for his."

A black coil of dread uncurled within my belly. He wouldn't have. "What?"

He'd bargained me away. My own brother. My other self. Indignation tore at my throat, showering sparks of anger. At him. At her. Why had she bothered with the pretense of a deal if Sam had already—

Her laughter was as bright as sunlight. "Of course I told him that wasn't possible. You can't go around pledging other people as payment for your own debts. Can you imagine? Oh, but how that infuriated him." She clicked her tongue. "Such different characters. Truly a wonder."

"But . . . what did he offer? It had to have been something special. He made it out of the woods. He's alive. Tell me," I insisted.

She paused, considering me. "He owes me a lie."

Laughter snorted out of me. "You didn't make a very good bargain. Sam lies about everything."

She shrugged. "This is a very special one. An important one.

427

One given at exactly the wrong—or right—moment." Her glee could hardly be contained.

"What do you mean? When?"

She tweaked my nose. "That, my girl, is entirely between your brother and me."

I squirmed away from her touch. Her fingers, so mangled and misshapen, felt wholly wrong against my skin, like the rough scrape of tree bark.

"Let's begin, then, shall we?" Dimples winked from her soft and rosy cheeks.

"But—"

"Now!" she snapped, and for the sharpest moment, her features blurred, chaos and discord screaming out over the beauty. I wanted to look away, to cower and sink into the earth. But it was over in less than a second, and the human features regained control, settling over her monstrous form like a costume cloak.

She ran the backs of her fingers along her jaw, as if reassuring herself that everything was put back into place, before offering a winning smile of contrition. "Now, honey-haired girl. My name."

Her name.

A name.

Any name.

Names are meant to have meaning.

My words from the flower field echoed back to me.

A name that meant something.

This thing before me. What summed her up? What resonated through her veins? What christening befit such a creature, so dark yet lovely?

Aphrodite, goddess of beauty.

It was the first thing to come to mind, but I tossed it aside. It wasn't quite right for this Queen. Her beauty was dazzling, to be sure, but there was a sharp edge beneath it, hard and calculating, twisted and cruel. Aphrodite was also goddess of love. This Dark Watcher exemplified many things, but affection was not one of them.

"Helen," I guessed, remembering the capricious queen whose beauty had brought nothing but destruction. It was a strong choice. One I felt neatly summed up this Queen.

"You think my face could launch a thousand ships?" She beamed. "I'm flattered, Ellerie, but no, that's not my name."

Two chances left.

I racked my mind, trying to remember every story in the book of myths that Sam and I had pored over as children. There were tales of heroes and rulers, gods and monsters. Some seemed to fit, but I remembered Whitaker's mention of the stars. It was another clue, I was certain of it.

"Cassiopeia," I tried, brightening. It was the constellation I'd pointed out to Whitaker at Christmas. The vain queen. I couldn't believe it hadn't occurred to me first.

Her smile grew into a wicked grin. "No."

"You're lying," She had to be. It made too much sense to not be true.

"One guess left."

I wanted to howl.

I thought through every constellation I knew, not just considering the shape—what it was meant to depict—but what the object really represented as a whole.

Orion and his famed belt did me little good, and neither did the sets of bears. My mind was dizzy with stars as I imagined their points and patterns, dredging up the stories Papa had told us when we were children and the summer nights were long and bright.

Whales and swans, foxes and dragons.

None of them were right.

But then . . .

The Harp.

Orpheus's harp.

Would you follow me to the underworld?

Whitaker had seemed so horrified when I'd told him of the doomed musician. Orpheus had had the chance to have everything but had lost it all.

All because he'd turned and watched.

Watched.

A smile curved over my lips.

This was it.

It had to be.

The Harp.

But it wasn't a harp exactly, not in the original myth. What was it called?

A lyre.

"Lyra," I said, remembering the constellation's proper name. Its right and true name.

She froze, and for one horrifying second, her whole façade fell away, revealing the true creature beneath the dazzling charms.

The jaw hanging too long, with too many teeth.

The frame, hunched and hulking.

Sinewy arms hanging past her knees.

Lank hair falling to her calves, matted and snarled.

For that split second, I saw the monster from Ephraim's journals, and everything within me quivered.

"What—what did you say?" she asked, pushing back a lock of hair, shiny and lush once more as she fought to keep herself together.

"Lyra," I repeated, more loudly this time. "That's your name, isn't it?"

She opened her mouth to reply but stopped short, her eyes darting to the other Dark Watchers in the glade.

Awareness burned in their eyes once more. They were no longer mindless drones carrying out their Queen's orders. When her control had slipped, it must have freed them from their catatonic state.

"How?" the man asked, taking a step toward the Queen—toward Lyra. "How did she know?"

"That fool must have tipped her off somehow," the older woman snapped. "It was stupid for us to have followed him here."

"He can't do that. None of us can. You made certain of that," the man said, whirling back to the Queen.

Lyra shook her head, denying everything. I could see her mind racing, trying to spin the situation to her favor, even as she lost grip on her mask of composure.

Other faces appeared in place of hers, their features morphing as fluidly as water over stone.

Twisted noses.

Inhuman ridges.

Exposed bone.

So many kinds of teeth.

"What now?" the older woman asked. "What happens now?"

Lyra balled her fists and, with a howl of frustration, grappled back to her previous form, even though it no longer seemed to sit on her correctly. Once you saw behind the illusion of a trick, it was impossible to believe it had ever been magic.

But still, she tried.

In a single motion, perfectly synchronized, every Dark Watcher's eyes fell upon me.

"Well, little honey-haired girl?" Lyra asked, her voice high and imperious. "You've won the game. What will your prize be? Go on, tell us the deepest desire of your heart."

I knew my answer.

Amity Falls.

But as I stared at her, unbidden thoughts entered my mind, sparkling madly like facets of a priceless diamond.

Pretty dresses, jewels, and charms. Eternal beauty, admiration, and praise. What would my life be like if I traipsed through the world as radiant and beguiling as the creature who stood before me?

She smiled as if sensing my thoughts, and I suddenly realized she knew exactly what I'd been thinking because she'd engineered them all in an attempt to distract me from my true mission.

"I want the madness to stop. I want my town to go back to how it was before you arrived. I want you to leave here and never return."

A frown marred her beatific face. "But that's impossible. The hatred, the violence—the madness, as you call it—was always there. It's been there, hidden away in the hearts of every person in Amity Falls. Our arrival didn't change that. We simply unlocked the door holding it back."

I shook my head. "I don't believe that. The Falls is full of good people. People who would never behave as they are now if they'd not been bewitched by you. By all of you." I shot a daggered glare toward Abigail and the others.

"I can't undo the past, Ellerie. No one can. Too many things are in motion already. It's like dye spreading across cloth—you can scrub till your knuckles are raw and bloody, but the two will never be separated again."

As if punctuating her words, a great rumble exploded through the forest, coming from the direction of town. Its force brought me to my knees as the ground shook. Little pebbles of slate and shale trembled free from larger rock faces, spilling down the incline with the loose clatter of an avalanche. A nearby pine, dead and dry and as yellow as a corn husk left after harvest, ripped free from its stagnant roots and crashed to the ground with a terrifying *boom*.

Other thuds echoed through the forest. The people of the Falls weren't the only ones suffering in this summer drought.

There was another explosion, closer to us, and giant comets rocketed into the sky, blazing orange and red. They arced high, blocking out the sun, before gravity pulled them back. They fell fast, plummeting to earth and pounding into the trees.

"Do you see now why I can't stop this?" Lyra asked. "There are too many wheels turning. Too much madness in the air. Too much hatred burning. Burning and churning and—"

Dark smoke rose out of the pines, pushed about by a hot wind. It wafted toward town, whirling with specks of ash and dancing embers. Dread bloomed deep within me, filling my rib cage, unfurling its dark fingers into my wrists, my knees, until all of my bones ached with its weight.

"We haven't had rain all year." My voice sounded flat and impossibly far away. "The whole town will go up like a tinderbox."

"That's our cue to leave you." She nodded to the others. Bloodlust danced across their faces, their eyes silver and hungry.

"No," I said, holding out my hand. "Stop."

The four Dark Watchers stilled. Lyra cocked her head.

"You may not be able to stop this madness, but that doesn't mean you're going to watch it play out. I banish you from Amity Falls. I want you to go far, far away, to where you can't hurt anyone ever again, and stay there."

The tall man bristled. "Who are you to—"

The Queen cut off his challenge with a sharp movement of her fingers.

"You want us to leave? This is your request?" she asked. Her voice was as light as silk, but her eyes burned with an acute re-sentment, flickering between me and the plumes of smoke. When another explosion went off, jolting the very ground we stood upon, her lips pressed together in a grim snarl, stifling back a howl of rage. "Then I suppose we're all done here."

"Wait," I said, throwing out my hand.

38

THE HOUSE WAS SILENT WHEN I ENTERED IT, TOO STILL
to be occupied.

"Merry?" I called out anyway, wandering from room to room.
"Sadie? Thomas? Ephraim?"

There was no answer.

The empty loft worried me the most. The bedsheets were
twisted and ripped, revealing the ticking mattress beneath.

Had Sadie's condition grown worse, necessitating a trip to town?
Or had they all been taken by force?

My footsteps crunched as I entered the dining room. A teacup
had fallen, and its ceramic shards lay shattered across the floorboards. I picked up a curved piece, examining the little flower
painted on the handle.

It was a lilac.

Mama's favorite cup.

Merry would have never allowed them to leave such a mess
behind. She would have swept it up and run a wet rag over the
floor to make sure none of the stray shards found their way into an
unsuspecting bare foot.

Taken, then.

I didn't want to imagine a mob of angry people marching to

the farm, searching for Sam and finding my sisters in his stead, but the images flooded my mind, each more horrifying than the last. I supposed I should have been grateful that the only damage left was one broken teacup.

I needed to go after them. Needed to find and save them all.

I spun around in the room, searching for anything that would make me feel less alone, less small. I needed something to fill my hands, to buoy my sinking confidence. The situation had spiraled far out of my control, and with every second that ticked by, I grew less certain I would be able to right anything.

Not with words.

Certainly not with reason.

It would have to be by force.

I stared at the empty spot above the mantel. Papa had taken the rifle with him, but his tools were still in the barn.

Hatchets.

Scythes.

Metal.

Blades.

I could do this.

I was halfway across the yard when a familiar hum rose, loud enough to break my grim thoughts, stopping me in my tracks.

The bees.

I couldn't leave the bees.

Not like this, with everyone else gone and the probability of my success dwindling.

They needed to be told.

I had to say goodbye.

I approached the hive boxes slowly, trying to push aside my worries and fears. They would sense them, and I had no time to waste putting on a veil.

I held my hands out, fingers softly splayed, showing them I meant no harm.

The bees drifted in and out of the boxes, seemingly unconcerned by my advance. I tapped gently on the middle box three times, as I remembered Papa doing whenever he had important news to share.

"Hello," I started, overcome by a strange sense of timidity. There was no one remotely close enough to overhear and judge me. And besides . . .

I stilled, watching the honeybees dance in the white-hot sunlight.

These were my bees.

The hive boxes and tools might still have belonged to Papa, but it had been months since he'd been near them. The colonies inside had shifted and repopulated many times since then. Even the queens could have changed, new ones born since I'd stepped into his duties.

Until this moment, I'd never stopped thinking of them as his.

But they weren't.

They were mine.

"It's me, Ellerie," I said, beginning again, with a fresh round of confidence and assurance. "I don't know how much you know about life outside your hives, past the fields and flowers, but things have . . . well, they've not been good lately. And they've gotten even worse today. I wish I could stay here, with you, and just go on tending to the farm, watching you grow and thrive, but I can't. My sisters and my brother—my hive—they need me."

I ran my fingers over the wooden lid, feeling the slight vibration of all the buzzing bodies beneath it.

"And a good queen always tends to her hive, doesn't she?"

A cluster of bees piled out of the entrance and crawled to the top. They were undoubtedly readying themselves for another forage, thinking of all the pollen to gather, but part of me hoped they'd come out to better hear my words.

"It's going to be dangerous leaving the farm and I . . . I don't know if I will make it back. It's strange to think about that—that this could be my last time here, with you, with the farm, with . . . everything. . . ."

Tears pricked at my eyes, and I looked away, blinking them back. I studied the porch steps, picturing Merry on them snapping peas, while Mama peeled potatoes in the rocking chair, singing and smiling. Papa was out in the fields, his big straw hat blocking the sun, while he chatted with the bees buzzing around him. Even Sam was there in my imagination, pushing Sadie on the rope swing under the oak tree. I drank the sight in, savoring the little details so ingrained in my memory. It was like reading a beloved old book. Would we ever be together like that again?

"If I don't . . . If something should happen to me . . . you will always have a home here, if you want it, but you're free to leave, free to swarm away if you need to. Do whatever you need for the good of the hive, all right?"

I wasn't sure how to end my speech, so I simply stepped away before the tears overwhelmed me.

As I trekked toward the barn, a trio of bees raced out in front of me, weaving around themselves. They hovered there for a moment, bobbing up and down, before rising into the sky, taking flight, and leaving me behind.

It felt like a blessing.

It felt like goodbye.

A miserable hot breeze swept by, carrying echoing cries and lingering screams from town. A dark haze blanketed the village, smoke and ash, dirt and debris kicked up from the explosions.

My resolve began to waver as I considered it. Nothing good would be discovered within such malignant murk.

I was in the barn for only a moment, grabbing what I needed from the wall.

With Papa's hatchet heavy in my hand, I made my way back to Amity Falls.

39

"Rule Number One: A rope of great cords will not fray, snap, or weather. The Falls stands strong if we all bind together."

THE SMOKE SMELLED OF BURNING TIMBER AND PITCH, vile and black. It hung thickly in the air, stinging my nostrils and eyes, turning the bright afternoon into a false twilight hellscape, and making it nearly impossible for me to see my surroundings. Though I knew I was on the outskirts of town—there were the Maddins' flower beds, withered away to ragged husks—I'd lost all sense of direction within the poisonous haze.

There were darker shadows that moved within the smoke, warped into nightmarish shapes and creations. I watched agape as an absolute giant swung back a scythe and brought it down upon a writhing mass again and again until the mass moved no more. The titan then turned, shifting its path toward me. I ducked behind a bush in time to see the small form of Mark Danforth hurtle past me. The scythe was easily twice his height. Its blade was slick with red and black and things I cared not to think about. His eyes were completely flat, unable to engage or understand anything that was going on around him.

"Where are you, Finnick?" he sang in an off-key taunt, all but whistling his glee. "I know it was you. You can't hide forever. I'm coming. Oh, I'm coming."

His head shot toward the left with a reptilian snap, and he listened to an approaching skirmish. Rather than flee, he took off after it, his curved blade raised high.

Shrieks rose from inside the Maddins' house, and moments later, a window on the second floor shattered from within. Deadly shards of glass rained upon the parched ground, followed by the meaty thud of a body pushed from the gaping hole. Bonnie let out a final gasping moan before she fell still.

"You there!" growled a voice from the window. A figure—too smudged in soot for me to clearly see—peered down at me.

Alarm flooded my chest, then raced up my throat like a splash of hot vomit.

It was Alice Fowler.

She'd been the one to push Bonnie from the window, killing the girl.

"Is that Ellerie Downing I see?" she called out. With the fire reflecting off her wide eyes, she looked crazed. Alice darted from the window, presumably on her way for me. I stumbled into the murk, heedless of where I was headed. I only knew I needed to get away.

I turned down the street to the right as the Maddins' front door swung open.

"Where are you? Come back here!"

Shouts rose across the road, and the schoolteacher raced after them, certain she was following me instead.

I pressed on, heading deeper into the Falls. Some houses were ablaze, having been caught by falling embers. Others were already gone, burnt down to charred remains. As I turned up Main Street, I found the source of the explosions.

McCleary's general store had been blown to pieces, bricks blasted out across the road like in a game of Trinity Brewster's jacks. The storage room must have caught fire, igniting kegs of gunpowder. The force of it had destroyed all the nearby houses, and the ensuing fires had raced to Matthias Dodson's livery.

Stallions galloped up and down the road, their eyes rolling madly as they tried to escape the inferno, racing like demons set loose upon the earth. Their screams rattled the air. I'd never heard a more horrible sound.

Behind me, hidden somewhere in the hazy madness, a fight broke out. Though unseen, I could hear every accusation hurled, every punch thrown. One of the men was Leland Schäfer. I would have recognized his nervous stutter anywhere.

"Get back, Winthrop, I'm warning you!" he cried. "I'll shoot, I swear!"

"Not if I shoot you first!"

Winthrop Mullins.

He blamed his grandmother's death on the Elder.

And now they both had guns.

I wanted to stop them, to somehow intervene, but I couldn't tell where they were in the shadowy mayhem. Their voices echoed off the walls of smoke, at my left one moment and my right the next.

A gun went off.

Once.

Twice.

The third shot zipped by, nearly grazing my ear as it sped past.

I had to get out of here.

But where to go?

Where would my sisters have been taken?

The Gathering House?

It seemed possible, given that the last Judgment had played out there, but all three Elders would be required, and Leland was too occupied with murdering or being murdered by Winthrop.

My mind skirted past the Gallows. If my brother was there—if all my siblings were there—I did not want to know, didn't want to imagine it, didn't want even a trace of it entering my thoughts, lest I somehow conjure it into existence.

With McCleary's and the livery stables destroyed, my list of public places narrowed considerably.

The tavern . . . or the church.

Squinting through the fiery haze, I picked my way closer to the center of town, dodging altercations, ducking every time I heard gunfire. My axe would do me little good if I found a rifle pointed in my direction.

I heard the shattering of glass as I approached the tavern. It was dark inside, lit only by two hurricane lamps, but I could make out overturned tables, bits of broken chairs, and cutlery strewn about. Whatever fight had broken out here was done and over with, save for one figure behind the bar.

Prudence Latheton scurried back and forth, smashing bottles of liquor with a manic zeal. Her eyes were crazed with a righteous fervor, and her laughter spurted, as deep as a bullfrog's cry.

I stepped inside. The room reeked of spirits and sour mash. It was a wonder the entire building hadn't already gone up in flames, as thoroughly doused as it was.

Prudence swung at a cask of ale with a hatchet of her own, and split open the oaken barrel with a cackle. I knocked into a fallen chair, and she froze, her movements sharp and alert.

"What are you doing in here?" I dared to ask, tightening the hold on my wooden handle. It was a risk, engaging her, but she might know where I needed to be.

"The Lord's work," she said proudly, striking the cask again.

I took an uneasy step closer. "Have you seen my sisters? Or Samuel?"

She raised one dubious eyebrow. "They found him hiding

away like a worm at Bryson's ranch. Carried him out kicking and screaming all the way to the stocks. I imagine he's still there. What's left of him anyway."

"He's dead?"

The words fell from me, dropping clumsily free.

Sam dead.

It didn't seem possible. He was my twin, the other half of myself. Shouldn't I have felt the moment when he left the world, without me by his side?

She shrugged, unconcerned.

"Prudence, please! What happened?"

"The parson wants to perform a cleansing, or some such nonsense. Says we need to make his soul right before he's sentenced. Me, I'm grateful he dared to bring the devil here. It let us see everything clearly, let us cleanse ourselves." She picked up a bottle of wine, examining it through slit eyes, before smashing it against the counter.

Pieces of glass ricocheted out and struck one of the lanterns farther down the bar. It teetered on the edge for a moment before shattering. The wick landed in a puddle of spirits. In a flash, they caught fire. Flames raced along the floorboards, up the bar, heading toward Prudence. She let out a scream as the fire licked at her sodden skirts.

"We have to get out of here!" I cried, grabbing a towel to stamp out the blaze.

"No! No! Not until every bottle of this devil's brew has been destroyed!" she protested.

"The fire will take care of that. Come with me!" She squirmed and twisted in my grasp, and I lost hold of my hatchet. It clattered to the floor and was kicked under a pile of debris as Prudence fought against me.

"Let me go!" she screeched, running back to the bar. "They must be stopped. They must be—"

A burst of fire blasted out from the counter, cutting off any words Prudence might ever have uttered again. The explosion threw us backward. I landed painfully on an upturned table, cracking my head against its leg.

The room went black.

Consciousness came back to me in little stirrings of awareness. The sharp scent of burning timber. The flicker of the dancing flames. But I was unable to move, too stunned to feel the building heat, too disoriented to save myself from the approaching inferno.

All I could do was watch.

Watch the angry golden red.

Watch the biting orange.

Watch.

Was it so very awful, sitting back and watching? There was a peace to it. An acceptance. It removed me from the situation, letting me examine it with an impassive detachment. I could almost understand its mesmerizing appeal.

It was so easy.

No.

My fingers twitched first, skittering over the motionless form of Prudence Latheton, searching for any sign of life. With a dazed groan, I pulled myself forward. The room swam in and out of focus. The furniture wouldn't stay still, and there were too many fires before me to make sense of where they were spreading.

How long had I been out?

Slowly my eyesight returned; the twin series of flames merged back together. The room was full of smoke, too murky to see through, and I had to feel about the floor for my hatchet. It couldn't have fallen far from me. Where was it?

At last, my fingers made out the metal curve of the head, and I strained to bring it closer.

Above me, the rafters groaned, too much weight supported on beams too far ravaged. When one splintered apart, sending fiery detritus down upon me, I bolted from the burning tavern as fast as my unsteady feet could carry me.

Down one street.

Down another.

I stumbled toward the church, pulled along by my unwavering belief that Sam was still alive. That I would find him, find my sisters, and that we all would somehow make it through this.

House after ruined house.

Wagons caught on fire.

Stinking messes of soot and charred flesh.

I hoped they were animals.

I couldn't bear to think of what else they could have been.

The Gathering House was nearly gone. The Founder Tree was a dark silhouette in front of a corona of flames. Its stumps seemed to reach up into the sky, begging for relief, begging for release.

I understood how it ached.

What would happen when it finally gave up the ghost, collapsing in a final pile of ash and soot? It had been the start of the Falls. Would its demise signal the town's end as well?

As I turned onto Sycamore Lane, an unexpected sight met my eyes.

There, surrounded by the smoldering husks of other homes, was the parsonage, seemingly untouched. My heart swelled with unrealistic hope. Perhaps my sisters had been taken here. Perhaps they were tucked away within those blessed walls, safe and untouched by the raging storm outside. Perhaps they—

A scream from within ripped apart my foolish thoughts before I could even start to wish them.

It throbbed, its vibrato standing the hairs of my arms on end. There was pain, yes, but something even darker, a primal urging of despair and grit, resolution and forbearance. It trailed off, as ragged as a torn cloth, only to mount again, louder and even more piercing than before.

"Rebecca?" I murmured, recognizing some small scrap of her in that horrible tone. What were they doing to her?

I pushed my way through the front door without knocking. Letitia Briard's parlor was an oasis after the horrors outside. Lanterns glowed cheerfully, and not a bit of furniture was out of place. There was even a tea tray laid out, cups still steaming, as if their owners had only just stepped away. When a volley of groans rose from the back bedroom, feverish and pounding into my temples, I almost wanted to laugh at the absurd juxtaposition.

"Get it out, get it out!" Rebecca howled, before letting loose a series of grunts.

Out?

I paused, terrified to conjure what was happening to her, before clarity dawned on me.

The baby.

Rebecca was in labor.

I glanced around the parlor, now unsure of what I ought to do. I was the last person Rebecca would want barging into her confinement room, but I couldn't leave her to do this alone.

I was spared having to make a choice as Letitia bustled out of the room, her arms full of bloodied linens. She dropped them as she spotted me.

"What are you doing here?" she demanded. Her eyes fell to the hatchet, darkening. "I'll scream. Simon is in the other room. Even if you reach me first, you'd never overpower him."

My face flushed. I was horrified that she thought so little of me. "I'd never . . . I wouldn't . . . I heard Rebecca and wanted to help."

"I think your family has done far more than their share of helping her."

A wave of uneasiness swept over me, and my feet itched to flee. "You know?"

"Anyone with half a brain could figure it out."

I glanced toward the back room, wondering who else was in the house. "Does Simon?"

She sniffed. "Of course not. My boy may be many things, but gifted with an ounce of sense is not one of them. . . . Have you come to kill it?"

"It?"

She looked at me as if I was impossibly slow. "The baby. I assume your brother sent you to cover up any evidence of their . . . congress."

My mouth fell open with horrified surprise. "I'd never!"

"Then what are you doing here?"

"I heard her cries—"

"There are a lot of people crying in the world right now. Go bother them instead."

Rebecca's screams grew higher in pitch, lengthening until I thought they'd never end, until they'd drown the world in their agony, driving everyone who heard them to madness.

But then, silence.

Until another cry sounded.

Softer.

Smaller.

And then, a laugh of delight.

"She's perfect!" Rebecca exclaimed weakly.

She.

A girl.

Samuel had a daughter.

"Just perfect," Rebecca repeated. "Look at her, Simon. She's just . . ."

"Blond," he finished. "She's blond."

The baby began fussing as heavy footsteps paced the room.

"Why is she blond?" Simon asked, confusion making him louder, looser, a cornered animal set to strike. "I've seen that shade before. . . . Where have I seen it?"

The bedroom door swung open, and I darted from the parlor before he could see me and piece everything together. I was across the yard before he emerged from the confinement room, and I ducked behind the little fence separating the parsonage from absolute chaos.

A thundering boom echoed through the hazy landscape. Another explosion? Or something even worse?

A trio of voices sounded from around the corner, arguing over one another. I pressed myself to the fence, praying the shadows would cover me.

"Who's that?" one asked, spotting me.

Rough hands grabbed at my arms, hauling me to my feet before I could flee.

"Isn't that one of the Downing girls?" Matthias Dodson nudged my chin, tilting me toward him for inspection. "I thought the lot of you were at the church, waiting on the parson."

Despite the perilous edge I was on, hope kindled within me. "Sadie and Merry are at the church?"

Calvin Buhrman wiped a hand over his runny eyes. They were red-rimmed, irritated by the smoke, and nearly swollen shut. "Don't even know why we need to go through this charade. We all know they did it."

"My sisters did nothing!" I protested. "Neither did Samuel. You have to release them! Matthias, *please!*" I pawed desperately at him, clutching at his cloak sleeve. My heart sank as I saw the scarlet Rules embroidered along its edge. He was dressed for Judgment.

"We follow the Rules, now and always," Matthias said, raising an eyebrow at the tavern owner.

"Where's Leland? We can't carry this out without Leland," Amos McCleary said, swaying unsteadily against his walking stick. It was gummy with drying blood, and I noticed a fine spray of droplets marring the Elder's face, turning his tufts of white hair to rust. The blood wasn't his.

"I heard him with Winthrop Mullins a few streets over," I said, hoping my information would grant me a bit of mercy. "They were arguing. . . . Then there was gunfire."

Amos puckered his lips, as grim as an undertaker. "We have to assume him dead, then. There's no time for speculation." He glanced to Calvin. "Should we appoint Buhrman to take his place?"

Matthias frowned. "That's not how things are done."

"We're past the point of doing things properly," Amos said. "Look around. There won't be a town left to save if we don't act quickly."

"I accept," Calvin said, jumping on the opportunity.

"Now, just a minute—"

"No time!" Amos cried, his eyes shining, bright and mad. "I said no time!"

He raised his cane, and brought it down on Matthias, clocking him over the head. Matthias released his grip on me and clutched his bloodied forehead.

"What the devil was that for, old man?"

"I should have done that an age ago. Don't think I don't know all about the secret meetings you and Leland held this winter, plotting and planning behind my back. You wanted to edge me out. Usurp my position on the council."

Matthias snorted, gurgling blood. "You were sick."

"That's no excuse!"

"The whole town couldn't stop to watch you die!"

"I'm not dying now, am I?" Amos struck him again. The carved Founder Tree smashed into Matthias's face, caving in half his jaw.

Matthias staggered back. The heft of his cloak and the nightmarish haze of the smoke made him appear larger than he was, strange and misshapen, making me recall the drawings in Ephraim's journals, Minotaurs and horned apes that walked upright through pine barrens, leathery wings on their backs.

It was this monstrous shape that hurled itself upon Amos McCleary, meaty fists striking into sunken cheeks. Calvin's eyes widened in horror as he watched the Elders pummel one another. After a moment, he shook his head and ran off.

"What is the meaning of this?" a voice roared, momentarily stopping the fight.

Parson Briard strode out of the burning darkness, his robes swaying behind him like a king's coronation vestments.

"I can't believe my eyes. The Elders, quarreling?" He stepped forward, squinting at what was left of Matthias's face. "That doesn't look good, Dodson. You'll want to have the doctor look that over. I think I saw him somewhere around the schoolyard. Parts of him, anyway." He shrugged. "Myself, I've never cared for modern medicine. I think the old ways still are best. Starve a fever. Feed a cold. Put a beast out of its misery."

There was a single gunshot, sharp and final, and I swallowed my cry as Matthias reeled back into an ashen heap. His cloak pulled away, revealing a fallen man and nothing more.

"That ought to cure what ails him, don't you think?" Briard asked, smoke still wafting from his pistol.

Amos leaned over, examining the still remains of his former

friend. "What have you done?" He turned toward the parson, his fingers tight around the bloodied walking stick. "Damn you, Briard. Damn you to hell."

A cackle of triumph burst from Amos as he swung his cane high. I turned away in time to avoid witnessing the bloody aftermath, but it didn't stop me from hearing it, like footsteps crunching through deep snow.

I broke into a sprint, praying the Elder would forget about me as he satiated his bloodlust elsewhere.

Rounding the corner, I could just make out the church's bell tower, rising among plumes of wreckage and ruin. In the little square at the base of the hill were the stocks. There was a dark mass huddled against the pillory.

Sam.

Before I could run to him, two shapes broke free of the shadows, hurtling into me.

"Ellerie? Is it really you?" Merry threw her arms around me. Her voice was rasped sharp. She'd breathed in too much of the smoke and ash.

Sadie squeezed me, sobbing, her head buried at my waist. "We thought we'd never see you again. We thought—"

"Are you okay? Have they hurt you?" I ran fingers over their soot-stained faces, brushing back loose, matted hair to inspect them. There was a line of red scratches down Merry's face, and one of Sadie's sleeves had been torn from her dress. They'd fought and struggled. I pulled them into another hug, tears falling over them.

Merry clutched my arm. "Parson Briard wanted to put us in the stocks with Sam, but Thomas charged at him. He told us to run, to run and hide."

"But then there was the ball of fire," Sadie cried, her cheeks scrunched. "And fighting, everywhere. Everyone has gone mad."

"I've seen."

"They're going to kill him," Merry said.

"We're going to find a way to free Sam, I swear we will."

I cupped her cheek, unable to stop touching my sisters. I needed physical assurance that they were here, with me, and safe.

"Not Sam," Merry said, pointing back to the stocks. "Thomas. And Ephraim."

I squinted. It had been too dark to make out before, but there were two figures secured in the stocks, not one. The heads hanging between the wooden boards had mops of brown curls, not Sam's bright blond hair.

"He lied," Merry said, her lower lip trembling. "Sam. When they brought us to the square, he told the parson that the devil had been summoned to the Falls—and that the Fairhopes were it." She let out a broken gasp. "They said the Gallows weren't good enough. That devils need to burn. They're building the stakes now, Sam leading them all."

"Sam did that?" I wanted to be shocked, to be stunned and outraged. How could our brother say such a thing? I knew he was capable of mistakes—big, horrible, awful ones—but this was beyond the pale. Lives were at stake. Innocent lives.

I froze.

There it was.

Sam's lie.

Given at exactly the wrong moment.

"We're getting out of here," I promised them. "All of us. The parsonage is still standing. I'll bet their stable is too. We'll take their wagon and make for the pass. We can try to find help and . . ." I glanced around, barely able to register the devastation. There would be nothing left to save, come morning. "But first we have to free Thomas and Ephraim."

"Briard has the key," Merry said.

Hot bile churned in my stomach as I remembered the crunch of his skull. I could not go back down that darkened street.

I raised my hatchet. "I've got something better."

My first strike at the stocks missed the boards and struck one of the metal hinges.

Painful reverberations from the thwack traveled up the axe, wrenching my shoulder back as I gasped. With a cry of determination, I swung the hatchet again, chipping into the frame.

Again and again, I unleashed my frustrations and furies onto the weathered boards.

Splinters and bigger bits of wood rained down on the parched earth until the stocks broke apart with a groan.

Falling to the ground, the men listed heavily, unable to stand. Thomas had been beaten badly, and his face was swollen and mottled. His eyes were glazed over, distant and unseeing, but when Merry reached out to support his weight, I saw him press his forehead to her temple, murmuring gratefully.

Ephraim's glasses were missing, and he squinted through the haze of smoke, his eyes raw and red.

"You brave girl," he said as I ducked under his arm, helping him lean on me.

"I figured out her name, but it didn't matter," I said, unable to accept any credit. "It was too late."

"What about Sam?" Sadie asked as we made our way toward the parsonage. "We're not going to leave him . . . are we?"

Whitaker's final words returned to me, floating in my head like a cork bobber, and I couldn't deny their ring of truth. Sam would abandon us, turn tail and leave without a spare thought.

But did that make it right to do the same to him?

"I . . . We should . . ." I let out a growl of frustration. "I'll go after him. Make your way to the parsonage. Ready the horses and search for whatever supplies we can take."

"We should just leave him," Merry said, surprising me. "After the things he said about Thomas and Ephraim . . . You didn't hear them, Ellerie. They were terrible and foul. And even worse . . ." She pressed Sadie close to her, covering her ears. "He blamed you for everything. For bringing them here. He wants to see you burn."

"He couldn't have meant it."

Sadie whimpered. "He doesn't know what he's saying. Something's not right."

"Obviously," Merry scoffed. "Please come with us."

"He's our brother."

She shook her head. "He's no brother of mine. Not any longer." She pulled me into a tight embrace. "Be safe, please, Ellerie."

I promised I would, pressing tearful kisses to her and Sadie before they stumbled off into the fiery dark.

I approached the square carefully, keeping beneath the blanketing shadows of the oaks, eyes darting and alert, my hatchet at the ready. All of the men looked indistinguishable from one another, and I bit my tongue to keep from calling Sam's name.

Their movements were efficient and purposeful. Two men stood on an assembled platform, hammering posts into place. The others brought piles of kindling and larger sticks. Some even carried full logs. It was a wonder the men bothered with kindling at all. The entire town was ablaze; little more than a spark would be needed to set their macabre bonfire alight.

A new figure raced into the square, panting loudly. "Samuel Downing!" he barked out. "Show yourself!"

"What do you want, Simon?" Sam asked, separating himself from the pack. He'd been holding one of the stakes.

Of course he had.

My brother narrowed his eyes, squinting against the haze.

"Your father has been looking for you. Says you're shirking duties here."

"I was with my wife, watching her give birth—to *your* daughter."

The other men stopped working, stilling to watch this unexpected confrontation play out.

Watch.

Sam jumped down from the platform and landed solidly on both feet. "Oh really?"

"You son of a bitch! Couldn't keep your hands off her, could you? How dare you even look at another man's wife!"

Sam smirked, fire reflecting in his eyes. "You poor simpleton. You truly don't get it, do you?"

A snicker rang out from the group behind Sam.

Simon's eyes darted wildly from Sam to the other men. "Get what?"

"I always wondered how she managed to get it past you. Did she hide a vial of blood in the sheets on your wedding night, or were you just too stupid to look for it?"

"What are you talking about, Downing?"

Winthrop Mullins let out a hoot from the platform, tossing his hammer from palm to palm. In the firelight, he looked absolutely feral, a wolf circling in for the kill.

So he had fired first.

Poor Leland.

"She was already pregnant when she married you," Sam said, snorting and buckling over with laughter. "And you were too dumb to notice."

Simon shook his head. "That's not true. That's not possible. We—"

"How's it feel to be the town's biggest cuckold, Simon Briard? The laughingstock of Amity Falls?"

Simon's jaw hardened as he fought back tears. He stepped away to leave, the men's mirth turning ugly and jeering.

Then Simon paused, his face twitching with a tic of rage. As he spun back toward Samuel, he removed something from the back of his trousers and hurled it into the darkness.

The hatchet flew through the air, spinning in tight circles around itself, glittering and bright and reflecting the flames of our ruined town.

It struck Sam square in his chest, lodging deep with a wet, pulpy *thwack*.

Sam looked down at the handle, blinking in confusion, before falling to his knees. His body trembled once, then fell forward and moved no more.

I did feel the moment when he passed, a pair of scissors snipping the tenuous thread connecting us, rendering it impossible to repair.

"Sam," I whispered, careful even in my grief to avoid being noticed.

Winthrop jumped off the scaffolding and flipped my brother over. I turned away.

"He's dead," he announced. Winthrop shot an uneasy look toward Simon. "You really killed him."

"Good. Only one more to go," Simon said, turning on his heel and running off into the night.

I drew a sharp breath, understanding his words.

Rebecca.

40

"REBECCA!" I CRIED, ARRIVING AT THE PARSONAGE. I'D run all the way, taking every shortcut I could. I had no idea if I'd managed to beat Simon back. Part of me had feared I was going to stumble straight into a bloodbath, but I'd pressed ahead, painful stitches stabbing at my sides. I'd already lost too many things I cared about. My heart couldn't hold another regret.

Letitia was nowhere to be found when I burst into the confinement room.

Rebecca lay on the bed, the room heavy with the metallic taste of blood, but she was alive and well.

"Ellerie!" she exclaimed, looking up from the small bundle in her arms.

A moment of uneasiness passed between us. I waited for her eyes to harden, for a scowl to form.

But she smiled.

"Do you . . . do you want to see her?" Rebecca pulled back the quilt, revealing the smallest, most perfect profile I could imagine.

I reached out, wanting to trace the curve of her chubby cheek, but noticed my fingers were caked with grime and soot, and with a trace of remorse, I pulled them away from my niece.

"We have to get out of here," I said. "Simon found out about Sam and—"

"I know," she said, her face falling. "I've never seen him so angry. He left—to talk to Samuel, I guess, and—"

"Sam's dead," I said, unable to pad the blow. "Simon killed him. And he's on his way to you."

Rebecca tightened her hold on the baby, bringing the bundle closer to her chest. "We'll hide. The Briards have a root cellar. We can lock it from the inside."

"We're leaving. Now. The town is caving in on itself. We have to get out of here before we're all swept up in it. My sisters have a wagon ready. You're coming with us. Both of you."

She glanced down at the bloodied bedsheets. "But—"

"We'll take every precaution we can, but we have to go," I said, grabbing at spare quilts and sheets, anything to help pad the back of the wagon. "Now."

⚜

The smoke from Amity Falls blanketed the whole of God's Grasp, embracing the valley in a dark, lingering handshake, and making the trail to the pass almost impossible to spot.

Sadie and I were at the buckboard of our stolen wagon, with me holding the reins. Merry was in the back, tending to Ephraim, Thomas, and Rebecca, and cooing to the baby girl.

"What about the wolves?" Sadie asked as we reached the end of the wheat field. The pines loomed ahead of us, peering down like grim sentinels.

"We'll be safer in here than back there," I reasoned with as much confidence as I could muster. I didn't know how long it would take for the creatures of the forest to return to their usual states, their usual sizes, now that the Dark Watchers were gone, or if they ever would.

Perhaps they'd all have to die before new life could return to this land.

After a pause, I nudged the mares forward.

Once in the sheltering arms of the woods, we dared to light the lanterns. With all the chaos in the streets, our flight from town had gone unnoticed, but I hadn't wanted to draw any attention to ourselves as we'd made our way across the fields.

The lanterns shone brightly, casting the shadows aside.

I thought of the sigil on Ephraim's trunk and all the knowledge left behind in his journals and notes.

There'd been no time to retrieve the crate, to retrieve anything from home. Would we ever again go back? Would the farm still be there if we did? Would any of the Falls remain?

I pushed aside my bleak thoughts, focusing on the crooked path before us. It wound through the forest, tracking back and forth as we ascended higher and higher up the mountain. It took an experienced driver a week to reach the pass. With all the scavenged supplies my sisters had pieced together, we had enough rations for four days.

Out in the darkness, a branch snapped, drawing my attention to the left side of the cart. The horses' ears instantly flicked toward the sound, their footfalls slowing till they plodded to a stop. I scanned the dark foliage, trying to pick out what had shifted there, but I couldn't make out much past the light's glow.

"Ellerie?" Merry asked, her voice low. "You heard that, didn't you?"

Keeping my movements as small as possible, I nodded. Sadie grabbed my knee, her fingers sinking into the folds of my skirt. I wanted to wrap my hand around hers, to reassure her, but I had to keep hold of the reins. We needed to get moving.

Rustling sounded, and the horses nickered uneasily.

"Come on," I encouraged, giving them a little start. They refused to budge. "Come on."

Another snap, more rustles.

Sadie tried to hold back a sob through bitten lips, but it squeezed from her. "It's the monsters, isn't it?"

"No, it isn't," I promised. "We're going to be okay. We're going to—" I slapped the reins across one of the mares' rumps. "Go!"

She backed up, causing the tongue to twist and push the wheels over a tree root, so that we landed at a wretched angle. We lurched, and I had the terrible notion that one of the spokes had broken.

We had no replacements. No tools.

If we tried to continue, more spokes would fracture and we'd be stranded. Neither of the Fairhopes nor Rebecca was in any condition to hike over the pass.

"Take the reins," I said, giving them to Sadie.

"What? No!" she protested even as I shoved them into her hands.

"I need to check the wheels."

"But the monster—"

I grabbed the hatchet lying forgotten on the footboard and jumped down.

Footsteps—decidedly human—grew louder, grew closer.

My mouth dried as I pictured Simon Briard stalking through the trees, his hatchet still dripping with my brother's blood.

I grabbed one of the lanterns and brandished it at the darkness. "Who's there?" I demanded. "Show yourself!"

"Ellerie."

I froze, the hairs on the back of my neck bristling as I heard the familiar tone.

A figure stepped into the circle of light, emerging out of the darkness. He had on his rucksack and travel hat. The brim's shadows shrouded his face, covering his eyes.

Were they silver, or his friendly amber?

"Whitaker."

His lips raised in a small half smile. "I suppose that name is as good as any."

He took another step closer, and I raised the axe, half-heartedly threatening for him to stop. He did, raising his hands in supplication. The green rings of his tattoos were gone, completely vanished, without a trace left behind.

I recalled the look in Lyra's eyes as I'd told her my ultimate demand—for them to flee Amity Falls and leave Whitaker free of the Kindred, his debts paid, his tenure broken. Disbelief mingled with such rage.

Seeing him here now—without her hold, without the weight of their claim—was a miracle.

"I don't know how you . . . I never would have thought . . ." He shook his head, knocking back his hat to reveal amber eyes, full of wonder, glossy with impending tears.

"It's done?" I clarified. "You're truly free?"

He nodded.

"No more debts, no more claims?"

He pressed his lips together and shook his head.

"Good."

There was so much more I wanted to say. So many questions I wanted to ask. Dreams I wanted to speak into existence.

But they weren't mine to presume.

Whitaker was free.

Finally free.

Free to make his way in the world. Free to pursue his heart's desires.

And though I hoped I'd be a part of them, I didn't want to push. Didn't want to assume.

He needed to make his own choices now. He alone.

And so I stayed silent, waiting, even as my heart split.

Whitaker looked away, studying the wagon behind me. "You're leaving?"

"There's nothing left of town. Maybe the farmhouse will still be standing, but . . ."

He nodded with understanding. "I was so scared for you when I heard the explosions, when I saw the flames." His eyes drifted to the back of the cart, counting people. "Sam?"

I shook my head.

"I'm sorry."

I raised my shoulders, shrugging. There would be tears—many, many tears—in the days to come, but for now, my focus needed to be kept on the trail ahead of us.

"What will you do next? Where will you go?" His voice was soft, his prying gentle.

"We'll go to the city. Find Mama and Papa. And then . . . I don't know." I shifted, the weight of the hatchet making my forearms quiver.

"I can't—I'll never be able to thank you for what you've done for me, but I . . . I thought this might be . . ." He took off one of his bracelets and held it out. "It's a hidden locket," he explained. "My sister's four-leaf clover is inside. I want you to have it." He glanced at the axe, still raised, however tenuously.

Without lowering my weapon, I took the little strap of leather. As I rubbed at the tarnished metal disk woven onto it, I felt the trace of an inscription.

I squinted at the spidery copperplate, surprised. "Josiah White."

It was so simple.

So plain.

So wholly not him.

He scratched his head. "I've not been that name for many, many years. I don't know who I am anymore. Not truly. Perhaps I'll stay as 'Whitaker.' Nothing else has ever fit so well."

He looked so uncertain, so young and yearning. His unflagging, otherworldly confidence was gone, replaced with a painful vulnerability that called out to me.

He looked human.

I lowered the hatchet, let it drop to the ground between us. "We could find out who you are . . . together."

"Together," he repeated earnestly. "I wasn't sure if you—"

I took the final step, filling the space that separated us, and pulled him into an embrace before he could finish the thought.

"Together," I insisted.

For a moment he remained still, too surprised to respond. But then his hands moved, drawing me closer as he pressed one soft kiss into my hair.

"You'll come with us?" I asked pulling away, keenly aware of Sadie's rapt attention.

"There's nowhere else in the world I'd rather be, Ellerie Downing."

His fingers slipped over mine and held on tight as they formed a promise.

I thought of the Buhrmans' tavern, the McClearys' store, Matthias's livery. The Gathering House and the church. The Founder Tree. The Rules. The whole of Amity Falls. All those buildings, those shops, those homes had once held such promise. Such expectation. Such dreams.

Gone now, all of it.

So I held fast to Whitaker's hand, letting my thoughts soften.

I almost felt cheerful.

Whitaker steadied me as I hoisted myself up and settled in beside Sadie, taking the reins. I waited until he was next to me before clicking my tongue at the horses. After a beat, they plodded forward, straightening out the wagon and leading us deeper into the forest, away from the smoke of Amity Falls and into the echoing chimes of the Bells.

ACKNOWLEDGMENTS

First, always. Grace. There's no one in the world I'd rather have pressed against my side as I work. Thank you for your patience, your excitement, and your love. I'm so proud to be your mama. "One more chapter!"

Sarah Landis, I'm still pinching myself in wonder. Your sharp insights and understanding helped turn a whole lot of straw into the best pile of gold! You are incredible, and I'm so, so lucky you're my agent.

To Wendy Loggia and the entire dream team at Delacorte—Beverly Horowitz, Hannah Allaman, Alison Romig, Noreen Herits, Alex Hess, Casey Moses, Kate Sullivan, Bara MacNeill, Sean Freeman—I would not be here without your care and love. Thank you, thank you, thank you! I owe each and every one of you a four-leaf clover and a generous slice of honey cake!

Writing is never a solitary act, and I'm so grateful to have an amazing group of friends, family, and agency siblings at my back. Your early reads, laughter, and support mean everything to me. Thank you so much to Erin Hahn, Sara Flannery Murphy, Kim Liggett, Alexis Henderson, Danielle Trussoni, Shelby Mahurin, Jeannie Hilderbrand, Elizabeth Tankard, Phoebe Booker, Peter

Diseth, Kate Costello, Sarah Squire, Jonathan Ealy, Sona Amroyan-Peric, Kaylan Luber, Charlene Honeycutt, Carol Craig, Josh Coleman, Chelsea Chandler, Adler Morgan, Melanie Shurtz, Ekpe Udoh and his most amazing book club, Scott Kennedy, Meredith Tate, Jess Rubinkowski, Jennifer Adams, Jennie K. Brown, Elizabeth Unseth, Lyudmyla Hoffman, and all of #TeamLandis.

Hannah Whitten, you have no idea how happy I am you tweeted out a call for fairy-tale-retelling critique partners. Gosh, what a difference 180 characters can make to a life! I'm so blessed to have you in mine! We may not have chocolate chip cookies or winged love interests, but we have each other. Love you so.

Mama and Daddy, Tara, Elias, and Ori . . . "thank you" is too small a phrase. I love you all and am so wildly glad to have you and your love supporting me every day. Thank you for trips to the library; for flashlights, and covers to read under; for endless reading, rereading, and re-rereading(!); and for never thinking my dreams were too big.

And for Paul, always. I love our life, our daughter, our home full of typewriters and mismatched chairs, and so, so, so many shelves of books. But most of all, I love you.

Chapter One

Billowing waves of smoke wafted through the air, caught in a balmy breeze. Papa pressed down on the bellows, releasing another cloud, raining it carefully at the hive boxes. He waited a moment. Then nodded toward me.

Even though my hands were completely covered, they shook reaching out to remove the lid. I'd never been allowed to help remove the honey combs before and I wanted to make sure I did everything exactly as Papa said. With a muffled groan, I strained to hoist the lid up, then set it aside in the grass, careful to avoid the three bees crawling drowsily across its top.

After puffing more of the smoke, sweet with burning pine needles, into the box, Papa stepped back, allowing me full access to the hive.

CHAPTER 1

This is the very first version of chapter one. I handwrite about 85 percent of my first drafts. Writing by hand helps me get out the big ideas quickly, and then when I go back to type them up, I can add nuance and more emotional beats.

BEEKEEPING TERMS:

Queenright - a hive w/ a queen
Queenless - a hive w/o a queen
Queen are only bee capable of laying fertilized eggs
Eggs can become workers or queens → depending
on what they are fed.
    Workers get royal jelly then switched to pollen + honey
    Queen only ever eat royal jelly
This means worker bees can convert any young
worker bee into a queen → an emergency queen

Symptoms of a Queenless Hive
    1) Lack of Eggs & Brood
        - also could be queen taking a "brood break"
    2) Drop in population
        When this is noticed, queen has been absent
        for many weeks
    3) An Increase in Honey & Pollen
    4) A change in temperament
        Irritated and nervous, make a high pitched
    whine combined with a low roar
    5) Queen Cells / cups
        queenless hives will attempt to make a replacement
    queen
    6) Laying workers
        - lay unfertilized eggs which become male
    bees or drones

If you place a queen bee in a queenright colony
they will kill the cage queen

BEEKEEPING TERMS

One of my favorite parts of writing is getting to research so many new
and interesting topics. Having read a stack of books on apiculture—and
subscribing to way too many YouTube beekeeping channels—I really
would love to try to keep a hive of my own one day!

THE TREES

One of the things that helps motivate me while drafting is to create a word count tracker. I draw up a little doodle—themed to the book, of course!—and then every time I write a thousand words, I get to color in something. For *Small Favors*, it was pine trees. I ended up coloring in 100 trees before deciding to go really crazy and embroider my word count—I ended up with 128 trees total, and a really special piece of art for my office!

THINGS TO RESEARCH:

~~[crossed out]~~
☐ Bee Keeping
☐ The ~~[crossed out]~~ Forest → wildlife. plants. etc
☐ Period clothing

NEEDFUL THINGS meets THE VILLAGE

- Everyone in the town is making bargains with Misfortune but no one talks about it or him
- Ellerie's father made some big final bargain that resulted in his and the mother's deaths
- Ellerie's first bargain is for wild flowers for the bees— one drop of blood "to see if you are brave"
- A big bargain for "her first kiss" given at a time and place of Misfortune's choosing
- The town is on course with Roanoke's disappearing colony. The mountains will crush them and no one will ever know what happened to them.
- or are villagers beginning to disappear one by one. prompting intervention from outside sources→ Thomas and father arrive w/ sheriff and other authorities?
- First kiss at the dance. First time Misfortune has openly entered / interacted with town.
- Supply trains used to be twice a year then once. then they started going missing. Town on verge of collapse, coming apart at its worn seams

THINGS TO RESEARCH

Once the seed of an idea comes to me, I fill up a bunch of pages jotting down notes that will capture the feeling and atmosphere of the book. I also leave myself little to-do lists for research. You can really tell how much some of my ideas changed in the drafting process!